ALEX MITCHELL was born in Oxford in 1974 and grew up in Belgium. He studied art and architecture at Strasbourg University and having completed his Masters there, he returned to Oxford and obtained a D.Phil in Classical Archaeology. His main field of research is the 'Archaeology of Humour', on which he has published several papers. His first book, *Greek Vase Painting and the Origins of Visual Humour*, was published by Cambridge University Press in 2009. He is now an Honorary Associated Researcher at the Institutes of Archaeology in Oxford and Brussels.

The 13th Tablet is Alex Mitchell's first novel in a trilogy of Mina Osman thrillers published by Haus Publishing.

THE 13TH TABLET

ALEX MITCHELL

First published in 2012 by Haus Publishing Limited

HAUS PUBLISHING LTD.
70 Cadogan Place, London SW1X 9AH
www.hauspublishing.com

Copyright © Alex Mitchell 2012

ISBN 978-1-908323-09-5
eISBN 978-1-908323-19-4

Typeset in Garamond by MacGuru Ltd
info@macguru.org.uk

Printed and bound by CPI Group (UK) Ltd, Croydon CR0 4YY

A CIP catalogue for this book is available from the British Library

To the scintillating Aurore,
whose love helped me ride the storm

And the waters overwhelmed the earth so greatly that all the tall mountains that were under the heavens came to be covered.

(Genesis 7: 19)

… and turned to blackness all that had been light. The land shattered like a pot. All day long the South Wind blew, blowing fast, submerging the mountain in water, overwhelming the people like an attack… they could not recognize each other in the torrent. The gods were frightened by the Flood, and retreated, ascending to the heaven of Anu.

(Epic of Gilgamesh XI)

[…] there is Old Nineveh, which is desolate. The whole land of Nineveh is black like pitch […] There is neither herb nor any vegetation whatever […] New Nineveh, opposite, is on the other side of the river. At New Nineveh is a large congregation numbering more than six thousand souls. It has two princes. The name of the one is Rabbi David, and of the other Rabbi Samuel. They are sons of two brothers, and of the seed of King David.

(Petachiah of Ratisbon, 12th century C.E.)

Prologue

Mina stepped into her living room. It was completely dark. She always closed the shutters against the fierce Iraqi sun but she didn't recall closing them this tightly. The air was stuffy and she couldn't see a thing. She flipped the light switch but nothing happened. She was about to try again when she heard a slight shuffling sound to her right.

'*Hal honaka ahad?* Is anybody there?' she asked hesitantly. A second or two passed but no answer came back. Suddenly someone yanked her arms backwards and bound her wrists with cable ties. She heard the zipping sound of the ties tightening around her wrists, before another person pulled a large plastic freezer bag over her head and held it tightly round the base of her neck.

Panicking, Mina gulped a breath which emptied the bag of the little oxygen it held and left her gasping for air. She started choking, sucking the plastic deep into her mouth. She fell to her knees.

As she felt her mind fogging, she heard the creaking sound of the shutters being opened slightly. In a blur she could make out three men in dark clothing, towering over her. One of the men bent down and yanked the bag from her head. She gasped for air, breathing so deeply she thought her lungs would explode. She burst into tears and shook violently, the body's natural response when given another shot at life.

The men didn't give her any time to think. They pulled her to her feet roughly and flung her on a chair. One man stepped up to her, bending low to stare into her tear-filled eyes and said in a cold voice, 'Miss Osman?'

Mina didn't reply.

'Miss Osman, you don't know us, but we know everything about you. Do you understand?'

'Yes,' she whispered.

'Good,' he replied slowly, 'so where is it?'

'Where is what?'

'Wrong answer,' he said and turned to one of the other men, 'You, the bag!'

'Please,' Mina begged him frantically, 'don't torture me! What do you want? I don't know anything…' She stopped talking abruptly when she saw her interrogator bringing a sharp knife towards her throat. It glinted in the single beam of sunlight peeking through the shutters.

He held the sharp edge of the knife under her ear and said, 'The tablet, Miss Osman, where is it?'

That's what they were after, Hassan's tablet? But how could they have known she had it? This was insane.

'So?' He asked, slowly pushing the blade against the skin below her ear until she felt it cut through. Pain flashed through her and she felt warm blood trickling down her neck. Instinctively she tried to bring a hand up to stem the bleeding but she was still tied up. She was utterly helpless. 'Please, please don't hurt me,' she sobbed, 'the tablet is in my rucksack.'

He pulled the knife away and turned to the other man, 'Pass me the plastic bag.' Taking the plastic bag, he turned back to

Mina and with a sinister smile said, 'We wouldn't want to leave any traces, would we?'

Mina felt the clammy plastic being pulled over her head once more and her mind begin to darken. 'This is madness,' she thought, as she began to lose consciousness.

PART 1

IRAQ

Chapter 1

Four days earlier
December 1st, 2004. Mosul airport

Hassan had been pacing up and down the arrivals area for almost an hour. 'The plane's landed,' he thought, 'why isn't anyone coming out?' He approached one of the guards standing at the gate and asked him what was going on. The guard glanced down at the round-faced youth and replied, 'Security checks.'

Hassan thanked him and sat down a little further away, 'Security checks, more security checks. What do they think, Bin Laden's on the plane? Will she ever come out of there?' Suddenly, he caught sight of Mina Osman's slender profile through the window and his face lit up.

Mina wore the tailored jacket and fitted jeans that Hassan and the other students knew so well from her classes. He had been wondering if she'd still be wearing a headscarf after spending time back home in America. At university she often wore a headscarf and made a point of always covering her hair on the streets of Mosul. He suspected Mina didn't like covering her head, but knew better than to ignore local customs. Hassan remembered a discussion they had had months ago, after a class on the representation of foreigners in ancient Babylonian art. The conversation had veered to female dress codes in different countries and she had told him that she often let her hair hang loose in the US. But when she appeared at the arrivals gate, she was wearing a dark headscarf, dashing his hopes.

Mina was the most beautiful woman Hassan had ever been close to. She had almond-shaped eyes that seemed to look deep into your soul. She was slender, but not as tall as the top models he had seen in magazines. She had a natural elegance, as if she breathed a more refined air than those around her. Yet there wasn't a hint of arrogance, other than a touch of academic pride. She was always polite and morally-speaking, irreproachable. Hassan was convinced that under her slightly stern scholarly persona, Mina hid a passionate nature. Half her students were hopelessly in love with her and the other half worshipped her as a goddess.

'Welcome to Mosul, Madam!' Hassan said with a large grin on his face.

'Hassan! What a pleasure to see you. Thanks for meeting me. I was afraid you hadn't received my text.'

'I did. But I was worried. Your plane arrived more than an hour ago! The security checks are worse than ever. I'm really sorry, Madam.'

She laughed, 'Don't be. You weren't the one rummaging through my belongings. It's funny really. As an archaeologist, I'd expect to be searched on the way out, not the way in!'

Hassan laughed and said, 'I thought you came to help us retrieve our looted artefacts, not rob them yourself.'

'I'm so glad to be back,' she said, speaking partly to herself. She added quickly, 'But let's get out of here. How are things, Hassan?'

'What do you mean Madam?'

'The news has been so distorted recently in the US, I have no idea what's really been going on,' she asked, looking concerned.

'Frankly? It's been awful, Madam,' he answered, as they fought their way through the crowd, Hassan taking the lead and carrying Mina's luggage. 'Fighter planes, bombs,' he went on, 'Police stations were blown up, insurgents from Fallujah came into Mosul and while all this was happening, the US army fought alongside the Iraqi National Guard. At university, the lecturers were either on strike or in hiding. We were wondering if there'd still be a university after the fighting ended.'

'I thought it had stopped?' she asked.

'Only on the 25th of November.'

'You mean things have only calmed down in the last week?' asked Mina.

'Yes. We didn't think you'd be returning,' he said, shooting rapid glances left and right before adding, 'I wouldn't want to be an American right now. The jihadists think that the US only support the Kurds, so they've been ambushing many American soldiers and civilian contractors. To tell you the truth I don't feel that bad about targeting some of those contractors, there's nothing *civilian* about them.'

'I'm sorry you feel that way,' said Mina tersely.

He looked at her, a little taken aback by her cold tone. 'On the other hand,' he stammered quickly, 'the jihadists are cowards. They've murdered Iraqi National Guard officers too. You know Muhammad, the short broody student who's in your class on cuneiform writing?'

'Yes, what about him?'

'His uncle was National Guard. He received insulting

letters, saying he was a traitor and warning that he'd better find another job. He dismissed the threats and they killed him. Do you know that bodies of beheaded officers have been found scattered all over the city?'

'My God, poor Muhammad,' she said, her eyes wide with fear.

'Madam?' Hassan asked, worried about her horrified expression, 'I apologise if I've scared you.'

'Aren't you scared?'

'There's nothing we can do about it,' he said with the resigned calm of a young man who had seen too much fighting in his short lifetime.

He changed the subject abruptly as he stopped in front of his battered car, 'So, Madam, what do you think of my new Mercedes?'

Mina suppressed a smile as she looked at the sorriest car she had ever witnessed. It looked like an art installation that had not quite made it to a contemporary art gallery. 'It's...it's... does it work?' she asked, trying to hide her doubts.

'Yes Madam. But you're missing the point. It's *mine*!' he added with a large grin.

'Oh. Right, my apologies. What a beautiful car! Listen, about the drive, I've changed my mind. Do you think you could first drop me at my flat in town and pick me up later? I should be ready in an hour's time.'

'No problem Madam.'

'And stop calling me Madam. Call me Miss, or just Mina.'

'Yes Miss Mina.'

'And...'

'Yes, Madam?'

'Speak to me in Arabic. We aren't in class right now, are we?'

'How will I practise my English?' he asked, wringing his hands in mock distress.

'And how will I practise my Arabic?' she answered.

He smiled and they drove off.

Mina loved speaking Arabic and listening to Hassan's comforting Mosuli accent. Her own accent had transformed beyond recognition. When she had first arrived she spoke classical Arabic, which she had learned at university. Although her parents spoke Arabic, they had always spoken English with her. It had taken her over a year to lose her literary turn of phrase and pick up the local dialect and, more importantly when in the field, the local slang. Even so, the incongruity of some of her sentences still made her students laugh. Luckily most of her classes were in English.

As she looked out at the familiar Mosuli landscape rolling past her window, Mina wondered whether she really was that glad to be back. She had a nagging feeling that she was running away from everything that made sense. Just over a year ago she had put her PhD scholarship at Columbia University on hold and left New York to take up a badly-paid lecturing position at the Department of Cuneiform Studies at the University of Mosul.

Nigel, her Columbia professor in Middle Eastern Studies had been very disappointed. She was such a promising PhD student and her dissertation on Early European explorers in ancient Mesopotamian cities would suffer greatly from her decision to leave so abruptly. Her parents too were appalled by her decision, despite being all too familiar with her passionate nature. This time it was different: they truly couldn't understand her motives. They had been born in Iraq, suffered under Saddam Hussein's rule and left the country to start a new life in America. Mina had been born in the US and brought up as a New Yorker.

Yet, Mina had felt uprooted and torn inside. Her parents had given her comfort, peace and freedom but for many years, she had felt betrayed, or more precisely, failed by them. They were unusual first generation immigrants; they didn't live within an Iraqi community and they worked very hard at trying to forget where they came from. In high school, Mina had never fitted in. With her long black hair and dark eyelashes, almond-shaped eyes and her chiselled nose, she was different from the other girls in her class. It was only at the age of fifteen, when she started reading about ancient Mesopotamia, the land 'between the two rivers' – the Tigris and the Euphrates – that she began to yearn to know Iraq properly. It was her way of coping with a fractured identity. A few years later she was completely immersed in the study of the archaeology of the Near East and cuneiform writing at Columbia. For the first time she was proud of her heritage and no longer felt self-conscious about her not-so-American surname.

Then the war in Iraq broke out. At first, most Iraqi people were filled with elation; it was an epic tale of liberation and the end of Saddam Hussein, the tyrant. But after a few years, with American forces still on the ground, Mina wondered what good came from their lingering presence. Depending on what news she read, she felt pulled one way or the other. She was finding it more difficult than ever to reconcile the two sides of her American-Iraqi identity.

When the terrible lootings of the Baghdad National Museum

occurred in 2003, she rushed to Iraq to help out in any capacity she could, leaving in her wake a confused ex-boyfriend, angry parents and a PhD on hold.

Of course, looters had been targeting archaeological sites all over the country for years. She remembered a scholar from Chicago University stating that gangs had been exporting ancient artefacts since the early nineties, and nothing had really been set up to challenge them; just like in Afghanistan, with the destruction of the Bamiyan Buddhas by the Taliban in 2001. The Taliban pretended to the world that those Buddhas were insulting to Islam, and declared that all idolatrous images of humans and animals were to be destroyed. Cowardice and lies. It had been a smoke screen; in reality they had been secretly selling ancient artefacts for years alongside heroin to fund their failing economy.

But the Baghdad lootings were a different story. Over 80,000 cuneiform tablets, some dating back to 3000 B.C.E. were stolen and hundreds of priceless statues and relics from the birth of civilisation had disappeared. The UNESCO director general, Koichiro Matsuura, had called for an immediate ban on the international trade in Iraqi antiquities and had sent a team of specialists to assess what action could be taken.

Mosul, where Mina's parents came from, had also been plundered and the museum there had suffered heavy losses. So, despite her parents' angst, she moved into their tiny flat in Mosul. Before emigrating to the US, Mina's father had passed on the flat to his brother and Mina moved in a few months after her uncle died. On arrival, Mina made it known at Mosul University and in more shady circles that she would help authenticate the many artefacts, and especially cunei-form tablets, which appeared sporadically on the market and return them to the city's museum, no questions asked. Many civilians had stolen art as an act of rage and hopeless revenge on Saddam. But many now wanted to return them, without getting into trouble with the new authorities.

Somehow Mina had so far managed to avoid being in the midst of terrorist attacks or full-blown battles. But for how long? While she had been away visiting her parents in New York for a month, Mosul had seen many gunfights and widespread destruction, and US intelligence believed there were worse times ahead. Everyone had urged her to delay her return to Iraq. But she had had her way, and here she was.

Hassan parked outside her block of flats. He helped her carry her suitcases up to the second floor and said he would return in an hour and take her to the Cuneiform Studies department.

Apart from the dust that had accumulated, everything was as she had left it a month before. There were piles of books in various parts of the flat, as the shelves could not handle any more volumes. She felt at home with the golden light streaming through the shutters and the unmistakable smell of old leather and wood. She dropped her suitcase and slumped on the couch, knowing that she'd have to get up soon or she would fall asleep. She had been invited for dinner by Professor Almeini, her departmental mentor. After a few moments spent staring at the ceiling, she mustered her strength and walked into the bathroom.

Chapter 2

December 1st, 2004

Mina threw a quick glance at her reflection in the side window to check her headscarf was properly adjusted before entering the department. Although she'd spent over a year in Mosul and had long forgotten the skirts and tight tops she used to wear in New York, she constantly felt self-conscious. After all, she was the only female lecturer in the department of Cuneiform Studies and had no female students. To add to her unease, Hassan had not accompanied her upstairs, saying that he had 'things to do'. Now that she thought about it, during the drive from her flat, Hassan had been evasive every time she brought up his studies. Mina realised that she was standing in the department's main corridor, lost in her thoughts, and quickly walked on through to her office.

An overweight and sour-looking man who was seated in the corridor, probably waiting to see one of the professors, threw her a disapproving glance. However demurely dressed, Mina guessed she was too voluptuous for this man's conservative ideas on how woman should be attired. She was about to tell him what she thought about his unwelcome gaze, when Professor Almeini appeared.

The elderly scholar took her hands in his, 'Dear Mina. How are you?'

'I'm fine,' she answered, feeling suddenly at ease in his presence. He was a short, thin man who exuded confidence and affability. Professor Almeini had a wiry strength, which had kept him going well past retirement age. University officials needed him to keep the department from falling apart, and he was rather reluctant to relinquish his office.

'Please wait for me in my office. I'll be just a minute,' he said in his calm voice.

Professor Almeini's office was a mirror image of his simplicity and scholarly nature: oak shelves, with row upon row of neatly arranged and well-read books, dappled light bathing his desk and an ancient rug underfoot. Although many colleagues had described to Mina how well-kept the University of Mosul was compared to a few years back, she only half believed their stories. The set-up was still quite basic in her eyes. Moreover, after the 2003 lootings, most lecturers had taken the library and departmental books home for safe-keeping. She was delighted to see that Professor Almeini had returned all his books to the office; it was a sign that things were somehow on the mend. She sat down in a chair at the far end of the office.

The professor's shiny Russian samovar was on its stand, the fire in its pipe smouldering. She smiled, thinking of the 'thousand and one nights' tales told by students about its origin. Her favourite story centred on the professor's imaginary involvement with the *mujahideen* in Afghanistan, she had overheard a young student in the university cafeteria telling his friends in hushed tones, 'he raided a Soviet stronghold and brought back the samovar. I swear, it belonged to a Russian officer.' Knowing the professor, Mina thought it more likely he had bought it in a bazaar while searching for some rare books. She heard his firm step outside the office. The professor shut the door and walked towards his favourite assistant.

'So, Mina, how was your trip to America?' he asked as he sat down opposite her.

'Refreshing. I attended a few seminars, I saw my parents... no bomb threats, no missing students or colleagues, you know, same old, same old.'

'Now, now. Don't be cynical, it's unbecoming. I remember when you first arrived. You were so starry-eyed, let's say.'

'I'm sorry Professor. I didn't mean any disrespect.'

'I could be mistaken, but you seem almost disappointed that work can continue at the university in such appalling conditions.'

'Yes and no. We teach students how to read ancient cuneiform, to understand their history but the recent past has caught up with us and I feel that there's little hope for their future. How can you be so peaceful when the world's tearing itself apart?' Mina asked earnestly.

'When you've known as many difficult times as I have my dear, you won't speak lightly of the work we do,' he said. 'You are in Mosul, ancient Nineveh, the city where the library of King Sennacherib was found.'

'I know Pr...'

'You do and you don't,' he said, cutting her short. 'Do I need to remind you of the importance of our mission here? I have a duty to safeguard what is left of the earliest writings in the history of the world.' Then, with much kindness in his eyes, he added 'Ah, Mina, with the meagre financial means I have at my disposal and with the war, all I *can* do is use my knowledge to further scholarship here and now. Look at all the academics who fled Baghdad and whom we've had to accommodate here in Mosul. They left everything behind.'

He seemed lost in his thoughts for a moment but Mina knew he was thinking the same thing as her; 'God knows when they'll be able to return.'

The professor collected himself and said, 'With last month's escalation in violence, I have no idea what will happen in the coming months. But as for you, you came here to help and you've achieved much Mina.'

'I don't feel I have, Professor. I promised myself I'd regain some of the stolen tablets, and return them to the museum, but I've only authenticated a few. Of all the shady people who've come my way, not one of their tablets came from the looted museums. They were either fakes that they tried to fob me off with, or artefacts looted from other sites.'

He looked at Mina's earnest face, amused by her youthful disappointment.

'Don't be so hard on yourself Mina. You've been a wonderful teacher for our students. You've done so much for this department. If anyone should be disillusioned it's me, with Hassan. He was such a good student.'

'What do you mean *was*?' Mina was surprised, 'He just drove me here. What's he done?'

'That's the problem. He hasn't done anything; he dropped out. Learned just enough to start working for those shady art dealers you were referring to.'

Mina was disappointed. She now understood why the boy had been so cagey when she'd asked him about his studies. 'I'm so sorry Professor. It must be very disappointing,' she said.

'Yes. But let's talk about other things,' he answered with a twinkle in his eye, 'I owe you a welcome dinner, don't I? My wife's prepared a delicious meal for your arrival. Let's go.'

ᔗ

Hassan was sipping tea in his favourite haunt. The establishment was renowned for surviving two Gulf wars and serving Mosul's finest coffee. Hassan didn't care much about the coffee but loved the café's atmosphere. He often conducted his business in the small backroom with its medieval windows framed by old marble slabs, which had probably been looted from some long-forgotten Roman building.

Life was a strange commodity these days. The war-torn country was on the brink of collapse, but Hassan seemed to breeze through all the horror. He had been brought up by a tough father and a doting mother and had quickly learned how to survive in a place that could be a war zone on Monday, a Green zone on Tuesday, and a survival zone the rest of the week. The constant sense of urgency made men either crumble or survive. War and its corollaries could bring out the brightest light or the darkest night in every person, but Hassan, like most people in the city, was focused on getting on with his day-to-day business.

The café owner gave Hassan a wink and nodded to a dishevelled man standing at the door. Hassan looked him over and waved him to approach. A year ago, he used to feel pity for the poor labourers who seemed out of their depth in the city. But in the last few months he had met so many of these poor souls, fumbling in their pockets, watching over their back, waiting for him to take a look at some ancient object that – without losing his kind nature entirely – he felt he had become more selfish and indifferent.

'Are you Hassan?' asked the hesitant man, whose weary eyes seemed older than the rest of him.

'Yes I am.'

The man sat down.

'Don't worry so much,' said Hassan affably. 'I work for the university, not for the police.'

The old man looked up at Hassan with a crooked smile. 'It's so difficult to know who to trust. I used to work my own land, now I try to survive in the city. They took everything from me, except my wife and children whom I need to feed.' He lingered on his last words to give them more meaning, but Hassan pretended not to notice.

'I know. Believe me when I say I've got nothing to gain from our meeting, except the pleasure of doing my work, which is to collect and catalogue all these objects.'

It was a fixed dialogue, rehearsed a thousand times and Hassan knew how to keep the upper hand. This was pretty easy when the seller was desperate and the buyer picky about what to purchase.

'Let's go to the backroom for privacy,' said Hassan, as if all he cared for was the labourer's reputation. They walked through to the backroom and sat down side by side on a bench. The man reached into his tattered satchel and brought out a rectangular object, tightly wrapped in a rag. He opened it carefully and Hassan, who had identified the object straight away, rolled his eyes. Yet another clay tablet. He took it slowly, pretended to read the cuneiform writing and nodded appreciatively.

'This is a very interesting tablet you've got here. I will take it to the university today. Thank you very much. You've done the right thing.'

The man looked embarrassed but was not leaving, so Hassan dug his hand in his pocket and gave him 30 US dollars. The man thanked him warmly and hurried away. Hassan turned over the object in his hands, he thought it was a little heavy for a clay tablet but did not make much more of it. He decided to call Bibuni right away.

'Yes?' asked a smooth, deep male voice.

'Salam Aleikum Mr Bibuni. How are you?' asked Hassan.

'Aleikum Salam my boy. I'm well. I've been told someone came to see you.'

'News travel fast,' said Hassan, thinking back to the café owner who had been fiddling with a phone while he was sitting with the old labourer.

'So, my boy?' asked Bibuni, unwavering.

'It's a beautiful tablet, with cuneiform writing. I'm sure it's an important text.'

'Scoundrel! Only a few months in the business and already trying to hustle me. Look here Hassan, find me sculptures, gold or silverware, even bronze amulets, but keep your wretched clay tablets. No-one wants to buy this stuff and those who do are more trouble than they're worth; before you know it, they show you an official UNESCO list of looted objects and refuse to pay up, or demand to see other tablets. You never hear the end of it.'

'So what should I do with it then?' asked Hassan.

'What do I care!?' Bibuni yelled down the phone. 'Use it as a chopping block, a wall decoration, whatever you want but don't try to pull that one on me again.'

'Alright Mr Bibuni, I'm sorry.'

'Have you got anything else?'

'Nothing for a couple of days, but I'm sure something will crop up. Any chance of a small advance?'

'Advance on what? Clay tablets? You must be joking. Call

me when you've got something decent and I will give you all the advances you could want.'

The line went dead. Hassan took a deep breath, put the tablet in his bag and left the café.

⤳

Mina and the professor walked briskly through the University campus, both tightly wrapped in traditional woollen shawls. Soon enough, they arrived at a block of flats. Mosul was a strange city: it had seen 8000 years of history and yet today, much of it was a concrete sprawl. The old city kept its charm of course, with its old Abbasid houses and romantic, meandering streets but many academics tended to live just off the campus. It was close to their workplace, cheaper and more secure than other parts of Mosul.

As soon as they entered the professor's flat, Mina recognised the mouth-watering smells of Mrs Almeini's cooking. The old scholar was almost toppled over by his grandchildren, who rushed up to the door to greet him. Their son's children often stayed with them during the day while their parents were at work. Both parents were interpreters for the US army and had a heavy workload. Mina always felt a pang in her heart when visiting the professor's home; there was so much warmth. It was very different from her own home, where her parents were busy trying to be 'American' and her mother rarely prepared Mosuli food. Despite the run-down location, the Almeini's flat was tastefully decorated. Mina knew that most of the silver-ware, rugs and paintings had come from another house, which the family had been forced to flee in an emergency. No-one ever talked about it. Mina suspected that the couple had had another daughter who died there but she had never found the courage to enquire about it.

The professor's wife, a delightfully warm and feisty brunette, was always impeccably dressed and constantly tried to fatten her up, 'You must eat more Mina,' she said, 'you seem so unhealthy.' To this, Mina ritually answered, 'I assure you, Mrs Almeini, I never felt better.'

Mina was always amazed by the old couple's ways. Although Almeini was a modern academic, aware of the latest theoretical twists in scholarship, he still lived traditionally at home. Mina had tried a few times to ask Mrs Almeini about her own thoughts on a variety of subjects but the old woman never engaged in intellectual discussion. Mina could not figure out if it was because she could not, or if she considered it inappropriate to do so in her husband's house.

After dinner, while they sipped tea and nibbled on small crunchy biscuits, the professor turned to Mina. 'Tell me about your research, Mina. Have you made any progress?'

'I have and I haven't. I applied for a travel grant from Columbia, to pursue my PhD investigations in Israel.'

'I guess it will be easier to get this grant than a visa for Israel.'

'Ah Professor, you forget I'm American!'

'True,' he answered. 'So, have you had any luck?'

'I don't know. Nigel hasn't given me much hope on this front. I think he feels that I've dropped out of 'his' programme since I've come here.'

'Would you like me to write to him?'

'No, thank you Professor. I'm sure things will straighten themselves out when I send him some substantial chapters to read. Until then…'

'Until then you're on probation!'

They both laughed.

In his office at Columbia University, Professor Nigel Haw-
thorn was pondering the letter of recommendation he had
promised Mina he would write to the travel grant committee
on her behalf. He was one of that peculiar brand of scholars who never left their office, certainly not to travel to the
country they worked on. He deciphered cuneiform tablets
from Nineveh but felt no need to know what Mosul looked
like, or engage in joint projects with Iraqi scholars. He did
not feel much of anything. In more ways than one, he was a
sort of Victorian scholar stuck in the wrong century. He didn't
understand Mina's need to travel, which he interpreted as an
unscholarly pursuit. He remembered an email she had sent him
when she had just moved to Iraq. It was full of descriptions
of Mosul, its monuments destroyed by the war, the flavours
and fragrances of the food. Her writing was more intoxicating
than persuasive. She recorded the romantic beauty of ruined
Abbasid homes in the old city and wrote at length about the
piled-up houses that overhang the banks of the River Tigris.
They seemed to her as though they had tried, at some point in
time, to race for the riverbank and to have been stopped – just
in time – by a magician's wand.

Nigel was tired of what he saw as Mina's inadequacies as
a scholar. She had been a good student whilst in his care but
he felt she had now strayed completely off rails and needed to
face up to reality. He knew how damning his letter would be to
Mina's application, but he did not care that much. Picking up
his fountain pen, he wrote quickly, and subtly in her disfavour.
Without the support of her own PhD supervisor, any chance
Mina had of getting this grant faded away.

Chapter 3

December 2nd, 2004

In the arid landscape of the Mosuli countryside, a young boy was running as fast as he could down a dirt track. The twelve-year-old was as scrawny as they came but quite resilient. He slowed down as he approached a group of workers, where he spotted his hero, the tallest, strongest, coolest guy he'd ever met. 'Jack, Jack!' he shouted.

The ruggedly handsome 35-year-old American turned around to greet the boy with a smile. Jack had a square jaw, thick dark hair and piercing blue eyes that always seemed to see and know everything. But what Muhad liked best about Jack was the crescent-shaped scar above his left eyebrow.

'Muhad? Catch your breath and tell me what all this excitement is about.'

'Jack,' said the excited boy, breathing heavily, 'we found the *qatan*.'

Jack laughed. 'The qa*n*a*t*. You found the *qanat*. Now that's great news. Take me there.' He turned to the villagers, 'Guys, take a break.'

Jack was relieved. He'd worked in this village and been around Muhad long enough to know that the young boy was not only very resourceful but usually spot on. At last, his small irrigation project might just take off. He had almost run out of funding and had he not met that old scholar at the university, he'd never have thought of looking for a *qanat*, one of the numerous ancient underground irrigation canals that crisscrossed entire regions of Iraq.

Muhad had run on ahead and was standing on top of a pile of debris, with a huge smile on his face. He was so proud to show off his find to Jack, whom he idolised. He had lost both his elder brothers in a roadside bombing a year earlier and Jack was the next best thing.

As Jack approached the small mound, he knew Muhad had found what they had been searching for. He unclipped his faithful trowel from his belt and started cleaning the clay canalisation. He looked up, trying to trace the progress of the *qanat* in an imaginary line. He wondered if it joined a spring or a subterranean river. He picked up his mobile phone and dialled a number.

'Hi. Jack Hillcliff. May I speak to Professor Almeini?' asked Jack, in his strong East coast accent.

'Yes of course,' said the secretary, patching him through to the professor's office.

'Hello Jack,' said Professor Almeini, always happy to speak to the engineer.

'Hi there Professor.'

'How's work going?'

'Very well; we found the *qanat*.'

'Wonderful! Was it in the quadrant we spoke of?'

'Yes. Young Muhad found it this morning.'

The old scholar laughed. 'I might borrow him someday; he could help me find some long lost papers in the departmental archives.'

'The problem is I can't see anything remotely watery in my line of sight. Also, even if I triangulate the potential direction it might have taken to find the water source, the landscape may have changed radically since antiquity.'

'I agree and as we discussed, some of these *qanats* go for many miles underground.'

'Yeah,' said Jack, 'I can't start drilling holes all over the place.'

Both fell silent.

'Jack, why don't you pass by my office later today, and we will go over the maps once again. Maybe there is something we missed. I'll also introduce you to someone who is more versed than myself in the archaeology of the region. I am a linguist after all.'

'OK. That's a good idea. See you later.'

He smiled at Muhad, patted him on the shoulder, and they walked back to the villagers.

⌇

Mina was a creature of habit. She always woke up at dawn, had a shower, spent half an hour doing yoga stretches, had breakfast and started work. But not this morning. It was past eight a.m. and she was still in bed, wide awake. She felt that Nigel, her PhD supervisor had let her down – after all, she had never officially interrupted her research.

She was trying to remember something that had troubled her in their last conversation when she visited him a few weeks before at Columbia.

'I need to spend a few weeks in Safed in Israel,' she'd said to Nigel.

'Why?'

'It concerns some odd discrepancies in the writings of Benjamin of Tudela.'

'The 12th century Jewish traveller from Spain?'

'Yes. You remember his descriptions of Mosul and the ruins of Nineveh?'

'Yes. I thought the other traveller was much more interesting. What was his name again?'

'Petachiah of Ratisbone. Yes, he writes more on Nineveh but hear me out, Nigel. On his way to Mosul, Benjamin de Tudela passed through many cities in Palestine. He recorded whether Jews lived there or not, described synagogues. He also recorded the numbers of Jewish inhabitants and did this throughout his travels.'

'And?'

'As you know, Safed blossomed as a centre of learning and mysticism for Jews later in the 16th century, the whole kabbalistic renaissance, and so on. But what I find surprising is that according to Tudela's writings, he found no Jews there in 1170.'

'What's so strange about that? Maybe there weren't any Jews then even if it did become an important place later on.'

'Maybe. But Tudela's other accounts were all accurate, except for this one. I found a piece of evidence in the British Library which contradicts it entirely: as you know, Tudela's *Book of Travels* was actually written by an unknown author who compiled his travel notes.'

'I know that, so what?'

'Well, a number of specialists believe that this anonymous compiler picked and chose the material and did not insert everything into the manuscript. I think they're right, and I can prove it.'

'Go on.'

'Among the other works bound to the manuscript, an essay by Maimonides and various other commentaries, there were a few pages of Arabic poetry. No-one has paid much attention to them until now because they were in Arabic and not in Hebrew and because they were never inserted in the compiled manuscript of Tudela's travels. But, I think Benjamin of Tudela copied these poems himself during his travels, because he also jotted down a few notes among them.'

'What do the notes say?'

'That he sent a letter to a certain Mordechai in Safed, on his return from Mesopotamia.'

'Really? How interesting,' Nigel suppressed a yawn. Mina looked at him. He didn't seem in the least bit interested.

'There wasn't much more, but I thought that the name Mordechai couldn't be anything other than Jewish, and the travel note states that he is 'in Safed'. That's how I made the assumption that there must have been at least one Jew in Safed.'

'So what? Aren't you seriously digressing from your thesis? You're supposed to be studying the writing of explorers in Mesopotamia, not Israel!'

'I think this deserves to be followed up. There might be more information to be gleaned in Safed. They have synagogues and archives that date back centuries… maybe I'll find more writings by Tudela?'

'Right. What do you expect from me?'

'Well, I was hoping that you could write as my referee to the travel grant committee?'

'Mina, as your PhD student status is suspended until you return to m…to the department, I'm not sure you will receive all the support you deserve. But I'll write on your behalf.'

'Thank you so much. I thought you didn't want to write any recommendations until I returned to New York?'

'Well, in this case, I'll make a small exception.'

Laying on her back, Mina reflected on these last words. Nigel was not known for his forgiving nature, and she had never known him to make exceptions. What did it all mean? She was not getting anywhere this morning. She got up, and had a shower.

～

An hour later, Mina walked out of her flat and proceeded to the backroom of Ibrahim's, a small art dealer in the market. She did this twice a week. The word was out through various channels that she helped whoever possessed illegal ancient artefacts to return them to the museum. She did not offer money, but she did offer anonymity and peace of mind. Unfortunately, in these times of need, very few genuine people came to see her. Many came by and tried to hustle her, and some actually came just to know if what they possessed was worth anything. She knew all this, but what else could she do? She had no money to offer these people.

'Hello Madam,' said an embarrassed voice.

'Hassan?' She was surprised to see him there.

'You don't seem very happy to see me,' he answered, disappointed.

'Of course I am,' and without beating around the bush, added 'but I still have in mind a chat I had with Professor Almeini about you last night.'

'Ah…'

'Yes. *Ah*. What are you doing? You're an excellent student. You should finish your degree and I'll find a way of getting you a scholarship to pursue your studies in the US. Life is so tough here. You need a break.'

She wasn't sure she could deliver on this promise, but she told herself she'd give it her best shot. Hassan seemed to hesitate and for an instant lost his usual cockiness.

'I would like that very much,' he said, looking down at his feet.

'What's the story about you working for 'art sharks'?'

He laughed heartily. He was the one who had come up with the expression one day during class.

'Honestly? They pay more than normal jobs, Madam, and I need the money.' He sat down, pulled out his bag and took out the rag-covered tablet. He handed it to her sheepishly, 'A gesture of goodwill.'

She was surprised, but did not show it. She removed the rag, and looked at the tablet.

'It's really heavy, Hassan.'

'Yes, I noticed that too when I first held it.'

'Weird,' she said.

'Can you read the inscription?'

'I'm amazed you didn't try to do so yourself.'

'I'm a little rusty,' he answered.

'Come on Hassan, don't be lazy. Let's have a look together. Is it intact?'

'No, it's missing the top part, and it was probably originally rectangular although only a large square remains.'

'Good. Language?'

'Akkadian.'

'Start at the top,' she said.

Hassan studied the tablet, 'We're missing the addressee, but the first few lines seem to describe the sale of a property between two distinct parties.'

'Good. You aren't that rusty Hassan. I'll take this to the department and catalogue it as Mos.Has.01 for tablet found in Mosul by Hassan, no.1.' He smiled, proudly. 'Any idea where this tablet was found?'

'No. I didn't think to ask the old labourer.'

'That's too bad. I'm off to the department now. See you in class?' She stood up, feeling quite excited.

⌒

As soon as Mina sat down in her office, she unwrapped the tablet and started reading. There was something strange about it. Although she agreed with Hassan's interpretation about the original rectangular shape of the tablet, this type of contract did not usually require many more lines than what was already here, so the original was probably not much longer than its current square shape. More importantly, the weight of this tablet felt wrong. She picked up the phone and called the small office of the janitor. Nurdin Muhammad used to be an art restorer at the Mosul museum, but in 2003, like many others, realised that the salary he had been waiting months for was not going to materialise. He had been forced to find different work, any work really. Now he was a janitor at the university.

'Hi Nurdin. Mina Osman here. I need to borrow a small pair of scales. Great. Half an hour? Thanks.'

There were enough student essays piled on Mina's desk to keep her up all night marking them. She picked up the first essay and started running through it. When she first started teaching at the department she had been aware of the students' poor English grammar, strange syntax and flowery vocabulary. But she had enjoyed their eagerness from the first instant and how uncontrived their writing was in comparison to some of her New York students. None of these boys followed a set path in the presentation of their essays or in their analyses. They enjoyed being given free rein to write in English about their own past, and they took full advantage of it.

A knock on the door brought her out of her marking reverie. It was Nurdin.

'Miss Osman?'

'Hi Nurdin. I see you have the scales. Thanks.'

'Can I have a look?'

'Please.' She knew all about Nurdin's former life and felt awful about his situation. His hands were strong and agile, and the assured way with which he picked up the tablet testified to the many priceless objects he had handled on a daily basis. He set up the scales on her desk, and weighed the tablet.

'You're right. The weight is completely wrong. I don't understand. It's much heavier than clay.'

'But it is clay?' she asked.

He passed his fingers on the surface.

'Yes it is. But the weight is more like that of a small stone slab. There must be an obvious explanation, but it eludes me,' he sighed, 'I have to get back to my daily chores, unfortunately.'

'Thanks for your help Nurdin.'

'Good luck,' he said as he left the room, shutting the door behind him.

Mina leaned back in her chair, puzzled. There was another

knock on the door. She quickly wrapped the tablet in its rag and put it away in her desk.

'Come in,' she said.

'Good morning Mina,' said Professor Almeini. 'How are those essays?' he glanced at the pile of paper on Mina's desk.

'They're quite good actually.'

'May I introduce you to my American friend Jack Hillcliff?'

Jack appeared behind the professor and stepped into the office. Mina stood up and shook his hand.

'Mina Osman.'

'Jack Hillcliff.'

She observed the handsome man in front of her. He seemed unpretentious and had a thoughtful air about him.

'Jack is in charge of an irrigation project in a small village outside Mosul,' explained Professor Almeini.

'You're American? It must be dangerous for you working on the outskirts of Mosul these days.'

'No more than working in downtown Mosul I guess,' he answered, smiling at her.

'Point taken,' she smiled back at him.

'People need water, especially in wartime,' he explained as if carrying out this kind of project while the war raged on was perfectly normal.

'Jack and I are working together on an aspect of his project and I thought you might be able to give him a hand,' Professor Almeini said.

'Sounds interesting. I didn't read anything about a departmental irrigation project?'

Jack answered immediately, 'Oh, it's nothing like that. I've got funding from a number of NGOs to bring water to this village and make it as self-sufficient as possible. I'm an irrigation specialist of sorts. And, until I ran into the Prof here, I was a little stuck.'

'How's that?' she asked.

The professor smiled at them, 'Mina, Jack, I need to get back to my office. I'm so glad you've met.' Looking at Mina, he added 'Don't forget we have a publication committee meeting this afternoon.'

'Of course not, Professor. See you there.'

Mina turned to Jack, 'So, Jack, have a seat and tell me all about how you met Professor Almeini.'

She was doing her best to be pleasant, but she was aware that her body language was a little awkward, always a sign that she was attracted to a man.

'I met the Prof through a mutual friend, a hydrologist in Baghdad. To be honest, I was a little nervous when I first met him but we started chatting, and before I knew it, we were talking shop.'

She smiled, 'He does tend to have that effect on people.'

'I came to him with questions about local *qanats*, you know those underground water canalisations. They're quite common in arid or semi-arid climates. Thousands of them are still in use in Iran and Afghanistan, and some since the Middle Ages. They carry water for dozens of miles without losing much through evaporation. But I couldn't find any around the village where I work. He suggested looking for ancient ones, going back to the time of King Darius.'

'You're kidding, right? Did he forget to mention that King Darius lived 2,500 years ago?'

'I know. It sounded insane at first but you know, irrigation specialists all over the world, and especially those working in developing countries, often investigate how things were done in ancient times.'

Mina thought about it and had to agree with him. Knowledge of water systems had not progressed that much over the last thousand years. All it took was keen observation of the water table, underground water and gravity over a long period of time. She had read somewhere about a *qanat* in Iran, in the city of Gonabad, which still provided drinking and agricultural water, 2700 years later. It was over 30 miles long.

'I'm totally under-funded and have little time to carry out my project' Jack continued. 'Although Mosul is built on the west bank of the Tigris and it's the major river in the region, we couldn't afford to set up a secure network all the way to the river. The Prof showed me some maps of the region's archaeologically excavated *qanats* and two of them happen to pass very close to the village I'm working in. He felt sure that if I found at least one of them, and could somehow follow its path, maybe I would find the underground water source, which this *qanat* used to tap into.'

Mina looked horrified. 'You want to use an ancient *qanat* to bring water to the village?'

Jack burst out laughing. 'No, I think I'd run into trouble with sanitary officials! If I could find that water source, I would lay pipes and a filtering system, follow the same track and bring at least one line of water supply to the village.'

'OK. I could give you a hand on the archaeological side of things if you're interested.'

'I'm very interested.'

'Great! I have some time to spare. Let's go down to the archive.'

They went down to the basement, into a small room which held the departmental map archive.

'Most of these maps are unpublished. As you can imagine, with the current state of affairs, there are more pressing needs.'

'I can. I'm also surprised the basement wasn't looted.'

'I know. It was seriously messed up though. We've spent months putting some order in the archive. The students have helped us tremendously. Where is the village?'

'About 30 miles west of the city,' he answered.

'What's it called?'

'Al-Bayaty Ninewa' he answered.

Mina started rummaging through the piles of maps, and pulled out a few.

'Here you are,' she said, pointing her finger at a dotted line on the map. 'There's the beginning of the *qanat*. And look! There seems to be a small pocket of underground water. Now, if we superimpose the first map…here's the village. Where did you find the *qanat*?'

'Roughly here' he said, pointing at a spot on the map.

'You're only about a mile and a half from the water pocket,' she said triumphantly.

'That's amazing. Can I have a photocopy of this map?'

'Of course. Just mention the help you got from the department to whoever funded you.'

As they walked back up to the main reception room, she asked him 'So Jack, you're an irrigation specialist?'

'Of sorts. I'm an engineer, with an interest in irrigation.'

'Your project strikes me more as a humanitarian one than the sort of job you'd normally go for with your expertise.'

A wave of sadness seemed to pass over his face.

'I…The village really needs it, and many more villages do,

too,' he answered. 'We should exchange numbers, if that's alright with you, Mina,' he said politely.

'Of course. Here's my card.'

'I don't have one, but I'll just write down my contact details the old fashioned way.'

'An engineer without a business card?' she teased.

〜

'We simply don't have enough funds to publish such drivel!' The head of department was fuming. He could not believe a woman was telling him what his department should or should not publish, 'With both departments running on half our usual staff we need to focus on what is most pressing. Even a tourist such as yourself should understand the difference between primary and secondary concerns,' he concluded.

Mina tried to fit in another word, but Professor Almeini cut her short. He turned to the head of department, 'Some books of a decidedly theoretical nature may have to wait until the more pressing archaeological reports are published. But we must be aware of the current changes in thought processes in our field, or...' his gaze hardened as he looked at his adversary, 'we may lose track complete of what we're supposed to pursue as scholars. Don't you think?'

'Of course Professor, of course.' The diminutive head of department was a mediocre scholar but an astute politician. 'I think this is as good a time as any to conclude this meeting. I will see you all in three months time. My secretary will send out a reminder two weeks before the meeting.'

He stood up, ignoring Mina and said goodbye to his colleagues. Mina had not felt like a woman for quite some time and it felt good to be recognised as one again, even in a negative context. When she first arrived in Mosul she had expected to be relegated to some horrid basement office and that being the only woman in the department, no-one would speak to her. A friend working in Pakistan had told her that every time there was a conference or committee meeting, the female scholars went to a different room from the men. But things could not have been more different. She wondered at first if she enjoyed her special treatment because of her connection with Columbia University, or her being half-American, but after a while she understood that being a woman was irrelevant to most scholars around her. She was a scholar herself, a third gender of sorts. Of course to some chauvinists like the head of department, there was no such thing as a third gender. She was a woman, nothing more, and nothing could be less.

'What a horrid man,' Mina muttered, as she walked out of the meeting room with Professor Almeini.

'Mina, Mina. You're so hot-headed. I wonder if you are at all suited for the world of academia and its little games of power, precedence and give-and-take.'

'I just want what is best for the department,' she answered passionately.

'I know,' he said, smiling. Then, with an air of innocence he asked, 'what did you think of Jack?'

'His project is quite thrilling,' she answered. 'Although similar projects are carried out in other countries, if this one works, it would be a first here and might even show the doubters in government that studying our past can benefit our present.'

'I like him,' said Almeini, 'he's bright and his heart's in the right place. There's more to this young man than meets the eye.'

Chapter 4

Hassan's clay tablet was on her coffee table. Mina felt a pang of guilt for having brought the ancient artefact back from the office but she often had her best ideas in the comfort of her own home. Sipping her favourite drink, a sweet mix of Bailey's and coffee, she ran through a couple of hypotheses. She brought in a brighter desk lamp, set it up next to the table, turned it on, and studied the tablet from every angle. One idea she had, however strange it seemed might answer the riddle. What if there was something inside the clay that made it heavier? She knew of tablets that had been found within clay casings, like envelopes. Granted they weren't usually covered in writing but if they were, they acted as seals to be opened by the recipient. Of course there were always exceptions. She could have it x-rayed. But that would require huge amounts of administrative paperwork, and she would have to wait weeks or even months before seeing any results.

Dispirited, she fiddled with the tablet. Suddenly it slipped between her fingers and hit the table. Horrified, she picked it up immediately to check for any damage. One of the corners had broken off. She looked at its cross-section but it seemed completely normal. There was nothing inside the tablet. She felt so embarrassed, both for dropping the tablet and for her mad conjectures. Maybe Nigel was right, and it was time she returned to the US.

◡

Mina stayed in bed, wide awake, for a few hours. Finally, at one a.m., she got out of bed, turned on the light and took a long, hard look at the tablet. She went into her study and picked out the smallest chisel she could find. Sitting down by the coffee table, she took a deep breath and tried chipping off another piece from the tablet. The sound was not that of chipping clay. There was something inside. She felt like an excited child about to rip open her birthday presents.

An hour later, she was soaking a slim and shiny tablet of black stone in warm soapy water. It was possibly basalt, and was roughly 22cm long and 15cm wide, snapped at the bottom in a diagonal break. She rinsed it carefully and dabbed it all over with cotton wool. One side was entirely covered in the most delicate cuneiform lettering she had ever seen. Mina was in a state of shock. She headed to her study and found her Akkadian and Sumerian dictionaries and grammar books.

After a few hours of work, she sat back in awe. Before her eyes was a version of the eleventh chapter of the *Epic of Gilgamesh*, written in Akkadian! The Epic was the most famous Mesopotamian literary text, and possibly the most ancient epic in the world. It dated back four thousand years. In its final form, also called Standard Akkadian Epic of Gilgamesh, edited by the incantation priest Sîn-lēqi-unninni sometime between 1300–1100 B.C.E., it ran on twelve tablets. The eleventh tablet was famous for recounting the story of the primordial flood. She went back to her study, picked up an English translation of the *Epic of Gilgamesh* and reread the story of the flood. She then looked over her translation of the tablet. It presented a strange version of the story: some passages from the usual narrative were missing and others seemed more detailed or contained new information. For instance, there were far more measurements of the ark than in the standard flood tablet. And the narration broke off during the construction of the ark, so all the descriptions of the actual flood and its aftermath, the famous scenes of Utnapishtim sending out birds to see if the waters had receded, were missing.

She sat back on her couch, thinking about the parallels between this Sumerian myth and the Biblical account of the flood and the story of Noah's Ark. The similarities had first been pointed out by an English scholar in the 19th century. She thought of the hundreds of scholars who, since then, had pondered the differences and similarities between the two accounts. She knew one thing for certain: the tablet she was holding displayed the only version of its kind in stone.

She could of course email the proper linguists and scholarly authorities, after all, she was not a specialist in epic textual analysis. But if she kept this tablet to herself and published a proper translation and commentary, it could be her making as an academic. She would have to explain how she got hold of it in the first place, and why it was encased in a fake clay tablet, but it would be worth it. The more she reread her rough translation the more she noticed how many odd elements there were in this text. A small detail suddenly caught her eye. Why had she not noticed this earlier? The beginning of the text conformed to other versions:

Gilgamesh spoke to Utnapishtim, the Faraway:
'I have been looking at you,
but your appearance is not strange – you are like me!

You yourself are not different – you are like me!
My mind was resolved to fight with you,
but my arm lies useless over you.
Tell me, how is it that you stand in the Assembly of the Gods,
and have found life?'
'Utnapishtim spoke to Gilgamesh, saying:
'I will reveal to you, Gilgamesh, a thing that is hidden,
a secret of the Gods I will tell you!

But then from here something had changed. Unlike the canonical Sumerian version in which the Gods are angry because the humans make too much noise and they decide to kill them all, this text was referring to humans having turned evil. Very much like the Biblical version. But this was impossible! The text couldn't have been inspired by the Hebrew bible as it was far more ancient. Plus she had never heard of such a typically Jewish moralistic view in an Akkadian version of the Flood. Furthermore, most stone or metal tablets were found in the foundations of temples. But this tablet was no foundation stone.

Who could she talk to about this? She could not confront Professor Almeini and explain that she had destroyed a clay tablet to get to the stone tablet. Gradually it dawned on her that by destroying the clay casing she had put herself in jeopardy. She could not talk about her find to anyone in her field. Of course, it was a fake clay tablet, whose only purpose was to conceal the stone tablet beneath, but it was still an ancient fake. In her eagerness, she had acted like an irresponsible child, against all the ethical and scientific methodology instilled in her over years of studying. She had committed the oldest sin the book: breaking something to understand it. This discovery, far from making her famous, could even turn out to be her undoing. Nurdin, the janitor, knew she had an unusual tablet, and it was only a matter of time before everyone would know she had a new unpublished tablet at the department. What a mess. She suddenly felt overcome by a wave of nausea and exhaustion.

Chapter 5

December 3rd, 2004

'Five more to go' thought Mina, stretching. She was correcting essays in her office, but from time to time she would glance at the thin stone tablet peeking out of her handbag. She was still unsure what to do about it. Why had it been encased in an ancient fake clay tablet? Obviously to conceal its importance, to make it look like any of the tens of thousands of clay tablets produced at the time. She could not understand what was so special about the stone tablet that would require such a sophisticated disguise. Moreover, the tablet was incomplete, yet still someone had found it necessary to conceal it.

What she really needed to do was speak to an independent scholar who would understand the importance of the find without questioning the particular context of the discovery. There was someone she remembered from a seminar she had attended at Harvard years ago. He was an old scholar in Hebraic studies who specialised in the philological history of Noah and his counterpart in the Sumerian tradition. He had an unusual name. She remembered thinking it sounded almost Japanese. What was his name? Shobai, Moshe Shobai. That was it.

With a bit of luck she might still have his contact details. She turned on her laptop, drumming her fingers on the table, cursing her old computer for being so slow.

'Bingo!' She still had his email address. He worked for a Jewish foundation in London, The Key to Tradition. She remembered that it was 'A very well-funded institution,' a colleague at the seminar had told her in hushed tones. She emailed a short summary of the translation to the old man with a few notes reminding him who she was and what the problem was with the tablet. Hopefully he would get back to her soon. As she sifted through her emails, she noticed one from Nigel. Anxiously, she opened it.

Dear Mina,
I'm sorry to be the one to give you this news. Your travel grant application was turned down. I don't think it has anything to do with your qualities as a scholar. There were many other high-calibre applicants and only two grants were offered this year. Don't hesitate to re-apply next year. You may be luckier next time…'

She couldn't read anymore. She slumped in her chair, crushed by the consequences of this news. She wouldn't be able to pursue her research on Benjamin of Tudela in Safed. She had been so looking forward to it. She wondered if the result would have been different had she remained in New York as a full-time PhD student. But she hadn't. It was idle thinking.

∽

The next step was to call Hassan and ask where she could find the old labourer who had brought him the tablet. Hassan would be curious about this. Could she trust him with such sensitive information? She would think about what to do when it came to it. First she needed to ensure that he would keep his mouth shut.

'Hassan?'

'Morning Madam Mina' answered the young man, sheepishly. 'I've just made up my mind to come and see Professor Almeini, to apologise for my behaviour over the last month.'

'That's great news. Listen, could you come to see me first? I need to talk over a few things with you.'

'Alright I'll come before lunch.'

She still had a few hours ahead of her to focus on research. Hopefully no-one would disturb her. She picked up her notes on Benjamin of Tudela. She was so disappointed not to have obtained the funds to travel to Safed. She would have loved to research the strange discrepancies in his stories. She'd left out a few details in her account of Tudela's manuscript when she'd spoken to Nigel. More importantly, she couldn't tell him about her intuitions as he clearly didn't seem to care. But like all researchers who spend a lot of time reading and deciphering every aspect of an author's work, she could almost sense what Tudela had left out in his accounts.

She refocused on Tudela, and on his travels in Palestine. She sensed he had intentionally withheld information in his account of Safed. There was a mystery here that she needed to unravel.

⌒

It was almost lunch time. Where was Hassan? The phone rang. 'Ah' she thought, 'he's calling to say he can't come'. But it was Jack.

'Hi there Mina,' he said in a cheerful voice.

'Hi Jack,' she answered, pleasantly surprised by the phone call. 'Was the search successful?'

'Yes, very. That's why I'm calling. Would you like to come over to the village tomorrow and see how your and the professor's deductions have created a lifeline for this village? We should hit the water source tomorrow, early afternoon.'

'That's great.'

'So will you come?' he asked again.

'Well…'

The department secretary put her head round the door and mouthed that the professor wanted to see her when she had a moment. Mina put her hand over the receiver and said she would be with him as soon as she could. She resumed her conversation with Jack as soon as the secretary left.

'Ok Jack, I'll see if I can leave the office tomorrow afternoon.'

'Could you ask the Prof to join us too? I haven't been able to reach him all morning.'

'I'll do that. See you tomorrow.'

'Oh, Mina?'

'Yes?'

'Don't leave Mosul much after lunchtime. There are loads of checkpoints on the road, but it's still dangerous. Parts of Mosul feel like the Wild West these days.'

'Thanks. I'll remind Professor Almeini about that,' she said ironically.

Mina was pleased Jack had called her and she was looking forward to seeing his work, but before long she was worrying again. What if Nurdin, the restorer-turned-janitor had told the professor about the tablet, or worse, Hassan had met him before seeing her? She felt miserable not being able to discuss her discovery with Professor Almeini. He had been so good to her and this is how she repaid his kindness. She heard a familiar voice in the corridor. It was Hassan. Mina hesitated for a second, then stepped out into the corridor. She beckoned to the young man to follow her into her office.

'Have you seen Professor Almeini?'

'Ah yes. I'm sorry. You asked me to come first to see you but I bumped into him, so I decided to talk to him there and then.'

'Oh dear.'

'What is the matter?'

'Nothing. Did you happen to tell him about the tablet you gave me?' She asked, avoiding his gaze.

Hassan was surprised by her tone. She was usually so direct but now she seemed changed, as if she was hiding something.

'No. We spoke of the courses I'd have to take and the readings I had to catch up with.'

She looked him straight in the eyes and said, 'I need to ask you two things. First, would you mind not telling anyone about the tablet you gave me until… until it's published?'

Hassan could tell she wasn't being entirely straightforward, but he couldn't work out what she was being so cagey about.

'OK Madam. And the second thing?'

'Where did you say the labourer found it?'

'I don't know,' he answered.

'That's really frustrating. You know how important context is in archaeology!'

'I can find out where the labourer lives if that's any help,' said Hassan.

She breathed a little easier. 'Yes that would be useful.'

Hassan felt compelled to question her. 'Madam Mina?'

'Yes Hassan?'

'…What's going on?' he asked.

This clever young man had returned from enemy territory to the difficult path of an honest, hard-working student. She owed him a straightforward answer. Somewhere inside her she also felt the need to share this find with someone, and who better than Hassan? She needed to come clean.

'You brought me something special the other day.'

'What, the tablet, Madam?'

'Can I entrust you with something? You must swear that not a word of this conversation will leave the room.'

He looked straight at her. 'Yes, you can. You know you can. I swear not to tell a living soul.' He felt a wave of pride that Mina was about to confide in him.

'You remember how heavy the tablet was?' she asked the young man.

'Yes.'

'There was something inside it.'

'Inside… you… you broke it?'

She blushed. 'Well. I think you should have a look at what I found.'

She pulled out the shiny black tablet from her handbag and placed it on the desk. Hassan's eyes widened in awe. 'What is it?'

'Hassan, this is probably the strangest account of The Flood that I know of.'

'You mean, stranger than the fact it was encased in clay?'

'Do you know Hassan, I'm glad you're back.'

He beamed with pride.

'Yes. Why would this have been hidden to start with? There must be something in the text… some secret information.'

'Now you've been reading too many mystery novels.'

'Why not? What else is strange about it?'

She described odd features of the tablet, pointing out to her wide-eyed student the various complex mathematical equations in place of the usual elementary Ark measurements, and the unexpectedly Jewish-sounding moralistic explanation of the Flood.

'This could be one of the most important finds in Mosul in decades,' Hassan stammered, clearly astonished.

'I know,' she answered, lost in her own thoughts.

'And to think I just handed it to you like that,' he said, looking utterly defeated.

'Yup,' she giggled. 'You could have made a fortune. Instead,' she added, 'you'll be famous.'

'At least my mother will be happy,' he answered with a smile.

Mina laughed. She was so happy to find that Hassan hadn't changed, he was still as sharp and funny as he had been in her classes. But she suddenly became serious.

'We need to keep this information to ourselves.'

'I understand.'

'You need to find the labourer's whereabouts. I don't think for a second that this tablet was stolen from a museum. He must have found it somewhere in an illegal dig.'

Hassan picked up his things. 'I'm on it Madam. I'll get the information by tomorrow.'

'Thanks,' she answered, relieved.

They left her office together and Mina walked on to Professor Almeini's office.

'Hello Mina' Professor Almeini said, smiling broadly.

'Hello Professor.'

'I don't know what you said to young Hassan, but he's back. I'm so glad. It really would have been a shame to lose one of our finest students to the criminals who plunder our national heritage.'

Mina took a deep breath. That's all there was to it. He had no idea about the tablet.

'I got a call from Jack,' she said, rapidly changing the subject.

'Ah?' said Almeini, pricking up his ears.

'He's invited us both to the village tomorrow afternoon. They are about to hit the underground water pocket.'

'Tomorrow? It's Saturday so I'll be at home with my family. I can't come unfortunately. What a shame.'

'Maybe we could go another day?' she asked.

'No no. You go. Tomorrow will be a great day for the department too. After all it is thanks to you that he found the source.'

'All I did was…' she began.

He brushed her comments aside.

'You should go there. How often do you get to meet handsome idealistic men in Mosul these days?'

Mina blushed from head to toe.

'Professor! Really. That's totally inappropriate!'

'*Inappropriate*,' he repeated, rolling his eyes. 'Maybe you haven't spent enough time in Mosul after all.'

He giggled and swept her out of his office.

Mina was mortified. Even her father had never tried a stunt like that one. Had he planned it all along, introducing Jack to her? She certainly hoped not.

Chapter 6

December 4th, 2004. Morning

Mina whistled as she checked her mailbox. Tucking the large loaf of bread she had just bought under her arm, she reached in awkwardly to pick up a small letter. Back in her flat, she went into her old-fashioned kitchen and made herself a pot of black coffee. As she watched the black liquid steaming in her mug, she thought of the ridiculous choices available in the coffee chains in New York: extra this, fat-free, a shot of this, half-that. Here, in an on-and-off war zone, you sat down in a café and a waiter came to take your order. Back home you queued for twenty minutes to be served in a Styrofoam cup. By the time you'd finished queuing you had to return to work.

She remembered an exchange between an elderly Indian Sanskrit scholar she had met at Columbia and a barista. The scholar had ordered a *chai* thinking it would be plain sweet tea with full-fat milk as you find in Benares, where he came from. The barista asked him if he wanted an 'extra shot'. The scholar smiled, not knowing what to answer. To the old man's horror the barista proceeded to add an espresso shot to his *chai*. Mina had laughed all the way back to the library that day.

She tore off the end of the warm loaf, spread a little butter and poured some honey across it. She closed her eyes and took a large bite. She loved this time of the day. She picked up the letter and opened it. It was a letter of apology from Professor Almeini. 'What a sweetie' she thought. She was not really angry with him and he probably knew it, but he had still taken the time to write to her about his peccadillo. When she thought how she in turn had failed him, she felt guilty as hell.

Mina was shaken out of her guilt as she suddenly remembered that she had to have her car serviced. She had been promising herself that she would get it done. The car was totally unreliable and did not always start when she turned the ignition. Hopefully it would not break down on her way to the village in the afternoon.

Mina decided to stay at home that morning. She had no teaching duties, and felt she needed to jot down some translation notes about the tablet, particularly regarding the mathematical references in the text. She could not understand what they referred to but hopefully someone would. She personally knew at least two scholars working on mathematical cuneiform texts who might help her interpret these formulas.

⌒

Mina hadn't progressed very far in her transcription of the mathematical equations when Hassan rang her doorbell. He seemed in a terrible hurry.

'Hello Hassan. Everything ok?'

'So, so…I got you the labourer's details. His name is Hassaf. I wrote down his address.'

He handed her a piece of paper. 'It isn't a nice part of Mosul. You shouldn't go there alone. I tried meeting him earlier but he was already out at work. No phone, no amenities. It's a terrible place.'

Noticing her scribbled notes and the tablet on her desk, he asked 'Any progress?'

'Not much. I've been trying to render the mathematical equations in the second part of the text, the one that's broken, but I don't have the necessary books here. I'll have to transcribe them as they are, work on the translation at the department and discuss these matters with a specialist later.'

'Right,' he said, a little disappointed.

'What about you? You seem a bit troubled.'

'I owe some money to someone, and I need to return it by today.'

'I'm amazed that anyone would keep to deadlines in this place.'

Hassan's face darkened. 'Some people do, Madam.'

He rushed off. Mina wondered what he had meant. He seemed so un-Hassan-like, so serious. It was as if she had been given a glimpse of another world of which she had no inkling. Perhaps Hassan was in more serious trouble than she had assumed. She wondered if she should discuss this with Professor Almeini.

By early afternoon, Mina had checked herself a dozen times in the full-length mirror in her bedroom. She had not worn her field archaeologist's outfit for months. It consisted of a pair of jeans with a *kameez* on top, head and neck covered with coloured linen scarves, and battered canvas army boots. She suddenly missed her life in New York where she could dress any way she wished. What choice did she have in Iraq? Particularly as she was going to a remote village. 'I'm not going on a date, after all,' she thought to herself. She checked herself one last time in the mirror and walked out of her flat.

Once she got into her car she closed her eyes, made a silent prayer, and turned the ignition. The car started. It had to be a good omen.

After many twists and turns, she finally arrived at the village. She parked her car by the side of the road, stepped out cautiously and knocked on the door of the first house. An old woman came out. Mina said she had an appointment with Jack and wanted to know how to get to wherever he was. After a while, Mina realised that the reason the old woman kept smiling was that she had absolutely no idea where the men were. Mina had no reception on her mobile phone, so she could not reach Jack that way. As she walked back to her car, feeling somewhat helpless, a young boy came out of another house to meet her.

'Hello Madam.'

'Hello.'

'I'm Jack's collaborator.'

Mina smiled at the boy's self-important tone. She immediately recognised him from the Professor's description of Jack's side-kick.

'He asked me to take you to him when you arrived,' he added.

'You must be Muhad,' she stated.

'Yes Madam,' answered the boy and beamed at her.

'Let's jump in the car then.'

This time, unfortunately, the car wouldn't start. She lost her temper and cursed the day she'd bought the car in every language she could muster.

'Don't worry Madam Mina. If you are up to it, we can walk there. It is only a few miles'.

'A few miles?' she said.

She could just imagine the state in which she'd arrive there, sweaty and covered in dust. She doubted she would find a shower at their destination. The day was getting worse by the minute. Muhad was smiling at her.

'What the hell,' she thought. 'Alright. Let's go,' she told the boy.

'Excellent, Madam Mina. Follow me!'

'Oh. Is it safe to leave the car here?' she asked.

'Yes. Everyone knows it's yours. No-one comes to the village, Madam Mina.'

'Just Mina, Muhad, Madam is for old ladies.'

'OK.'

The more they progressed on their route, the more jovial Muhad became. He kept peppering her with questions, 'Where is New York? Do you drive a S.U.V.? Are you an engineer? Are you married?'

'You ask a lot of questions, Muhad,' she said, trying not to smile.

'I know. Jack always says that I ask too many questions. The boy puffed up his chest and took on a deep voice, 'If you want to be a man, Muhad, you need to ask fewer questions and acquire gravitas'. He turned to Mina, 'What's *gravitas* Mina? Jack won't tell me.'

She laughed. She could just imagine the daily banter between the man and this young boy. What a pair they were, the American engineer and his small, questioning associate. She understood why the professor spoke with such fondness of Muhad. He was very endearing.

As she gazed at the desert landscape surrounding them, the dusty road and detritus on either side, she thought of an article she'd read about the neurosis of Arab *émigrés* longing for the cleanliness of the desert. When she first read this sentence she thought to herself that it had reminded her of the line in *Lawrence of Arabia*, 'Why do you love the desert so, Lawrence?' 'Because it is clean.'

She herself had often felt a longing for the desert when stuck in a traffic jam or when submerged in problems back home. She had even gone travelling to New Mexico with a friend, hoping to find some solace in the emptiness of the landscape. But she had not found it, and instead had ended up here, in the real desert.

She realised she hadn't gone walking like this since she'd first arrived in Mosul. She remembered the first days, visiting every corner of the city, her joy at being there among her fellow countrymen. But slowly, without becoming 'one of them' in the least, she had lost herself in work at the university and somehow forgotten the reason behind her deeper desire and longing to be here. Would she have been the same person back in New York? Would she have forgotten who she was, for the greater good of the university? Possibly. It was a strange conundrum she'd noticed among many university lecturers, who'd arrive as scholars but retire as administrators.

'We're almost there Madam Mina,' said the young boy, who was practically skipping with excitement. His elation was contagious. Mina was looking forward to witnessing the moment the water gushed out. She was already thinking over the outlines of an interesting paper she would write on ethical scholarship and the overlap between archaeology and humanitarian work.

As the road twisted to the right, a group of men hard at work appeared in the afternoon sun. Digging like this would have been unthinkable during the summer but it was winter and the temperature was bearable, even in the early afternoon. The men were eager to find the water source and Mina thought that they would probably have braved the summer's dazzling heat with just the same dedication. Jack looked up and noticed two figures approaching. He stopped what he was doing and walked towards them.

Despite his jeans and shirt being coated in dirt, he had the same rugged and handsome air about him as he had at their first meeting in the more rarefied confines of the university. She couldn't help but notice his thick brown hair and his firm chest, shoulders and arms, all seemingly carved out of wood. His lack of pretension and unpretentious walk made him all the more attractive. He was definitely the strong, silent type. With every step he took towards them, Mina felt her heart beating faster.

'Mina, I'm so happy you could make it,' he said, looking straight at her with his piercing blue eyes. 'Why didn't you drive up here?'

'My car broke down in the village,' she replied, slightly embarrassed.

'Man, you must be exhausted!' He turned to his sidekick, 'Muhad, where's the Prof? Did you leave him in the village so you could keep Mina to yourself?'

Muhad blushed and dropped his head. Mina struggled not to burst out laughing. 'The professor couldn't make it, but I'm sure he's as anxious as me and young Muhad here to see the result of your work.'

Muhad looked up at Mina and gave her a large, toothy grin.

'You drove to the village alone? That was really dangerous,' Jack said to Mina, trying not to seem too concerned.

'I said I was coming,' she answered, 'So I came'.

Mina wasn't quite sure, but she thought that Jack did not seem overly disappointed about Almeini's absence.

'Right!' he replied quickly in an effort to change the subject. 'Let's join the workers. We've almost cracked it!'

When they reached the elevated spot where the men had been digging, Mina could feel the expectation in the air. She stood among them for what seemed an eternity, with little Muhad jumping around the trench. The men seemed so hopeful and absolutely focused on what they were doing. Suddenly, in the settled stillness of the air, they heard a gurgling sound, then a trickle of muddy water appeared.

Great cries of 'Allahuakbar!' went up and the workers yelled with joy. They had found the water pocket. Some were crying, others laughing madly. Jack was running left and right shouting orders to the various workers. He was smiling broadly, but had not lost his head: they needed to make sure that the water was channelled immediately, and he was already calculating the potential supply to the village from the flow of the water. The men got back to work with renewed vigour.

After a while, covered in mud, Jack waved to Mina and smiled. She smiled back. There was a feeling of elation in the air, a sense of easiness. Here in the middle of nowhere, in the most basic conditions, they had witnessed and shared undiluted joy. 'Water gushing from the bowels of the desert...It's like a tale from the thousand and one nights,' thought Mina.

Hassan was on his way back to the small flat he shared with his mother, more light-hearted than he had been in months. Mina believed in him, valued his opinion and had confided in him. He would tell his mother to stop worrying about him, that he would make amends and resume his studies. He was in such a dreamy state he did not see the two men waiting in the side alley beside his mother's block of flats. They grabbed him as he passed by and flung him into the alley. A huge man punched Hassan hard behind the ear and he was knocked off balance. The man held him against the wall, while his skinny partner took out a flick knife.

'You are two days late.'

'I'm sorry! I was going to pay you two days ago, but I was not paid by my boss. I'll have it soon.'

The huge man punched him again, hard.

'You were warned. Three weeks, not one day more,' he said, and brought the knife up to Hassan's throat.

'Please!'

The skinny thug winked at the huge man and punched Hassan full in the face. His nose broke and blood gushed down his face.

'I can get the money! In two days, I'll have the money,' begged Hassan.

'How's that?' asked the thug.

'My boss owes me money. I'll explain the situation to him. Two days. Please!' The man glared at him, hesitating over what to do next.

'Right. You know what two extra days means?'

Hassan nodded.

'We add ten percent to the total.'

Hassan nodded again.

'You have two days. If you don't have the money then, we will be visiting your mother.'

They left him bleeding in the alley. Hassan shivered on the ground, curled up in pain. There was no other way out. He would have to contact Bibuni and tell him about Mina's tablet.

Chapter 7

December 4th, 2004. Evening

Mina sat on a flat rock, watching the villagers at work, taking photographs and writing in her diary. The sun had almost dipped below the horizon. She felt conflicted; she loved this beautiful country but her relationship with it was uneasy. 'Probably like any second-generation immigrant returning to their country of origin,' she thought.

She felt angry when she observed dispossessed men and women walking by her in the bombed streets. There were so many people with makeshift houses, jobs and lives. Although she had not seen any bombings or gunfights, the bullet holes in every other building said it all. A sense of utter ruin was everywhere. It literally hung in the air, burnishing the whole country with an intense sadness.

On the other hand, she knew perfectly well that road-side bombings and kidnappings were carried out by terrorists. It was as if the US had stumbled into a hornet's nest, between the Kurdish separatists who used the war to further their own agenda against the Turkish government and the Christian Armenians who probably wondered how long they could survive in an increasing 'Muslim versus the West' conflict.

People of various denominations and sects fought each other constantly since the end of Saddam's reign.

Those who had been oppressed under Saddam's regime, longed to rise stronger after their lengthy ordeal. After Saddam, the power vacuum had been quickly filled by the US, but it could not last. America would have to leave soon, before the people's frustration and resentment turned to uncontrollable anger.

Yet, the presence of American troops in Iraq did not deserve to be compared to the tyranny of living decades under Saddam Hussein. Mina's parents had left Iraq long before the first Gulf War in 1989 but she remembered her father saying at the time, 'Bush is calling for the Iraqi people to rebel against Saddam, but he won't step in to get rid of him. Bush is no idiot, he won't get involved in internal Iraqi politics because he's got no-one up his sleeve to replace a tyrant. Iraq is not ready for democracy, not as we experience it here. Tribalism, corruption and internal wars cannot be dealt with through formal debate.'

'Not yet', thought Mina, 'Not yet'. She really hoped that things would improve sometime soon.

The heat had gone, and there was a slight chill in the air. It was time to return to the village. Jack gathered his maps and various calculation sheets and then started rounding up the villagers. They all looked tired but happy after a rewarding day's work. Jack joined Mina and walked by her side, silent but contented.

'Are you satisfied with the amount of water at the village's disposal? Will it be enough to supply everyone?' she asked him.

'Hopefully. I still have to make further calculations when I return to the village. I'm so pleased we found this water pocket, but I'm slightly worried about the distance from the village and its altitude: as you know, in a *qanat* the water flows under its own gravity. I really hope it works. I told you how we couldn't set up a water system all the way to the Tigrus, but what's worse is that there is no point connecting our water pipes to the Mosul water system'.

'Why is that?' she asked, genuinely interested.

'Two reasons. The first is that during the summer, there is hardly any water in the water network anyway, so people tend to use water-pumps.'

'And the second?'

'Purifying and sterilizing the water would cost too much.'

'I hadn't realised the situation was that bad in Mosul.'

'God yeah. The pipes are at a lower level than the ground-water. The pipelines are fractured and lots of stuff has got into them that shouldn't be there. You can't imagine the amount of germs and infectious diseases that have appeared in Mosul in recent years.'

'That's a bleak image of Mosul,' she replied.

'Yeah. Listen, as you are staying overnight in the village—'

'Am I?' she asked with a raised eyebrow.

'Well…yeah. Your car's broken. I've lent my jeep to a friend in the next village and no taxis will drive outside Mosul at this time of night. It's too dangerous.'

'It's just that I didn't plan…' she started,

'Oh I'm sure Muhad's mother will lend you everything you need. You can stay with them.'

He stuck his hands in his pockets and mumbled 'I'd invite you to stay at my place, but everything is very traditional out here and unmarried men and women simply don't sleep under the same roof.'

'I know. It's much better like that,' she replied.

They walked on in silence. After a while Jack cleared his throat, 'As I was saying earlier, I won't be working tonight as you are here, and I think we should join the villagers for a small feast they've organised to commemorate this special day'.

'That would be wonderful.'

They continued to walk side by side, slightly self conscious and all too aware of their proximity. When they finally arrived at the village, the women were crying out the joyful and guttural sound which one hears all across the Middle East, at weddings or occasions of great mirth. A magnificent fire, set up near the biggest house, was blazing up to the stars. The men and children sat down on thick woollen blankets, while the women cooked and brought food. There was laughter, chattering and loud calls for more food. All of it was almost drowned by the sound of traditional Arabic music. Someone had brought a stereo cassette tape player. Jack and Mina were guests of honour and were seated on cushions laid out on the richly-patterned rugs. Mina was beaming with pleasure.

The music was turned down a little as an old woman walked towards the fire, holding something wet wrapped in a white cotton cloth. She opened the cloth ceremoniously and brought out a fish. She then sliced off the fish's head and tossed it into the fire all the time muttering words in some long forgotten language. The men clapped and the women cried out. The old woman walked back slowly, and vanished into one of the neighbouring houses. The music came back on again, as though the scene had never taken place.

'I've never seen anything like it,' said Mina.

'Neither have I. I was hoping you might be able to tell me more about it,' replied Jack, looking quite surprised.

'Not really. Maybe it's an old ritual which has passed down

through the ages. The old name of the capital of this region is Nineveh, the city of the goddess Nina.'

'And?'

'She's the goddess of fish. The cuneiform symbol for Nineveh is a fish pictogram.' Jack seemed at a loss, so Mina added, 'cuneiform, you know, the most ancient and common writing form in this part of the world'.

'I've heard of cuneiform. Tell me more,' he said, leaning back on one elbow to look at her.

'The word comes from the Latin *cunei* for wedges, as the writing takes the shape of permutations of wedges or nails in soft clay tablets or inscribed on stone.'

'Wow. That was a pretty clear and concise explanation. Do you speak like that to your students?'

She laughed and thought of friends back home, anthropologists who would have killed to witness the fish sacrifice scene. She imagined how they'd be writing theories on the 'anthropology of fish', fighting epic scholarly battles over the bones of an ephemeral custom.

She looked up at the stars and sighed, 'I'd love some wine right now.'

'Yup. So would I, but you won't get any of it here!'

She knew as much, but it was still disappointing.

'Wait a second, you Christian heathen. I've got an idea. Stay put. I think I have a bottle in my house. You pinch two glasses, and meet me at your car in ten minutes'.

He walked off, chatting with a few villagers on the way, thanking them for their hard labour all day. She waited a few more minutes before casually picking up two glasses and then sauntering off in the direction of her car. Jack was already there, hiding a bottle of wine under his jacket and carrying a shawl.

'You don't propose we sit in my car and hope no-one notices us?' she asked.

'No, no. They're lovely people, but they wouldn't like that much. We need to be out of sight. Let's walk a little way away from the village. It's a bit of a steep walk up some rocks but there's an amazing view when we get to the top. The moon and stars can be our drinking buddies.'

The walk was steeper than she thought but they eventually reached the top. He was right, the landscape was breathtaking. As there was no man-made light for miles, the stars shone like beacons in the night sky and the moon illuminated the desert in a mesmerising way. They sat down on his jacket and Jack proceeded to open the bottle of red wine. He poured her a glass, then one for himself.

'What shall we toast to?' he asked.

'To the cleanliness of the desert,' she answered looking out over the sands.

He laughed, 'To the cleanliness of the desert,' he echoed, smiling.

'What a place. Do you come here often?' she asked.

'Not that much. Sometimes at the end of the day to gather my thoughts.'

'How did you end up here? I mean, here in Iraq?' she asked.

'It's a long story. What about you?'

She told him about her despair when the lootings began in the museums in Baghdad and Mosul, how she'd flown out here and had worked at the university ever since.

'What do you think of the war?' he asked.

'I hate war.'

'Who doesn't?' he answered with a sigh.

'I don't understand how anyone would want to be a soldier.

How could anyone want to learn how to maim and kill other human beings?'

He remained silent, but pulled out a heavy embroidered shawl with which he covered Mina and himself.

'Never mind,' she continued, 'no-one's fighting out here. You said you were an engineer, but you seem to me more like a poet, lost in an Arabian tale, far from home.'

'I thank thee, oh beautiful Princess Scheherazade!'

They both laughed. As they gazed out into the desert and sipped the wine, Jack felt his attraction to Mina growing, but relied on the wine to help him overcome his unexpected shyness towards the beautiful scholar. He edged his hand ever so slightly towards her and reaching out with the tip of his fingers, gently stroked her leg, but she didn't respond to his touch. Should he be more forward? He hesitated but eventually decided to keep his hands to himself and just enjoy the moment.

When the wine was finished they walked back to the village and he introduced her to Muhad's mother. He parted from her a little reluctantly, and wondered how the night might have turned out had they met in the US instead of this village.

'What's wrong with me? I'm acting like a schoolboy,' Jack thought to himself, unsettled. 'Maybe it's the setting, after all, even the fanciest bar in New York couldn't compare to drinking wine with a beautiful woman in the middle of a desert under the vastness of the starry Iraqi sky.'

⏴⏵

'Miss Mastrani?' asked Mr Bibuni over the phone.

'Ah, Mr Bibuni,' answered a cold voice.

'I'm sorry to call you at such a late hour,' said the shifty art dealer.

'It isn't late here,' replied the matter-of-fact voice.

'Of course, of course,' he replied, adding 'what a pleasure to hear the sound of your voice.'

'Have you found anything interesting?' she replied curtly, knowing perfectly well that hearing her steely voice brought no pleasure at all.

'I have come across something that might interest that special client of yours. The flood collector.'

'What is it?' she asked, coolly.

'A very unusual artefact with an inscription relating to the Babylonian flood.'

'Unusual?'

'Yes. It is not a clay tablet and I'm told by my young assistant Hassan that this version differs from the canonical version in more ways than one.'

'Where did it come from?'

The art dealer winced. This was turning from a business proposal to an interrogation.

'Somewhere in Mosul.'

'Email me a photograph of the object.'

'I am so sorry Miss Mastrani, but I can't have any traces of this transaction on the internet. I'm sure you understand. All I can say is that it is the most important discovery since the 19th century when the Gilgamesh tablets were found in the Library of Ashurbanipal here in Mosul.'

'Hmm.'

Natasha Mastrani paused. She was fantasising about how, if she had it her way, she'd watch this fat crook slowly roasting, rather than barter with him.

'Of course, this is just a courtesy call,' said Bibuni. 'Your client was very generous last time we did business but if he is not interested, I'm quite sure others will be.'

'Is it in your possession?' she asked.

'Yes,' he lied.

'I'll be in touch.'

Just before Bibuni put the phone down, he thought he heard a faint clicking sound in the background. He did not give it a second thought.

⤳

A man sitting in a car with all the lights out outside Bibuni's shop, took the miniaturised listening device from his ear and dialled a number on his mobile phone.

'Master?' said the man in a deep voice.

'Yes?' came the reply in clipped tones.

'Bibuni, the art dealer in Mosul, has the object we seek. What should we do?'

'Nothing. Observe and report to me.'

Chapter 8

December 4th, 2004. Malibu, California

Oberon Wheatley, the powerful owner of a corporation worth hundreds of millions of dollars, was jogging back to his Californian mansion. He always thought best when running. At this moment he was thinking about what Natasha had told him a few hours ago, that this artefact might be the one he had been seeking for years. Wheatley trusted her; she seemed to have a sixth sense about such things. She had scouted artefacts from all over the world on his behalf for many years. She also dealt with other, less *artistic* aspects of his business, when the need arose. A seasoned professional, her involvement was always utterly discreet. She was well-mannered and kept her mouth shout. Even her name, Natasha Mastrani, was a cover. He had asked her once what her real name was before she had quit her ruthless past as a CIA operative. She had answered with a smile that implied she could tell him, but if she did, she'd have to kill him. To secure her services and guarantee that she would go above and beyond the call of duty, he paid her a very handsome salary.

The fact that the tablet had been found in Mosul was good news, but he had to be careful this time. He had been indirectly involved in the looting of the Baghdad Museum, and although no-one had pointed a finger in his direction, many people knew that the lootings were too well organised to have been as random as it might have seemed at first.

He stopped on his front steps to catch his breath and measure his pulse. Excellent. He did not smoke, hardly drank, had a trainer and a dietician working for him round the clock and enough money to last him, his three ex-wives and their descendants for generations to come. He was clever, handsome and rich. But, what he really craved was power and he did not yet have enough of that to satisfy him. As much as he lied to the world, he was always completely honest with himself.

$\backsim$

Showered and refreshed, Wheatley walked into his private museum. The walls were covered with exquisite paintings by Braque, Monet and Picasso. But these paintings were merely a screen for his real passion. He pushed a button on a remote control and a large mirror glided silently to one side, uncovering a hidden metal door. He punched in a code on his remote, and the door clicked open. He strode down a glass corridor. At the far end stood another door and beyond it, a bank of monitors linked to complex seismological, barometric and humidity measuring devices. He closed the door tightly behind him and walked through to the end door. As he pushed it open, dimmed lights automatically came on throughout the large room.

This was the place where he kept his most valuable treasures. Even Natasha, who knew so much about his quest, was rarely permitted to enter this vault. In the back room he had hung famous paintings of the Biblical flood story. It had taken him almost two decades to buy or steal these paintings, most of which had been replaced by the faithful copies now admired by curators and the public alike in many illustrious museums and galleries. A series of glass cabinets snaked their way through the room. They contained dozens of cuneiform tablets, stone fragments, Chinese oracle bones, European papyri and manuscripts, all with some relevance to the primordial flood. Over the years he had wasted precious time researching the lost continent of Mu, a hypothetical landmass that allegedly existed in one of Earth's oceans, but disappeared at the dawn of human history. But he had soon concentrated all his efforts on ancient Mesopotamia. If the piece Natasha had told him about really was the one he had been searching for for so long, it would be the crowning jewel in his Flood Room.

He had the perfect shrine for it at the back of the room; a large gold casket, near his marble desk. Once he had the tablet in his keeping he would have all the time he wanted to decipher its wonders. After all, in his line of work, he had access to the most powerful computers in the world.

Natasha had asked him how much he was willing to pay to obtain it. 'Any price,' he had answered. Then she had asked how far he was ready to go if money could not buy it. He had given her a look that told her exactly how far.

Chapter 9

December 5th, 2004. Mosul, Iraq

Hassan woke up with a start. His mother had opened the shutters in his room and catching sight of his battered face, had started to scream. He hoisted himself up gingerly and tried to calm her down but she was inconsolable.

'What happened? Who has done this to you? Why are you not studying? How much more pain can God send me? He took my husband away, then my beloved sons. What am I to do with you?'

She would not stop the wailing and questioning, and Hassan did not know what to answer. He could not bring himself to explain the danger he had placed her in. He had had such wonderful news to share with her before the money-lender's henchmen stopped him outside his home. He felt as if any attempt to get back on the straight and narrow was thwarted at inception. His good intentions were crumbling under the weight of the reality of his situation. His head was pounding with pain and anguish. As he lay there, mute, his mother eventually stormed out of his room, muttering age-old imprecations under her breath. He dressed quickly and made himself some breakfast, as his mother left the house for work.

How was he going to convince Mina to sell him the tablet? He felt miserable. She would never accept. The academic stakes were too high. He would have to find a way to steal it. And do it pretty soon as Bibuni thought he already had the tablet. He had tried calling Mina a few times the night before and this morning but her mobile was out of range or switched off.

He had to be very careful. He did not want Bibuni to know about Mina. It was one thing to betray her trust, but quite another to involve her in the dangerous underworld he was forced to engage in. He refused to have that on his conscience. As he was planning how to break into Mina's flat, his mobile phone rang. It was Bibuni.

'Hassan?' the dealer gasped.

'Yes Mr Bibuni?'

'Where are you right now?'

'At home, why?' asked the young man, apprehensive.

'Get the hell out of there,' Bibuni screamed.

'What's happened?'

'I've made a terrible mistake, my boy.'

Hassan thought Bibuni's voice sounded different, a little slurred, as if he were drunk.

'Some people are on their way to your flat. They're after your tablet.'

'Who are they?'

'I barely survived their visit myself. Run!'

Hassan ended the call and tried to think as quickly as possible. The first thing to do was phone his mother at work. She would have to stay with her sister for a few days in their ancestral village near Kirkurk until things calmed down. He rushed out of the house and slammed the door. He had just reached the corner of his street, when he heard the screeching tyres of a van stopping just behind him. Two men in dark suits ran up, grabbed him and pushed him into the van. Inside the vehicle another man punched him in the side of the jaw. They climbed into the back after him and slammed the door shut. A few seconds later, the van was gone. Everything had happened so quickly that passers-by hadn't noticed a thing.

〜

Jack came by Muhad's house in the morning. Mina had slept wonderfully well. Muhad's mother had practically adopted her, and they had been chatting all morning over breakfast. Jack walked in smiling.

'Morning Mina,' he said, giving her a quick hug.

'Morning Jack.'

He sat at the table and sipped the cup of coffee that Muhad's mother had offered him.

'I got my jeep back,' Jack said. 'Do you want a ride into Mosul? I need to get some spare parts for your car and a few other bits and bobs.'

'Thanks, that would be great. I was also going to ask you a small favour.'

'What is it?'

'I need to meet an old man to ask him a few questions about an artefact I'm researching. He lives in a dodgy part of the old town and I'd feel safer in your company.'

'My pleasure,' he answered. He turned to Muhad and handed him an envelope, 'Can you give these written instructions to the village elder? Just so he knows what to do while I'm away for a week or two.'

'Of course Jack,' said the boy solemnly, as if he'd just been appointed Secretary of State.

Jack and Mina took their leave from Muhad's mother after much hugging and headed back to Mosul. The road was in a sorry state and even though they had less than thirty miles to cover, the drive took a long time. They passed two check-points, where Jack showed his papers. Both times the guards let them through without even asking who Mina was. 'How typical of this place,' she thought to herself. 'Women are invisible.'

When they finally entered the city, Jack parked the jeep near the US army base and told her they would have to walk from there, as it was impossible to drive through the narrow streets of old Mosul. They moved at an easy pace through the maze of medieval streets.

As they walked, Mina showed Jack various architectural remnants of Mosul's past glory. She told him about the far-reaching origins of the city, then called Nineveh, and known in texts as a place of worship of Ishtar, the Babylonian goddess of sex and war. Back in 1800 B.C.E. the goddess's temple was crammed with 'sacred prostitutes' offering their services to the city's male devotees. She told him about King Sennacherib, who transformed Nineveh into the new lush capital of Assyria around 700 B.C.E. She recounted the extraordinary discovery in the 19th century of the Library of Ashurbanipal, which contained hundreds of tablets, including the Standard Akkadian Epic of Gilgamesh. The tablets found in this library were still the subject of research today.

'Look at this door Jack. You see how the stone threshold doesn't seem to fit?'

'Yes?'

'It's a marble slab, probably dating to the 13th century or even earlier. If you were to turn it over, you might find a cross, or something like that.'

'Where did it come from?'

'Probably from one of the many Armenian churches you'll find in Mosul.'

'Many of the local buildings were constructed with material from ancient Roman and Early Christian monuments, which were carved and re-used in a Muslim context.'

'So Christians were here before Islam?'

'Oh yes! Most of Nineveh's pagan inhabitants converted to Christianity. There were also synagogues and temples of all sorts long before the Muslims came into the picture. I suppose all this is long forgotten.'

'I had no idea.'

'Today the population is a strange mixture of Kurds, a large minority of Aramaic-speaking Christian Assyrians, and a smaller minority of Turcoman.'

'That I do know. It's funny how they all seem to live together today, working together, intermarrying. I was a little surprised when I first arrived. We have such a warped impression of this place back home, you know, as if the city was teeming with Islamic terrorists.'

'Which home is that Jack?'

'West Virginia. Couldn't you tell from my accent?'

'No. You seem to have lost all trace of it. How?'

'I studied hard.'

'Engineering?'

'Yes and other things. Ah. Here we are.'

They entered a down trodden street, where crippled houses leaned one against the other, their front doors seeming to sink into the ground. Hassan had not been wrong in his description. She could just imagine the labourer leaving his village in the hope of finding work in Mosul and ending up in this miserable area, surviving among numerous family members huddled together in tiny rooms.

As they arrived at the house described by Hassan, Mina turned to Jack.

'By the way, you said to Muhad you'd be away for a week or two.'

'Yes?'

'Are you thinking of taking a vacation in Mosul?'

'No,' he laughed. 'I received a call the other day and need to sort out a few things.'

'I see. That's a very Jack-like answer: to the point, yet utterly vague.'

She didn't wait for a further explanation and knocked on the door. An old woman peered out shyly. Mina explained who she was, and after much smiling and comforting words, the old lady let them in. She turned out to be the labourer's sister and after she had fetched him, they sat down for tea. Mina never failed to be moved by Middle Eastern hospitality. In this poverty-stricken home, where brothers, sisters, cousins and grand parents all lived in two small rooms separated by a curtain, they still offered tea to visitors.

'You work for the university?' the labourer asked Mina.

'Yes. I teach there. My student Hassan showed me your tablet and I just wanted to know where you found it.'

The old man looked apprehensive, 'He told me that I wouldn't get into trouble'.

'I assure you that you're not in trouble at all. I'm asking you these questions because if I know where the tablet was found, I could learn more about it'.

'I don't think the man understands what you're on about,' Jack said to Mina.

'There may be more similar objects where you found this one,' she said to the man.

'Oh no. You won't find anything there,' he replied.

'What do you mean?' asked Mina.

'My son found the tablet in the rubble of a bombed house,' he explained.

'A house?' Mina asked, trying to hide the growing excitement in her voice.

'Yes, but I think it came from a building buried under the house which was bombed. And since then, the whole area has been bombed again.'

'Could you show us where it was? We will pay you for your time of course,' Mina added quickly.

'Follow me please,' he answered immediately.

They left the house and moved through squalid streets. Rats roamed freely and the rubbish gave off the horrendous smell of decay. They walked on and on. With each step Mina felt more uneasy. She looked at Jack, as if to say 'I'm sorry... and I'm worried'. But his relaxed demeanour calmed her.

'Is it much further?' she asked.

'Not much. We're almost there,' replied the labourer.

The street lead to a large open space, the size of a football field. They walked over the rubble. The old man hadn't lied. An entire block had been razed to the ground by at least two air strikes. It was a horrific scene of destruction. Like everyone else, she had heard about the air strikes, but she had not fully realised their awesomely destructive power: they simply obliterated everything in their path.

The old man stopped, half way across the area, and pointing his finger to a spot on the ground, simply said 'here'. She paid him for his time and he walked away, thanking God for his luck. Jack watched Mina getting down to work, rummaging among the stones. After a while, she picked up a stone, and her face changed, screwed up in intense thought.

'What's up Mina?' asked Jack.

'What's up? I'll tell you what's up. Look at this,' she said with cold fury, showing him a small piece of stone covered with inscriptions.

'Yeah?'

'It's Hebrew, Jack. Hebrew.'

'And?' he asked again, with a look of total incomprehension.

'It means our wonder boys up there bombed a house which must have been built over an ancient synagogue. Then they bombed it again. We won't find anything useful now.'

She sat down on a pile of rubble, exhausted and defeated, and started to cry. Jack let her cry for a moment, then sat down beside her and put his arm around her shoulders.

'I didn't know you were Jewish. I had no idea.'

'I'm not Jewish. My father's Muslim and my mother's Christian', she answered between sniffles.

'So…why are you crying?' he asked, bewildered.

'I'm crying because this must have been a long lost synagogue that Benjamin of Tudela described in his travels. And, as if it wasn't enough, this was the very place that my stone tablet came from.'

'Time out! I'm totally lost right now. You're going to have to tell me more or nothing at all.'

'OK. But I need to get out of here,' she said, wiping the tears from her face.

'Right. I know a nice café in the old city. I'll take you there.'

Chapter 10

Mina sat across from Jack in his favourite café. She took a sip of tea and started talking almost immediately. 'I'm researching the travels of Benjamin of Tudela, a Jewish merchant who lived in Spain in the 12th century. He left his country in 1166 for a long series of travels that lasted almost a decade.'

'That's some holiday.'

She pretended not to have heard his joke and continued.

'Well, although he wrote a lot, and his *Book of Travels* is a very learned account of the socio-political world of his time, he was nevertheless a merchant and as such, spent a long time in Baghdad, which was a thriving and opulent Jewish centre.'

'OK. So the man was a clever merchant.'

'Are you going to interrupt me all the time?' asked Mina.

'No no, just get to the point.'

'Fine. His writings were already disseminated in his lifetime but proper publications and most translations date from the 16th century onwards. The original and oldest manuscripts date back to the 12th century and are in the British Library, and the libraries of Rome, Vienna and Oxford. The British Library's manuscript is the finest of them all, and the purest.

'The purest?' asked Jack, desperately trying to keep up with Mina's account.

'Yes, the other manuscripts contain pieces inserted by other writers. The British Library manuscript is bound with very few other works. Anyway, when I accessed it at the British Library for research, I noticed in the catalogue that there was another manuscript with the same number, 27.089.'

'You actually remember accession numbers of manuscripts?'

Of course I do. I only worked on a few manuscripts by Tudela. I asked the librarian about this, he checked and said I had misread the number, which was actually 27.089bis. It was a sort of adjunct manuscript, a bundle of pages with Arabic poems. To cut a long story short, among them I discovered unpublished travel notes written by Benjamin of Tudela himself.'

'Can we call him Benny? I'm not an academic.'

'No we can't. Don't you respect anything?' she replied, irritated.

'Yes. You.'

She smiled and pulled her pocket computer out of her bag.

'Here's my rough translation of his travel notes: *Free at last. This morning I took my first deep breath since that fated day in Nineveh. Who would have thought that keeping this secret would burden me more than my travel bags? Maybe I should not have read what I read; maybe I should have tried to turn my gaze away. Who knows? I have sent a letter to my dear friend Mordechai in Safed explaining my findings in the old synagogue in Nineveh. Maybe he will choose to pursue this quest. He is young, vigorous and learned. I am too tired to pursue anything but my young nephews who like to play hide-and-seek among the orange trees in our orchard. I will leave it to Mordechai and others to find out whether it is true or not. If it is, and the object is indeed found, it will be of the greatest importance not only for Jews, but for all mankind.*'

'Wow. What a story!' Jack exclaimed. 'Couldn't you have begun with this? Which synagogue was it? I mean, where in Mosul?'

'He describes a number of synagogues. Let me check the notes I've got on here.'

She searched for the right document on her pocket computer, 'Here's the passage, *Travels* 118–120:

It is a very large and ancient city, situated on the river Tigris, and is connected with Nineveh by means of a bridge. Nineveh is in ruins, but amid the ruins there are villages and hamlets, and the extent of the city may be determined by the walls, which extend forty parasangs to the city of Irbil. The city of Nineveh is on the river Tigris. In the city of Mosul is the synagogue of Obadiah, built by Jonah; and also the synagogue of Nahum the Elkoshite.'

'So, which one is it?' asked Jack impatiently.

'I think it's Jonah's synagogue as it would have been the older of the two, but who knows? What's really important is that we just stepped on the ruins of an old place of Jewish worship that corresponds to Tudela's description of ancient synagogues and that this is where my weird tablet comes from.'

'I'm sorry, why would Jonah's synagogue have been the older one?' asked Jack.

'He was an important figure in Mosul.'

'Wait, you mean *the* Jonah? The one who refused to do God's work and ended up in a whale?'

'The very same,' she answered. 'Jonah is still revered by Muslims in Mosul. Anyway, his "synagogue" was bombed by our fellow Americans'.

It was early evening when Jack drove Mina back to her flat. She invited him upstairs to freshen up before going out to dinner. As they climbed the stairs, Jack dropped his shoulder bag, spilling most of the contents and sending all manner of things tumbling down the stairs. Mina bent down to help him. 'No, don't worry about this,' he said, collecting up the bits and pieces, 'You head on up, I'll be there in a minute or two.'

Mina was actually grateful, as it would give her just enough time to tidy up a few things in her flat. Jack had never been to her place and she did not want him to think she was a messy academic.

Mina stepped into her living room. It was completely dark. She always closed the shutters against the fierce Iraqi sun, but she didn't recall closing them this tightly. The air was stuffy and she couldn't see a thing. She flipped the light switch but nothing happened. She was about to try again when she heard a slight shuffling sound to her right.

'*Hal honaka ahad?* Is anybody there?' she asked hesitantly. A second or two passed but no answer came back. Suddenly someone yanked her arms backwards and bound her wrists behind her with cable ties. She heard the zipping sound of the ties tightening around her wrists, before another person pulled a large plastic freezer bag over her head and held it tightly round the base of her neck.

Panicking, Mina gulped a breath which emptied the bag of the little oxygen it held and left her gasping for air. She started choking, sucking the plastic deep into her mouth. She fell to her knees.

As she felt her mind fogging she heard the creaking sound of the shutters being opened slightly. In a blur she could make out three men in dark clothing, towering over her. One of the men bent down and yanked the bag from her head. She gasped for air, breathing so deeply she thought her lungs would explode. She burst into tears and shook violently, the body's natural response when given another shot at life.

The men didn't give her any time to think. They pulled her to her feet and roughly flung her on a chair. One man stepped up to her, bending low to stare into her tear-filled eyes and said in a cold voice, 'Miss Osman?'

Mina didn't reply.

'Miss Osman, you don't know us, but we know everything about you. Do you understand?'

'Yes,' she whispered.

'Good,' he replied slowly, 'so where is it?'

'Where is what?'

'Wrong answer,' he said and turned to one of the other men, 'You, the bag!'

'Please,' Mina begged him frantically, 'don't torture me! What do you want? I don't know anything…' She stopped talking abruptly when she saw her interrogator bringing a sharp knife towards her throat. It glinted in a single beam of sunlight peeking through the shutters.

He held the sharp edge of the knife under her ear and said, 'The tablet, Miss Osman, where is it?'

That's what they were after, Hassan's tablet? It couldn't be. This was insane.

'So?' He asked, slowly pushing the blade against her skin below her ear until she felt it cut through. Pain flashed through her and she felt warm blood trickling down her neck. Instinctively she tried to bring a hand up to stem the bleeding but she was still tied up. She was utterly helpless and screamed, 'Please don't hurt me! The tablet is in my rucksack.'

He pulled the knife away and turned to the other man, 'Pass me the bag.'

Taking the bag, he turned back to Mina and with a sinister smile across his face said, 'We wouldn't want to leave any traces, would we?'

Mina felt the clammy plastic bag being pulled over her head once more. She felt her mind darkening. 'This is madness,' she thought, as she began to lose consciousness.

The three men stood over Mina did not notice Jack creep into the room behind them. Edging up to the nearest one holding the knife, Jack suddenly sliced his left hand through the air with lethal speed and hit him with a knifehand strike to the throat.

They all heard the disgusting popping sound as he fell to the ground. One of the men pulled out a gun and aimed it at Jack, but Jack anticipating this move, flung himself to one side and narrowly avoided the bullet. With a grunt of effort he spun around and put all his force into a kick that smashed the gunman's right knee. The man dropped the gun and crumpled to the floor, groaning in agony. The third man looked at his colleagues scattered around him on the floor, paused for a second, and then ran out of the door as quickly as he could.

Breathing hard, Jack rushed over to Mina and yanked the bag from her head to let her breathe again. He swung around, quickly picking up the gun and aimed it at its previous owner's head. 'Who the fuck are you? What are you doing here?'

The man looked up at him and a twisted smile flickered across his face. In the hushed room they all heard the muffled crunch of breaking glass coming from the man's mouth. The gunman twitched slightly and his eyes rolled back into his head. Two seconds later, he was dead.

'Cyanide – shit,' Jack said, furious.

He turned to Mina to check how she was coping. She was in shock. She looked at him, eyes wide with bewilderment. He took two quick strides towards her and reached out to touch her arm, she shrunk away from him and started sobbing hysterically.

'Mina! Try to breathe slowly. Are you ok?' he asked, as calmly as he could manage.

'Who are you Jack?' she stuttered.

'We don't have time for this. We need to get out of here Mina.'

He peered cautiously out of the window. 'It's clear. We can move out,' he ordered.

'But…the police.'

'You can call the police once we're out of danger. Mind you, I'm not quite sure what you're going to tell them. These men are professionals, and they came after you for a reason.'

He took her gently by the arm and led her down the stairs. Her face was growing paler by the second. As soon as she made it into the passenger seat of his car, she passed out. Jack fastened her seatbelt and drove off. He couldn't quite believe what had just happened. After a while, he pulled the jeep up at the main gate of the US military barracks, showed his credentials, and drove onto the base.

⤜

The third man was sitting in his car, still panting. He dialled a number on his mobile. 'Miss Mastrani?'

'Yes? Do you have the tablet?'

'No.'

'What happened?'

'We turned the place upside-down, there was nothing in the flat. We waited for her to get back but then while we were interrogating her, some guy barged in. He killed Guslin with one stroke to the throat, smashed Anderson's knee with a kick and disarmed him. I ran for my life.'

'You…ran?' she asked, softly.

'Sorry. I only had a split second to decide what to do,' he answered, already realising from her tone that he'd made the wrong decision.

'Where is Anderson?'

'I think he's dead too.'

'You…did well,' she said. 'I'll deal with you later,' she thought to herself. 'Where are Mina Osman and that man now?' she asked, neutrally.

'No idea Miss Mastrani.'

'That won't do.' He shuddered at her glacial tone.

'What do you want me to do?' he asked her desperately.

'Return to the flat. Clean up the mess. Did anyone hear the gun shots?'

'Don't worry about that,' he answered, finally being able to offer some good news. 'It's a war zone. People are kidnapped and murdered on a daily basis.'

'Right. When you're done, wait for further instructions at the agreed location.'

'Yes Ma'am.'

'I hope this Hassan is still alive. I need to…' she paused, searching for the right word, '…speak to him when I arrive tomorrow'.

'You're coming in person to Mosul?' he asked hesitantly.

'Yes,' she said, and hung up the phone.

The man thought about his options. He would clean up the mess at the flat, but that was it. He would be long gone before Mastrani arrived. He had worked with her long enough to know exactly what was in store for him, having failed his mission.

Chapter 11

December 6th, 2004

Mina woke up in a small room with white-washed walls. Looking around her, she saw her clothes hanging neatly on the back of a chair. She tried to work out how long she had been there, or recall who had undressed her and put her in bed, but she was groggy and could not remember a thing. She was thinking so slowly, what was wrong with her? A knock on the door startled her.

'Miss Osman? May I come in?'

'Yes' she answered, gathering the sheet under her chin.

A doctor came into the room. 'Hi. My name is Dr. Slotter. How are you feeling?' he asked earnestly, a picture of good manners and efficiency.

'Where am I?' Mina demanded.

'You're in the infirmary on base. You're safe here.'

'But how did I get here? I don't remember anything.'

'You were brought here unconscious. I was told you had gone through a traumatic event, so I administered you some sleeping drugs. Our female nurses took care of you. Do you mind if I check you over?'

Without waiting for an answer he took out a tiny torch, shone it into her eyes and made her look up and down, left and right, then checked her blood pressure and pulse.

'You seem fine. Is your pulse always so slow?'

'Yes. I've practised yoga for many years. How long have I been out?'

'The whole night.'

'The whole night? Where's Jack?'

'Jack? I'm sorry, I don't know any Jack.'

'Jack Hillcliff,' she insisted. 'He must have brought me here.'

'Major Hillcliff?' he asked.

'Major...Yes. Can I see him?'

'Why don't you rest a little while I try to get hold of him? He may not be on base right now.'

'Thank you Doctor,' she answered.

When the young doctor had left, Mina sat up and tried to recall what had happened. Her head felt like a huge pumped-up football. And as if that wasn't enough, she was beside herself with anger. Jack had lied to her. 'A Major in the US army,' she thought. Professor Almeini had said, there was more to Jack than met the eye. 'You got that right,' thought Mina, 'he's a lying bastard too.'

She thought of the magical evening they had spent on the rocks in the desert. She ran through every moment she had spent in his company in her mind, and every image left a bitter taste in her mouth.

Suddenly the events that led up to her waking up in the hospital came rushing back to her; she remembered those terrifying men were looking for the tablet. The only person she'd ever spoken to about the tablet with was Hassan. He must have told them. Had he been violently interrogated too? She had to speak to him. She threw off her covers, and jumped out of bed. Losing her balance for a second, she sat down on the bed again. She rummaged through her things, but could not find her phone. She was about to call out to the doctor, when Jack walked into the room.

'Where's my phone Jack?' she yelled.

'I've got it here,' he said calmly, handing it to her.

She snatched it off him. 'So you're a Major are you?' she asked, barely trying to conceal her anger.

'Well, a Major on indefinite leave.'

'You don't seem 'on leave' around here.'

'I left the army over three years ago. I'm not wearing a uniform, am I?'

He was trying to make her smile, but his efforts just infuriated her more.

'You *lied* to me Jack. You fucking lied to me.'

'I tried telling you that night in the desert.'

'What? You didn't try anything. What are you talking about?'

'You asked me about my past and—'

'And you avoided answering my questions.'

'Well. Yes. You seemed to hate the military so much I didn't know how to broach the subject.'

Mina changed the subject herself.

'Why did you take my phone?'

'I had to check a few things.'

She picked up her phone angrily, and tried calling Hassan.

'No reply. What's happened to him?'

Jack looked away.

'Oh God, what's happened to him? I'll try calling his mother.'

She dialled another number, and was relieved when a woman's voice answered.

'Salam Aleikum. I'm Hassan's teacher from the university. I'm trying to get hold of him. Is he at home?'

'No Professor. He hasn't been at home for two whole days. I'm very worried.'

'Please don't worry, I'm sure he will come home soon. Could you ask him to call me when he comes back? My name is Mina Osman.'

'You're Professor Osman?'

'Yes,' she answered.

'He's always talking about you.' The woman's voice cracked with emotion, He's a good boy, Professor Osman.'

'I know. He's also one of our finest students. Please ask him to call back when he returns.'

Mina hung up, and burst into tears.

'So, you can lie too,' thought Jack to himself. He wanted to take Mina in his arms and comfort her, but he had a feeling it would only make matters worse. He observed her from a distance and all he saw was a woman in shock, blowing her nose and apparently trying to compose herself and retain some dignity under difficult circumstances.

'Jack, or whoever you are, I can't stay here. I've got to get back to my flat, talk to the police, the department.'

'Mina, listen to me, I've talked to the Iraqi National Guard. I returned with them to your flat; the bodies were gone and so was all the evidence of the fight. To make matters worse, someone must have bribed an important police official because they're dropping the case altogether claiming lack of evidence.'

'My god. Who are these people? They weren't even Iraqi.'

'That's the real question.'

'I have to go back there. I have to change my clothes, pick up some things.'

'Mina, you can't go back to your flat! Don't you understand? People are trying to kill you. Do you have any idea why?'

She didn't reply immediately, 'I don't know, Jack.'

'I heard them mention a tablet. C'mon Mina,' he said, taking her hand in his.

She wrenched her hand from his and shot him a cold look that firmly reminded him where he stood with her.

'Drop the sweet talk, Major Hillcliff. I'll stay somewhere else. Anywhere. But not here. Please…just leave me alone.'

He stood up slowly, 'Alright. You're angry right now. Please call me if you want my help in any way. You know how to get hold of me if you need to.'

She did not answer and with a sigh he left the room.

Mina put her clothes back on and made a phone call.

'Professor?'

'Mina! I've been trying to get hold of you for over two days now. Where are you?' he asked, frantically.

'It's a long story. I can't talk right now. Can we meet at the university cafeteria in an hour from now?'

'Of course Mina. I'll be there.'

She bumped into the doctor in the corridor as she left the room.

'Miss Osman? Where are you going? I think you should remain here for at least another day, until you feel well enough to leave the base.'

'I'm fine doctor. Can I ask you a small favour?'

'Of course. What is it?'

'You know the computer in my room, is it connected to the internet? I need to check my emails.'

'Yes. Just click on the web browser.'

'Thank you.'

'I'll be next door if you need anything,' he said.

'Thank you so much.'

Mina logged onto her webmail quickly and found dozens of new messages. She skimmed through the unimportant ones, as well as Almeini's, and was left with two emails, one from Shobai, the Jewish scholar she'd contacted a few days before and the other from her former department at Columbia. She opened the latter first. It was from Nigel's secretary.

Dear Mina,
I have tried reaching you since yesterday at your department in
Mosul, but I couldn't, so I've emailed you with all the details.
I have some excellent news. An academic foundation, The
Foundation for Academic Excellence, has offered to pay your
research grant in full and any extra funding you may need
during your stay in Israel. They only require you to meet them for
a formal interview in Tel Aviv in four days time. You'll find all
their details in the attached word document.

Kind Regards,
Alma Fitzhenry

Mina was overjoyed. What wonderful news. It was like a gift from heaven; she could escape from this twisted situation with Jack and from the thugs who were after her tablet. Also, she could take a break from Mosul and pursue her line of enquiry on Benjamin of Tudela with proper funding. She looked up the foundation online and found out that it belonged to a conglomerate, which was composed of a number of multi-million-dollar corporations, dealing with anything, from cosmetics to the fuselage of airplanes. They were at the technological forefront in each of their fields and had vested interests in related businesses all over the world. She wondered why they had decided to pay for her grant, but thought better than to look that gifthorse in the mouth.

As with all huge corporations, they probably had dozens of people working around the clock to find ways of obtaining tax-relief for their companies, and funding academic projects was an excellent means to do so. She knew that some scouted universities and even took on failed applications which they deemed interesting, just like hers. She checked the date of the email. It was a day old, which meant she had three days to get to the interview on 8th December. She would have to leave right away.

She quickly checked Shobai's email. It was an automated out-of-office reply. Hopefully he would get back to her soon. She needed information and quickly. She wrote back to him immediately saying that she would be travelling in Israel for her research and that she would love to meet if he was free at any time over the next few weeks. As she finished writing the email to Shobai, she began to wonder what she should do about the tablet. Obviously, she couldn't leave it in Mosul, but nor could she travel with it to Israel. She'd never clear customs with an ancient artefact in her luggage. The answer to her dilemma came in a flash of inspiration. She smiled to herself, it was a mischievous yet elegant plan.

Before leaving the base, she knocked on the door of the doctor's office and asked if she could send something by special military courier on behalf of Major Hillcliff. He assured her that once it had been x-rayed and passed security, it would not be a problem. He could do it for her if she was in a hurry.

She suddenly wondered if she should trust him. He sensed her hesitation, and hurriedly added that he would be honoured to take care of Major Hillcliff's mail. He was dead serious. She thanked him, gave him the small package, and walked away.

＄

A young officer appeared at the door and saluted Jack. 'Sir. Miss Osman left the base, sir.'

'Thanks. Good job. That'll be all,' said Jack.

'Yes, sir.'

Jack rushed back into Mina's room, turned on the computer and, using special software, retrieved the log file of every key-stroke Mina had made during her visit. He read her emails, and then found the hotel in Safed where she had made an online reservation for two weeks. What was going on? Was Mina really going to Tel Aviv to attend an interview and then on to Safed for research? Or was all this just a cover?

＄

Mina was early. She waited at the university cafeteria looking around her constantly. She had been here so many times, and had felt completely safe and carefree. Now, everyone seemed suspicious. What would she tell the professor? He would want to help her, but what if he ended up like Hassan? She could not let that happen. She opened her bag, took out a sheet of paper and wrote him an apology note. It would be better not to meet him at all. That way he would not be involved.

Chapter 12

December 6th, 2004

Hassan had managed to sit up and was assessing his situation. He'd been kidnapped and forced to tell the American thugs all about Mina and where she lived. He hoped with all his heart that she had managed to flee before they got to her. His jaw ached and his right eye was so bruised, he wondered if it would ever see normally again.

They had put a canvas sack over his head, bound his hands, and beaten him in the back of the van until they had arrived at this basement flat. He guessed that they were in the suburbs, they would have needed a secluded place to conduct their dirty work. They had kept the sack over his head and two men held him on the ground, while a third poured water over the sack and into his mouth. So much water. He felt like he was drowning. With his lungs bursting and every muscle straining against his captors, he had felt death approaching fast. When they had eventually yanked the sack from his head he told them everything they wanted to know.

Having got all the information they needed, they had dumped him in an empty room, with his hands still tied behind his back. As far as he could tell, he had been here for at least two days, drifting in and out of consciousness. He had to find a way out. They had kept him alive for a reason; they certainly were not the sort of men who would let him live after they had got what they were after. Perhaps they had kept him as a back-up plan, in case they couldn't get hold of Mina. If this was true, and he'd been here for at least two days, there was some hope – she must have eluded them. He had to get out of there before they returned.

What could he do? First and foremost, he needed to untie his hands. He looked around and noticed for the first time that the walls were made of rough concrete blocks. He dragged his arms across the jagged surface and before long he found a particularly sharp edge near the door. Pushing himself against the wall, he managed to stand up. He couldn't help looking down at his soiled trousers. Hopefully, one day, he would forget all this. He started rubbing his bonds against the concrete block. A couple of hours later Hassan had picked the door lock and was running down a Mosuli suburban road.

⌣

'The airport please' said Mina, getting into a cab. She had a long journey ahead of her. There were only domestic flights leaving Mosul – she would have to fly to Baghdad, then take a connecting flight to Amman in Jordan and from there to Tel Aviv. She would buy herself proper clothes in Amman. She had been so dazed when she woke up in the infirmary that she had not noticed that Jack had brought her laptop and some clean clothes from her flat. She found them on a chair against the wall before leaving. But they were hardly interview material.

She had her passport, which she always carried with her, and that was all she cared about for now. As the cab headed out of

the city, she tried to gather her thoughts but found it very difficult. She was still in shock after the events of the past few days,
and she was terribly worried about Hassan. She could still hear
his mother's voice telling her what a good boy her son was.

She had a pounding headache. 'It must be the drugs they
gave me,' she thought. She couldn't get over the fact that Jack
had deceived her. He had lied through his teeth about more
than a decade of his life; that was no small fib. What else was
he hiding?

Walking through the airport's busy main entrance, Mina
spotted a bearded man looking directly at her. Something about
his dark suit made him seem out of place. Their eyes met, and
he quickly looked away. Mina checked herself; she was being
paranoid. She glanced again in the direction of the man, but
could not see him anymore. She looked around, but there was
no trace of him. He had simply vanished. She quickly bought
her tickets and walked through customs.

The plane took off and Mina felt relieved to be on her way.
Her heart still raced at the thought of what she'd been through
but she was safe now, on a plane, flying far away from all this
madness. She suddenly felt American again and wanted to hug
a US flag or dress up as Wonderwoman, her favourite super-
heroine. She was also an immigrant of sorts, with long black
hair, who had left the Amazons to embrace America. Mina was
tired of feeling guilty or ashamed of her American heritage,
tired of being a woman in a man's world. 'No-one will miss
me,' she thought.

She was looking forward to spending time in Israel, where

few people knew her. A good opportunity to stop rehashing what she'd gone through and instead focus on her research. Maybe she would even find time to write a scientific paper on the tablet.

What would she do in Tel Aviv? The interview was taking place at the Sheraton Tel Aviv Hotel and Towers, a five star hotel overlooking the Mediterranean sea. The foundation had paid for her room in advance for three nights. The corporate world certainly knew how to take care of candidates. She had never been to Israel but she did have a friend there who worked at the Eretz Israel Museum in Tel Aviv.

Liat was an Israeli archaeologist who had studied with Mina at Columbia for a Master's degree. They had had a small falling-out over their political beliefs, but she liked Liat both as a scholar and as a friend. Hopefully Liat would feel the same when she called on her. She would just pop by the museum on arrival. Mina thought back to that year, when she was going out with Charlie, whom Liat had introduced her to. He had been heartbroken when she left for Iraq. She did not feel she had a choice, and to be honest – hindsight can be cruel – she doubted whether she had ever really been in love with him.

Charlie was a lawyer with an international firm in New York. He spoke a number of languages, was fun to be around, quick-witted and handsome. But Mina had always felt there was something missing. Their relationship was too easy-going. They could have gone on for years before realising that they were not really meant to be together. She thought back to the last time they had spoken, in a small Italian restaurant in the Village. Charlie could not understand why she wanted to leave the country, she had such great prospects in New York. She could do anything she wanted, even leave academia and write for a living. He had offered to help her out if she wanted him to. She toyed with the idea, but it was neither in her character nor her upbringing to be financially dependent on a man. She told him as kindly as she could that she needed a clean break and that their relationship was not significant enough to make her change her mind. He told her she sounded phoney, and she smiled sadly and said that she was sorry. Thinking back to how sure she had felt about her decision then, she worried that she might never find what she was looking for. She had felt a flicker of promise, of something meaningful emerging between her and Jack but the revelation about his past had left her feeling deeply betrayed by him.

After changing planes in Baghdad, Mina flew on to Amman. She thought back to the wonderful trip she had taken there years ago with her parents, they had even rented a Jeep to visit Petra's countryside. They were so proud of her and wanted to share her passion for the archaeology of the Near East. Mina had been studying the civilisation of the Nabateans, the ancient inhabitants of Petra, and she had begged her parents for months to let her take a trip there with a group of girlfriends. They had refused outright, it was too dangerous. Instead, her father had come into her room one day and told her he had arranged everything and they would take the trip together as a family. She had discovered aspects of her parents she never knew. Her father was a doctor but seemed ill at ease in most circumstances. Her mother had been a journalist in Iraq, but now worked as a translator. For the first time, Mina saw her parents totally in their element. It had been a lovely trip.

She decided to buy a few clothes in the duty-free shops in Amman's airport. She had a few hours ahead of her before the next plane to Tel Aviv. She bought a new handbag, chose a pair of fitted trousers, a serious blouse and cardigan for the interview, and a top, jacket and boots for travelling to Safed. She would buy whatever else she needed once she had the grant money in hand.

Having completed her shopping, Mina sat down in a café for a much needed break. She sipped the hot coffee and looked around her at the bustling throng of travellers. Suddenly she saw the bearded man again. He passed in front of her for just a few seconds, but she was sure it was him. One thing most archaeologists have in common is a nearly autistic capacity to notice small details among huge bodies of evidence. Here, among the thousands of travellers, she was convinced she recognised the man from Mosul.

Arriving in Amman and buying new clothes had made her feel light-hearted again. But she was back in hypersensitive mode, observing everyone around her. Now that she thought about it, since she left Mosul she had felt that she was being followed a few times, especially in Baghdad.

It must have been this bearded man. Who was he? He did not resemble the thugs in her flat at all. His features seemed more refined and his complexion was definitely Middle Eastern. Just for a moment, she wished Jack were around.

᠆

Back in Mosul, Natasha Mastrani, in a red tailored dress and slick knee length boots, was standing near her car. She took off her sunglasses and tapped them gently on the bonnet of the car while waiting to be patched through to Oberon Wheatley's phone. She caught her reflection in the tinted window, and seemed pleased with her look, especially how her icy blue eyes glinted under her platinum blond hair.

'Sir?'

'Ah, Natasha. What's the update?'

'Not the best of news. I wish I'd stuck to the usual operatives.'

'You're slipping Natasha, you're slipping.'

He was obviously amused by her uncharacteristic incompetence and enjoyed teasing her.

'I'm really sorry sir. However, the flat was cleaned and the right people were paid off. There will be no sign of our involvement.'

'So what's worrying you?'

'The surviving operative disappeared and so did the young man, Hassan. And we still don't know where Miss Osman is.'

'The story gets funnier by the second. Clearly the operative did not want to face the music on your arrival.'

'Probably not, sir.'

'Do I need to remind you that I am paying you far more than the CIA ever did because you have accustomed me to perfect results? There is no red tape with me. You have full latitude to carry out your missions.'

She tried to sound as contrite as she could.

'Yes sir. There are still unanswered questions. I need to work out the whereabouts of Miss Osman and this Hassan and find out who the man was who killed our two operatives.'

'No. Please make preparations for my arrival tomorrow.'

'You're coming here? I wouldn't advise that sir.'

'No. Tel Aviv. Make sure security is tight in the harbour, around and on my yacht.'

'Is there something I should know?'

'Mina Osman will be visiting Tel Aviv for a few days.'

That was why he sounded so amused. She knew better than ask questions. Oberon Wheatley hadn't become one of the most powerful men in the world by twiddling his thumbs. He didn't wait for events to pass. He was always one step ahead. She got in her car, and drove off to the airport.

PART 2

ISRAEL

*The apple cannot be stuck back on the Tree of Knowledge;
once we begin to see, we are doomed and challenged to seek the
strength to see more, not less.*

(Arthur Miller, 1915–2005)

Chapter 13

December 6th, 2004. Tel Aviv

Mina landed at Ben Gurion Airport late that evening. If Mosul seemed security conscious it was a walk in the park in comparison. Luckily she had the invitation for an interview and a reservation at the Sheraton Tel Aviv Hotel & Towers to explain her presence there and her route from Baghdad via Amman. She noticed how many policewomen guarded the airport. It was a change from Iraq to see women in uniform. They were fit and aggressive, much like their gun, the famous Desert Eagle. Half-asleep she hailed a cab under the starry winter sky.

When Mina arrived at the hotel she was duly impressed. Walking through the plush lobby, she felt for a moment like a high-flying businesswoman and wondered briefly if she was not in the wrong line of work. But she knew all too well that she was only thinking that way because of the stark contrast between the conditions of the last few days spent in a wartorn country and those here, in this luxurious five-star-hotel. As soon as she got to her room, she had a quick shower and then collapsed on the bed, still in her bathrobe.

The next morning, Mina woke up fully energised, ordered a light breakfast to be brought up to her room, she had a shower and did her stretching exercises. She followed a complex chain of yoga asanas she had learned from a young Indian yogi, who had since become quite a celebrity. She had worked with him every day for three months and remembered the first month, when she thought she would never be able to stretch into the positions he demonstrated. As he was as relentless as she was driven, eventually, by the end of the three months she had managed to stretch into every position in his programme. She would have pursued their work, but he had fallen in love with her and she had had to explain to him, as kindly as she could, that she was not interested in him in that way. Unfortunately, he had been very hurt and they parted on a bitter note.

After breakfast, she started preparing for the interview. It was her understanding that the grant had been practically offered to her, but you never quite knew with these things and it was not in her nature to go anywhere unprepared; she would express her gratitude for the offer, try to show off the little she knew about the Foundation's goals and explain what her project encompassed. If the grant was as substantial as she thought it might be, she would need to add all the post-fieldwork expenses: various expert opinions, chemical analyses, thermo-luminescence, 3D digital scanning, the whole works. She needed to put together a much more extensive budget than she had first planned when applying for the in-house grant at Columbia.

She did a couple of hours' work and then decided to take a break and walk around Tel Aviv. Mina still had a day to get ready and loved discovering new cities. She went downstairs and picked up a few flyers and a map of the city in the lobby. She walked along the beach for a while thinking how disappointing it was she had not come during the summer, as she would have loved to swim in the Mediterranean. Instead, she headed resolutely into the city, following the directions on one of the leaflets to the best shopping areas. After some pleasurable window shopping on Dizengoff Street, she arrived at the crossroad with Gordon Street, where she saw a café with a large bay window and people sitting out on the terrace. She sat down and ordered a double espresso. It was brought to her promptly, along with a glass of water, by a charming and clearly gay waiter in an extremely tight t-shirt and designer sunglasses; in fact, all the customers looked somewhat flamboyant. She was surrounded by artists, media people and intellectuals – it was so different from Mosul. Mina felt almost reborn, back in a mini-New York. She looked on her map and found the Eretz Israel museum, but it was quite a hike from where she was, so she thought that she would take a taxi and surprise Liat. She hoped her friend was at work today and could spare some time.

'Are you a tourist?' a young man seated at the next table asked her in English. He said he'd be delighted to take her sightseeing. Mina thanked him and told him she was waiting for a friend. He did not insist. She really wasn't interested in him, but she was impressed by the direct yet courteous way in which he had approached her. The truth was that she could not help thinking of Jack. Had she been too harsh with him? She kept replaying their last meeting on the military base, over and over again. As she often did when she felt lost, Mina took out her notebook. It was her preferred method for clarifying her thoughts and feelings – she would often make detailed lists of pros and cons. In Jack's case, she had been brutally direct with him and had made it clear she did not want to see him again. And yet she had a nagging, irrational feeling that she might have been wrong. Even though he had lied to her, she had loved that magical evening with the villagers, and their walk up the hill in the desert. And above all, he had saved her life. Something told her she would be seeing him again, whether she liked it or not. More pressingly, she knew that she was in deep trouble with the department and needed to email Professor Almeini to clear things up. She would email him once she knew the result of the grant interview. She also had to try to find out what had happened to Hassan, but doing so would make her relive her ordeal at the hands of the three men in the flat.

⌒

Natasha was at Ben Gurion airport, waiting for Oberon Wheatley. She had spent the previous night checking and re-checking every aspect of security at the harbour. No-one could approach the yacht uninvited, nor leave it for that matter. Natasha could not help but admire how her boss gathered information on everyone. Mina Osman had arrived at her hotel just as he said she would. Wheatley suddenly appeared outside the main entrance, saw her, and walked straight to the car. She took his luggage, put it in the boot and together they drove off immediately to the harbour.

Oberon had bought his yacht from the famous Italian yacht designer Benetti, for an obscene amount of money. With its steel hull and aluminium superstructure, the 230ft *Rêverie* moved at a maximum speed of 16 knots, weighed 1600 tons, had seven decks and an interior designed by John Munford. Oberon had had his eye on the boat for some time and once it became his, he had had his technicians transform it into much more than a dilettante's pleasure vessel. One sensed that under the aristocratic veneer of absolute comfort and luxury, dark mahogany and top-quality marble, the yacht possessed every technological amenity that the modern world had to offer.

Oberon had not said a word to Natasha since his arrival making her feel exceedingly uncomfortable. He climbed to the upper deck, into the yacht's saloon, sat down in his favourite Chesterfield armchair and nodded at the barman to make him his usual drink, a dirty martini. He waited silently until the man brought it to him then, taking a sip, he finally uttered his first word.

'Natasha?'

'Yes sir?'

'Is everything set?'

'Yes, sir. Miss Osman has checked into the hotel.'

'Excellent. That's my girl.'

He smiled at her.

⤳

The taxi dropped Mina at the entrance of the Eretz Israel Museum. From reading a leaflet she had picked up at the hotel she knew that it presented the history and culture of Israel through a number of varied exhibitions, including the ethnography, folklore, cultural history, traditional crafts and archaeology of the land. It was very much a model of avant-garde museography, Mina thought, and decided to take a quick tour before calling on Liat.

Although she thought the Planetarium was a tad gimmicky with its 'Voyage through the Universe' show, she really enjoyed the inner gardens. The entire museum was built like a beautiful shrine around an ancient mound, Tel Qasile. She soon realised that a proper visit of the museum would take hours, so she went to the main desk and asked to speak to Liat Hoffman. The lady at the front desk asked her to wait in the lobby, 'Dr. Hoffman will be with you in a few minutes'. 'Dr. Hoffman…!' Mina thought, 'well she didn't waste any time'. Liat had only been studying for her Masters' degree when they last spoke in New York. Mina felt slightly envious of her friend's academic achievements, but the feeling quickly passed as Liat entered in the lobby. They rushed into each others arms and Liat gave her a long hug.

'Mina, I'm so happy to see you! It's been so long. When did you arrive?'

'Last night. I thought I'd surprise you.'

'You did,' Liat laughed 'OK. Let's get out of here.'

'Can you leave your office just like that?' asked Mina.

'It's the first day of Chanukah today. Things are a little lax. You know, people leaving early to be with their family.'

'Of course, Chanukah. I totally forgot. What about you?'

'You know me… I enjoy lighting a candle from time to time, but I'm not really into religion.'

'Oh. I thought Chanukah was all about fighting foreigners?' replied Mina, with a glint in her eye.

'Mina, Mina. Had you said, 'Oh Liat, I thought it was a pagan festival of lights that you find everywhere from here to Timbuktu during the bleakest time of the winter season,' I would have thought, 'she hasn't changed one bit.' But political sarcasm?'

'I'm sorry. I've been through the mill recently.'

'Don't worry. You're in my town and I know it's your first time in Tel Aviv, so I'm going to take you on a tour! We'll get drunk and talk about all the boys we never slept with in New

York.' Mina giggled, she felt like a feisty graduate student all over again.

'Oh God, Liat, I'm so happy to see you.'

The two women squeezed into Liat's car, a ludicrously bright yellow reconditioned Fiat Cinquecento, and drove towards Yafo, in the south of Tel Aviv. Liat knew her audience well, so she began her history of Tel Aviv with its biblical origins. Mina learned that Yafo was mentioned in the Old Testament as a border city of the Territory of Dan; that timber from the fragrant cedar trees of Lebanon was shipped to Yafo to build the temple of Salomon in Jerusalem. Some scholars even thought that the city, also known as Joppa or Jaffa or even Yafo, was named after Japheth, one of the sons of Noah.

Noah again! Mina wondered if she would ever escape the Flood saga.

Liat parked the car and as they started walking she reminded Mina that before getting swallowed by a giant whale, the prophet Jonah had left his hometown Nineveh for Yafo where he had hired a ship to flee 'from the presence of the Lord'. 'You know why I've brought you to Yafo?' asked Liat.

'Yes, of course. You want to show me the origins of Tel Aviv and its Arab quarter.'

'Nope. As usual you're wrong. We are *here* because this is where we'll get the best hummus in town.'

Mina remembered vividly how during their time in New York Liat talked relentlessly about hummus, and had been on a mission to find the finest hummus in the World.

'So, your hummus quest ended here?'

Liat put on her most serious face and said 'Yes. Why do you think I took the job at the museum, if not for the hummus?'

'You're mad.'

'Of course I am, mad about hummus.'

They entered a tiny kebab joint, and the Arab owner's face lit up when he recognised Liat. He smiled at her, flashing all his golden teeth and said in Hebrew:

'Ah. My favourite customer. I've kept you the best of the best!'

'Hi Ahmed. This is my good friend Mina, she's only visiting Tel Aviv but what sort of visit would it be if she didn't taste your falafel and hummus?'

'Quite right. Take a seat and I'll be with you in a minute.' They sat down on mismatched plastic chairs.

'Liat, this is the tackiest sandwich shop I've ever sat in.'

'Yes. A true pearl in a sea of mud.'

'Is that a political statement?'

'No, a culinary one.'

'Just checking.'

'Thanks. I remember the last time we had a political discussion. I thought I was going to tear your eyes out.'

'I was pretty close to slapping you.'

'But we're all grown up now, aren't we?'

'I don't know. Are we?' They laughed, then, without any warning, as was her habit, Liat launched into a monologue on the modern history of Tel Aviv. Mina smiled at her old friend, thinking that people don't change much over time.

'The name itself, *Tel Aviv* ' Liat began, 'means 'the hill of spring'. In a way, it is an apt description of a city that sprang from the desert. Although it began as a suburb of Yafo, an association called the 'Ahuzat Bayit' founded Tel Aviv in 1910 on sand dunes north of Yafo. A good example of the early socialist beginnings of Israel, the land was divided into parcels

Mina dropped her bags and gave Liat a big hug. They sat
n and as Mina looked at the drinks menu, she spotted the
e of the bar. It was called Noa.

the name of this place really Noa?'

s, like the builder of the ark. Isn't it funny?'

na didn't respond. She could not help noticing these small
which were starting to stack up like an omen. Maybe
oice of studies and her recent adventures had more to
han a mere scholarly pursuit. Was she fated to track
ory of Noah? Her rational mind usually fought against
perstitious ideas, but she could not shake the strange
he was part of a larger story here. She had thought she
owing in the footsteps of Benjamin of Tudela. Maybe
ld have checked first if he had been following someone
tsteps himself.

u alright Mina?' Liat asked her brooding friend.

course. Let's order some drinks pronto.'

the rush?' Liat asked, half-yawning.

uch time spent in a non-wine-drinking country,
!'

⮑

of wine and some tasty nibbles later, Liat and
d back into one of the sofas. They propped their
e coffee table in front of them and admired their
Ferragamo high heels.

ely, Liat,' Mina slurred.

e.'

t mind my asking…'

d Liat.

---

by drawing lots. Believe it or not, commercial enterprise was
banned throughout the new city, it was practically communist!
But the emigrants did not stick to these principles for long, or
it might have become a hill of winter rather than one of spring.
The book *Alteneuland* or *Old New Land* by Theodor Herzl,
who is, after all, one of the founders of the Jewish emigration
movement, was a tale of rebirth. In that sense, it's pretty close
to the Hebrew meaning of Tel Aviv. In the early 1950s, the
two cities of Tel Aviv and Yafo merged into one to form Tel
Aviv-Yafo'.

'That's what's surprised me so far,' interjected Mina, 'the
contrast between old Yafo and Tel Aviv's high towers and
modern buildings '.

'Yes. The architecture of Tel Aviv is linked to the influx of
German Jews after the modernist architectural movement was
banned by the Nazis in the thirties. The immigrants built hundreds of Bauhaus constructions, all white or yellow, which gave
rise to Tel Aviv's nickname: the White City. Today Tel Aviv is
the second largest city in Israel, and because of its odd Old
New culture, its beaches and swanky cafes, it has a youthful
and hip feel to it.'

'You're not referring to this snack-bar, I hope.'

'Duh.'

⮑

The two women walked the old, narrow streets of Yafo,
talking about the good old days. After a while they arrived
at Tel Yafo, also known as 'ancient Yafo'. The site dated back
thousands of years and had been excavated by many archaeologists since the 1950s. The remains of a gate were found

there with an inscription by the Egyptian Pharaoh Ramses II, dating back to the time he conquered the region. A replica of the gate lintels had been erected by archaeologists in their original location.

Mina was enraptured by the abundance of history in Israel, the rapid succession of events and the inexorable downfall of great empires. The Egyptian empire was countered by the Hittites from Anatolia in modern Turkey, but was not finally vanquished until Alexander the Great invaded it in the 4th century B.C.E. Then it was the turn of the Romans, who gave the names of Syria and Palestine to the region. Israel was the name of Jacob in the bible. In a way, it was both an ancient and a recent name. Crusaders followed, then the Ottoman Empire and finally the British took over, until they relinquished their Palestinian Mandate in favour of the creation of the new state of Israel in 1948. What a wonderful mess! Liat seemed to guess what Mina was thinking.

'I've always thought of Israel as a palimpsest,' said Liat.

'I know exactly what you mean, the way history is written over and over again on the same parchment.'

'Mina, I know I should wait patiently for you to tell me about Mosul, but I really want to know what's going on.'

'Things are in a terrible state. You wouldn't believe the daily tragedy.'

Liat was about to say that things weren't exactly rosy in Israel, but thought better than to comment.

'Although I've never been in the line of fire, and luckily I was in the States last month when most of the carnage took place, I've witnessed the results. The bombed areas, the distraught families.'

Mina went on to describe the continuous fear that people

wore on their face like a grimacing mask, and
had portrayed the destroyed monuments, the
little hope she had that anything would im
future.

'I narrowly escaped being shot myself.' S
'What do you mean? On the street?'
'Yes, on the street,' Mina lied.

There was no way she would invol
ongoing troubles. Liat sensed there was
on, but she let it drop. Mina would
now.

'So tell me more about this intervie
'I'll tell you tomorrow, after I've
haven't prepared for it enough really.
'What are you going to wear?'
'I bought a few things in Amma
'Your usual stuff?' Liat asked, w
'I'm a bit short of cash until I g
'Well, I'm not. I'm taking you
the hand and they walked back

After a few solid hours of
laden down with bags and v
happy and giggling like so
other sorely, but had not re
'I'd forgotten how tiri
exhausted,' Mina said.
'But happy?' asked Lia
'Oh yes. Very happy.'

dow
nam
'Is
'Ye
Mi
signs,
her ch
them
the his
such su
feeling
was foll
she shou
else's foo
'Are yo
'Yes of
'What'
'Too m
that's wha

Two bottles
Mina slump
feet up on th
newly bough
'They're lo
'Yes they a
'If you don
'What?' ask

'With the fortune your parents left you, do you still need to work for a living?'

'What you really mean is why am I working?'

'Well, yeah.'

Liat thought about it for a moment, and then simply replied, 'Because I enjoy it.'

'Good answer!' She could sense that Liat was about to ask her what she was hiding and the amount of alcohol she had drunk would make her an easy prey to thorough questioning. But Liat was as tipsy as her. Instead she asked her about Charlie.

'It just didn't work out,' said Mina.

'Liar. He wrote to me at the time. You dumped him when you decided to go off to Iraq.'

'Alright. I did. So what?'

'You were a great couple, you could have stayed together. You're twenty-nine, you know! Time's ticking. Didn't you think you should have waited for him? I know he'd have waited for you.'

'No. That was part of the problem. Charlie and I would never have stayed together. Do you remember Susan and her Italian boyfriend? Remember the hours she spent on the phone talking to him instead of being with him? Remember how she was never free but alone all the same? It was painful to watch. Long distance relationships? No thanks.'

Both girls went silent.

'You seemed to get along.'

'There was no passion, Liat. Not on my side anyway. I loved him, don't get me wrong. But in the end, it was like having a good friend and living in the hope it would turn into something greater.'

Mina didn't know if it was the alcohol or the talk about former lovers, but Jack's image had entered her head and would not leave. 'I hardly know him,' she said softly.

'What? Who are you talking about?' Liat asked, her gossip antennae quivering.

'No-one,' replied Mina.

'Yeah. Like I'm gonna let that one slip. C'mon, talk to Auntie Liat.'

'OK. There is someone.'

'What's his name?'

'Jack.'

'American?'

'Yes.'

'Kind, supportive, does the dishes after dinner...or a bad boy?'

'You're being silly', laughed Mina.

'Fine. Where did you meet?'

'In Mosul.'

'Journalist, diplomat or military?'

'Are those the only American men available there?'

'Oh, let me guess; you found yourself the only American archaeologist mad enough to work in a war zone.'

Mina smiled, 'I don't want to talk about him.'

'Liar.'

'Not as much of a liar as he is.'

'Bad boy then,' concluded Liat.

'I guess so.'

'Any regrets?'

'Yes. We never even kissed.'

Liat was about to laugh, but saw the genuine sadness on Mina's face. She gave her a long hug instead.

Another bottle of wine later, in the early hours of the morning a very drunk Mina stumbled into the Sheraton Tel Aviv Hotel & Towers.

Chapter 14

December 8th, 2004

Mina woke up at 08.00, still exhausted. She had overslept and was suffering from a monumental hangover after her drinking session with Liat. She felt more disorganised than she had ever been and desperately wondered how she would cope at the interview under these conditions. The only course of action was a long, hot shower and by the time she had finished drying her thick black hair, putting on her make-up and choosing an appropriate 'interview skirt' among the clothes Liat had bought her the previous afternoon, it was 10.15.

As she sat in the restaurant to have breakfast, the waiters kept glancing at her while she poured herself some tea. She jotted down a few notes in preparation for the interview as a means of refreshing her memory. She had always made a point of never reading her notes at presentations or during teaching sessions as it helped her moderate her talk based on her audience's reactions. She checked the interview venue in the document emailed to her by Nigel's secretary. It read '11.a.m. Foundation Grant committee – The New York Hall Meeting Room.' She asked a waiter how to get there and found that it was on the eighteenth floor.

by drawing lots. Believe it or not, commercial enterprise was banned throughout the new city, it was practically communist! But the emigrants did not stick to these principles for long, or it might have become a hill of winter rather than one of spring. The book *Alteneuland* or *Old New Land* by Theodor Herzl, who is, after all, one of the founders of the Jewish emigration movement, was a tale of rebirth. In that sense, it's pretty close to the Hebrew meaning of Tel Aviv. In the early 1950s, the two cities of Tel Aviv and Yafo merged into one to form Tel Aviv-Yafo'.

'That's what's surprised me so far,' interjected Mina, 'the contrast between old Yafo and Tel Aviv's high towers and modern buildings '.

'Yes. The architecture of Tel Aviv is linked to the influx of German Jews after the modernist architectural movement was banned by the Nazis in the thirties. The immigrants built hundreds of Bauhaus constructions, all white or yellow, which gave rise to Tel Aviv's nickname: the White City. Today Tel Aviv is the second largest city in Israel, and because of its odd Old New culture, its beaches and swanky cafes, it has a youthful and hip feel to it.'

'You're not referring to this snack-bar, I hope.'

'Duh.'

∽

The two women walked the old, narrow streets of Yafo, talking about the good old days. After a while they arrived at Tel Yafo, also known as 'ancient Yafo'. The site dated back thousands of years and had been excavated by many archaeologists since the 1950s. The remains of a gate were found there with an inscription by the Egyptian Pharaoh Ramses II, dating back to the time he conquered the region. A replica of the gate lintels had been erected by archaeologists in their original location.

Mina was enraptured by the abundance of history in Israel, the rapid succession of events and the inexorable downfall of great empires. The Egyptian empire was countered by the Hittites from Anatolia in modern Turkey, but was not finally vanquished until Alexander the Great invaded it in the 4th century B.C.E. Then it was the turn of the Romans, who gave the names of Syria and Palestine to the region. Israel was the name of Jacob in the bible. In a way, it was both an ancient and a recent name. Crusaders followed, then the Ottoman Empire and finally the British took over, until they relinquished their Palestinian Mandate in favour of the creation of the new state of Israel in 1948. What a wonderful mess! Liat seemed to guess what Mina was thinking.

'I've always thought of Israel as a palimpsest,' said Liat.

'I know exactly what you mean, the way history is written over and over again on the same parchment.' 'Mina, I know I should wait patiently for you to tell me about Mosul, but I really want to know what's going on.'

'Things are in a terrible state. You wouldn't believe the daily tragedy.'

Liat was about to say that things weren't exactly rosy in Israel, but thought better than to comment.

'Although I've never been in the line of fire, and luckily I was in the States last month when most of the carnage took place, I've witnessed the results. The bombed areas, the distraught families.'

Mina went on to describe the continuous fear that people

wore on their face like a grimacing mask, and before long she had portrayed the destroyed monuments, the lootings and the little hope she had that anything would improve in the near future.

'I narrowly escaped being shot myself.' She bit her tongue.

'What do you mean? On the street?'

'Yes, on the street,' Mina lied.

There was no way she would involve her friend in her ongoing troubles. Liat sensed there was something odd going on, but she let it drop. Mina would talk to her…, but not now.

'So tell me more about this interview? Are you ready?'

'I'll tell you tomorrow, after I've made a fool of myself. I haven't prepared for it enough really.'

'What are you going to wear?'

'I bought a few things in Amman.'

'Your usual stuff?' Liat asked, with a raised eyebrow.

'I'm a bit short of cash until I get the grant money.'

'Well, I'm not. I'm taking you shopping.' She took Mina by the hand and they walked back to the car.

⌒

After a few solid hours of shopping, the two women were laden down with bags and walked into a bar. They were both happy and giggling like schoolgirls. They had missed each other sorely, but had not realised it until today.

'I'd forgotten how tiring it was to shop with you. I'm exhausted,' Mina said.

'But happy?' asked Liat.

'Oh yes. Very happy.'

Mina dropped her bags and gave Liat a big hug. They sat down and as Mina looked at the drinks menu, she spotted the name of the bar. It was called Noa.

'Is the name of this place really Noa?'

'Yes, like the builder of the ark. Isn't it funny?'

Mina didn't respond. She could not help noticing these small signs, which were starting to stack up like an omen. Maybe her choice of studies and her recent adventures had more to them than a mere scholarly pursuit. Was she fated to track the history of Noah? Her rational mind usually fought against such superstitious ideas, but she could not shake the strange feeling she was part of a larger story here. She had thought she was following in the footsteps of Benjamin of Tudela. Maybe she should have checked first if he had been following someone else's footsteps himself.

'Are you alright Mina?' Liat asked her brooding friend.

'Yes of course. Let's order some drinks pronto.'

'What's the rush?' Liat asked, half-yawning.

'Too much time spent in a non-wine-drinking country, that's what!'

～

Two bottles of wine and some tasty nibbles later, Liat and Mina slumped back into one of the sofas. They propped their feet up on the coffee table in front of them and admired their newly bought Ferragamo high heels.

'They're lovely, Liat,' Mina slurred.

'Yes they are.'

'If you don't mind my asking…'

'What?' asked Liat.

'With the fortune your parents left you, do you still need to work for a living?'

'What you really mean is why am I working?'

'Well, yeah.'

Liat thought about it for a moment, and then simply replied, 'Because I enjoy it.'

'Good answer!' She could sense that Liat was about to ask her what she was hiding and the amount of alcohol she had drunk would make her an easy prey to thorough questioning. But Liat was as tipsy as her. Instead she asked her about Charlie.

'It just didn't work out,' said Mina.

'Liar. He wrote to me at the time. You dumped him when you decided to go off to Iraq.'

'Alright. I did. So what?'

'You were a great couple, you could have stayed together. You're twenty-nine, you know! Time's ticking. Didn't you think you should have waited for him? I know he'd have waited for you.'

'No. That was part of the problem. Charlie and I would never have stayed together. Do you remember Susan and her Italian boyfriend? Remember the hours she spent on the phone talking to him instead of being with him? Remember how she was never free but alone all the same? It was painful to watch. Long distance relationships? No thanks.'

Both girls went silent.

'You seemed to get along.'

'There was no passion, Liat. Not on my side anyway. I loved him, don't get me wrong. But in the end, it was like having a good friend and living in the hope it would turn into something greater.'

Mina didn't know if it was the alcohol or the talk about former lovers, but Jack's image had entered her head and would not leave. 'I hardly know him,' she said softly.

'What? Who are you talking about?' Liat asked, her gossip antennae quivering.

'No-one,' replied Mina.

'Yeah. Like I'm gonna let that one slip. C'mon, talk to Auntie Liat.'

'OK. There is someone.'

'What's his name?'

'Jack.'

'American?'

'Yes.'

'Kind, supportive, does the dishes after dinner...or a bad boy?'

'You're being silly', laughed Mina.

'Fine. Where did you meet?'

'In Mosul.'

'Journalist, diplomat or military?'

'Are those the only American men available there?'

'Oh, let me guess; you found yourself the only American archaeologist mad enough to work in a war zone.'

Mina smiled, 'I don't want to talk about him.'

'Liar.'

'Not as much of a liar as he is.'

'Bad boy then,' concluded Liat.

'I guess so.'

'Any regrets?'

'Yes. We never even kissed.'

Liat was about to laugh, but saw the genuine sadness on Mina's face. She gave her a long hug instead.

Another bottle of wine later, in the early hours of the morning a very drunk Mina stumbled into the Sheraton Tel Aviv Hotel & Towers.

Chapter 14

December 8th, 2004

Mina woke up at 08.00, still exhausted. She had overslept and was suffering from a monumental hangover after her drinking session with Liat. She felt more disorganised than she had ever been and desperately wondered how she would cope at the interview under these conditions. The only course of action was a long, hot shower and by the time she had finished drying her thick black hair, putting on her make-up and choosing an appropriate 'interview skirt' among the clothes Liat had bought her the previous afternoon, it was 10.15.

As she sat in the restaurant to have breakfast, the waiters kept glancing at her while she poured herself some tea. She jotted down a few notes in preparation for the interview as a means of refreshing her memory. She had always made a point of never reading her notes at presentations or during teaching sessions as it helped her moderate her talk based on her audience's reactions. She checked the interview venue in the document emailed to her by Nigel's secretary. It read '11.a.m. Foundation Grant committee – The New York Hall Meeting Room.' She asked a waiter how to get there and found that it was on the eighteenth floor.

As she arrived at the entrance of the meeting room, a young blonde woman introduced herself as one of the Foundation's secretaries. She thanked Mina for coming, and told her not to be intimidated by the grand appearance of her surroundings. It was the only appropriate room available for interviews. She then explained that only two members of the committee would conduct the interview and that they were already inside. Mina entered the room and felt increasingly apprehensive as she approached the two men, both dressed in dark suits, pink shirts and silvery-grey ties. They were sitting at the very end of the room, at a table covered with a variety of papers and files. Mina noticed that the secretary had followed her into room and taken a seat by the door.

Mina thought the men looked slightly odd, more like businessmen than academic interviewers. Maybe it was the fact they worked for a corporate foundation. They suddenly noticed Mina and rose to greet her.

'Miss Osman. Thank you for attending this interview. My name is John Gridlam and this,' pointing at his shorter, fatter colleague 'is Bill Rowley.'

'Thank you for inviting me, I'm honoured to be here. It was quite unexpected and I only received the invitation by email a few days ago.'

They seemed surprised and concerned. 'Do you feel up to it? Would you like more time to prepare?'

'Not at all,' lied Mina.

'Let's begin then,' said the taller of the two men.

They ran through her former application for the internal grant at Columbia, and asked her what she intended to do and how she would carry out her research. She answered as fully as she could. They asked her about her future projects, and seemed happy with her answers. She then spoke about all the extra funding she might need. They nodded appreciatively. She was surprised at how easy-going the whole thing was. 'I wish I'd known earlier about this foundation,' she thought to herself. But still she felt a little uneasy; she had anticipated most of their questions but everything seemed a bit vague, and long-winded, as if they were playing for time.

Suddenly, the secretary's mobile phone rang. As she replied, she walked towards them.

'Mr Wheatley is in the building,' she said.

The men stood up immediately, straightened their jackets and tightened their ties. Mina wondered what this was all about and turned to the secretary questioningly.

'Mr Wheatley is the founder of our academic organisation, the Foundation for Excellence. He's in Tel Aviv on business,' the woman explained, 'and he likes to pop in from time to time during interviews to meet candidates.'

Mina was startled. The secretary saw her face and added, 'Don't worry. I think,' turning to the two men, who nodded at her, 'that everything has gone very well. Mr Wheatley is a very kind and cultured man, who takes an interest in all aspects of his business.'

She then walked back across the room and took her place by the door. Mina felt her hands begin to shake as she stood up beside the two men.

Oberon Wheatley arrived a few minutes later. As soon as he entered the room, his electrifying energy seemed to cast a spell on all those present. He was taller than both men, who had rushed up the room to meet him, followed more discreetly by Mina. He was wearing a tailored winter suit, evidently from

Saville Row, and smiled as he greeted Mina, showing off his gleaming white teeth and strong jaw.

'What a pleasure to meet one of Columbia's most promising students.'

'Thank you sir,' said Mina.

'I have read your resumé, and was mightily impressed. Do you know that with your languages and intelligence, you could easily get a very well-paid job in the business world?'

Mina smiled.

Turning to the men and the young woman, he asked, 'How did it go?'

The men were about to answer, but the secretary was faster.

'We are happy to say that Miss Osman has made a very satisfactory impression on the committee, and confirmed our original thoughts on the matter. We just need your signature to approve the grant and release the funds immediately.'

She showed him the papers.

'Excellent,' said Wheatley, signing the papers. 'Right. That's sorted,' he concluded as he glanced at Mina. 'Are you free for lunch?' he asked, straightening up.

Mina was flustered, the whole thing had moved so fast.

'Yes, of course,'

He turned to his secretary, 'Would you be so kind to book a table at the Olive Leaf for Miss Osman and myself?'

She nodded and walked away to call the hotel's famed restaurant.

'I've just arrived from California. It's awfully cold here, don't you think?'

'Yes it is. Do you come here often on business?'

'Sometimes. Mind you, it can't be much of change for you,

coming from New York. I spent one winter in the big apple, and decided never again!'

'I agree, but I've actually just arrived from Iraq, not from the US.'

Wheatley seemed quite taken aback 'How on earth did you get through customs?'

She smiled, 'I travelled via Jordan.'

'What an intrepid and charming young woman! You must tell me all about it over lunch.'

He turned to his secretary who confirmed with a nod that the table was booked.

⤳

The restaurant was a welcoming modern space, with an off-white ceiling, panoramic sea views and leafy plants encased in large terracotta pots. Mina and Wheatley were seated at a table near one of the wide bays, from where she could admire the open sea.

Surveying the room, Wheatley said: 'The carpet is quite tacky and the furniture is a little too modern for my own taste, but the food is quite acceptable.'

'I'm glad to hear that,' said Mina, feeling completely out of her depth.

He ordered a bottle of champagne and they drank to her success.

'Mr Wheatley, I would like to thank you for funding my research.'

'*De rien*. Mina, if I may call you Mina?'

'Of course.'

'If the rich men of this world do not fund those who further our knowledge of the past, our outlook on the future would be a mixture of gloominess and ignorance.'

He looked at her, smiling. The background music changed to the French song *La Bohême* by Charles Aznavour. He looked at her and asked if she spoke French. She understood a little. He quoted the first lines of the song,

'*Je me souviens d'un temps que les moins de vingt ans ne peuvent pas connaître.*' What a wonderful song. I remember the days when I studied in Paris. I was young and wanted to conquer the world.'

'And have you?' she asked, mischievously.

'Not yet, not yet, but I'll get there.' Hs eyes flickered coldly for a moment.

'You seem quite young, Mr Wheatley, to be the C.E.O. of such a huge corporation,' she said smiling at him.

'Please, call me Oberon,' he said, smiling back at her.

After a while Mina excused herself and felt his lingering look on her tight skirt and toned legs as she brushed past him. Ten minutes later, as she walked back from the powder room, she felt slightly guilty, as if she was cheating on Jack. 'How stupid,' she thought, unconsciously running her fingers through her hair as she approached Oberon. He smiled at her and she smiled back, undeniably charmed by this powerful man's manners and culture.

He asked her more questions about her work, and her thoughts about the current war in Iraq. She tried to answer as naturally as she could but was thinking, 'He's almost too smooth.' After the delicious lunch of a delicate porcini risotto followed by grilled sole with creamy pommes dauphinoise, he invited her for drinks on his yacht that evening. It would be a fun and select party. Could she arrive slightly earlier, maybe 8 o'clock, so they could discuss her work a little further before the other guests arrived? Mina accepted the invitation gladly and Wheatley took his leave. A waiter opened the door to the terrace for Mina, who felt like walking in the fresh outdoor air before returning to her room. She was on top of the world.

∽

'Sir, you should have worked for the CIA' said Natasha to Oberon.

'Who says I haven't?'

She looked at him, taken aback. He let her hang for a while and then laughed out loud.

'You should have seen your face my dear. It was quite amusing. Had I worked for the CIA, operations would have run a little more smoothly I believe, and would have had some chance of success.'

'If you are referring to Mosul, Sir, I can assure you it won't happen again.'

'I know it won't.'

She tried not to think about what he meant by that.

'Back to the yacht. Let's get out of this godawful place.'

∽

Mina was lying on her bed, balancing her shoe off the tip of her toes. She picked up her phone and dialled Liat's mobile number.

'I did it!' she said.

'I knew you would.'

'It was quite amazing. Well, the C.E.O of the Wheatley Forecast Corporation, Mr Oberon Wheatley himself came by and then invited me for lunch.'

'Oh my god! You lucky bitch!'

'Language Liat, language. Oberon is quite the gentleman, and would, I'm sure, be utterly shocked by your poor choice of words!'

'Oberon, is it?'

'Yes, Oberon.'

'Is he hot?' asked Liat, matter-of-factly.

'Yes, he certainly is. In his mid-forties, dazzling charm and richer than Rockefeller.'

'And…?'

'And he invited me for a party this evening on his yacht in the marina.'

'I can't believe it.'

'Well believe it, but I need your help,' pleaded Mina.

'What? You need me to lace you into your finest negligee before you meet him?'

'No! But I will need your help in choosing an appropriate evening dress. This time I have loads of money.'

'No problem. I know just where to go. I'll pick you up in the lobby in half an hour!'

'Liat …?' Mina interrupted her.

Back in his room, just opposite Mina's, Jack had heard enough of Mina's thoughts to last him a lifetime. He was devastated. He leapt off the bed and rushed out of the room, but as he was about to knock on Mina's door, he hesitated, and then walked furiously back down the corridor. He never heard the end of the conversation.

'Yes Mina?'

'During the lunch, Oberon was exceedingly charming.'

'And?'

'But I can't stop thinking about Jack.'

'Oh, Mina!' sighed Liat.

'I know. I know. I can't help it. Never mind. See you in half an hour.'

⤳

When Mina returned from her second shopping spree with Liat, she checked her emails in the hotel's computer room. Nothing from Hassan. She still harboured a tiny hope that her resourceful student had somehow managed to evade his pursuers and was in hiding. There were a number of emails from Professor Almeini, but she could not find the courage to read them.

Her attention suddenly focused on one email – she opened it. It was from Shobai. He was thanking her for her email and wanted to discuss the content of the tablet further. He was an old man, so he could not travel much, but would be delighted to meet in London. The last lines of Shobai's email sent a shiver down her spine. *Finally, my dear girl, I entreat you not to discuss your discovery with anyone you do not trust absolutely. There is danger in playing with century-old riddles.*

How prophetic his words were! She had to meet him. The poor old man would be terrified if she told him about her ordeal in Iraq. She suddenly felt thrown back into the turmoil of her last days in Mosul. She had avoided thinking about what had happened completely, but suspected she was still in shock. Were the three men assassins? According to Jack they were "professionals", whatever that meant. She shuddered, remembering the dead eyes of the man who had questioned her. If only she knew why these men were after the tablet. Its discovery was clearly a philological breakthrough, but she could hardly imagine academics hiring assassins to get hold of a tablet for publication purposes. Mina was out of sorts after reading Shobai's email, but she had not spent three hours with Liat searching for an evening dress for nothing. She thought of Scarlett O'Hara in *Gone in the Wind* saying, 'Tomorrow is another day'. Mina took a deep breath and decided to put all her concerns on hold and have fun tonight.

Chapter 15

Mina stepped out of the lift wearing a gorgeous evening dress and very expensive high heels. When she brushed past the reception desk, the entire male staff fell over themselves to greet her, open the door and wish her a good evening. She was enjoying herself immensely, smiling at each one of them in turn. She left the hotel feeling like a princess out of a fairy tale, her shawl flowing in the wind. As she headed towards the marina, slowly because of her long dress and heels, she half-expected a genie to rise from the sand and offer her three wishes. What would those wishes be? She would love to meet Jack again. That would certainly be her first wish. As for the other two, she would need to think a little more about them. Money wasn't a particular issue for her but the large grant she had just been awarded would go a long way for her research. She also felt much freer in her travel plans.

What a strange world, the world of business. She had checked her bank account online, and found that the Wheatley Forecast Corporation had wired her $11,000 instantly. According to the agreement she had received that afternoon, her original travel grant had been transformed into a yearly fellowship of $45,000, paid quarterly. She could also send them requests for up to $30,000 over the next two years for scientific testing of various archaeological material in the course of her research.

Mina walked a little faster to arrive on time to meet Oberon before the party began. At the pier, a young man in full uniform hailed her.

'Miss Osman?'

'Yes?'

'Please step in the tender. I am to take you to the *Rêverie*. She is anchored slightly out of the harbour tonight to offer more privacy to Mr Wheatley's guests during the party.'

A few minutes later, one of Oberon's men invited Mina to come aboard the *Rêverie*. She walked across a temporary platform that jutted out of the aft deck. Red Chinese lanterns had been strung up all around the yacht for the party and, as she climbed the winding stairs, she noticed soft up-lighting and outdoor heaters on the aft deck. Oberon appeared out of the dark.

'My dear Mina, you look absolutely ravishing.'

'Thank you Mr. Wheatley…Oberon.'

He smiled at her and gestured her to sit by his side.

'What will you have to drink?' he asked softly.

'Champagne, please.'

'Champagne it is.' He turned to the barman, who nodded back at him.

'May I thank you again for your generosity? Your funding will seriously further my research.'

'I had no idea archaeologists could be so charming. Had I known earlier, I would have funded many more projects.'

'I'm beginning to wonder why you funded mine.'

'Please don't. There was no photograph on your application. I'm happily surprised, that is all.'

'In that case, I'll be honest too. Since my interview today, I have felt like I was lost in a fairy tale. I thought to myself, am I in Tel Aviv or in *A Midsummer Night's Dream*?'

'I suppose that being called Oberon doesn't help.'

'Well, no. Where's Puck? Is he hiding behind the bar?'

They both laughed. The barman brought the champagne flutes, and served them Oberon's best champagne.

'Thank you Dominique, leave the bottle. Please make sure everything is ready for the party.' As the barman was leaving the room, Oberon called him again,

'Dominique, please ask Natasha to join us.'

He then turned to Mina. 'I propose a toast to your success in finding out what happened to Benjamin of Tudela during his stay in Israel, and to the end of the war in Iraq.'

Mina was surprised that Oberon had actually read her grant application.

'Those are two toasts I will happily drink to.'

Mina drank her champagne and closed her eyes for an instant. She was enjoying being transported into a world of luxury after her last gruelling days in Mosul. When she opened her eyes, she recognised by Oberon's side the blonde woman who had introduced herself as his secretary before the interview. Two men in dark suits had appeared on either side of the table. Oberon made a gesture and one of the men pulled Mina backwards by the throat while the other tied her hands behind her back.

'What's going on?' cried Mina.

'I'll show you what's going on,' said Natasha in a low, cruel voice.

Mina went mute. She tried to cry out but was unable to utter a single sound. She watched on, hopelessly, as Natasha slowly slipped on a pair of black leather gloves then slapped Mina hard across the side of her head. A spasm of pain shot through her cheek and eyes. All she could hear was a hissing sound. Had she gone deaf? Suddenly another hard strike from Natasha's leather clad hand whipped across Mina's face. This time her cheek went numb, and she fell out of her chair, hitting her head hard against the wooden deck.

The two men picked her up, and made her stand. Natasha balled her fist and punched her hard in the stomach, leaving Mina retching from the impact. She wouldn't be able to sustain much more of this onslaught. But the pain had numbed her mind. Only one thought remained: the hopelessness of her situation. She looked pitifully at Natasha, entreating her to stop, but she just punched her right under the solar plexus in response. For a few moments, Mina couldn't breathe, and collapsed to the ground. Her torturer knew exactly how far to carry out the beating. The men sat her down firmly on the chair.

Mina's face was starting to bruise and she was bleeding from her nose. When she tasted the blood on her split lip, she fainted. One of the men shoved a bottle of ammonia under her nose, and she came to in a matter of seconds. Oberon had a strangely detached look on his face. He turned to Natasha, 'Is it done?' She nodded in return. He looked at Mina and spoke very slowly, all charm gone from his voice.

'I'm going to ask you a question. If you answer me truthfully, you keep your full grant, and walk away. If you don't, Natasha will continue her own particular brand of questioning.'

Mina looked at him, more terrified by his cold stare than anything she'd known before. She broke down in tears and heard him sigh with irritation. She saw him raise a hand to signal to Natasha to start beating her again.

'No, please! I don't know anything,' she spluttered through her tears, 'anything about anything. Please let me go.'

Oberon didn't seem to hear anything she said.

'Where is the tablet?' he asked.

Realisation dawned on Mina. This is what it had been about all along. The interview, the lunch, the invitation to the yacht…to seduce her into giving up the tablet. Now she was properly terrified. If Oberon had sent the three men to her flat in Mosul, her chances of leaving the yacht alive were slim.

'In my room at the hotel', she answered, trying to steady her voice.

'No it isn't,' he replied.

Mina's heart sank. How stupid. They had had all afternoon to search her room.

'Should Natasha pursue her delicate work? Do you want to end up like your friend did', turning to Natasha, 'what was her name?'

'Liat Hoffman, sir,' she answered.

'Oh Liat, no!' sobbed Mina.

He looked back at Mina, deadly serious. She saw his blank eyes, without an ounce of humanity left in them. This man was a calculating machine, who would stop at nothing to get the information he wanted. He'd spoken of Liat in the past tense. Had they murdered her? She knew nothing. Mina hadn't told her a word. She couldn't keep up this charade any longer.

'I sent it by special military courier to a hotel in Safed.'

'Which hotel?' Oberon asked matter-of-factly.

'Central Merkazi', she answered.

He turned to Natasha. 'Call the hotel. Ask if Miss Osman has a reservation there and if they've received a package for her.'

'Yes sir.'

'So, Mina, have you deciphered that delightful tablet?' Oberon asked.

'I…I just translated it' she stuttered.

'And?'

'And it's a version of the flood in the Gilgamesh's Epic, the eleventh tablet.'

'That's it?'

'Yes. Should there be something else?'

'I'm the one asking questions, Miss Osman,' he replied icily.

Natasha returned, and whispered something into Oberon's ear. He smiled and turned to Mina.

'Well Mina, I'm sorry we need to part at this point in time. It would have been a pleasure to know you more…intimately.'

He paused. Then, savouring every word, he added,

'Too bad, really. Had I been less pressed for time, we might have discussed the myth of the sacred tablets of Nineveh that enable their possessors to predict natural disasters.'

'Tablets? There is more than one?'

'Oh yes my dear.' He paused. 'I'm not in the habit of blabbering away, but as you will not be talking much in the foreseeable future…the myth and purpose of this sacred tablet is described on an ancient Chinese oracle bone I have in my modest collection. I'm told it dates back to 1500 BC and refers to a stone tablet *from the land in the West between two mighty rivers, the text of which was copied onto four clay tablets that were sent East and West*…and you seem to have stumbled upon the only surviving one, and quite evidently the original one. As the Epic of Gilgamesh runs on twelve tablets, one might call your stone tablet from Mosul the "13th Tablet". All in all, thank you very much.'

He nodded at the two men and then shot a meaningful look

at Natasha. They brought Mina to her feet and forced her down the stairs, back onto the platform. Stepping up behind her, one of the men knocked her unconscious, while the other prepared a large canvas sack, which they filled with heavy rocks. While they worked, Natasha scanned the location to make sure there were no witnesses. The men slipped Mina into the sack and tied it up. They then loaded it onto the tender. Before long they were out in the open sea.

Natasha was looking through her binoculars, and from afar saw the two men throw the sack into the dark waters. No-one would ever find her body. Oberon looked at her inquisitively. She nodded back to confirm the men had done their job. He relaxed visibly and picked up his champagne flute.

'I think we should finish this excellent and rather rare champagne.'

'Yes sir,' she said, sitting down next to him, 'It would be a shame to waste it.'

'Well, that's all sorted. My guests should arrive soon. Take the day off tomorrow, then make your way to Safed with your men and pick up the tablet. Call me when you've got it.'

Natasha seemed thoughtful.

'What's on your mind?' Oberon asked, putting his hand on her knee.

'I was wondering how the girl managed to send mail through a special military courier.'

'She's a resourceful one,' he answered, as if he were talking about his clever golden retriever.

'Was, sir.'

'Of course, was.'

'Should I cancel the standing order to her account?'

'No, keep it running. It's a great alibi. Had I planned to murder this delightful creature, would I still be paying her?'

He smiled as he thought about the bright young woman he had just disposed of. 'Perhaps I shouldn't have been in such a hurry. Maybe she knew more than she let on.' His doubts lingered, but only for a moment. He glanced at Natasha as she crossed her legs. She knew that look well and rose slowly from her chair. Turning around to face him she unbuttoned her top. She was not wearing any underwear. She pulled a silver clasp from her head and let her blond hair sweep over her bare shoulders and breasts. He watched her, breathing heavily as she walked around the table. He sat back in his chair and held her eye as she leant down and gripped him by his tie. She brought her face close to his, and slipped the tip of her tongue between his lips. He grabbed her from behind, trying to pull her down. She held him at a distance while she slowly slipped out of her skirt. He was overcome with desire for his deadly assassin. Leaving her thigh-length boots on, she stepped forward and straddled him. She moaned gently as she sank into his passionate embrace.

⌐

A few hours later, a man standing on a small boat in the darkness of the harbour made a phone call.

'Master… she went on the yacht but it's back in the harbour, and she hasn't returned. We believe she was disposed of by Wheatley.'

'That would be very unfortunate. Keep watching Wheatley and his men.'

Chapter 16

December 9th, 2004

Mina woke up shivering. In a daze, she looked around and thought she saw metal walls. 'Where the hell am I?' She tried sitting up, but she was zipped up in a sleeping bag, and covered with a pile of duvets. Her head felt like it had been pumped up with pressurised air, but it was nothing compared to the pain she felt on the left side of her face and at the base of her skull. Her whole body ached. In the dim light she could make out the figure of Jack looking at her.

'Hi Mina.'

'Jack? Where am I?'

'You're safe. Take these, and drink some water.' She took the proffered tablets and swallowed them as told, then finished the whole glass in a bid to cool her aching throat

'You're in the back of my van. Stay still. You almost died of hypothermia.' He stroked her face and smiled at her.

'I'm in your van? In Mosul?' She felt nauseous, and tired beyond belief.

'No. We're in Tel Aviv. Sleep Mina. I'll watch over you.'

She dropped back onto the floor of the van and fell into a deep sleep. Jack watched her and thought about the past few hours. He'd been waiting in the water for two hours by the tender while Mina was on the yacht. Powerless to prevent it, he had watched her being beaten up by Natasha and bided his time. When they put her in a sack, he knew the time to act had come. He hooked his belt to the tender and was towed along until Oberon's men stopped, far away from the yacht. He swiftly detached himself as soon as they had slung Mina into the sea and turned the boat around to return to the yacht. He plunged after her. The water was icy cold but he was wearing a full scuba diving outfit he had rented that afternoon. He had a powerful torch but could hardly see a few feet ahead. A seasoned diver, he knew that if he did not find her in the next few moments, it would be too late. Suddenly he could make out the shape of the sack, dropping fast into the murky abyss. He reached out but missed it. He plunged further down, thrusting himself down as hard as he could, and caught it by the cord. He pulled out his knife from his ankle sheath and cut through the length of the sack, yanking Mina out and bringing her back to the surface in a few kicks. Placing his mask over her face, Jack made her breathe his oxygen, and tried to resuscitate her, but despite coughing up some water, she was still unconscious. He knew he would have to swim very quickly to the harbour, before hypothermia set in, which worried him more than anything else. He was furious for not anticipating Wheatley's sadistic streak and how far he was prepared to go. Jack would make him pay for every bruise on her beautiful face.

～

'Morning Mina,' said Jack, offering her a warm drink, as she sat up sluggishly.

She looked at him with blank eyes, then, remembering

fragments, her hands started twitching, she felt a long shiver shooting through her spine, and suddenly burst into an uncontrollable flood of tears. Jack held her in his arms. She cried for a long time while he slowly explained what had happened and how he had saved her.

She finally took a sip of coffee from the Styrofoam cup, grimacing from the pain in her jaw, and looked up at him.

'Thank you Jack. Thanks for everything…but what were you doing there? What are you doing *here?*'

Jack looked down, feeling uncomfortable. 'I've been following you since you left Iraq.'

'Why?'

'Well, I was worried about you, and obviously with a good reason. That bastard Wheatley had you thrown into the open sea, tied up in a sack. Had I not been there, we wouldn't be talking right now.'

'Don't think I'm being ungrateful here, but I can't possibly,' she swallowed hard, and tears sprung to her eyes again, '…I can't possibly explain how much I need you to be honest with me right now.'

'What do you mean Mina?'

'I mean, who follows someone to a different country because they're worried for them? Don't lie to me. I've been beaten up and almost murdered by people I trusted, and Liat… they murdered her.' Mina was racked by sobs.

'Mina, listen to me! Your friend Liat is in a sorry state, but she's not dead. I took her to a hospital and she's recovering. They told me she'll be OK in a few weeks.'

A wave of relief washed over Mina.

'She's alive?' she stuttered, 'Oh thank you Jack, thank you. I have to see her, I need to explain.'

'No, Mina. I convinced her not to talk about what happened, as it would be too dangerous to do so right now.'

They both remained silent for what seemed like an eternity. Mina stroked Jack's hand, 'I'm sorry I said the things I did in Mosul. I didn't mean them.'

'Yes you did. I'm sorry I lied to you.'

She looked at him inquisitively.

'The reason I followed you was that I couldn't make out if you were a player or a victim back in Iraq. As I said to you, those men in your flat were serious mercs.'

'Mercs?'

'Mercenaries... and there you were, half-Iraqi, half-American, beautiful, clever, apparently out of place in that university, involved with mercs and off to Israel.'

'Beautiful?' She arched an eyebrow. He smiled.

'Well, very sexy too, but that wouldn't be a prerequisite to be a spy.'

'Why don't you tell me everything, from the beginning.'

'Alright, here goes. I knew from your last email...'

'What? You went through my email?'

'I'm sorry. I promise never to do it again.'

'You promise?' she asked him.

'Yes. Can I continue? I thought you were a spy then.'

'OK. Go on.'

'So I followed you to Amman and then to Tel Aviv. I booked a room in the same hotel under an assumed name...I have a number of passports. Anyway, the information I had gathered on Oberon Wheatley warranted some serious concern. I needed to check the hotel and its immediate surroundings. One of my contacts told me that Wheatley's private yacht was anchored in the harbour marina and that usually meant that he was aboard. I thought it was a strange coincidence that you should both be here at the same time. So when he suddenly showed up at your interview, I knew the whole thing was a trap.

'How did you know he was there?'

'I placed a bug in your handbag.'

'Oh man, you're in so much trouble. This story is getting worse by the minute.'

Jack pretended not to have heard her and continued talking, 'the harbour was under surveillance, especially the area around Wheatley's yacht. I would either have to make contact with you directly or find a way to approach the yacht without raising suspicion, which would be difficult. If the surviving attacker at your flat in Mosul worked for Oberon, he'd recognise me immediately. I can't tell you how anxious I was waiting all night for your drunken return after you left to party with your friend. I was worried that your enemies had decided to act before the interview, so I was pretty relieved to see you stagger into your room at last. To tell you the truth, I did think to myself then, 'here I am, in Israel, trying to protect a woman I hardly know from people I know even less about. I must be mad.' Then again, I guess that's part of the reason I joined the army, and never completely left it…to be in a position to protect and defend beautiful women in peril! Jack grinned.

'How very gallant of you!'

'Besides, I've been known in the past to thrive on danger. Anyway, after your interview, while you paced on the terrace without a care in the world, I was fuming back in my room. The listening device I'd placed in your handbag had picked up your entire conversation. You'd fallen into Wheatley's lap. I knew you'd never leave his yacht alive; I was absolutely sure of it. The obvious thing to do was to meet you in your room and tell you it was a trap. But, as things stood between us, you'd almost certainly not believe me. I'd also have had to explain why I'd followed you and bugged your bag.'

'Yup.'

'It all came down to bad timing. Had I met you before the interview I might have been able to warn you, but it was too late. So I stuck to my original plan. I got some scuba gear, hid by the yacht and waited for them to…well you know the rest.'

'Listen, I don't know why Wheatley tried to kill you, but if you want my help, I need to know everything.'

'I agree.'

Mina leaned on Jack's shoulder and started telling him about the meaning and importance of the tablet and how Oberon was desperate to get his hands on it. She suddenly sat up in anguish, 'I actually told him where the tablet is. I sent it by courier to a hotel in Safed. We need to get there now or all of it will have been for nothing.'

'But we have an advantage.' Jack answered, grinning.

'What do you mean?'

'He thinks you're dead. You know, Mina, I feel I'm on a strange quest in foreign lands, just like the good book says.'

She looked at him, quizzically. 'The good book?'

'The Bible, silly! Solid Baptist upbringing. Difficult to shake off.'

She smiled at him. He seemed to think for a second and suddenly burst out laughing.

'Are you alright Jack?'

'Yeah. Yes. I was just thinking about Jonah. You know how he left Nineveh, went to Yafo, and ended up in the sea.'

'Yes?'

'Well, it just occurred to me that I'm your whale in the story.'

She saw herself leaving Mosul, travelling to Tel Aviv and being thrown off a boat into the sea. They both laughed hysterically.

'OK. After I've returned the wet suit and diving gear, I think we should get going. I looked up the best way to get to Safed. It's a two and a half hour journey by car. You'll have all the time in the world to fill me in on background information. Also,' he added, 'I managed to salvage your suitcase from your hotel room. Get changed, and let's go.'

As they were driving out of Tel Aviv, Mina checked herself in the mirror and was shocked at her appearance.

'The bruising looks terrible!'

'Don't worry. The anti-inflammatory cream should reduce the swelling.'

She really hoped he was right: even speaking was painful. As she looked out at the landscape unfolding beyond the large windscreen, it occurred to her that she could just let the tablet quest go. She had survived her ordeal. She was alive against all odds. But no, she craved justice for what Oberon had done to her and Liat out of greed. For the first time in her life she longed to make someone else suffer.

'Are you OK? You look like you're about to murder someone.'

She did not reply, but Jack knew exactly what she was thinking.

'We're going due north into the mountains of Upper Galilee. Mina, I think it's a good time to assess our situation,' he said, changing lanes. 'One, you found a mysterious stone tablet hidden within a clay casing. Two, what you translated didn't make much sense to you. Three, as soon as the word got out about the little you did translate, Wheatley gets hold of you and Liat in order to steal the tablet.'

'On the yacht, just before they knocked me out…' Mina faltered, 'Wheatley mentioned an ancient Chinese oracle bone that listed…'

'Excuse me?' said Jack, interrupting her, 'what the hell is an oracle bone?'

'I am not really sure. All I know is that the oracle bone script is the oldest form of Chinese writing. They were used to predict events in imperial China, that's why they are called oracle bones'.

'Right', said Jack, 'so what's engraved on Wheatley's doggy bone?'

'According to Wheatley, it lists a stone tablet 'from the land in the West between two mighty rivers', and four clay copies which were sent to the four corners of the world. He said this tablet enabled their owner to make accurate predictions.'

'Hmm I see. From what I gathered about Wheatley's line of business, I assume it would have to do with weather forecasting.'

'Yes, and I now wonder if doesn't specifically have to do with flood forecasting.'

'Why?'

'The tablet I found… it's a version of Noah's story.

Jack raised his eyebrows.

'A good Bible student like you should remember the story of Noah.' Mina continued, ironically.

'Yes of course, something about a flood and a pretty big boat as I recall?'

'Right. The world of men has become evil and God is displeased. He finds only one righteous man.'

'Noah.'

'Yes, and He entrusts him with the future of mankind, animals and plants. Noah builds an ark and the flood destroys everything. For many days and nights the waters do not recede. Eventually the rain stops and Noah sends out a dove to see if there is land in the vicinity. The bird returns with an olive branch in its beak, proving that the waters are receding, and the cargo on Noah's ark is safe. God decides to make a covenant with Noah never to destroy humanity again, and produces a rainbow as a sign of it.'

'Lovely story. I always did wonder where rainbows came from. Right. What about the Sumerian version?'

'Well, there are many historical layers to the Sumerian version. It's a little complicated. Some fragments of the flood narrative date back to the turn of the second millennium B.C.E. in Sumerian poems. Others are found in *Atrahasis*, an epic written in Akkadian dating back to 1750–1650 B.C.E. But, the most complete story is revealed in the eleventh tablet of the Epic of Gilgamesh, the Standard Akkadian version. And that one is the most recent one, dating back to 1300–1100 B.C.E.. It's pretty much the same story as the biblical one with a few twists; some Gods are displeased with the continuous noise that humans make and decide to destroy humanity, but others are on the humans' side and entrust Utnapishtim, their 'Noah', to build an ark, they get into the ark, he sends out the birds, yada yada yada.'

'OK. What about the tablet?'

'I'm impressed. Last time I spoke to you, you kept interrupting me.'

'You're obviously getting better at telling stories.' He grinned broadly at her. 'The weather is getting worse. Do you know that Safed sometimes gets snowed in? I read that on the Internet yesterday. That's if I was looking at the right place; there is a ton of different ways of spelling Safed.'

'It's Tsfat in Hebrew but it's confusing, as sometimes it is also spelled Sefad or Sfad. It's a really important town. It has been a prestigious centre of learning for over four hundred years and it's one of Israel's four sacred cities, together with Jerusalem, Hebron, and Tiberias…Did you say snow?'

'It is over 900 metres above sea level.'

'I hope you found us some coats and gloves?'

'Mina. I'm a soldier. Preparation, preparation, preparation. Of course I have. So, the tablet?'

'Yes. It differs from the Standard twelve tablets in philological ways that I can't explain entirely until I've seen it again, but I don't think that matters so much. What I find most intriguing is how different it is from the eleventh… there are loads of weird calculations.'

'Calculations?'

'Well the Sumerians were very advanced in mathematics and….'

'Really? I thought the Greeks invented all that stuff?'

'You're doing it again.'

'What?'

'Interrupting me.'

'Sorry. Go on.'

'"The Greeks were thinkers. They theorised about everything. The Sumerians and Chaldeans were quite different, they were obsessed with astronomy and astrology, which involved advanced mathematics. What is weird is that both the Sumerian and Hebrew original flood narratives contain the measurements of the ark, but nothing more in terms of mathematics.'

'What do you mean?'

'God tells Noah or, in the Sumerian version, different Gods tell Utnapishtim how to build the ark, how long it should be, how wide and so on. But the tablet I found provides lots of other calculations and formulas, which are far beyond my capacity to understand.'

'Maybe I can help on that. Engineering and math, that's me.'

'You mean you don't just shoot people and save damsels in distress?'

'Now you're being silly.'

'I know.'

Mina stopped talking for a little while. Jack observed her from the corner of his eye. She seemed to be pondering something.

'What are you mulling over?'

'There may be another group of people after the tablet.'

'Why? Oberon's not enough for you?'

'When you followed me, were you wearing a disguise?'

'No.'

'There was another man following me at the airport in Mosul and in Amman. He looked Middle Eastern, wearing a dark suit and with a long beard, I'm sure it was the same man.'

'I remember that man in Amman,' said Jack all of a sudden.

'You saw him?'

'I saw you watching someone ' he said.

'What if he is part of a Muslim sect trying to retrieve the tablet for their own purpose? Who else grows such beards?'

'The Amish?'

She giggled. Jack had a wonderful way of taking the tension out of the worst situations with a joke.

'And Noah is referred to over 40 times in the Qur'an; he is an important figure in Islam.'

'So what? You sound like some people I know: they're wearing headscarves, so they must be terrorists!'

'OK. I'll tell you another story. According to Muslim belief, the ark is supposed to have circumnavigated the Ka'ba in Mecca before the waters of the flood receded.'

'You're kidding right?'

'No. And another tradition holds that Noah's grave is in the mosque in Mecca. Maybe my research has attracted the attention of a Muslim group completely unrelated to Oberon Wheatley.'

'Maybe. But even if you're right, these guys haven't made a move, so, let's concentrate on what we know.'

'Oberon obviously believes the tablet would be worth millions if he could use it to forecast events ahead of competitors.'

'Using the calculations you spoke of?'

'Maybe. The other really weird element is that the tablet relates the Jewish moralistic view that humanity turned evil and was in need of radical cleansing through annihilation.'

'Yes, you have told me about that before, but what do you make of it?"

'I don't know.'

'Maybe it's a rebus of some sort. You know, like a code?' Jack said.

'You sound just like my student Hassan right now.'

'I'm really starting to warm to that boy!

After a few miles he got off the road, stopped at a small petrol station, and parked near the restaurant area.

'Let's take a break. I can't see anything ahead with this rain. The weather's awful. I don't know about you, but I need a coffee and something to eat.'

'I do too, but don't you think Oberon could get his hands on the tablet before us?'

'No, not in this weather. Besides, he thinks you're at the bottom of the sea. Remember?'

⌒

They ordered coffee and two goat's cheese sandwiches and sat down.

'I'm famished. I haven't eaten since lunch yesterday.'

Mina froze, hit again by an onslaught of memories of the events that had lead her to be rescued by Jack from the depths of the sea.

'Thank you for saving my life Jack... twice.'

'Let's not make too much of a habit of it. I value my own life too you know.'

'Hmm. So, mystery man, tell me about you.'

'What do you want to know?'

'Are you really an engineer?'

'Yup. The army realised early on I had a special aptitude for maths, so they enrolled me in their engineering and water management courses.'

'How long were...Are you still in the army?'

'I joined in my late teens, and sort of quit a few years ago.'

'Sort of?'

'Well, I quit officially but since then I've participated as an independent contractor for certain missions.'

'Like a mercenary?' She asked, taken aback.

'If that's how you want to see it, yes. But it isn't really like that. It's well paid and I can choose my missions and work with people who won't screw them up.'

Jack seemed to hesitate but then added, 'I've also worked for non-military agencies over the years for which I received special training, but that's all I can say about them.'

Mina let the information sink in and then swiftly changed the subject.

'So, why did you quit the army?'

'For a number of reasons but mainly because the job felt repetitive. I'd go in with a team, do the job, and leave. I never exchanged a word with civilians on the ground. One day I woke up and just felt that people and missions had become figures and statistics.'

'Were you only stationed in Iraq?'

'God no. I've worked in many hot spots: Bosnia, Somalia, on the Thai-Burmese border, you name it. But I spent the last few years in and out of Iraq. I heard of the many water-related humanitarian projects, like the one at the village where you met me. I had engineering knowledge and the military training to pull it off. I saw an opportunity for change and I quit.'

'I'm glad you made that choice. I may never have met you otherwise.'

'It felt good, you know; I felt in touch with people again, not just fellow soldiers. Your arrival changed everything. I was suddenly catapulted back into special forces mode.' He winked and added, 'but it wasn't all bad.'

After a silence, Jack said, 'I hope when all this is over we can go for a stroll in the moonlit desert. I know a nice spot close to a village outside Mosul.'

'I'd like that very much,' Mina beamed.

It was time to get back to the van. They dressed up warmly with coats Jack had stacked up in the back, alongside sacks she did not dare ask about. 'Probably more soldiering toys,' she thought to herself.

'Tell me more about the flood,' Jack said when they were back on the road. 'It's obvious that it's the root of all our problems right now. And what's this Chinese oracle bone Wheatley spoke of? I'd love to see it for myself.'

'The first thing you need to understand is that almost every ancient civilisation has its own flood myth.'

'Don't be so superior. Obviously there must be other flood myths around. Even today, there are floods all over the world, every day.'

'I'm not being superior! God you're touchy. There's just so much to explain. I don't know where to begin.'

'OK. Just pretend I'm one of your pubescent students. I'm sure it will help to simplify all this.'

'Now who's being superior?'

'Sorry,' he said.

'Alright. I'm not referring to floods in general. I'm talking about *the* flood, the original one. The flood story from the Bible that you know so well involving Noah and his ark is found in different variations all over the world: the Greeks, for example, have the myth of Deucalion and Pyrrha who survived the flood.'

'Why would that Greek story be *the* flood?'

'Funny you should ask that. Most Christian authors in Antiquity felt the same way, as if *the* flood was their very own and only made sense within their religious framework. St Jerome believed that the Greek flood was a local flood and not the primordial flood described in the Bible.'

'I like that. You're comparing me to a saint.'

'Yeah, that's wishful thinking. I'm pretty sure you're no saint. I managed to do some reading on this subject last week, so let me tell you all about it while it is still fresh in my memory. No interruptions?'

Jack pretended to zip his mouth. She put on a serious air and explained, 'There's a Chinese Book called the *Shujing*, which was probably written around 700 B.C.E. It describes Emperor Da Yu controlling the flood waters that reached to the Heavens. Other parts of Asia have flood myths too. In Vietnam, the Sre people believe a horrific flood came from the sea and covered the earth, destroying everything. Of all humanity only a young man and his sister survived. They floated in a drum, and as the waters abated, they were left high and dry on the top of Mount Yang-La. In India, the flood story begins with terrible winds and rain which last a hundred years. Closer to home, the Native American Hopi explain that the swelling of the primordial river brought about the flood after everyone had become evil and gone mad during the 'first world': young men would make love to old women, old men with young girls, people killing each other, people becoming sick, etc. Then comes the flood. In South America, the Aztecs believed that humanity was devastated by a flood during the Fourth sun. All survivors were transformed into monkeys.'

'Amazing. What about other continents? Africa, for example?'

'In Africa, Bantus believe that a genie called Nzondo first provoked a terrible flood, at the origin of river Zair, and then disappeared. Should I go on Jack?'

'OK. But if everyone has a primordial flood story, obviously some global physical disaster must have that triggered it? Was it a destructive comet?'

'Maybe it is the mythical rendering of the end of the Ice Age and the coming of global warming.'

'I see what you mean…the amount of melted ice must have caused tremendous floods all over the planet.'

'Who knows? The Sumerians, Hebrews and the Native Americans saw the flood as a punishment for human wickedness, but for others, it marks the unavoidable end of a Golden Age and the passage to darker times.'

'Thank you Professor.'

'You're welcome, young man. What I don't understand is what Oberon told me before he… he…'

It was no use, she burst into tears again. Jack stopped the car on the side road. He unbuckled his seat belt, turned towards her and stroked her hair as he spoke to her in a deep and soothing voice.

'Hey. You'll be alright. Just focus on one thing – you're still alive. You beat him.'

He gave her a tissue to dab her lip, which had started bleeding again.

'Mina, what were you saying before? What didn't you understand?'

She breathed in deeply and said 'Why a Chinese text would mention the existence of five tablets from Mesopotamia.'

He thought about it for a moment, 'It beats me. We should ask a specialist when we are back to the US.'

As they drove higher in the foothills, Jack slowed down considerably, because the rain had transformed into sleet, and visibility was much worse than at the outset of their trip. Including their half-hour stop, they had already added an hour and a half to the route.

'We should be getting quite close to Safed now,' Jack said eventually. 'I hope the sky will clear. I've visited the north a few years ago with a friend. I'm sure that from the top of this hill you can see the Golan Heights to the East and Mount Hermon to the North – you know people ski there, but it would probably be cheaper for Israelis to fly to Switzerland.'

'I didn't know about Mount Hermon. Around here, what you can see for sure is Mount Meron, the burial place of Shimon Bar Yochai, the author of the *Zohar*, the mystical book of the Jews.'

'The what? I thought their sacred book was the Bible? The Torah?'

'The *Zohar* is a mystical book and central to the study of Kabbalah. It is said that people who aren't trained long enough in the study of the Torah and try to read and understand the *Zohar*, will lose their mind in the process. It's a dangerous book.'

'Come on, Mina. We're grown ups. That's a bedtime story.'

'I'm not joking. This is what I've read. I don't know much about Kabbalah but it seems that this saintly man, Bar Yochai, was fleeing the Romans in the 1st century C.E. He hid himself in a cave. He eventually emerged enlightened and wrote this magical book. Well, that's the story anyway. Some scholars think Bar Yochai was a bit like Homer with the *Iliad* and the *Odyssey*; you know, a sort of mythical writer ascribed to a book that is actually multi-layered and written over a long period of time by many authors.'

'I'm sorry, I've heard this magical stuff all over the planet; India, South America and even back home with the Mormons and their golden plates. I simply don't buy it.'

'Well, you'd better buy it fast because we're almost in Safed, kingdom of Kabbalah. And it isn't popstar Kabbalah either. It's the real deal.'

After twenty more minutes of driving, they finally saw Safed's hill. As they approached, they were gradually entranced by the calm atmosphere of this 'magic' mountain. How better to describe a place which rises almost 3,000 feet above sea level, surrounded by forests and the purest of air, so conducive to meditation and clear thinking? By this time, the entire city was covered in a white mantle of snow. Mina thought of the kabbalists' belief that the *Schechina* or the Manifest Presence of God rested above the city. With so little water in the Promised Land, this vision of purity must have felt to some like a divine presence. After all, did not certain sages believe that the Messiah would appear first in Safed before travelling to Jerusalem?

Chapter 17

December 9th, 2004. Safed

While Mina waited in the van on Jerusalem Street, Jack picked up the stone tablet from the Merkazi Central Hotel and cancelled Mina's reservation. He walked back to the van with the package, which Mina tore open. She breathed a long sigh of relief when she found the stone tablet, unscathed. Jack drove them through the Old Town. Mina expressed surprise at the large number of art galleries they were passing on the way and Jack explained that Safed had been at the forefront of contemporary Israeli and Jewish art for many years. The Old Town was not only home to some of the oldest of the seventy synagogues scattered around Safed but it was also famous for its so-called Artist's Colony. New galleries appeared like mushrooms throughout the cobbled streets. Jack parked the van outside a small internet café.

As they walked into the café, Mina to Jack, 'I remember reading about a nice guest house not too far from here, Bar-El. We could stay there.'

'Frankly, I think we should get the hell out of here.'

'Come on Jack. I have nothing to fear with you by my side.'

'Mina, we've got the tablet, we're safe. But Wheatley will find out today or tomorrow that you're still alive and that you have the tablet. We should be on the other side of the planet right now.'

'Give me two days to complete my research on Safed and then we can leave. I haven't been through hell and back to go home empty-handed.'

'I don't like this. But if you must, here are my conditions: no sightseeing and we need to be as discreet as possible.' Mina batted her eyelashes in agreement and smiled sweetly at him.

'Women! I don't know why I fall for this.'

'You can't help it. And anyway, there is no reason why Oberon would stick around if the tablet isn't here any more.'

'And you do still have his money...' They both burst out laughing.

Jack felt as if he were looking at Mina for the first time. They were slowly warming up, drinking green tea in the brightly decorated internet café. Mina seemed full of life now and she had some of the sparkle back in her eyes. Jack could not deny it; she was stunningly beautiful, even with her wounded lip and bruised cheek. For a moment he wondered if, back in Iraq, he had ever believed she was a national threat, or if the real reason he'd followed her to Israel was simply because she was the hottest and most intriguing woman he'd met in a long time.

'Jack, we've chosen the worst time of the year to come to Safed.'

'Why's that?'

'Well, for one thing it's the Chanukah holiday and tomorrow evening is Shabbat. I hope all the guest houses won't be booked up. Maybe we should leave Safed and return in a few days?'

'No. Let's manage with the time we have.'

'OK. One more thing – I think you and I should pretend to be Jewish. I'm worried people might not answer my questions openly if they realise I'm half-Iraqi.'

'I don't think we'll fool anyone, Mina.'

'You'd be amazed how welcoming orthodox Jews are, especially during festivals. They're always trying to bring their non-religious brethren into the fold. They call it doing a *mitzvah*, a good deed. Listen, just go with the flow, be yourself and don't engage too much with anyone. I'll do the talking. I'll be Miriam and you... Josh, both from New York.'

'Are you sure you're not a spy? You're devious. I'm in, Miriam.'

They were silent for a time, then Jack said:

'Mina? May I ask you a personal question?'

'Of course.'

'Your father is Muslim and your mother's Christian. Right?'

'Not much of question, but yes.'

'So how come you know so damn much about Jewish customs and culture?'

Mina looked a little embarrassed. She took a deep breath and said:

'You've obviously never lived in New York for a long period of time. There are so many Jewish communities there.'

'So? One of my best friends lives near Chinatown in San Francisco, it doesn't make him almost Chinese.'

'OK. My ex-boyfriend is Jewish. His family in New York practically adopted me for a time. I became fascinated by Jewish culture.'

'Right...sorry I brought it up.'

Now Jack felt embarrassed.

'It's fine, really. I broke up with him a while ago.'

She noticed Jack's smile from the corner of her eye and continued, 'besides, I've been researching the life and works of Benjamin of Tudela for years for my PhD, as well as other Jewish travellers of his time. So I've done some extensive background reading on many aspects of Judaism.'

They moved to one of the computer terminals and looked up information on Safed. Mina thought she should start her investigations with the oldest synagogue; it was the one most likely to have information about Benjamin of Tudela. It seemed that the Abuhav *shul,* the Yiddish word often used for synagogue, was the oldest.

After printing out a map of central Safed and a few other documents, they made their way to the Abuhav *shul.* They walked through charming meandering streets covered in snow, with colourful posters on the walls, old women opening window shutters, young Jews walking to *shul.* People were preparing for Chanukah everywhere around them. What Mina enjoyed most though, were her own muffled footsteps. It felt like she was walking in a dream, where no-one could hear her arriving nor leaving, except for the occasional crunch in the frosty snow. Looking up, she noticed many houses had domed roofs, the shape of which was emphasised by the weight of fallen snow. Having passed the main square, they arrived at an open courtyard. They walked through a narrow lane, framed on either side with tall walls and finally arrived at the entrance of the synagogue. They were surprised at the height of the building; it was at least four storeys tall. As they passed through the entrance, out of the silent courtyard and into the warmth of this place of learning, they felt blood rushing through their bodies again. It was like walking through a small orchard of stone trees, with beautiful cupolas and finely carved pillars dividing the internal spaces of the building. At the centre of the mosaic floor was a platform from which the Torah scroll was read. Mina's trained eye immediately noticed the unusual elements of their surroundings; the ceilings were painted blue, to remind the visitors of the celestial vision; there were three holy arks instead of one. Mina picked up a crumpled leaflet at the entrance that gave a few explanations to visitors. One of the arks enshrined a *sefer* Torah, a Torah scroll that was over five hundred years old, brought back by Rabbi Isaac Abuhav from his native Portugal.

A young Ethiopian Orthodox Jew came up to them and told them in his broken English that the women's place of worship was elsewhere. Mina told him that they just wanted to visit the synagogue and possibly talk to the person in charge of the archives.

'You wanting administrator?'

'Yes,' she answered.

As he walked off, Jack turned to Mina.

'I've never seen a black Jew.'

'Huge numbers of Ethiopian and Russian Jews have emigrated to Israel in recent years. The law is such that all Jews can emigrate here, almost no questions asked. The Jewish diaspora is amazing. They're come from everywhere, from China to South America.'

'Wow. So they can just return from wherever they have lived for centuries?'

'Yes, it's called the *Aliya*, the Law of the Return.'

'Too bad it doesn't work for the Palestinians too…'

'Jack, I've got more reasons than you to feel for the Palestinians, but I think you're being naïve on that count. Anyway, I've come here for information and not to insult people so please back me up. Shhh. He's coming back.'

The young man had returned with a jolly looking man in his late forties, so corpulent he seemed to roll down the stairs.

'Shalom. My name is Ezra and you are?'

'Shalom. My name is Miriam and this is Josh. We're from New York and we're visiting Safed for Chanukah. Your synagogue is a real jewel.'

'Thank you.'

He beamed with pleasure and kept looking at Jack, as if he expected him to speak. Mina realised that being a woman she was less likely to get answers than Jack, but it couldn't be helped. She said to Ezra, 'I've also come here to do some research for my PhD.'

'How fascinating. What are you working on?'

'Well, I'd be interested in any information, texts, documents of any sort you may have on or by Benjamin of Tudela. You see, I thought since your synagogue was the oldest in Safed, you may have old records that other synagogues don't.'

'Benjamin of Tudela? I don't think so. But, there is someone in Safed who might be able to help you. Old Eli, Eli Ben Mordechai. I remember he was obsessed with Tudela for some time, but I can't recall why.'

'Is he in Safed?'

'Yes, at the Ari *shul*, the old one where Ari prayed, the Sephardi one.'

'Would it be possible to meet him?' asked Mina.

'Of course, I can arrange for you to meet him tomorrow morning. Would 10 o'clock suit you?'

'Yes, that would be perfect.' Mina said. They thanked him profusely and left the synagogue. They would have to rush if they wanted to book a room for the night. They retraced their steps through the Old Town to Bar-Yochai Street. Back in the van, they drove up Jerusalem Street, past the upper end of the citadel park and parked as close as they could to the guest house. They hurried down a narrow path of the Artists' Colony and arrived at a wrought iron gate.

They passed the vine-covered stone courtyard of the Bar-El guesthouse and into the hundred and fifty years-old restored house, where they spoke to the owner, who confirmed that there had been a last-minute cancellation for a suite, which had a view of Mount Meron. It would cost $160 a night. Mina winced, so the lady said she could reduce the price if they stayed more than one night. Jack jumped in and said they were staying at least two nights and would take the suite.

She reminded them that it was almost time to light the Chanukah candles. They could of course go to any of the many synagogues of the old town for the lighting, but they would be welcome to join the others here and take care of their luggage later on. Jack and Mina followed her into the darkened dining area. The atmosphere was heavy with mystery. Jack turned to Mina and asked her in a whisper what they were all waiting for.

'For sunset. When the lights will be lit,' she whispered.

Mina picked up a *kippa*, a small, round skullcap, which she discreetly passed to Jack. He quickly placed it on his head like all the other men standing in the room. They mingled with the people surrounding the *menorah*, a brass candelabrum with eight branches. There were three candles waiting to be lit. A young man sang blessings as he held the *shamash*, the separate candle which would be used to light the other candles. Mina could not help thinking that while *shamash* meant 'to serve' in Hebrew, as the candle served the other candles by lighting them, it was also the name of the ancient Sun God in Sumeria. She marvelled at how all things were so interconnected in the Middle East.

Everyone smiled as the young man sang the blessings in a beautiful baritone voice and when he was finished, they all joined in singing songs, accompanied by a group of *klezmer* musicians, Eastern European Jewish clarinet players who then performed variations on the traditional songs. Jack and Mina were moved by the atmosphere, and for a while, were able to forget the ordeal of the past few days and the reasons that had brought them to this enigmatic city.

After the meal, Jack and Mina picked up their bags from the van and walked back to the guest house climbing the few steps up to their suite. It was a delightful room, with stone walls, tile floors with Moroccan motifs and the ubiquitous deep blue decorations. While Mina went to the bathroom and ran herself a bath, Jack retrieved his laptop and set up an internet connection. He started reading about the Ari synagogue. The more he read, the more he felt utterly out of his depth. He left one of the pages on the browser for Mina to read later then shrugged off his coat and snowy shoes and stretched out on the bed. He was exhausted.

When Mina came back into the room she found Jack fast asleep. She gazed at her handsome travel companion and wondered how he would react if he woke up and found her naked by his side. Tempted as she was to find out, she knew there was work to be done. She picked up the stone tablet from her bag and worked on it for some time, taking a few notes. She noticed the open laptop on the desk and had a look at what Jack had been up to. She found the page open on the Ari Sephardi synagogue. It dated back to the 16th century and had been named after Rabbi Isaac Luria, also known as the 'Ari' or 'the Lion' in Hebrew. His name was actually an acronym for Adoneinu Rabbeinu Isaac, one of the greatest kabbalists of all times. He'd arrived in Safed in 1570 and died there in 1572. He was buried west of the city.

The Ari had prayed in this synagogue and was said to have been visited by the Prophet Elijah in a small recess at the back of the building. According to tradition, the two of them discussed the mysteries of the Torah. Today, the tiny room is kept as a shrine, where people light candles during the day. The synagogue was destroyed in an earthquake in 1837, but was rebuilt twenty years later. Mina wondered how much of the Ari's sacred room had remained intact over the years.

Mina's attention drifted as she marvelled at the centuries of mysteries surrounding this city. What amazing luck that this Eli they were going to meet was 'obsessed' with Tudela. He'd probably have documents to show them, maybe even a small archive. She closed the laptop, picked up a large woollen blanket, and covered Jack with it. She then walked to the other room and opened her suitcase. She pulled out some of the clothes Liat had bought her in Tel Aviv, caressed the fabric and sighed, thinking about her friend. At least she was alive. Mina hoped one day Liat would forgive her for what she had unwittingly put her through. She sat down on the bed as she felt tears welling in her eyes. Pulling herself together, she undressed and slipped under the covers, where she fell asleep almost instantly.

Chapter 18

December 10th, 2004

Jack woke at dawn, still fully clothed. His first thought was for Mina and her safety, so he dashed to the other room and peered through the doorway to be met with a lovely morning sight. Mina's jet-black hair was strewn about her face as she breathed slowly, deep in sleep. He stared at her for a while and then crossed to the windows and gazed out at Mount Meron. Reassured, he went back to his own room, found a spot in a pool of morning sun, sat down and started stretching.

Mina woke up when she heard Jack taking a shower. She walked up to the bathroom, and took a guilty peep through the open door. Her heart was beating as fast as hell, as she savoured Jack's toned body. She had already noticed how fit he was back in Mosul but now she noticed the many battle scars in his back. God only knew the things he had done in his life. She probably didn't want to know. If he'd chosen to leave the army, why should she inquire?

'Morning Jack...do you always leave the bathroom door open?'

He turned the shower off, and picked up a towel to wrap around his waist.

'Yes. An old habit; you never know who's about to come in while you are in a vulnerable position.'

He raised an eyebrow at her. She blushed and wondered if he had known she was there all along.

'Let's have breakfast and then go to the Ari synagogue,' he said.

'OK. I'll be ready in a second,' she replied.

⌒

Natasha had already arrived at the Merkazi Central Hotel. She approached the front desk and said that her name was Mina Osman and there was a package waiting for her. The receptionist looked deeply embarrassed and told her that a man had already picked it up. There was nothing here. Natasha was furious. She asked him to check again. He called his colleague at home, who confirmed that a man in his mid-thirties had picked up the package and cancelled Miss Osman's stay. Natasha stormed out of the hotel and walked back to the car, where three men were patiently waiting for her. She picked up her phone.

'Sir?'

'Yes Natasha?'

'I don't know how to say this. Someone has already picked up the package. According to the concierge, it was collected yesterday afternoon. The man also cancelled her room reservation.'

'Damn it! She tricked us. She'd planned for this person to pick up the tablet all along.'

'Could she still be alive, Sir?'

'She's not that resourceful, Natasha. Then again, leave a few men there for a day or two. Give them the girl's description and tell them to check out the place. Maybe they'll find out more about that man who picked up the parcel.'

'Should I stick around?'

'No, take the first flight back. The trail's cold.'

～

Jack and Mina arrived early at the Ari *shul* and decided to have a look at the small recess where Ari was said to have met the prophet Elijah.

'Mina, we need to be really careful,' Jack reminded her. 'Wheatley's probably on his way to Safed as we speak. Hopefully he won't go sightseeing after failing to find the tablet.'

'Right. I might not have your training but I can be discreet, I assure you.'

An old man walked into the synagogue and sized them up. He walked straight up to them.

'Josh, Miriam? Are you the youngsters who wanted to meet me?'

'Yes,' said Mina, surprised at the old man's New York accent. 'Are you from New York?'

'Yes. A long time ago, mind you. Let's sit down over there.' They walked to a bench to the side. 'So, how can I help you?'

'We've been told by Ezra from the Abuhav *shul* that you are the person to speak to about Benjamin of Tudela.'

His eyes widened a little, and he seemed almost annoyed.

'What else did he say?'

'Nothing' she lied.

His face brightened slightly.

'Well, what would you like to know?'

'I am PhD student at Columbia and I am researching the travels of Benjamin of Tudela, especially with regard to his discovery of Nineveh, as my work focuses on the first European travellers to visit Mesopotamia.'

The old man nodded without saying a word, as seems to be the habit of all sages when listening to young scholars.

'I learned from unpublished travel notes by Tudela that he sent a letter to a certain Mordechai in Safed. Now, until then I really believed Tudela when he wrote in the *Book of Travels* that there were no Jews in Safed. Obviously, if he sent something here later, all the way from Spain, he was being untruthful. So I thought there might be a small but exciting mystery to uncover here.'

'When is Tudela thought to have passed by Safed?'

'1170 C.E.'

'Hmm. Young lady, that would have been about the time the crusaders came here and built their citadel on the hill. It was their custom to expel the Jewish or Arab populations from their newly built fortress cities.'

Mina smacked her forehead. 'What an idiot! Of course, the crusaders. Why didn't I think of that? I was so engrossed with Tudela's personal voyage that I overlooked the context. So there is no mystery. Maybe there were just one or two Jewish families still living within the city at the time of the crusaders. Maybe he wasn't the author of this passage. End of story.'

The old man looked very troubled. 'Not quite. There is more to this story than you imagine. But first, what are these travel notes you're referring to? I've been researching Tudela for a long time and never heard of them.'

'There's a good reason for that. I found them by accident in the British Library while working on the compiled manuscript. These travel notes were never inserted into the canonical edition of Tudela's *Book of Travels*.

'Fascinating, who'd have known…' said Eli.

'It seems that Tudela hoped his friend in Safed would pursue a quest about an important item he had learned about in Mosul.'

'I think we have both been looking at the same story from two different ends,' said Eli.

Mina and Jack looked at him in surprise, then with anticipation.

'When I first arrived in Safed, I was still a young bible student. Every day I learned more on the saintly scholars who shaped our destiny. I was especially interested in the Ari and his disciples. I read avidly, day and night. Blessed was the time when my eyesight was keen and my hand steady. Never mind, as you probably know, the Holy Ari didn't write much himself, his disciples wrote down all his teachings.'

'No, I didn't know that', said Jack ironically, 'but please go on,' he added quickly, after Mina kicked him in the shin to shut him up.

'Well', continued the old man, 'when Chaim Vital, Ari's favourite disciple wrote the famous book *The Tree of Life*, which compiled his master's teachings, there were only manuscripts, no printed copies. Each disciple had to make a vow, under the threat of excommunication, not to allow any copy to made and sent to a foreign land and to keep the knowledge secret. It did get out eventually and was published, but I always wondered how accurate the printed copies were.'

Eli took a deep breath and continued: 'After years of patience and dedication, I was finally introduced to a small group of men in Safed who let me read from one of the original manuscripts. There I was, in a small room, reading feverishly through the ancient pages of *The Tree of Life*, when I suddenly came across a short marginalia, you know, a tiny commentary in the margin. It was so strange that to this day it is still branded in my memory.'

'What did it say, Eli?' asked an excited Mina.

Eli quoted: *'Was it God's plan? Rabbi Benjamin the Traveller divided our community, but the Lion cast out the Dark Ones. Beware of their return. In the holy room.'*

'It's like a warning in riddles' said Mina feeling a shiver of excitement run down her spine, 'but how do you interpret it?'

'Well, it took me some time to figure it out and unfortunately I was never allowed access to the manuscript again but I am pretty sure "Rabbi Benjamin the Traveller" is Benjamin of Tudela who wrote about his travels in the 12th century. As *The Tree of Life* was written over 400 years after his death, Tudela couldn't have divided the community in person, it must be something he did or wrote. Something concerning God's plan.

Eli took in another deep breath and continued: 'I read Tudela's *Book of Travels* over and over again but I never found out how he divided their community, nor who the Dark Ones were, nor why one should beware their return. But, it is clear that they were evil enough to be "cast out by the Lion", that is to say excommunicated by the Holy Ari himself. The last part of the passage troubled me for days on end. There is only one "holy room" that makes sense here and it's in the Ari's synagogue. It's the recess in which it is said that the Ari pondered deeply on the mysteries of Kabbalah and received instructions from the prophet Elijah himself. But I have never found anything there, not even peace of mind.'

Jack and Mina looked at the old man in wonder. Mina's research was taking the strangest turn.

'Still, you were right', Mina added passionately, 'this commentary you read in the margin of *The Tree of Life* is verified by the travel notes I found in the British Library: Tudela clearly states that he wrote to Safed about an object of the greatest importance to mankind.'

The old man looked at her and sighed. 'Don't mistake my tone for a lack of enthusiasm at your endeavours: whatever the content of the letter Tudela sent to Safed, it must have been quite significant to divide such a learned community. But I spent many years gathering useless information on Tudela, looking everywhere in this synagogue for a sign. I even went to Egypt, to the small island where the Ari is said to have spent time in a cave as a young man. I found the cave: I searched every inch of it with great reverence, but it was to no avail. I'm tired now.'

Mina shook her head, dispirited. The old man rose to his feet.

'I'm sorry I couldn't be of more help. Here's my phone number. Get in touch before you leave Safed. I would love to talk some more about these matters. Maybe I've missed something?'

Jack laid a hand on Mina's slumped shoulder and tried to comfort her, but she was too depressed to listen to him. They thanked Eli and slowly left the synagogue. Mina looked for a last time at the recess where Ari had met the prophet Elijah, and they were out in the cold streets once again.

Mina and Jack strolled aimlessly through the Citadel and the park for two hours. The cold air cleared their minds and numbed their feet. Although Jack was disappointed for Mina that they had not found out more about her research, he was mainly relieved that they would soon be on their way, far from Wheatley's grasp. They entered an art gallery and while Mina asked a few questions, Jack looked out of the store's window and suddenly froze. Springing into action he pushed Mina into a corner of the gallery and waited there for a few minutes. She asked him what the matter was but he just told her to stay there and not to leave the gallery. He had just recognised Wheatley's men from the yacht, on the other side of the street. He quickly deduced that they had already been to the Merkazi Hotel and were now asking around about him, and possibly Mina, if they thought she might still be alive.

Leaving Mina safely in the gallery, Jack discreetly followed the two men. Hopefully they would not sense him on their trail; the narrow and winding streets made it easier to conceal oneself, but he still had to keep his wits about him. He followed them for half an hour, street after street, watching them as they questioned owners of art galleries and people coming out of synagogues throughout the Old Town. He had a fleeting impression he was being watched too and turned round, but there was no-one there. He wondered if Oberon had sent more than two men, or if he was in Safed himself.

The men were approaching the Abuhav *shul*. Jack thought of Ezra, the synagogue's administrator. He would definitely remember Mina and himself from the day before. He would send the men to the Ari synagogue and straight to Eli. He calculated he had about fifteen minutes to deal with this. He picked up his mobile phone and called Eli's home number to warn him of the danger. He did not tell him much, just enough to scare him out of staying at home and convince him to meet Mina and himself at the guest house in thirty minutes.

He then rushed back to the art gallery, picked up Mina and brought her up to speed on the latest events as they made their way back quickly to the guest house.

Mina paced up and down their room, waiting impatiently for Eli.

'Don't worry Mina. I'm sure he'll make it.'

'I just don't understand, all I did was ask a few questions.'

'Sometimes questions can have dangerous consequences.'

'It reminds me of something…That's it! I'd totally forgotten to tell you about it.'

She explained who Moshe Shobai was and the email he had sent from London, warning her about playing with century-old riddles. Jack agreed she should get in touch with Shobai once they were sure Eli was out of danger. They heard some huffing and puffing and finally the old scholar made it up the stairs to the suite, carrying a small shoulder bag. Mina rushed to greet him and apologised profusely for putting him in danger. The old man simply shook his head and told her not to burden herself with the shameful actions of other men. He said he'd brought some precious documents on Tudela so they would have an opportunity to talk more about her fascinating research.

He reminded them that sunset was fast approaching and that tonight would be a special Shabbat, as it was Chanukah. Members of his congregation would be surprised not to see him officiate on this special night but Jack advised him not to return to his house tonight, nor to the Ari synagogue during Shabbat. He suggested that Eli could participate in the Shabbat dinner at the guest house instead. Surely it would count for something? Mina felt a little embarrassed by Jack's blunt way with the old scholar, but he was right.

After the Shabbat meal, Mina and Eli went to sleep in separate rooms in the suite, whilst Jack stood guard. Several hours later, in the dead of night, he heard the old man scream. He raced down the corridor and went into the old man's room. Mina followed in a matter of seconds, as she too had been awoken by the screams.

'What's wrong, Eli?' asked Jack.

The old man was visibly shaken. 'I had a dream. I saw a rabbi. He spoke to me. He said his name was…I can't say.'

'What?' asked Mina bewildered. The old man sat up against the wall to gather his thoughts.

'I have the answer. We must go. Now.'

'Where?'

'To the Ari *shul*.'

To Jack and Mina's surprise, he leapt from the bed, hurriedly put on his shoes, coat and scarf, and rushed out of the room.

Chapter 19

Eli had the keys to the synagogue. But still, they all felt as if they were trespassing and being sacrilegious, but then again, nothing could have stopped them now. The old man walked right through the main area to Ari's room. It was still illuminated by the dozens of candles that had been placed there during the day. The old man knelt at the very bottom of the furthest wall and using a small penknife, began to scratch the old mortar all around the only protruding stone in the recess' masonry.

'You want to pull out that stone?' asked Jack.

'Yes.'

'I'll run to the van and get a crowbar,' he ran back through the synagogue.

The old man continued clearing the stone's mortar.

'Can you tell me what you dreamed of, Eli?' asked Mina.

'I dreamed that the Ari came to me. He was pointing at the inscription affixed to the façade, outside.'

'I didn't pay much attention to it. What does it say?'

Jack had returned with the crowbar. Eli stood up to let him do his work and continued his conversation with Mina.

'It says the original synagogue dates back to the 14th century but that it was damaged in an earthquake in 1759 and then destroyed in 1837 after a much stronger earthquake. The building was restored and rebuilt in parts a few years later thanks to a donation by Rabbi Yitzhak Guetta of Trieste. The inscription on the façade refers to this Italian rabbi. Recently, a team of surveyors started a restoration project here and one of the specialists showed me which parts of the building pre-date the two earthquakes. This stone I am trying to loosen is the only original stone from the Ari's room. I just thought that maybe someone stumbled on documents among the rubble and respectfully put them back behind the new wall when it was reconstructed.

'We'll know soon enough,' said Jack.

With a strong pull he managed to prise the stone out of the wall. Eli and Mina joined Jack on their hands and knees. Eli brought a candle a little closer to the empty space and pulled out a bundle of papers wrapped in an oil skin. The old man was trembling all over and kept repeating, 'It's a Chanukah miracle, it's a Chanukah miracle.'

Eli was so excited he immediately proceeded to translate the text written in a mixture of Aramaic and Hebrew to his two avid listeners. Mina jotted as much as she could from his live translation in her own notebook.

'Safed, 2 Kheshvan 5332'. Eli thought for a while and said 'I may be wrong, but that would approximately be October 1571.'

> *'I will recount here faithfully the events that occurred during the last week, so that these extraordinary events do not come to pass into oblivion.*

'The opening words of the text clearly identify it as a chronicle.' Eli said, 'I have to skip a few lines; the document is illegible.'

'...*months ago, I was putting some order in the archives of our synagogue when I came across a bundle of papers which seemed much older than the documents I usually deal with. As I opened the bundle, the typical musty smell of old paper momentarily took me aback. I delicately prised open the papers and to my astonishment realised it was a lengthy letter written by the eccentric traveller, Benjamin of Tudela three centuries ago, to Morderchai of Safed. I could not understand what these letters were doing there. I felt much enthusiasm at the discovery of such a correspondence. It has always been my dream to travel to far-away lands, and I looked forward to reading some of Tudela's accounts, from his own hand. After the usual civilities, and business issues, the tone of the letter became very enigmatic. And, when I got to Tudela's description of an ancient and spellbinding tablet kept in the Jerusalem Temple that had survived the coming of the Romans I immediately brought the whole bundle of papers to my master.*

Eli stopped and said, 'This is extraordinary. A tablet...in the Temple in Jerusalem! If it survived the Romans, he means that the tablet was still there after the Jerusalem Temple was destroyed by the Romans in 70 C.E. This next part is illegible.'

'*... that night. There was our beloved Ari, my holy master Rabbi Chaim Vital, myself and...*'

'That's strange,' Eli said, 'A name has been crossed out. I'll continue.'

'*[XXX], who we all thought had lost his mind, was sitting on a chair at the back of the room as he always did. On the main*

table, my master had spread out for all to see the remains of
Tudela's letter. After a while seven other rabbis came to join the
session. There was…'

'Illegible' said Eli, sighing with frustration.

'*… in his letter to this Mordechai, Benjamin of Tudela entrusts*
his friend with a secret. In the archives of a synagogue in
Nineveh. he read about an enigmatic clay tablet that had been
sent from Nineveh to Yerushalayim and hidden… in the Kodesh
Hakodashim.'

Eli murmured, 'that's the name for the holy of holies, the most
sacred part of the temple in Jerusalem.'

'*As soon as my master uttered these words, the room seemed to*
bustle with energy. All the rabbis started talking at once. Our
beloved Ari stood up…'

'I can't read any of the following. Let me jump to the next
paragraph,' said Eli.

'*… all eyes focused on his radiance, as he seldom speaks and his*
words inspire our every thought. He said 'Thank you Chaim.
Rabbi Benjamin's letter describes a tablet written in the old
language of the Sumerians, from a time preceding the destruction
of the first temple. The Babylonian King's advisers recorded odd
discoveries while trying to read omens of floods and earthquakes.
According to this letter, the tablet is a Babylonian rendering of
Noah's Mabul.'

'Mabul means a flood or a river, but here it means *the* deluge,' Eli explained.

'It enables its possessor, if he can decipher its inner knowledge, to observe nature's secrets, and prepare for the next…'

Eli stopped for a moment and said, 'I'm not sure how to translate the next phrase, but "Godly changes of nature" is about as close as I can get.'

'… Godly changes of nature. We were all in shock. I shuddered, as I half-envisioned the mystical consequences of our beloved Rabbi's last words: 'The next Godly changes.'

My holy master was the first to speak. He turned to our beloved Ari and said, 'Master, I have also read the letter, and do not doubt its veracity nor Benjamin of Tudela's assessment. Yet I wonder about three things. First, where is the tablet at present, if it survived the Roman destruction? Two, I am troubled by the idea that there could be more Mabuls to come. Finally, even if we were able to predict when the next Mabuls were to occur, and this is a problem in itself, as it would involve divining practices, which are forbidden to us, who are we to disturb His Holy Will?' My master had unravelled everyone's thoughts in the methodical fashion he had learned from his own master.'

'Here's another damaged passage I can't decipher,' said Eli.

'… we can be sure that if we are all seated in this room tonight, The Holy One Blessed be He… saved the tablet from the Romans, so that we would find it at the right moment in time. Everyone agreed with the speaker.

My holy master reminded us all of King David's psalm: "Like rivers they raised, O HASHEM, like rivers they raised their voice, like rivers they shall raise their destructiveness". 'This means that the tablet can only refer to other Mabuls not The Mabul, as The Holy One Blessed be He had promised Noah that The Mabul would never happen again'.

Then, Rabbi Tammim…'

'I don't know of this rabbi,' said Eli

'*…who was tapping his foot impatiently as was his habit, cried out that just as Noah was saved because he was the only just man of his time, no-one should interfere with His Holy Will. When these Mabuls would happen the survivors would, once again be the only just ones. He paused, and then hammered out each word: The Holy One Blessed be He is Gevurah Shebechesed…'*

'In Kabbalah,' said Eli, 'there are ten revelations of the Creator's will. They are called *Sephirot* in Hebrew. What we have here is a combination of two revelations: strength and kindness or *gevurah bechesed*. He's saying that God acts with the firmness and benevolence of a father who can see further than his children.'

'*He purified humanity in forty days, with strength and kindness'* concluded Tammim.

My holy master asked Tammim 'No-one doubts His Strength and Kindness, nor his divine Plan, Tammim, but what of those who will not survive, the men, women and children who will die in the process?'

Rabbi Tammin did not answer. My master pursued his

argument, 'as Avraham bargained with The Holy One, Blessed be He for every soul in Sodom, not merely the just ones, but the fallen ones too, it is our sacred duty to choose to save ALL life, good as well as evil.'

I thought of the discussions we had had with my holy master only weeks before on Ramban's commentaries on miracles and free will. We were all part of The Holy One, Blessed be He's, plan. All was written from all time, and Nature is both illusion and one form of reality. There was no contradiction between our having free will and being the instruments of His Holy Will. Had I wanted to answer to Rabbi Tammim, I would have reminded him that The Holy One, Blessed be He, was justice. I had also noticed that when Rabbi Tammim spoke…'

'A name is crossed out again' said Eli, 'I think it is the same person. Clearly he must have done something very wicked for his name to have been obliterated in this way.'

'[XXX] stirred. He had not spoken a word for more than a year, since the time he had, in youthful exuberance, and against all the forewarnings of our master, tried to unravel the Zohar's teachings. He was no longer glassy-eyed. It was as if the conversation he was witnessing had brought back his soul from the depth of madness to the tip of his tongue. He did not speak. Had I only known what would come to pass, I would have tried to speak to him then, but we were all so confused and focused on Tudela's letter and how to find this magical tablet that I did not pay any attention to him.'

'I'm sorry,' said Eli, 'the next passage is illegible.'

'… *but the blessed Ari spoke: 'As it is written* "as in water, face answers to face, so the heart of man to man". *If we decide to act to save lives, this action is just. As it is written*, "*whoever saves one* life *saves* the entire world".'

His last words still hung in the room, as prophetic beams of light. He hummed to himself in the surrounding silence, and his hands waved gently over the table. He then opened his eyes, and very matter-of-factly said: 'these mabuls will not occur in our times. I will send a search party to Jerusalem. If they find the tablet, we will conceal its existence until the time is right.'

I think we all silently interpreted his vision in the following way: if the simple people knew of the mabul before it happened, humanity would turn to chaos, and we all shared the wisdom of his words.

By now night was upon us, and my holy master considered the matter concluded. He left Tudela's letter on the table overnight for us all to meditate upon His Holy Will. I dared not touch it, not even to put it in safekeeping back in the archive.

When I woke up the next morning, I returned to the study. The letter had disappeared.

'I'm sorry,' said Eli, 'the next passage is illegible.'

'… *A month had passed since our beloved Ari sent the search party to Jerusalem with special instructions to locate the tablet. Finally, last night, they returned from their quest. I watched in awe as the five cautious and watchful men, their clothes still dusty from their travels, entered, silently, one-by-one the study of our blessed Ari. I watched, as the last one locked the door behind him. We all gathered in the hall, disciples and masters, trembling with anticipation, and in utter silence, impatient to know the outcome of their search, like young men on their wedding night. I still remember my excitement, my heart pounding in my chest at the idea that this tablet, which had caused such disturbance in our scholarly community was perhaps just a few feet away, in this small study, a small crack in the divine plan.*

At last the blessed Ari opened the door and from the way he looked at us, each in turn, we all knew without a doubt that the search party had been successful. A wave of relief swept over me. I felt tears running silently down my cheeks. Yet, this profound joy lasted but a few seconds for suddenly ...

'The crossed out name again,' said Eli.

'[XXX] whom we thought had disappeared, came storming in the hall accompanied by Rabbi Tammim and a few other disciples, and pushed us aside to get closer to the Ari. [XXX] stepped forward, with darkened brow, his eyes rolling in angst and his body shaking with fury. He pointed his finger at the Ari and screamed at him like a rabid dog: 'Hand over the tablet, Rabbi, give us the tablet, as it must be destroyed'.

Everyone stood frozen in horror. It was all too clear now that it was he who had stolen Tudela's letter from the study. But the blessed Ari, raised his hand in a sign of peace, and said to [XXX] 'You were given the grace of recovering your sanity and returning to life, yet you still turn a blind eye to His Will. Know this, that the tablet you crave for is out of your reach and that it is with sadness and humility that I cast you out of this community. You shall become dark like the night and be nameless, as shall be your descendants for all the years to come'.

'The rest of the document is totally illegible' said Eli, 'and I can't see any signature at the bottom which could tell us more about the author of this chronicle.'

Mina and Jack were dumbfounded. They were incapable of uttering a single word. Eli just kept repeating 'It's incredible!' over and over again, his face beaming with ineffable joy.

⤳

Jack carefully placed the stone back in its place in the wall. Eli, holding the bundle of papers under his coat, close to his heart, walked hesitantly out of the synagogue, followed by Jack and Mina. They walked down the cobbled path towards the main road. The night was pitch black. Jack told them both to wait for him there while he picked up the van.

'I'm speechless, Eli,' said Mina.

'I understand. It is as if one had stumbled on a sacred gathering and felt still under its spell. I know I feel this way.'

'Yes but there is a detail you don't know yet.' Speaking quietly and slowly, she said, 'I have the tablet they speak of. I have it here, in my bag.'

'You have what?' Eli dropped all the papers in the snow.

He got slowly to his knees and started gathering them with Mina's help. She went on, 'I have one of the tablets. It's actually a stone tablet, but that's a story which I'll tell you some other time. I believe there is more than one tablet. I think that the one described by the Safed rabbis was a clay tablet sent to Israel long ago, maybe even before the building in Jerusalem of the first temple of Solomon. I suppose we'll never know how Tudela found out about all this'.

Eli looked at Mina in amazement and then sunk deep into

thought. Suddenly his face lit up. He seemed relieved as if he had finally understood something but was reluctant to share it. He turned to Mina and confessed 'I haven't been entirely truthful with you either.'

'What do you mean?' asked Mina.

'Let's wait 'till we're out of the cold and in Josh's van.'

As they drove off, Mina looked at Eli. She felt miserable about lying about their identity. She was about to tell him her real name when he spoke.

'Miriam', he began slowly, 'Over the years I've collected many documents relating to the Ari. Among them I found a short letter which only makes sense to me now. It's in my bag, which I left at your place. It dates back to 1755. It's a letter from a Jewish gentleman in England to his brother living in Safed. I know it by heart.' The old man began to recite,

> *'Dear brother,*
> *I hope the printing business is picking up as you hoped it would*
> *when you left for Safed. I am writing to reassure you. As you*
> *probably know by now, we had to leave Lisbon in a hurry.*
> *Everyone is alive and well. As for the clay tablet, I followed*
> *father's instructions. I keep it with me at all times. Let's hope that*
> *when the time is right, our sons or their descendents will receive*
> *a sign from G'd, and return this burden to its rightful place,*
> *wherever it may be. I miss you brother and I pray G'd we can*
> *be reunited before long. If you wish to write to us, we're now in*
> *Cambridge. Hildersham'*

I remember thinking it was a rather odd letter, but not until now did it make any sense'.

'Well, I still don't understand…' said Mina.

'I do', said Jack, 'the tablet which was found by Ari's search party was entrusted to this guy or his family in Portugal, and the tablet's now in England'.

'Exactly', said Eli, 'or at least it was there in the 18th century.'

'But where in England? And what were their names?' asked Mina.

'The man signed his letter 'Hildersham' from Cambridge, so I guess we have the answer.

Eli sighed. 'I am too old for all this. But you should continue.'

'We will,' said Mina.

'Then go to Cambridge at once. A number of scholars from Cambridge came to visit Safed years ago. They worked at a Research centre in the University Library. I'm sure they could help.'

Suddenly, Jack braked hard and the van juddered to a halt. A car was blocking the road up ahead and because the road was very narrow he could not do a U-turn. Three men had jumped out of the car and were flashing their torches up the road in their direction. They were armed and pointed their guns at the van.

'Oh my god,' said Mina.

'Maybe it's the plain clothes police,' said Eli.

'I don't think so' hissed Jack, 'Stay still!'

The men slowly approached the van. Jack waited until they were almost at arms length from the passenger door, then suddenly reversed at full-throttle. One of the men fired his weapon, but the van was already out of range. Mina and Eli cringed in terror, as Jack drove the car backwards at high speed into the darkness, scraping against the walls on either side of the road. The men had run back and jumped into their car and were driving fast down the alley after them. They were almost back to the cobbled stone path that led to the Ari shul. There was no way out.

'I'll stop the van in the middle of the road, and we'll have to run for it,' yelled Jack, 'Eli, go back to the Ari synagogue and find a place to hide. We'll hide in the old cemetery.'

The poor man, still clutching his papers, hobbled out of the back of the van and Jack and Mina watched him hobble as quickly as he could back to the synagogue.

'He'll be alright. Let's go,' said Jack, pulling Mina by the hand.

As they rushed towards the cemetery, they could hear the men climbing over the van. They ran as fast as they could, trying not to fall on the uneven ground.

Safed had known a number of earthquakes and the cemetery was a chaotic assemblage of tombs and paths from different ages. They could hear the men's heavy steps thumping the ground in hot pursuit. Mina hid behind a tombstone as Jack slowly crept to one side, gun in hand, waiting for the men to arrive. As the first one appeared, he shot at him but missed. Mina started running again. He could not rush after her as he was cornered by two of the gunmen. The third man was catching up with Mina. Jack saw her stumble and lose balance. She dropped her bag in her fall, and for an instant hesitated to pick it up. But as she saw the man fast approaching, she left it where it had fallen in the dust and ran further on. The man stopped to pick up the bag. Jack watched him as he searched with one hand while holding his flash light in the other. He pulled out something and dropped the bag. He then turned round and signalled to the other two to follow. Jack understood at once what this meant. They had the stone tablet. There was no need to pursue Mina or him any longer. They had what they'd come for.

Eli hid in the only place where he felt truly safe, in the Ari's room. A candle was still burning, but he couldn't summon up the courage to put it out, even at the price of his own safety. He waited in absolute silence for what seemed an eternity. Suddenly he heard footsteps coming towards him. A tall dark shape entered the softly lit room. Eli clutched the bundle of papers as tightly as he could under his coat. When he saw who the man was, he was surprised and started to rise to his feet, but the man pushed him violently against the back wall and held him there by the throat. Eli's eyes widened in shock. The man grabbed the scarf from around the old man's neck and slowly tightened it around Eli's neck until he was gasping for breath. Eli's last sensation was that of his precious papers being wrenched out of his helpless hands.

PART 3

ENGLAND

There are more things in heaven and earth, Horatio,
Than are dreamt of in your philosophy.

(Shakespeare, Hamlet, Act 1 Scene 5)

Chapter 20

'Two whiskeys and a coke, please,' Jack said to the flight attendant, smiling meekly. Mina was sitting next to him, brooding. He reckoned she would need more than a few drinks to shake off her mood, but he did not want to get her drunk. Her dark eyes were lost in a world of despair and hatred. He understood how she felt; everything had gone so horribly wrong in Safed.

They had discovered so much information about Tudela and the tablet in just a few days and then, within hours, Wheatley's men had retrieved it and murdered Eli. Jack would never forget the pitiful sight of Eli's frail body propped up against the wall in the Ari's room. Luckily, they had been using false identities while in Safed, so no-one knew who they really were. They'd be long gone by the time the local police found out about the young couple that had wanted to meet Eli. Their quest now hung by a fine and mysterious thread: a short letter written from Cambridge about a tablet being safe. They didn't even know if it was linked to 'their' tablet. Jack had found the letter in Eli's shoulder bag and taken it with him. Eli's death had plunged Mina into a deep melancholy.

Jack had done the only thing he knew how to do. He channelled his grief and guilt into a cold rage aimed at one person: Oberon Wheatley. He missed Eli and knew they would mourn his loss, but right now they had to bite the bullet and pursue their journey. Wheatley's men were assassins. Where Mina's first reactions to Eli's murder had been to freeze up with guilt and shame, the effect on Jack had been the opposite; it had spurred him on to pursue their search. Based on sparse information from an 18th century letter and an ancient kabbalist chronicle they were now travelling to England. With any luck, what the letter hinted at was true and the mysterious tablet was still in England.

Even though he knew it was seriously inappropriate at a time like this, Jack couldn't help but look at Mina's desolate face and think she looked more beautiful than ever. He felt sick to the stomach. He needed to focus right now, not start thinking like that. Mina raised her head and noticed his expression. She turned her head away as if she knew just what he was thinking.

'Here you go,' he said, serving her a whiskey and coke, 'drink up.'

'Thanks.'

'So, what now?' asked Jack.

'I don't know. I thought you had great plans for us in England.'

She was angry with him. She had noticed his look earlier on, and could not believe how insensitive he was. How could men think of sex at such times? But she also felt guilt, grief and frustration at their situation. She knew her anger ought to have been directed at Oberon, but Jack was the only one around. It was unfair, but she was not in a state of mind to think properly.

'We're on a plane now. So, why don't we just think through what's happened in the last few days?' Jack said.

'You think we can make matters any worse?'

'Mina, all I mean is we need to assess the situation. I don't think it's that bleak.'

She did not answer and instead looked through the round cabin window into the open sky.

'Right. I'll talk then.'

'Knock yourself out.' She said, and instantly wished she hadn't.

Jack looked hurt. She guessed he did have some feelings after all.

'I think you're as shocked as I am to realise that your initial academic interests are connected to the tablet and our current quest. You were looking for information on Tudela, and you got much more than you bargained for.'

He did not wait for her to answer. He was trying to force her, not very subtly, to re-engage with the matter at hand.

'Although I didn't really follow everything Eli translated,' he continued, 'I think I got the gist of it. Feel free to fill in the details where you see fit. After all, you took notes while he spoke to us.'

He heard her sighing and went on, 'Tudela knew about the tablet you found in Mosul and…'

'No, my tablet is in stone. He found information about a clay tablet.'

Jack smiled to himself, 'Right, the one which was sent to the Temple in Jerusalem?'

'Yes,' answered Mina.

'Can we assume this Jerusalem tablet is a copy of the same tablet you found in Mosul?'

'We have no choice. Let's assume that.'

'Well, that arrogant bastard Wheatley did say that there were four copies of the tablet. There's no reason to believe he lied to you. He couldn't imagine you'd rise from the abyss,' Jack said, trying to make her smile.

'He might have been wrong. Let's focus on the two tablets we know of.'

'OK. Not only does Tudela find out about the Jerusalem tablet, but also that it can be used to forecast natural disasters. He sends this information to a friend in Safed and it's lost and forgotten until some archivist finds it in the 16th century.'

Mina had mixed feelings. She didn't want to pursue the discussion because she was still angry with Jack, but her mind had already started racing through various hypotheses. Reluctantly, she picked up her bag and took out her notebook. Luckily Oberon's men were only interested in the tablet and had ignored the remaining contents of her bag.

Jack sighed with relief. She was back in the world of the living. Mina leafed through her notes while Jack pursued his analysis of the situation.

'The next part is all described in the chronicle. The rabbis agree that Tudela's letter wasn't a fake. They spend the whole night discussing what to do if they found the tablet and apart from one guy...'

'Rabbi Tammim,' interjected Mina.

'Yeah. Apart from that rabbi, they all agree to search for the tablet because they believed it could save lives,' said Jack.

'Yes. But with one caveat: not to disclose this information to anyone. I still don't understand why. If they wanted to save people from future disasters, why keep it secret?' Mina wondered out loud.

'They were quite shrewd. Today, you'd call it 'crowd control.'

Just imagine the panic that such information could produce: riots, plummeting stock-markets worldwide.'

'Right. I get it. Then a search party is sent to Jerusalem to find the tablet.'

'And,' said Jack, 'my guess is that this Ari character – I really like him by the way – gave instructions to send the tablet into the diaspora, as far as possible from Safed.'

'Yup and he picked Lisbon', replied Mina.

'Then, someone called "The Dark One" steals the letter…' said Jack.

'No. He stole Tudela's letter after the initial meeting and he wasn't called dark or nameless until *after* the search party returned from Jerusalem. His name is crossed out everywhere, so there is no way of tracing who he was.'

'What do we know about him?'

She read from her notes and summarised, 'He'd been in some sort of catatonic state for about a year but came out of it during the conversation between the rabbis. Who knows what went through his head but evidently he was in violent disagreement with the council and decided to take matters into his own hands, literally.'

'What do you think happened to Tudela's letter?' asked Jack.

'If I'm right about his motivations, after having stolen the letter he would have destroyed it, as it went against his understanding of God's Plan.'

'I think I agree with you,' Jack said, 'and now the proof that any of this actually occurred has been stolen – for the second time in history.'

He suddenly paused. Mina looked at him inquisitively, 'What are you thinking Jack?'

'Since Eli's death I've been wondering about something.

Something that just doesn't make sense. You would agree that as far we know, Wheatley isn't aware of Tudela's letter or the Safed chronicle. Remember how in the cemetery his men stopped pursuing us as soon as they had your tablet in their hands?'

'Yes. And?'

'For Wheatley's men, Eli was just a means to an end, to get to us. So why did they look for him in the synagogue? And why was there hardly any sign of a struggle in the Ari's room?'

'It's a tiny room. Eli was a frail old man. He'd have seen them coming towards him, abandoned all hope and succumbed to his fate,' Mina said.

'I don't buy that. He had searched all his adult life for this chronicle. I'd bet a dollar to a dime that he would have put up some sort of fight.'

'Maybe. So why didn't he? And should we suppose that Oberon knew about the Safed chronicle?'

They both remained silent and deep in thought.

'Eli, what happened to you? Why didn't you fight back?' Mina thought to herself as she shed a tear for the old man.

'I think we should stay in London for a few days' Jack resumed, obviously trying to focus on something practical. 'And meet this old scholar researcher who warned you about the tablet. He obviously knows something.'

'Yes. His name is Moshe Shobai. The poor man, when he hears what we've been through he won't believe how prophetic his words were.'

'How did you get to know him?' asked Jack.

'I met him at a conference a few years ago. A really lovely old man.'

'He might be really lovely, but if he knew how dangerous

this tablet was, he would have told you more about it. Didn't he strike you as suspicious?'

'In comparison to everything we've gone through, no I don't think he's particularly suspicious,' she answered sharply.

'Are you still pissed off at me?' he grumbled.

'I'm sorry. It wasn't you. If Oberon disappeared from the face of the earth in a pool of his own blood, I'd feel less angry.'

'Don't despair, it could still happen. But for now we should concentrate on what we can do. I was trained not to worry about or wish for things that are out of my present remit. Why don't you sleep? We'll be in London in a few hours.'

She nodded in agreement, breathed in deeply a few times and closed her eyes. Jack recognised the years of yogic training in the way Mina relaxed all her muscles by a simple act of will. He had learned to do the same but the hard way, during military ops when he had to force himself to relax and sleep for a few hours before springing back into action. He picked up Mina's notes and read through the last pages. Who was behind Eli's murder? He had downplayed this subject in front of Mina, but he was not satisfied with their conclusions.

→

Same day. New York.

Natasha stepped through the glass revolving doors of the Wheatley Forecast Corporation building, into the main lobby. The security guards greeted her as she walked to the main lift. As the elegant glass lift ascended, she smiled at the irony of a glass building that housed within its walls a business that was anything but transparent. When she reached the thirty-second floor, she inserted a key into a slot next to the lift buttons and the lift rose to the thirty-third, Oberon's floor. She proceeded through the main lobby decorated in an art deco style, with a mixture of glass and metal ornaments, and veered left into the sophisticated waiting area outside Oberon's private office. His secretary, Miss Dawson, was a sixty-year-old Oxford-educated English spinster, always immaculately dressed and totally *au fait* with every aspect of Oberon's official business. She looked up impassively at Natasha, 'Mr Wheatley is expecting you.'

Natasha knocked on the door and walked into his office.

Oberon was on the phone, closing a deal with a major weather broadcast channel, for special rights on advanced meteorological information. A single glance at Oberon's hunter's smirk, was enough for Natasha to guess that he was forcing his deal down the other person's throat, and enjoying every bit of it. He finished his call and looked at Natasha with glee, eyeing up the metal attaché case she held in her hand.

'So my dear, what have you brought me?'

'A certain stone tablet' she answered.

She slid the attaché-case on his desk and opened it. He looked at the cuneiform tablet, picked it up and examined it on all sides.

'What sort of stone is it?' asked Oberon.

'I'm looking into it,' said Natasha. 'We'll have the results of the analysis in a day or two.'

'Excellent. Send it to Professor Manfred this afternoon, under the usual confidential terms. I want the translation as soon as possible.'

'That won't be possible, sir.'

'Just double his fee.' Then, noticing that Natasha was avoiding his gaze, he asked, 'Why not?'

'He passed away three months ago.'

'How unfortunate.'

'I only found this out yesterday. Since then I've looked for a suitable translator, but I'm not sure we'll get someone as amenable as Professor Manfred, when it comes to the sort of confidentiality we require. I don't think we can trust any scholar faced with such a tablet not to publish their results or let alone refrain from talking about it.'

'Oh. Is that all? In that case, we'll just use the Vatican procedure.'

'Sorry sir?' she said.

'When Vatican officials find an apocryphal gospel and feel that it may harm the orthodoxy of the Catholic faith, they don't give it out to one translator. They divide the work between three or more.'

'So that no-one but the officials have the full knowledge of the text's importance,' she answered.

'Exactly. Photograph the inscription and split it between three scholars you have already listed. Make them sign the confidentiality agreement before sending anything.'

'Yes sir.'

'It was a stroke of luck, leaving those men behind in Safed', he added.

'Yes.'

'What amazes me is that Mina Osman's still alive.'

'There was a man with her in Safed,' Natasha added, 'he might be the same one who was in Mosul. I suspect he has been protecting her all this time. I think I should find out who he is.'

'No,' he answered, 'you have enough on your plate as it is. What can they do? Try to steal the tablet back? I think not. Miss Osman will probably return to New York and cash in her quarterly research funds. I don't think we'll hear from them again.'

'Right. I'll go then Sir.'

Natasha's intuition was that Mina Osman and her mysterious helper would be back on the scene. Oberon had already made a mistake talking to Mina on the boat about his Chinese oracle bone. However clever he might be, he was too arrogant to be considered wise.

～

Same day. Safed.

'Master?' said a man. He was dressed in dark clothing and sitting in a car with tinted windows that concealed him from passers-by.

'Yes?'

'We have recovered a parchment describing the council of rabbis in Safed.'

'Good. Where is it?'

'Ephraim is on a plane as we speak, bringing it back to you.'

'It should have been destroyed.'

The man hesitated, then said, 'It will be done Master, but the tablet is in Wheatley's hands.'

'Retrieve it.'

'It will be difficult master. He is well guarded. I may need some…*special*…help.'

'Do not fret. I will pray for you and I will send you instructions.'

'Thank you Master.'

'Your labours will soon be at an end,' the voice said, and the line went dead.

Chapter 21

December 13th, 2004. London

Mina woke up alone in the hotel room. Jack's bed was untouched. He hadn't returned since the night before. She retraced their steps from the moment they landed at Heathrow airport; they'd taken a train to Paddington station in West London, then walked through Paddington Green to Maida Vale and come to the Colonnade hotel, where Jack had booked a room for a few nights. 'We'll be safe here,' he had said. They were a few streets away from Little Venice, with its beautiful mansions and canal barges. For a millionaires' haven, it was a wonderfully discreet part of London.

Mina had been exhausted when they'd arrived at the hotel but Jack had 'people to see,' as he put it enigmatically. She didn't ask any questions and hadn't seen him since. She couldn't find her mobile phone anywhere. Had she forgotten it in Safed? No, she was sure she still had it in Ben Gurion airport in Tel Aviv. She remembered turning it off. It was the last time she'd handled it. Had Jack taken it? Again? She found a note stuck to the bathroom mirror. 'Morning Mina. Meet me for lunch at one p.m. at the Waterway, on Formosa Street. Xx, Jack.'

She was a little miffed at his bossy tone, but she couldn't deny that she looked forward to going on a date with Jack, if this was what he intended. They had been through so much pain and misery since they had met, a change of pace would be welcome. She lay half-asleep in the large, warm bed, all alone, thinking about Jack. She felt a growing desire for Jack's muscular body. She wanted to feel the weight of him crushing her, wanted his strong hands to pin her down as he made rough, passionate love to her. She snuggled deep under the sheets, and closed her eyes.

Mina left the hotel an hour later to grab a coffee in Little Venice and gather her thoughts while she waited for Jack. She had asked for directions in the hotel lobby but expected to get lost in a matter of minutes. It was only her second visit to London and she had not spent much time walking in the city back then.

Two years ago, she had attended an academic conference on the ancient Near East at University College London, which housed one of the largest institutes of Archaeology in the world. She had been offered accommodation nearby, in Russell Square, from where she had visited the British Museum a few times, as well as Covent Garden. That was the extent of her knowledge of the British capital.

She strolled down the broad streets of Maida Vale. It was a delightful part of London; central but secluded all the same, five minutes walk from Paddington station but cut off from the bustle of London traffic. As she walked past large white mansions lined with expensive cars she knew she was nearing her destination. She arrived at the canal, on Bloomfield Road. She walked across a bridge towards a barge-café. It was painted in a glossy maroon finish and ivy tresses hung down from the upper deck on either side.

The weather was chilly, so she walked onto the barge and into the café. She ordered a cappuccino and a croissant. The Buena Vista Social Club soundtrack was playing, which put her in a good mood. She had an hour before meeting Jack. She took out her notebook and placed it next to her coffee mug, leaned back and watched the cyclists shooting by, using the local network of canal routes to get to Paddington station. She remembered Jack saying that one could access most of London and avoid all traffic by using the cycle paths along the canals.

She thought back to their conversation in Tel Aviv the day before their departure to London. Jack could be very persuasive but she would not have left for London had she not felt deep down that he was right. She still felt utterly devastated about Eli's death. She kept repeating the words that Jack said: she had neither wanted him dead nor had she killed him. Someone else had: Oberon Wheatley. He might be legally untouchable, as Jack explained, and would never stand trial for the crimes he had perpetrated, but by going to London she could at least make sure he would never learn about the other tablet. She would get there first for Eli and for all those who believed in saving mankind rather than annihilating them or holding them to ransom.

Right now, Wheatley had the stone tablet and most likely the rabbi's chronicle as well. But they held the upper hand, as they already knew the contents of both and knew where to head next: Cambridge. Clearly the letter between the two brothers, from Cambridge to Safed, indicated that an 'item' was safe, and would one day be returned to its rightful place, the temple in Jerusalem. What else could this item be but the Jerusalem Tablet? She would have loved to know how the tablet had come to be a family heirloom of sorts, cared for by these two brothers. But first she had to speak to Moshe Shobai. Whatever Jack's misgivings about the man, she would meet him. The whole world was not after them, Jack was being over-cautious. One couldn't be so naïve as to think that academic pursuit was not fraught with danger. Shobai probably knew something about the tablet as a scholar deeply immersed in the field and was wise enough to keep away from what he sensed to be dangerous. He had kindly told her to leave it well alone but she hadn't heeded his warning.

Her thoughts had drifted so much she'd almost forgot the time. She paid the waitress and left her a generous tip. Walking briskly across the bridge, she turned left down the street towards the restaurant. Jack was waiting for her out front holding a beautiful bunch of roses.

'Hi Mina,' he said, offering her the flowers.

'Hi Jack. Thanks,' she answered, taking the roses and kissing him on the cheek. 'Now can I have my phone back?' she added, smiling sweetly.

He grinned and pushed her gently into the restaurant. He had made a reservation for a table by the window. As they sat down, Mina looked out at the canal through the glass. Jack ordered a bottle of red wine and some sparkling water. They looked at each other without a word until the drinks arrived.

'What should we toast to?' asked Mina.

'To the success of our quest! By the way Mina, if you'd checked your mobile you'd know that Hassan's fine.'

'He's fine?'

'Yes, he is. I'm not quite sure how he escaped Wheatley's grasp but he did and he texted you to say he and his mother were staying with relatives in the countryside. I texted back saying it was good news and that you'd get in touch sometime soon.'

'Thanks for that Jack. Now, seriously, where's my phone? Are you a kleptomaniac? It's the second time you've taken my mobile while I've been asleep.'

'Technically, you fainted the first time. Does that really count?'

'Just give me my phone.'

'Here you are,' he said, handing her a brand new one.

'That's not my phone.'

'I know. Yours wasn't safe to use any longer. We need to stay under the radar for the time being. Here's a British passport by the way.'

'A passport? You *have* been busy,' she answered.

'Let me explain.'

The waiter came to take the order. Jack chose the salmon, and Mina who hadn't paid attention to the menu, said she would have the same.

'Please, do explain,' said Mina, sarcastically.

'We have no idea how powerful Wheatley is,' Jack said, 'my guess is his area of influence is huge; politics, finance, police. We don't know that he won't try to get hold of you again. I couldn't do anything about it while we were in Israel, but in London things are different. I met a contact last night, and he sorted out a few things for us including fake IDs and a car. I bought us two pay-as-you-go mobile phones and I found Moshe Shobai's office address in St. John's Wood. It's a funny place to have an office, as it is mainly a residential area but there it is.'

Mina was trying to assimilate all the information, but was struggling, 'Jack?'

'Yes?'

'I know you told me Oberon is a powerful guy. But with all your 'connections,' can't we get some more help? Why can't you contact the proper authorities and have Oberon arrested?'

'Well…'

'What?'

'Back in Iraq, when you were in the hospital…'

'Yes?'

'I called it in.'

'Can you be less cryptic?'

'I talked to a friend, Stella, my former superior officer and discussed your situation.'

'So? That's good, isn't it?'

'Then in Israel, the day we left, I was contacted again but not by her.'

'By whom?' she asked.

'Someone I didn't know, from a different service. Intelligence. He asked me about you but I played dumb. I then tried contacting Stella but she was unreachable.'

'I still don't understand,' Mina said, with growing anxiety.

'You have to understand how these people in the intelligence business think. Their ears prick up at the smallest bit of information, especially in wartime Iraq. The little they know of your story is weird enough to interest them. They're paranoid, ever-doubting and obsessed with secrecy. Maybe my conversation with Stella was intercepted, or maybe she spoke to someone she shouldn't have. I don't know. The important thing is that before you know it, Mina, you'd be locked away somewhere, for reasons of 'National Security.' The whole affair would be taken over by some agents and I'd never see you again.'

Mina was pale as death. She was about to say something but Jack continued.

'Let me finish. That's one worry, but from the moment our business became known to more than one person, I realised it could be leaked to more people and eventually Wheatley could find out about our whereabouts too. I'm sorry, Mina.'

'There's nothing we can do about this, is there?' Mina asked, depressed.

'No.'

'So, what now?'

'We go all the way; we find the clay tablet, we may even discover the other three clay tablets, you unlock their potential and then…'

'Then?'

'Then we'll be in a position of strength to bargain with them all,' Jack said, trying to reassure her.

'So, we're on the run?'

'Yes. But don't worry about it. I'm on top of things.'

'Yeah, sure.' She felt like running out of the restaurant that very instant.

'Mina, look at me,' Jack said, firmly but kindly, 'this is what I was trained for, all these years, doing all these special operations, enduring pain and anguish, for a time like this. I won't let anyone harm you, or hinder us. Let them try.'

For a second she saw the hardness in his eyes and shivered slightly, she knew what Jack was capable of.

The waiter came back with their poached salmon, watercress, and sweet potato and carrot mash, and Jack tucked in immediately.

'I'm famished,' he said. 'I haven't eaten since last night.'

'Go ahead,' she said, pushing her plate towards him. 'You've worked hard enough for two meals. Jack?'

'Yes?'

'Don't do that again.'

'Which part?' asked Jack, sheepishly.

'You know which part. I understand your reasons for taking my phone and all the rest, but just tell me about it before acting.'

'I'm sorry. I won't do that again next time.'

'OK. So what should we focus on now?' asked Mina.

'Well, I think we should meet Dr Shobai as soon as possible.'

'I want to meet him alone.' she replied.

'Mina, I don't think that's a good idea. Last time you met someone alone you almost ended up at the bottom of the sea.'

'Wow, you're paranoid Jack. You really need a reality check.'

'I need a reality check?' he said, raising his voice in frustration.

'We're talking about a really old man, a scholar, not a power-hungry billionaire or a military operative.'

'All right, but I think you should surprise him at his office,' said Jack.

'I'd probably give him a heart attack barging in on him like that.'

'His office is real, but there's something weird about his foundation, *The Key to Tradition*.'

'What do you mean?' she asked impatiently.

'I did a few background checks and it looks too clean.'

Mina was taken aback, but remained calm. 'Jack, I know you've lived in a world of deceit and double agents and whatever else, but believe me, this is my world and whether the foundation has *clean* or *unclean* records, is irrelevant.'

'Mina, let's meet half way on this. You see him at his home

and I'll stay in the car. I'll give you an earpiece, so that we can communicate.'

She thought about it for a minute, played with her food absent-mindedly and finally looked up at Jack, 'Agreed.'

'Good,' he concluded, 'this salmon is delicious; maybe you should try it rather than just torture it. Now, we need to discuss what you'll talk about, but more importantly, what you're going to omit.'

'Now why would I do that?'

'First, we don't want him to get involved and second, you don't really know him and I don't trust him,' Jack said.

'Alright. So what should I omit?'

'Don't tell him about Cambridge or the guy who sent the parchment, this Hildersham dude.'

'Why not?' asked Mina.

'Because we're the only ones to know about this right now and no-one should know what we're up to.'

'Ok. What else?'

'I'm really not sure you should talk about anything frankly. Personally I'd hear what he has to say. I wouldn't volunteer anything.'

'Oh that's great. I can just imagine the conversation. "Hello Dr Shobai, how are you? Sorry I'm calling on you like this, uninvited. Why don't you tell me everything you know about a tablet you seem to be terrified by. Why? Just 'cause I'd love to know." That's great, Jack.'

'Just don't volunteer too much, that's all. Don't talk about Wheatley trying to kill you or your friend. Don't mention him at all.'

'When do you want to go?'

'I thought we could go later in the afternoon, when he's

back from his daily walk. It seems that Dr Shobai is still quite fit for his advanced age.'

'Is there anything you don't know?' she asked Jack, smiling.

'A smile, at last. Praise the Lord!'

'One last thing?'

'Yes?'

'I'm not going to barge in on him like that. I'm calling first to tell him I'm coming,' said Mina.

'I think it's a mistake.'

'It's plain rude, Jack. Give me the number.'

'Alright. Here's it is.

She dialled the number under Jack's irritated gaze. A young male voice answered, 'Hello. *The Key to Tradition*. How may I help you?'

'Hi. My name is Mina Osman. I'd like to see Dr Shobai today if possible.'

'Let me see if he is available.' She heard him flicking through a diary. 'I'm sorry, Madam, he won't be available until two weeks from now.'

'Could you tell him I'm in London right now, and am staying over here only a short while?'

'Yes of course. Shall I call you back on this number, madam?'

'Yes please.'

The line went dead. Jack was observing her, with an 'I told you so' look written all over his face.

'I'm sorry Jack, I had to do this,' she said.

'Now, you're going to have to wait for the guy to call back, and maybe he won't be free for days.'

She didn't reply. They ordered coffee, and waited.

Half an hour later, the mobile phone rang. Mina picked it up.

'Hello, Miss Osman?'

'Yes, it's me. Any luck?'

'Yes. I spoke to Dr Shobai, and he managed to postpone a few meetings to be able to see you this afternoon.'

'Fantastic.'

'Could you come by at five o'clock?'

'Yes of course. Thank you so much', said Mina.

'My pleasure. Goodbye.'

'Goodbye,' she replied ending the call. 'See Jack? Feminine charm. Beats devious spy methods every time.'

⤚

Moshe Shobai had just returned to the Foundation, a reconditioned semi-detached house on Boundary Road in St. John's Wood. Jack's contact had said he wasn't too surprised to find that the old Jewish scholar had opened shop in this part of town, as there was quite a large Jewish community in that neighbourhood.

Shobai was dressed as a typical scholar, with corduroy trousers, a tweed jacket and a turtleneck jumper. He was in his early seventies and he walked slightly bent, but one could still make out his former tall physique. He had short white hair and a trimmed beard; his hands were old and refined and he seemed to measure out every one of his movements. In a blue Ford Escort parked opposite Shobai's house, Jack observed the old scholar entering the house, walking up the stairs to the first floor, turning on the light and sitting down in an armchair.

Jack turned to Mina fidgeting in the passenger seat, 'It's

time, Mina. He's alone. Here's your earpiece. I'll be right here in the car. If things go wrong, just cough twice.'

'A good thing I don't have a cold right now,' she joked.

Jack smiled but didn't laugh. She was nervous and he knew it.

'Good luck Mina. Maybe he is just an old scholar after all.'

She walked up to Shobai's front door and rang the bell. Jack watched him stand up from his armchair and call someone from the landing. Mina took a step back and waited for someone to open the door. A young man appeared.

'Hello. You must be Miss Osman?'

'Yes. Is Dr Shobai in?'

'Of course. He's waiting for you in the library area on the first floor. May I take your coat?'

'Thank you.'

'It's the first door on your right when you reach the landing.'

Dr Shobai was waiting for her at the door, with a large smile.

'Welcome Mina, what a pleasure to see you again.'

'You too Dr Shobai.'

'Call me Moshe,' he said, as they walked into the library. 'I was surprised to hear you were in London. The last time I heard from you, you were teaching at Mosul University.'

'I've been travelling quite a bit these last few weeks, you know, doing research.'

He smiled at her.

'You haven't changed one bit. The same wide-open eyes, as driven and passionate as when we met at Harvard.'

'Dr…Moshe, we need to talk.'

'You seem quite out of sorts my dear. Does it have anything to do with the tablet you found?'

'Well, yes.'

'Let me make you some tea first and then we can sit comfortably and talk.'

He had not said much but his Eastern European Yiddish accent was quite distinctive under the British veneer.

'I thought you were Israeli?' she asked. 'Your accent has more Yiddish in it than *Ivrit*.' 'Is it that obvious?' He wrung his hands and said, '*Oy smeir.*' She laughed at his impersonation of an Eastern European Jew.

'Actually, I was born in Israel in a very orthodox family. Tell me about yourself while I make us some tea.'

'You're doing well Mina,' thought Jack.

Mina sat back in her armchair and looked around the library. She was struck by its large wooden tables, where she guessed many students and scholars came to pursue their research. There were a few thousand volumes in this room alone. Row upon row of beautifully bound books covered all the walls, resting on mahogany wood shelves. Dr Shobai poured her a cup of Assam tea.

She took a sip and said, 'You have a magnificent collection, Dr Shobai.'

'Please call me Moshe, Mina. We're scholars, not administrators.'

Mina felt totally at ease with this sympathetic old gentleman. 'Jack is completely paranoid,' she thought.

Back in the car, Jack felt the meeting was proceeding well. Still, he was tempted to beep her to remind her to keep on her toes.

'So, do you have the tablet here?'

'Unfortunately no. To cut a long story short, it was stolen from me.'

'How awful. I suppose Iraq is going through a terrible time right now. With all the lootings.'

'Yes.' She decided to let him believe it had been stolen in Iraq.

'If you want my opinion, it's good riddance, Mina.'

'I'm sorry Moshe, but could you explain what you mean? You've been cryptic about this tablet since the beginning and I want to know why.'

'Well done,' thought Jack.

'Well,' said the old scholar, 'the moment I read the rough translation you sent me and the description of how the stone tablet was dissimulated inside a clay case, I made the connection with an account I read years ago in a late 16th century manuscript kept in Coimbra, in Portugal.'

He took a sip of tea and went on. 'The main text was a complex kabbalistic commentary on a *sephirot* on God's *Gevurah Shebechesed*. It is an aspect of God which means 'strength' and 'kindness'.'

She shuddered. Mina remembered Eli's words, 'God acts with the firmness and benevolence of a father who can see further than his children.'

Shobai continued, 'In the margin was a cryptic sentence about a tablet written in Ur, a dangerous tablet, with which one could unravel God's plan. Many men had sought this tablet in vain and had died in its pursuit. I remember wondering at the time if the men in question had died because of the tablet or simply had died vainly in a hopeless quest. But my main thought was that it was a dangerous text, something that shouldn't be trifled with. That's why I wrote you that email.'

'But Moshe, if the tablet I discovered is the same as the one you're talking about, which I believe it is, we have a text that enables humans to predict natural disasters. That's a major breakthrough.'

'Mina, I believe there are some things scholars should keep well away from. However good *your* intentions, what if it fell into the wrong hands?'

'Even so, what is the worst that could happen?' asked Mina.

'I don't think anyone should try to peer into God's mind, for want of a better word.'

Mina was surprised at his response. Shobai had not struck her as a very religious man.

'Don't mistake me,' he said quickly, as he noticed her expression. 'The tablet was hidden for good reasons I'm sure. It's an accident that this tablet was found. If it hadn't been for the war and all the destruction, you may never have located it.'

'One second you believe that the tablet can give its possessor the knowledge of God's plan and shouldn't be trifled with, and the next second you believe in *accidents*?'

Shobai laughed softly. 'Mina, Mina. You've cornered me. I feel like a foolish young yeshiva student. Let's keep away from theology. You're alive, I'm alive, so obviously I must have been wrong about the tablet. Maybe it isn't that dangerous.'

'My god, the man is more slippery than an eel,' thought Jack. 'He jumps in and out of arguments.'

'What I wonder, Mina, is why you came to talk to me, here in

London. Of course, I'm delighted to see you again. But why travel so far? Has something happened I should know about?'

Mina was troubled. He was asking obvious questions, but she didn't like the turn the discussion was taking. She'd have to say something soon.

Jack said into the mouthpiece, 'Mina, do not mention Wheatley. Don't mention Cambridge.'

'Well. I've found another text,' she began.

'Another text?'

Mina noticed Shobai squinted slightly when he pronounced his last words.

'It's a 16th century chronicle describing a discussion between rabbis in Safed.'

'Yes?'

'A discussion about the tablet.'

'Extraordinary. Do you have this here?' he asked.

'No. It was also stolen from me,' she said, looking down at her tea cup.

'Dear me. Mina. You want to give this old man a stroke? Next thing you'll tell me you've found the original Ten Commandments, but that you lost them on the Tube.'

Back in the car, Jack laughed. He was starting to warm up to the old man.

Mina blushed. She was about to say 'it's real, Moshe. An old man just like yourself died because of it', but she held back. Instead, she said 'Well, not everything was stolen from me.'

Shobai looked up at Mina, curiously.

'Mina, no!' Jack blurted out in the mouthpiece.

But Mina didn't care. She felt wounded in her academic pride and she blurted out 'I still have a fragment of a letter which seems to indicate that there is another tablet, somewhere in… in Britain, but it was torn, so I have no idea where.'

'How interesting. What does it say exactly?' leaning in.

'Oh, for that I'd need to have a better look at the fragment. I can't remember off by heart.'

She was lying miserably and she sensed he knew it, but he didn't comment.

'Why would it be in Britain? Maybe you're wrong about its location?' he asked.

'Maybe. But if I weren't, where should I start searching?'

'Do you mean "in which library"?' he asked her, tentatively.

'I don't know. You tell me.'

'Well, I really don't have a clue. I'm baffled,' said the old scholar.

Mina looked disappointed. Shobai tapped her gently on the arm.

'Mina. Don't worry so much. I'm sure it will all turn out fine. Do you need a few letters of introduction to London libraries?'

'No, but thanks for your offer. I have all the credentials I need.'

'Of course you do. Well,' he said as he stood up after Mina, 'I'm delighted to have met you again, but I'm only sorry not to have been able to help you more in your current search.'

'Thank you for your time Dr Shobai.'

The young student brought Mina her coat, and then left them. Dr Shobai walked her back to the door, and waved her goodbye as she left. Mina searched for Jack's car, and his voice in her ear said, 'Just walk down the pavement to the left. I'm on the corner of the street.'

As Mina turned the corner, Jack opened the passenger door and she jumped in. He seemed irritated, so Mina did not speak. When they reached the hotel, and Jack had parked the car, he finally looked at her and said:

'It went pretty well didn't it?'

'Are you being sarcastic?'

'No, why?'

'Why? You haven't said a word since I got in the car,' she said angrily.

'Oh, that.'

'Yeah, that.'

'I'm pretty sure we were being followed,' he answered.

'Oh my god. Who?'

'I don't know. This is the second time I sense we are being followed but I can't see anyone.'

'Maybe we're not being followed then,' said Mina cheerfully. But her smile froze when she saw Jack was dead serious.

'You don't understand, Mina. Not only was I trained by the best to pick up on someone tailing me, but I am particularly good at it. I know we're being watched.'

'So who are they? What are they after? Wheatley already has the tablet.'

He did not answer. Instead, he got out of the car. She followed him into the hotel. A crowd was waiting at the lifts, so they climbed the stairs. As they reached the third floor, he said,

'Mina, as soon as we get to our room, grab your things. The hotel isn't safe anymore. We need to move.'

'OK.'

'We need to get to a place with loads of people, and lose these bastards there, before leaving for Cambridge.'

'How do we get there?'

'We take a train from King's Cross.'

'Can't we lose them at the train station?' asked Mina.

'We don't want them to know we're leaving London.'

They entered the room. Mina went straight to her case and started sorting her things, but Jack took a moment to sit on his bed and plan the next step. She suddenly had an idea and stopped what she was doing.

'Jack, why don't we go to the British Museum? It's usually crawling with tourists day in and day out.'

'Perfect. You're right. Are you ready to go?'

'Give me ten minutes.'

A quarter of an hour later, Mina walked to the reception, where Jack had just finished paying for their room. He rushed her to the exit. Jack felt like alarm bells were ringing all around him.

'They're here, Mina. I can't explain, but I know they're here. Transfer any valuables and your notes about the tablet in your small rucksack and when I tell you, drop your suitcase and run to the car. Don't forget Hildersham's letter.' Jack watched her transferring all her things. He paused, 'Now!'

They both ran as fast as they could but before they could get to their car, a blue Mercedes drove up and double-parked in front of it. Two motorbikes, driven by men in dark suits and helmets appeared out of nowhere. One was revving near the double parked car and the other had mounted the pavement. Jack reacted with lightening speed. He ran towards the biker on the pavement and kicked him square in the chest. The man flew backwards off his bike onto the pavement. Before he could pick himself up, Jack had turned the bike around, Mina jumped on the back, her rucksack dangling on one arm, and they were off.

Jack accelerated towards Little Venice and drove over the bridge Mina had crossed the same morning. Looking in his mirror, Jack saw that the Mercedes and the second biker were behind them and without a second thought he took a sudden hard right turn into a one-way street. They nearly crashed into a utilities van that was heading in the same direction but at a much slower pace. Jack slowed down as he turned right again onto the canal tow path. The Mercedes screeched its tires as its driver hit the brakes to avoid crashing into the front of the Bridge Pub, but the biker followed the same route as Jack.

Mina was on the verge of passing out in fear but she held onto Jack as they sped down the narrow bicycle lane at full throttle, dodging benches and terrified cyclists. She thought she heard a cracking sound. Jack shouted at her not to turn her head around, and to duck low. The biker was shooting at them. Even at this speed, Jack managed to drive in a zigzag so their pursuer couldn't get a clear shot. He suddenly saw an opening in the hedge to their left, just as a group of cyclists was coming towards them. He missed crashing into the group by a hair's breadth and he catapulted into the small path leading away from the canal and towards the main road. Their pursuer was not so lucky. He lost control of his motorbike, skidded on his side and all Mina heard was a loud splash as he crashed through the cyclists and into the canal. As they reached the main road, they dismounted the motorbike and Jack hid it in a convenient bush as Mina hailed a passing taxi. The cab slowed down and pulled up beside them. They rushed inside.

'British Museum, please,' said Jack.

'Right you are,' replied the cabbie.

'Oh my god, oh my god,' Mina kept repeating, as Jack held her hands and tried to comfort her.

'We're safe for now, Mina. Let's stick to the plan.'

The driver of the blue Mercedes had watched the whole scene from a nearby bridge. He waited for a few cars to pass by, and calmly started tailing Jack's cab.

⤿

The black cab entered Great Russell Street and slowed down as it approached the main entrance of the British Museum. Jack got out first, helping Mina out of the car. A cold wind was now blowing. Jack tightened his scarf around his neck and looked up to the sky. Dark clouds were forming above them. It would start raining soon and from the looks of it, it would be a heavy downpour. 'It might just work for us,' thought Jack, as he followed Mina through the great gates.

Just ahead of them was the outer courtyard, and beyond it the enormous building that had been a landmark in the London landscape since its construction in 1753, when Sir Henry Soane offered his private collection to the British public. It was much smaller then, the collection being kept in Montague House, but over the next centuries, more than sixty houses surrounding the museum were pulled down and a central edifice appeared with large gallery wings. The museum extended all the way to Montague Place, and housed the millions of objects that had been added each year to the initial 18th century collection. After much construction work, there rose a building of huge proportions, with a tremendous neoclassical facade, eight perfect ionic columns crowned by a pediment and flanked by a colonnade on either side.

As Jack walked past the guards, he gave a sidelong glance back to the main street and noticed the blue Mercedes driving slowly past the gates. Their pursuers had caught up with them and were not even bothering to hide anymore. Jack immediately assumed they'd have men near Montague Place, the other exit of the Museum, which was more discreet for a stakeout. They'd have to lose them at the museum's main entrance. As they walked through the outer courtyard, Jack stared at the façade, and for a few moments felt almost dwarfed by the edifice and its awesome presence. To him it resembled a Greek temple, standing fast in the coming storm, towering above London's streets and his own personal problems. They seemed so petty in contrast to this monument dedicated to past ages and to the memory of ancient and great civilisations. They climbed the stairs into the main lobby. Mina walked straight into the Great Court.

'Mina, walk slowly. There's no rush.'

'Alright. Where do you want to go?'

'I don't know. Why don't you show me the flood tablet you mentioned.'

'OK. Don't you love this glass dome? It's so clever.'

Jack did not respond. He silently cursed Norman Foster, the architect. When Mina had mentioned the British Museum, he had thought it was a perfect idea; he remembered awfully crowded corridors which were used both for museum visitors to circulate and to exhibit ancient artefacts. But walking through the museum today felt quite different, much less crowded, spacious in fact. No, he did not share Mina's wonder at the cylindrical tower of the Reading Room, and the over-arching glass dome, it would make their task considerably more difficult.

'Follow me,' said Mina, 'the room's upstairs.'

They climbed the stairs around the Reading room, up to the swish Court Restaurant on the upper floor. They proceeded straight through to Mesopotamian Room 56, and then right into the other Mesopotamian Room 55, where an unassuming glass case held some of the most famous cuneiform tablets in the world.

'Jack, take a look. Here it is, Tablet XI of the Gilgamesh Epic. Because it was found among the other tablets at the library of Ashurbanipal in Nineveh, we date it to the 7th century B.C.E.'

'It's clay, right?'

'Yes?'

'How is it that it was so well preserved?' asked Jack.

'Well, you see, Ashurbanipal was a king after my own heart. He loved scholars and kept adding copies of important docu-ments to his library. We even have tablets describing how scholars were trained themselves. Anyway, when the palace eventually burned down, the tablets did not dissolve or burn like parchment or papyrus, they baked. And that's why we still have them today.'

'Fascinating. So this text is a copy?'

'Yup. Also, it's written in Akkadian, whereas a much older version, which is in the room we've just walked through, is in old Babylonian and dates back to the 17th century B.C.E.'

'Sorry to interrupt you Mina, but don't you smell some-thing odd?'

'What do you mean?'

'Something strong, like musk, but not the artificial stuff. I can't quite put my finger on it.'

'Yes, I do… and I think I've smelled the same thing not long ago.'

'I know! It was outside the hotel. Let's get the hell out of here.'

They rushed back to the central tower. A tall man with a black beard and smoked glasses was resting against the railing, pretending to read a leaflet. Jack quickly grabbed Mina's hand, feigned going right but then rushed down the left hand staircase. Unfortunately the man caught up with them within a few seconds. Jack urged Mina to run away, as he turned around to face his opponent. She took a few steps down the stairs all the time trying to look back to watch the men wrestle above her. Amazingly, nobody seemed to notice the fight. Jack had bent the man's arm behind his back and when he heard it crack he shoved his head into the wall. As the man crumpled to the floor, unconscious, a small vial fell out of his pocket and shattered on the marble steps. Jack and Mina immediately recognised the pungent fragrance they had smelled earlier. Jack picked up a shard of the vial and hurried down the stairs with Mina. They slowed their pace somewhat as they passed guards in the main lobby hurrying towards the staircase. Jack discreetly snatched a sopping wet umbrella, which a man had put against a column while shaking his trench coat.

They ran down the steps into the outer courtyard, heavy rain still falling from a darkened sky. The driver of the blue Mercedes was waiting near the gates, but did not see Jack and Mina dashing by shielded by an umbrella like any young couple keen to get out of the rain. They ran ahead, down Museum Street, and dodged into an occult bookshop.

Mina, who by this time was beyond physical and mental exhaustion, could hardly stand upright. Jack helped her sit down on a large and ancient-looking leather chair and pretended to browse through the books, all the while keeping a close watch on Museum Street. The shop owner barely glanced at them, as they did not seem like genuine seekers of the dark arts, just passers-by trying to escape the rain.

Mina was so anxious she could feel her hands shaking. To try to put her mind at rest she focused on at the collection of books, placed haphazardly on the shelves around her. Some of the books had the weirdest titles but she was too frazzled to understand what she was reading.

'Mina?' Jack hissed from the corner of his mouth. She did not hear him. He spoke again, louder this time and placed a hand on her shoulder. 'Mina?' She was startled, and looked at him with scared eyes.

'What is it?' asked Mina. Jack sighed and took her hand.

'Mina, we have to separate. We haven't shaken them off yet.'

'No Jack. Please, no,' she begged him, tears welling in her eyes.

'We have to lose them. I'll draw their attention, and while they follow me…'

'Please Jack. Don't leave me. I can't do this alone.'

'You can do it, Mina. You have to, OK? Wait for ten minutes after I'm gone, then walk out of here, right, into New Oxford Street and get in the first cab. Go straight to King's Cross and catch a train to Cambridge. I'll call you in an hour.' He looked deep into her eyes and kissed her wet cheek softly, 'You can do this Mina.'

He looked out of the front window for a few seconds, turned round a last time and walked out onto the street. 'Good luck,

Jack,' Mina murmured, but he was already gone. While she looked at her watch and waited, an odd-looking man, wearing a large-brimmed hat with a feather stuck in its side, started talking to her, oblivious to her anxious state.

'Do you know,' he began, 'that you're standing in a genuine occult bookshop? It was once run by the head of a lodge called The Order of the Hidden Masters,'

Mina looked at him with a blank expression on her face.

'And, one of the patrons of this order was Alistair Crowley,' he added mysteriously.

Mina didn't answer so the man walked towards another customer and started chatting to her. Mina checked her watch and noticed that ten minutes had gone by. She did as Jack had told her. She hailed one of many cabs passing down New Oxford Street, and after a few minutes ride, was at King's Cross station. She bought a ticket to Cambridge and enquired about the next available train, which was leaving in twenty minutes. She treated herself to a takeaway cappuccino, sat down on a chair next to the other travellers and sipped her coffee. She was utterly drained and incapable of thinking about anything. When the Cambridge train was announced she stood up, and numbly walked in the direction of platform 9A.

Jack felt stupid. No-one appeared to be following him. He had changed cabs three times, and was walking down Portobello Road in Notting Hill. Had they managed to lose their pursuers at the museum after all? Why hadn't he checked to see if they were still lurking around before leaving Mina? How stupid. They'd have both been on the Cambridge train by now.

He tried phoning her, but the call went straight to her voice-mail. 'Oh god, I hope she didn't leave it in the suitcase' he thought. He went for a beer in a nearby pub and looked at the happy faces of men and women meeting for a drink after a hard day's work. What was wrong with him? Why did he always end up running for his life? By now, his face had probably been retrieved by the police from CCTV camera footage in the museum.

He waited half an hour and tried calling Mina, again unsuccessfully. He got in a cab and drove to their hotel in Maida Vale, hoping to get hold of the suitcase and check what had become of the mobile phone. An employee at the front desk explained that a man in a dark suit and sunglasses had just come by and picked it up. 'I should've gone straight back to the hotel' thought Jack, increasingly angry with himself. He walked around Maida Vale for a while to gather his thoughts. He wondered if their separation could prove to be an asset after all; maybe he could sort out their other problem. He would contact Stella and ask her why Intelligence was interested in Mina. Stella was stationed in Germany. Maybe she could leave her base for a day, and they could meet up at the drinking den in Soho.

Mina had finally arrived at her destination. She felt much worse now than when she'd embarked on the train. Twenty minutes into the trip, she had searched her rucksack thoroughly looking for her new phone, but it was not there. She must have left it in her suitcase, or in the hotel room. How was she going to get in touch with Jack or Jack with her? She did not even know his email address. She walked out of the station, in the direction of Tenison Road where she saw a few guest houses. She picked one and booked a room for two nights, hoping to find something nicer within the next few days. She walked up to her room. Her hands shook as she opened the door. She dropped her rucksack on the floor, sat on the bed and cried silently, in the gloomy winter light filtering through the stained curtains.

Chapter 22

December 14th, 2004. Cambridge

Mina woke up late in the morning, wishing it had all been a dream. But there she was, in the same seedy guest house in Cambridge, alone. She took a quick shower and after laying out the bed sheet on the floor, slowly stretched through a series of yoga *asanas*. Later, pulling on her last pair of jeans she was reminded she would have to buy clothes, again. She left the guest house, her small rucksack hanging from one shoulder. A few builders wolf-whistled her as she walked down Tenison Road. She felt like telling them off but instead looked straight ahead to Mill Road. She entered a café at random and ordered a cappuccino, croissants and jam. As she drank her coffee, warming her hands around the mug, she looked out of the window at the grey street. It was raining again. The miserable weather was starting to depress her even more than her current situation.

Around midday, she walked into the city centre. She bought a few clothes and an umbrella. When she passed the main market place and reached King's Parade she stared in wonder at the spectacular walls of King's College. Seeing its gigantic chapel and the peacefulness of the scholars walking about the college grounds, she felt her spirits lifting slightly. She asked her way to the University Library.

The library was the only place Jack and her were set to visit in Cambridge, after Eli told them about it in Safed. It would be his first point of call. A helpful young man who introduced himself as a student at King's College walked with her through the college's main quad, and over its private bridge onto Queen's Road.

He asked her what brought her to Cambridge, so Mina told him that she was doing research for a week or two. He was very excited about the University Library and explained that it was a copyright library, like the Bodleian in Oxford and the British Library in London, which meant that it stocked almost every book published in English.

'The great advantage of this library over the other two,' he explained 'is the fact that it is an open stack library. One wastes an awful amount of time at the Bod or at the BL requesting books that you don't really need in the end.' He joked about the building, comparing it to an erect phallus, with its huge central tower whereas the Bodleian in Oxford was more womb-like, with many subterranean floors where its precious volumes were held. He told her all she needed to do was to walk straight on, along the pedestrian path and she'd get to the library.

At the library reception desk, a clerk told her she'd need more credentials to get a reader's ticket. She sighed with irritation; she'd have to email Columbia to request a letter from her department stating her research need and that meant leaving the library. So she walked back towards the city centre through Silver Street hoping to find an internet café but lost her way. She stopped at a sandwich shop to get a bite to eat. There were no internet cafés close by so she hopped into a cab and returned to Mill Road where she'd spotted a couple earlier on.

She entered the Jaffa Net Café and emailed her department. She waited for an answer while sipping a mint tea in the courtyard, sitting among hookah smokers lost in volutes of apple tobacco fumes. After a while she checked her email. Her department had sent her the requested letter. She printed it out and decided to return to the library the next day. Although the café was pretty downtrodden, she enjoyed being there, surrounded by Arabs from all over the globe. Had the weather not been so dreadful, she would have almost felt at home, drinking tea and listening to fleeting conversations in Arabic. A few men were sizing her up, but let her be all the same.

Jack had slept most of the afternoon in a cheap hotel off Edgware Road. He'd managed to contact Stella the night before and they had made plans to meet in Soho later in the evening. Jack took the tube to Piccadilly Circus. As he walked through Soho's bustling streets, he smiled at the memory of their last meeting in the dingy, smoke-filled pub. He remembered Stella's joke. 'Careful Jack! Just make sure you sit down opposite the right girl when you get back from the restroom.'

He spotted Stella immediately, sitting at the bar. He walked up to her, and they gave each other a warm hug. She was as sexy and sophisticated as the last time they'd met. She had short blond hair now and looked slightly older, but she still seemed as fit as a Marine leaving boot camp.

'How long has it been, Jack?' asked Stella.

'Too long, Stella. So tell me, why is Intelligence onto me?' asked Jack, going straight to the point.

'Well, they're not exactly onto you – more onto your lady friend. She seems to have something that interests them.'

'It was stolen from her,' said Jack.

'Oh. Were you there when it happened?'

'Sort of. They weren't Intelligence.'

Stella seemed surprised but did not question Jack about it.

'Listen Jack, the less I know, the less I can tell. I came to warn you to be careful and to lose the girl. Why get involved? I thought you were done with all this stuff.'

'Stella, do I detect a twinge of jealousy in your tone?'

'Don't even go there! So what's the story?'

'I care about her.'

'So? Send her a postcard. It wouldn't be the first time, hmm Jack?'

'Not this time.'

'That's a pity.' There was just the slightest hint of wistfulness in her voice but she smiled at him broadly and so Jack pressed on.

'What did you find out from the CCTV footage at the British Museum?'

'Nothing.'

'Nothing?'

'Yeah. No fighting, no body, not a squeak…that's good news, right?' said Stella.

'Damn.'

'Jack. What the hell have you got yourself into?'

Jack didn't answer. He noticed a young man on the other side of the bar had been listening to their every word.

'Well, as soon as Intelligence is satisfied that the girl's got nothing, they'll drop it. You know how they are. Too much on their plate to worry about what-ifs.'

'Who did you speak to, Stella?'

'That's the weird thing. No-one. But you quit the service in a hurry. Maybe they kept a tab on you, just in case.'

'Maybe. Anyway. It's all over now. She doesn't have whatever they think she had. I just want to make sure she's safe.'

As he said those words, he turned to look at the young man but he was gone.

'Dear Jack, I think you'll be fine.'

Stella was smiling now. Jack smiled back at her. Now that the young Intelligence agent had heard what he wanted to hear, they should leave Jack and Mina alone. One less thing to worry about. But he couldn't ask Stella or anyone else for help, or they'd come back after Mina with renewed strength. He laughed out loud.

'I'd forgotten how sneaky those guys were,' he said, 'that's a relief. Let's go for dinner.'

'Great. I know this fantastic Greek place in Coptic Street.'

Chapter 23

December 15th, 2004. Cambridge

Mina walked through the revolving doors of the University Library. After obtaining her reader's ticket, she walked up to the first floor. She passed the Catalogue Hall and entered the Reading Room. The Library itself was a modern edifice, but the oblong Reading Room's white walls, large windows and its high wood panelled ceiling gave it a peculiar and ancient feel. Mina chose a seat among the many available for readers and sat down. She wondered what she was supposed to do now. Maybe she should email Dr Shobai and ask him for help? She felt lost without Jack. She decided to focus on the research units housed within this huge library. Poor Eli had told them about a group of scholars from the University Library in Cambridge on the very night he was murdered in Safed. She returned to the main desk and was given a small booklet with information for first time users of the library. She ran through the various research units and one caught her attention, The Taylor-Schechter Genizah Research Unit. She knew what a *genizah* was, a depository used for worn-out sacred Hebrew texts, but why here in Cambridge? 'The 140,000 fragments of Hebrew and Jewish literature and documents rescued from the Ben Ezra Synagogue in Cairo cover every aspect of life in the Mediterranean area a thousand years ago,' she read.

Perfect. The scholars Eli had met must have come from this unit. She called them from an internal phone at the front desk and made an appointment to meet a research assistant after lunch.

⌒

Mina walked into The Taylor-Schechter Genizah Research Unit. She introduced herself as a scholar in Jewish studies from New York, looking to meet a researcher specialised in the history of Jews in the British Isles. Soon enough she was shown into an office by the unit's secretary.

'Hi,' said a portly woman wearing an awful purple turtleneck and a matching pair of trousers, 'how can I help you?'

'Well', said Mina, 'thanks for seeing me at such short notice. It may come as a surprise to you, but I was told about your unit by some scholars in Safed, in Israel.'

'That makes sense, we work with scholars all over the world. Tell me about your research, Mina.'

'I'm working on a small 18th century letter written by a Jewish scholar from Cambridge. I thought someone at the Research Unit might be able to point me in the right direction.'

'Hmm. That's strange. You see, there were no Jewish scholars, well not officially, in 18th century Cambridge. They only became eligible to study and teach at the University in the late 19th century. The earliest scholar I can think of was a Hungarian rabbi by the name of Solomon Schiller-Szinessy. But we're talking about the 1860s, not before…what is the name of the scholar?'

'Hildersham,' said Mina.

'I don't know any scholar by that name. Are you sure about it? It sounds German, a little like Hildersheim or Hildesheim?'

'No. It's Hildersham, from Cambridge' replied Mina.

'You know, there is a village called Hildersham, about ten miles east of Cambridge, beyond the Gog Magog hills. Maybe your scholar lived there?'

Of course! Mina felt so stupid. She hadn't even bothered to check if Hildersham was a place. She could easily have googled it and found the answer within a few seconds.

Mina was about to leave and thank her profusely, when the woman remembered one of the unit's associated researchers.

'Daniel Bamart is from Hildersham. He might be able to help you out. I'll give him a call at his office.'

She picked up the phone and dialled his number. While she waited for him to pick up, she asked Mina where she would be in the next two hours. 'In the Reading Room', Mina replied.

'Hi Daniel. How are things? Excellent! Really? Well, I have someone here who might need your help. Are you free later on? Great. Her name is Mina Osman. She'll be in the Reading Room. In an hour. OK. Thanks. See you around,' she said. Then she turned to Mina.

'There you go. He'll pop by in an hour or so. I hope it helps.'

'Thank you so much!' replied Mina, and she walked back down to the Reading Room.

An hour later, Mina noticed a lanky young man observing her from afar. He seemed to be in his late twenties, with a wild mane of ash blond hair and a dreamy air about him. He was handsome in an academic sort of way. Eventually, with much hesitation and an odd mixture of 'ehms' and 'ahhs', he asked her if her name was Mina Osman.

'Yes, that's me. Are you Daniel?' asked Mina.

'Yes Daniel Bamart.' They shook hands, 'Are you working at the Genizah?'

'No. I'm doing some research based on a letter I found related to Hildersham. What about you?'

'Oh, I'm a Hebrew scholar. I was brought up in Cambridge but I studied in Jerusalem. I'm currently working on a joint research project at the unit. To tell you the truth, the person who is most likely to be able to help you is my father.'

'Really? Why's that?' asked Mina

'He's a retired medical doctor but his passion is local history. He could probably answer any questions you have about Hildersham.'

'Fantastic. When do you think I could visit him?'

'What about right now?' Daniel asked her tentatively.

'Great!'

'OK. I'll drive you down there, I was off to see him anyway,' he lied.

'You're sure he won't mind me arriving unannounced?' Mina asked.

'No. Really. He's retired you know; lots of time on his hands.'

'OK. Let's go then.'

⸗

They drove for twenty minutes in a slight drizzle. Mina watched the countryside rolling by on the eastern road out of Cambridge. She looked up and noticed dark clouds gathering in the sky. Daniel turned off the main road into Hildersham. They passed a small bridge, a few houses and he parked the car outside a charming old cottage, with a small brass plaque that read 'Mulberry Cottage.'

'The door's always unlocked. My dad doesn't believe in break-ins,' Daniel said with a sigh.

They entered the cottage and walked through to a comfortable living room. Its centuries old white-washed walls were covered in black-and-white framed landscape photographs. Daniel's father was asleep in an armchair, a book lying across his lap. Daniel woke him up gently.

'Hi dad. It's me.'

Dr Bamart smiled at his son.

'Hi Daniel. I didn't expect you until this evening.'

Daniel blushed.

'I've brought a friend, Mina,' he said to his father.

The old man rose from his armchair to take a closer look at Mina.

'Daniel, where are your manners?' said the man to Daniel, then, turning to Mina 'Good afternoon, I'm Joshua Bamart, Daniel's father.'

'And I'm Mina Osman, from New York. I'm doing research at the University Library, partly about Hildersham. Your son told me you might be able to help me and kindly drove me here to meet you.'

The old man puffed up his chest.

'I'd be delighted to help you. I have huge archives upstairs which concern the history of this village and some of the neighbouring villages. I'm sure you'll dig out your answer somewhere in there. Would you like a nice cup of tea first?'

'Yes please,' said Mina.

An hour and several cups of tea later, Mina was feeling guilty again. The more Dr Bamart was kind to her, the more she felt phoney and guilty about her lame research topic. The man was clever and so was his son. They were bound to realise she was lying. Bamart asked her where she was staying.

'In a guest house off Station Road,' Mina replied.

'Oh. How dreadful. How long do you intend to stay in Cambridge?'

'Two weeks. Actually, it is pretty depressing. You wouldn't know of any nice accommodation in Cambridge?'

'Why don't you stay here, with us? We have two guest bedrooms. You wouldn't be in the city centre but you'd have peace and quiet.'

'That would be very nice. How much do you charge per night?' asked Mina.

'No no, dear me, I don't usually rent out the rooms, they're for guests.'

'Oh, I see. I couldn't, Dr Bamart.'

'Hush hush. Call me Joshua. Frankly, now that I'm retired I miss company and if you promise to cook a Middle Eastern meal for me one evening, you're most welcome to stay here for two weeks.'

Mina was moved by the old man's kindness and thinking back to the horrible room that awaited her, was relieved to accept his offer.

'In that case, I accept, on condition that I can cook more than one meal before I leave.'

Daniel felt over the moon as she said those words.

'Well, now that's all settled, you ought to bring your belongings from your guest house,' said Joshua. 'Daniel, can you drive Miss Osman back into town?'

'Of course dad,' he answered, and to Mina, 'Come on Mina, I'll drive you now.'

'Thanks Daniel,' she said.

As they got into the car, Mina thanked Daniel for his hospitality.

'It's a real pleasure. I should have thought of it myself. By the way, I'm really sorry about this, but you'll need to catch a bus on the way back here. I've got things to take care of, but I'd love to have lunch with you tomorrow if you're around.'

'Of course. That would be great,' answered Mina.

Mina spent a very entertaining evening in Joshua's company. Her host had cooked a delicious vegetarian feast. They drank wine and talked about the many countries they had travelled to. He seemed so different from his son. He wore thick rimmed glasses, and was as short and plump as his son was tall and slim. He was a funny old man and was totally at ease in her company, probably due to his many years as a country doctor, used to seeing patients at home. He told her about his wife, Esther, a beautiful New York artist 'with a dreadful temper,' She'd died ten years ago but they had shared thirty blissful years together. He never remarried and since her death he rarely entertained guests. He enjoyed living with his memories and seeing his beloved Daniel whenever he was in the country.

After dinner, they went for a walk along the river towards the nearby village of Linton. The night was cold and damp but the stars were shining in the pitch black sky. Mina wished Jack were there with her. They could have walked together under the stars. 'God I miss you,' she thought, looking up at the night sky and wondering where he was.

Chapter 24

December 16th, 2004. Cambridge

Jack had been tossing and turning in his king size bed since five a.m. He'd spent the previous day in London making sure he wasn't followed and had driven off to Cambridge in the evening. He felt much happier for having seen Stella and knowing that, for the time being, the spooks were off his back and Mina's. That left Oberon Wheatley and the other mysterious pursuers. But now that he was in Cambridge, he kept wondering how he was going to find Mina. He had opted to stay in a comfortable hotel on the banks of the River Cam, right in the city centre. He had asked discreetly after Mina at various hotels and guest houses near the train station, but no-one seemed to remember her. He only had one choice left, which was to go to the University Library and wait until she showed up.

⤔

Mina called the Genizah research unit and spoke to the secretary. She explained that she was Daniel Bamart's guest and if someone called Jack Hillcliff came by the unit asking for her, she would be very grateful if they could give him Daniel's address in Hildersham. Later that morning, Mina and Joshua had their first serious conversation about her research. She explained that she was looking for a Jewish gentleman who had lived in Hildersham or in Cambridge in 1755 and for any correspondence that may have existed between Hildersham and Safed from the 18th century onwards. Joshua looked at her strangely and said he wasn't aware of any such correspondence. They were sitting in Joshua's office, which contained a huge archive made up of filing cabinets and shelves upon shelves of documents that lined the walls. He said it was all at her disposal. He then explained that she would have to search the archives from different angles, as he didn't have a specific 18th century section. It was thematic, divided according to parish records, public records, land ownership and so forth. She thanked him and got down to work. He smiled at her, and walked out of the office.

Daniel returned from Cambridge at lunchtime, carrying extra wellington boots for Mina. Father and son lead her through Hildersham's muddy fields to Linton for a pub lunch. At least it wasn't raining that day. Mina was trying to be cheerful but she kept wondering if Jack would find her. Daniel seemed more embarrassed than usual as they walked back to the house together chatting, as Joshua lagged behind.

'Mina, can I ask you a personal question?' asked Daniel with difficulty.

'Yes, of course,' she replied.

'Do you have someone in your life? I mean, you seemed a bit sad today and I just wondered if…' he broke off.

'Daniel, can I be frank with you?'

'Don't be too tough on me. I know you American girls can be blunt as hell.'

They both laughed.

'I'm sort of involved with someone.'

'Ah,' said Daniel sadly.

'I hope I wasn't too blunt?' she asked.

'No, no. A direct answer to a direct question.'

'Daniel, can we be friends? I think we could be good friends and right now, I really need one,' said Mina.

Daniel was disappointed but respected her frankness and genuine offer. He straightened up, and shook off his infatuation.

'It's a deal.'

～

Same day
St John's Wood, London

In a dark room an old man was sitting at his desk, deep in thought. A shadowy silhouette had crept into the house from the garden. Thinking that he heard an unusual noise, the old man left his desk and stepped into the corridor. Nothing seemed out of the ordinary. He returned to his study…the shadow moved up the stairs, then unhurriedly and noiselessly stepped onto the landing of the second floor. He walked down the corridor to the old man's study. He knocked on the door. The old man looked up to face a bearded man in a dark suit.

'Master,' said the bearded man, bowing respectfully.

'Good,' said the old man, 'You're back. Are our people posted at all the major libraries?'

'Yes master, Oxford, Cambridge, London, Aberystwyth and Edinburgh. One of our men thinks he recognised Miss Osman's friend outside the University Library in Cambridge.'

'Hmm. Send more men there immediately. We can't afford to lose their trail again. What about Ephraim in New York?'

'All is in place, he will act tonight.'

'Any digital copies?'

'They've already been destroyed.'

'Good. We may not be as *dark* and *nameless* as we were in the olden days, but we certainly know how to vanish in the night. Clear out this place. I'm moving to the other house.'

❧

Jack had explored the main reading rooms of the University Library but Mina was nowhere to be seen. Since then, he'd been sitting patiently in his car, waiting for her to show up at the library's main entrance. He was trying to guess what she might have done if she'd already been there and left. It was mid-afternoon when he plugged his mobile phone into his laptop and started surfing the internet, reading about the library and its various research units. He came to the same conclusion as Mina and decided to ask after her at the Genizah Research Unit. Maybe she'd already been there and they would remember her. Half an hour later, having learned all he needed to know, Jack was on his way to Hildersham.

❧

Same day. New York.

Natasha knocked on Oberon's office door.

'Come in,' he said, looking up from his computer screen.

Natasha walked into the room. Oberon glanced at her sideways. She seemed nervous.

'What's the matter, Natasha?'

'I'm going to need to access the vault, sir.'

'Why?'

'The tablet is back in Malibu, isn't it?'

'Yes it is. What's going on, Natasha?'

'Something very strange, sir. The three translators have disappeared, as well as the camera I used to photograph the tablet.'

'Did you copy the digital images on our server?'

'Yes sir.'

'And?' he asked patiently.

'They're gone too', she answered, looking away.

'What? How is this possible?' he blurted out.

'Someone hacked into our system and deleted the files and that same someone stole my camera from my own office.'

'Don't we have security systems?' he asked.

'I checked last night's CCTV recordings but all they show is a blank image. Either they were all out of order or someone disabled the cameras.'

Oberon was furious.

'You're in charge of security!' He screamed at her, 'That's why I pay you so much. And you don't have a single god damn answer?'

'I need to fly right now to Malibu and check the vault.'

'You'll leave this office when I say so. I want you to get to the bottom of this. The vault's security is state of the art.'

'But…' began Natasha.

'But what?' asked Oberon.

'This is the work of someone who is highly trained and extremely clever. I think he or they are after the tablet. It could be Mina Osman and her friend.'

'Mina Osman? You must be joking,' he spat with contempt.

'No, her partner. He handled three of my best men in Mosul as if they were boy scouts, retrieved Mina Osman from the bottom of the Mediterranean Sea and shot his way out of Safed. I'm sorry sir, but I think we're dealing with a tough son of a bitch.'

'OK. Find out who he is. We leave for the mansion tomorrow morning. Set up the flight. Make sure there is extra security at the mansion tonight.'

'I'm on it,' she answered and left the room.

Oberon tapped nervously on the mahogany desk, and then picked up his laptop and hurled it against the wall.

⌇

Malibu suburbs. Early afternoon.

Ephraim had left New York a few hours earlier, having successfully erased all data pertaining to the tablet from Oberon's offices. He'd been lying naked on his bed for hours in this tiny Malibu motel room with the curtains drawn. Two guns were carefully placed on the bed stand as well as a set of darts, the sharp end covered in a dark substance. Standing up, he had read Shobai's email over and over again, until he knew its lines by heart. He opened up his suitcase, and reached for a vial. He pulled out its stopper and a pungent fragrance immediately filled the room. He poured some oil into the palm of his hand and started applying it to his skin. When his entire body was covered in oil, he stood in the middle of the room and faced east. He closed his eyes and began chanting an incantation in a low, rhythmic voice.

'Great Caliel, I adjure thee by thy great name, thee angel of clarity and justice, *Shofteni betsidkekha adonai elohay ve'al Yismekhu li.*'

He then moistened his skin with pure water from another vial and continued his incantations:

'Make me invisible, lord Caliel, in the presence of any man from sunset till sunrise. Amen.'

He sat down, crossing his legs, and remained utterly still. A few hours later, he rose from his seated position. Outside, the sun was slowly setting. He moved so slowly that the contours of his body seemed to fade, or blend somehow with the surrounding darkness. He flexed his muscles and thought to himself, 'It is time.'

⇝

Hildersham, Mulberry Cottage

Joshua Bamart was bringing wood from the garden into the house, when he heard someone knocking at the door. He called out to Mina from the bottom of the stairs, 'Mina, could you open the front door, please. I've got an armful of fire wood right now.'

'Of course Joshua, I'm coming down.'

Her mind still lost in various letters she had been reading in Joshua's archive, Mina climbed down the stairs, and opened the front door to find Jack standing on the doorstep, with a beaming smile. She thought her heart had stopped beating.

'So? You're going to leave me standing here?' asked Jack.

'Oh Jack, I can't believe you're actually here!' She said and threw her arms around him.

Old Bamart was building a fire while Jack and Mina sat comfortably in their armchairs. When he was satisfied the fire had picked up momentum, Bamart sat down.

'A cup of tea Joshua?' asked Mina.

'A nice cup of tea, Mina, a nice cup of tea. Yes please,' he smiled at her.

He turned to Jack, sizing him up.

'So, Jack, are you also a scholar from New York?'

'No sir, I'm from Washington and I'm an engineer.'

'Please, have a scone,' Joshua said to Jack, offering him a plate covered with scones and another with a pot of thick clotted cream and raspberry jam.

'Thanks. I'm so glad I found Mina in the end. She lost her mobile phone and I found out she was staying with you from the people at the Genizah Unit.'

'Well, we'll have to find you a room in the house as well, I suppose.'

'Well, thanks. I was going to stay at a hotel in Cambridge. Are you quite sure?'

'Of course I am.'

'That's mighty kind of you,' Jack replied.

Jack thought Joshua seemed sad, as he left the house with Mina to go for a walk in the village.

'What's his story, Mina?'

'He's such a lovely person. He reminds me in some ways of Professor Almeini. You'll get along just fine. I think he's sad because he probably thought I'd be a good match for his son. He also seems to think I'm Jewish and I haven't really had the opportunity to correct him.'

'His son?'

'Yes, Daniel, he's a Hebrew scholar at the UL. He's a really nice guy, a bit on the geeky side. It's thanks to him that I found this place.'

'That was quick thinking,' Jack said, trying not to show his displeasure at the notion of a 'nice guy' inviting Mina to live with him, and his father's matchmaking plans. His sarcastic tone didn't escape Mina.

'What do you expect? You abandon me in London and you think I'm just going to sit in some nasty guest house and wait for Oberon Wheatley's assassins to murder me?'

'I'm sorry. I wish things were different. You did the right thing. And no-one would think to look for you here.'

They walked up the main street towards the local church. Mina opened the gate leading into the church yard, and she led the way to its side entrance. They stood outside as she spoke.

'I came here yesterday already and there's something strange about this church. In fact, everything about this church is weird. Especially the paintings inside, which are made to look like they come straight from the Middle Ages, but in fact were produced in the 19th century. Mind you, the building itself goes back many centuries.'

'It's beautiful,' said Jack.

'It's even more beautiful inside. You'll see. But before we enter, look up at the coats of arms which line the upper walls,' she said.

'Right. And?' he asked.

'Look at this one, with the circles and the lines between them.'

'Is it a coat of arms? Who does it belong to?' asked Jack.

'I don't know, but it doesn't matter. This is a simplified version of a really famous diagram, the Kabbalistic tree of life.'

'Come on Mina, I think we've spent too much time conspiring together. You're seeing things.'

'No. I know I'm right. Check it later on. You'll find it on any website about Kabbalah. It represents many things, including the mystical *sefirot* that Eli told us about in Safed'

'And in English?'

'Think of these circles as spheres of knowledge, or *sefirot*, to approach the divine, step by step.'

'OK. I agree. It's weird to find this here. What about the rest of the church?'

'That's where it gets interesting. Let's go in.'

As Jack and Mina walked into the church, a dark shape moved out of the trees and closer to the building. The man was holding a small device in his hand which he had been pointing towards the couple since they started their walk. It was a 'shotgun' microphone, a directional sound-locating device. It was specifically designed for medium range frequencies, which allowed its user to isolate and pick up distant human voices. He hadn't missed one word of Jack and Mina's conversation so far. It would be more difficult to hear what they said now that they had entered the church.

'This church's amazing. It's like a precious jewel lost in the fields,' said Jack.

'Yes. Don't you feel it's all *too* good? asked Mina. 'What do you think of those wall paintings?' she asked.

'The colours are so vivid. But the style of the paintings is medieval. Were they restored?'

'That's the point, they're made to look medieval, but they're not. No. Everything's fake here. The most ancient thing in this church is the altar slab.' She let the word hang, waiting for Jack's reaction.

'No…' said Jack, 'You're not trying to tell me that the Jerusalem tablet is right here, under our noses?'

'Why not? Why couldn't the tablet be hidden under the altar slab, or be the altar slab itself?'

'There's only one way to find out. We'll get some tools from Joshua's shed and return tomorrow to check it out.'

'Alright,' answered Mina. 'But if we do, we must be very careful not to break anything. If the tablet is part of the altar, we just take a photograph and put it back in its place. I feel uneasy about desecrating an altar but especially because Joshua is the keeper of the church.'

'I thought he was Jewish?' asked Jack.

'He is, but he makes sure the church is cared for and plays the organ from time to time. Never mind. You'll be careful, won't you?'

'Of course, Mina.'

In the evening, after dinner, they all sat by the fire. Joshua spoke of the magic of the Gog Magog hills just outside Cambridge, of the strange stone circle nearby and the ancient Roman road you could still follow from Cambridge to Linton. Jack and Mina were fascinated by their host's every word.

Chapter 25

December 17th, 2004. Hildersham

Jack and Mina both woke up to a loud wailing coming from downstairs. They rushed out of their respective rooms and bumped into each other in the corridor.

'Did you hear that?' asked Jack.

'Yes. It's Joshua,' she said alarmed, as she ran down the stairs.

The old man was sitting in his armchair. Mina approached him carefully.

'Joshua? Is Daniel alright?'

'Oh God, oh God,' he kept repeating.

'What is it Joshua?'

He looked at her with vacant eyes and said, 'It's gone.'

Mina and Jack looked at each other in total incomprehension. They both knelt next to Joshua, and Mina held his hand.

'Talk to me Joshua,' she whispered to him kindly.

A car pulled out near the house. A few moments later, Daniel opened the front door. He saw an expression on his father's face that he hadn't seen since the day his mother died. Mina was by his side with another man.

'What's going on here?' he shouted.

Mina walked up to Daniel and said, 'I don't know. We just

came running down the stairs when we heard your dad screaming. He's been like this ever since!'

'And who are you?' Daniel asked Jack.

Mina answered for Jack, 'This is my friend I told you about. He arrived yesterday afternoon.'

'Hi, I'm Jack,' he said.

'Daniel', replied Daniel quickly before kneeling at his father's side.

'Dad, what's happened?'

Old Bamart took a deep breath, and sighed.

'I went to the church early this morning and…' he broke off.

'And?' asked Mina.

'And the church was vandalised during the night.'

'What?' said Jack and Mina simultaneously.

Daniel looked at them suspiciously.

'The altar was smashed and…and an object I care about was stolen,' said Joshua wearily.

'What was stolen, Dad?' asked Daniel.

'I can't speak of it here,' he replied, glancing at Jack and Mina.

But Mina quickly interjected, 'You can Joshua. I think I know what you're talking about. Was a cuneiform tablet stolen from the altar last night?'

He looked at her in wonder.

'You knew?'

'What does she know, Dad? What the hell's going on here?' asked Daniel.

'I think it's best if Mina and I filled you in on what we're really doing here,' Jack suggested.

An hour later, after much talking, all four sat in silence, their faces drained of colour.

'So you've been a keeper of this Jerusalem tablet all your life and you never told me a thing,' Daniel asked his father in disbelief.

'I'm sorry son. I was not to share this secret until I felt my life ebbing away, like my father before me and his father before him. I'm still in shock to learn that Mina and Jack found a letter from my ancestor.'

'How did all this begin?' asked Mina.

'Well, the letter you found was written by Alejandro Cardozo, my ancestor who settled at Mulberry Cottage in the 18th century. He was a Portuguese Jewish scholar whose real name was Yeshua Ben Moshe. He probably came from a Marranos family, you know the 'secret Jews' who remained in Spain and Portugal after Jews had been outlawed there in 1492 but took on a Christian name.'

'Hmm, certainly not one of Portugal's finest hours… talking of which, I thought Jews weren't allowed at Cambridge University until at least the 19th century?' Mina said.

'He wasn't working for the University. He first arrived in London where he stayed with the large Sephardi community which had settled there centuries earlier. And, just like it says in the letter you found, one of the Cardozo brothers had moved from Portugal to Safed where he set up a printing business. Yeshua was the eldest, and as such was entrusted with the tablet. That's how it ended up in England.'

'What happened then?' asked Daniel astonished.

'He was employed by the local vicar, here in Hildersham.'

'To do what, Dad?' asked Daniel

'The churchman was an antiquarian of sorts, and as many

other Christian biblical scholars of the time, he had been trying to go beyond the Vulgate, to unlock the full potential of the Jewish Bible.'

'Sorry guys, what's the Vulgate?' asked Jack.

'It's the name for St. Jerome's translation of the Old Testament in Latin,' replied Mina.

'He must have entrusted the vicar with the tablet he brought from Portugal, and ended up becoming the unofficial keeper of the Church of the Holy Trinity...and now it is gone.'

They all sat in silence, deep in their own thoughts. Daniel wondered why and when his family name had changed from Cardozo to Bamart.

'Who did this Jack?' asked Mina.

'I don't think it's Wheatley, he doesn't have a clue about the clay tablet. I guess I was followed from the library to Hildersham by our mysterious and relentless pursuers, I'm so sorry!'

There wasn't much more to add. The tablet was gone forever. Whoever these men were, they'd won. Jack was furious at having been duped but there was nothing he could do about it.

⌒

Same day. New York. Private airfield.

Natasha and Oberon were waiting in the car for the private jet to land and fly them to Malibu. As the jet finally made its descent onto the airfield runway with a screeching sound, Oberon's mobile phone rang.

'Yes?' answered Oberon.

'It's John, sir, in Malibu. I don't know what to say.'

'What is it? We're about to leave.'

'Someone was in the vault last night. The concealed door was open when I entered the house.'

'What? What did they steal?' Oberon spluttered… his precious private collection…

'I don't know sir.'

'Right. Walk back to the vault right now and call me when you're standing near the large wall painting with a tower.'

'Do you think the tablet's gone?' asked Natasha anxiously.

'I certainly hope not,' he snapped.

The phone rang.

'It's me sir. I'm in.'

'On my desk. There should be a thin stone tablet.'

'I can't see anything of the sort, sir.'

'A shiny flat stone, black.'

'No. Nothing like that, sir.'

Wheatley felt his heart plummet, 'And you didn't see anyone approaching the house?' Oberon asked.

'No sir. I don't understand. We had two teams of four men guarding the house and the grounds throughout the night.'

'Go through all the CCTV footage and get back to me within the hour.'

'Yes sir.'

Oberon felt like strangling someone right now.

'Natasha?'

'Yes, sir?' she answered, taking a step backwards.

'Any luck finding out who Mina Osman's partner is? Did you call our friend in Intelligence?'

'Yes. All he knew was that someone called Jack Hillcliff may be involved but it was unconfirmed.'

'Find out everything you can about him, his family, everything!'

﹏

Hildersham. Evening.

'You know Jack…the more I think about it, the more I'm convinced our pursuers might be Jewish. It's as if some age-old biblical tale is unfolding before our very eyes.' Mina and Jack were chatting quietly in the kitchen.

'So you don't think it was Wheatley's men or Muslim fanatics?' asked Jack.

'No.'

'That doesn't make sense Mina. All the Jews we've encountered or read about want the tablet deciphered.'

'Not all of them Jack. Remember Eli's translation? There was a rabbi whose name was crossed out, the one who'd stolen Benjamin of Tudela's letter. What if he had created around him a following? A kind of sect who aimed to eliminate all traces of the tablet and now their descendants are after us?'

Jack went mute for a moment and then said, 'It's pretty far fetched, but it would explain a number of things. Remember the commentary Eli had found which warned people against the "Dark Ones"?' We are still not sure what that means.

He seemed to be deep in thought.

'What are you thinking Jack?' she asked.

'I think we haven't yet met our fiercest enemies.'

Chapter 26

December 18th, 2004. Hildersham

Wearing warm overcoats borrowed from the Bamarts, Jack and Mina walked on the icy pavement to the church to look at it one last time. It was late morning and the sky seemed vast and empty. Mina felt as if she were on a pilgrimage to a desecrated relic. They sat in the church, on the front pew, side by side.

'So that's it, Mina. We should make tracks.'

Mina didn't seem to have heard what he'd just said.

'It's amazing to think that the tablet was here since the 18th century, and no-one ever thought of looking,' she said, pondering out loud.

'Clearly, our not-so-mysterious enemies did think about it!'

'What do you mean by not-so-mysterious?' asked Mina, suddenly more attentive.

'I acted on your hunch last night. I called Shobai.'

'And?'

'The phone line was disconnected, so I asked my contact in London to pass by Shobai's house.'

'And?'

'He was gone, as was all his furniture. He moved out, without leaving a trace.'

'So you think he was behind it all?' asked Mina.

'Possibly. He had the knowledge and the means to plan it and carry it out.'

'I don't know. He was strange of course…the way he avoided some of my questions.'

'I'm sure he knew much more than he let on.'

'That's possible, I suppose, but I still find it difficult to see him as our Nemesis,' said Mina.

'If he is, I wonder how long he's been after the tablet.'

'Well, if you're right about him, since around the 16th century,' Mina exclaimed. 'And that means Shobai is the descendent of the man whose name was crossed out so many times in the rabbi's chronicle,' she added in disbelief.

Jack didn't reply.

'Can you imagine how fanatical Shobai would have had to be to relentlessly pursue and destroy all records of the tablet, and with such ruthlessness?' said Mina.

'Yes, I can,' said Jack, very seriously.

'Well I can't picture it. Call me naïve, but he may have left his house in a hurry because he was terrified by the very people who are after us.'

Jack kept his thoughts to himself. They walked out of the church, across the yard and past a barren mulberry tree. Mina reflected she would never be there to taste its fruit. She would probably return to New York and get her life back together. They walked down the street heading back to Mulberry Cottage. As they crossed a small bridge, Mina stopped to look at a local area map stuck onto a wooden notice board. It had started to rain and dark clouds were gathering in the sky.

'Come on Mina,' said Jack, 'we should get going. The weather's changing.'

'Just a second,' she replied.

Jack watched Mina, standing in the middle of the road, thoughtful and completely oblivious to the rain. She suddenly started running to Mulberry Cottage and he followed closely. They walked into the house, soaking wet, and Mina rushed up to Joshua.

'Joshua, do you know of a place called Noah's Ark?' she asked him impatiently.

'I'm sorry?' he replied, looking up at a drenched Mina.

'In the fields, not too far from the bridge?' she added.

'Ah, yes. Noah's Ark. It's a very small patch of land.'

'Why is it called that?' she asked.

'The local farmers call it that.'

'But why?'

'I'll show you,' he sighed. 'I need a walk anyway.'

'I'll come too,' said Daniel.

The four companions walked out into the fields, the rain beating hard against their umbrellas. They followed the river bank for about a hundred meters and then Joshua pointed to a slightly raised patch of land with an ancient and magnificent tree standing at its centre, its branches dark and long, stretching into the wind.

'It's a strange thing really,' Joshua said. 'We often get flash-floods here, even in the winter and what happens is truly amazing. As you know, this is the Fens region, flat lands, with fields as far as the eye can see, so locals know every mound, hill and dip in the landscape around them. Anyway, when flooding occurs in Hildersham, all the sheep flock as one to this spot, which is on slightly higher ground. Probably for that reason, it has always been called Noah's Ark. It isn't much of a hill, but enough not to be covered with water when the river overflows its banks.'

Mina had noticed a large quantity of nettles surrounding the mound. She made a small sign to Jack and Daniel to follow her to the other side of the tree.

'We need to come back here tonight,' said Mina 'discreetly, with shovels. We shouldn't tell your dad anything, Daniel. I don't want to raise his hopes, just in case I'm wrong about this.'

'What are you on about, Mina?' asked Daniel.

'This is no ordinary patch of land. This is what we call a 'tell' in archaeology, a mound, and the nettles here are a sign that the earth contains high levels of nitrates. Human bodies may have been buried here and perhaps other things too.'

She turned to Jack, 'I don't believe in coincidences anymore.'

∿

Same day. Hackney warehouse, London.
Shobai was furious. The tablet his men had brought back was an ancient wedding contract written in Akkadian.

'Ephraim was successful in Malibu, which means that this is your last mission. You two need to return to Hildersham tonight and follow Mina Osman. Find and destroy the tablet. Now go.'

∿

Hildersham. Mulberry Cottage
'So what do you work on exactly, Daniel?' asked Mina. 'All you told me was that you were in Hebrew studies.'

'I work on a number of magical papyri found in Alexandria.'

'Wow. Greek or Jewish papyri?' she asked.

'Both,' he answered, with pride.

'You know there are loads of similar magical Akkadian inscriptions' she said.

'I know. I've read many translations of omens you guys have found on cuneiform tablets. They're fascinating,' Daniel replied.

'Academics,' thought Jack, and he rolled his eyes. 'They might be standing on the brink of disaster but they'll chat about *fascinating inscriptions*. Unbelievable.'

'Well, if you're into magic, Daniel,' said Jack, interrupting the scholars, 'there's still something I don't understand.'

'What's that?' asked Daniel, lying back against the couch.

'How those bastards eluded me so many times,' said Jack.

'They're well trained, I suppose,' said Daniel.

'I'm sure they are but believe me Daniel, I'm well trained too,' Jack replied.

'Well, how do you explain it?' asked Daniel, with an air of satisfaction.

'I can't,' said Jack, 'all I can say is that although I couldn't *see* them until it was too late, I could *sense* their presence. At the British Museum, Mina and I both realised that whenever they were close to us, we caught a whiff of a strange smell. That's probably how I was sensing their presence, without being aware that it was their smell.'

'What sort of smell was it?' asked Daniel.

'It's difficult to describe. Wait a minute,' he searched his pockets and retrieved the shard of the vial he had picked up after the fight at the British Museum. He handed it to Daniel.

'I know this smell,' said Daniel.

'You do?' asked Jack, genuinely impressed.

'Yes, it's oil,' replied Daniel, feverishly, his eyes lit up.

'Duh. Thanks Daniel, I'd never have guessed.'

'No, it's *the* oil,' Daniel whispered. 'It's temple oil, Abramelin's oil, whatever you want to call it.'

'What's wrong with the two of you,' said Jack, looking at Mina and Daniel. 'Don't you ever speak English?'

'I'm pretty lost myself,' admitted Mina.

'OK,' said Daniel, 'I'm sure you've seen countless images of witches stirring weird magical potions in large cauldrons, right?'

'Yes,' replied Jack.

'Well Abramelin's oil is the ultimate potion. I'm no expert in this, as I'm interested in ancient magical texts, but *The Book of Abramelin* is a treatise on magic. It was given by an Egyptian magus, Abra-Melin, to Abraham of Worms, a German Jew who lived in the early 15th century. It was used in the last century by people like Alistair Crowley and his secretive followers. According to some scholars, the text itself might have been the invention of another German Jewish Talmudist, Rabbi Yaakov Moelin, who also lived in the early 15th century.'

'So what?' asked Jack, impatiently.

'All in good time,' said Mina, smiling at Daniel to continue.

'What else can you expect from an action hero?' Daniel answered.

Jack scowled at him for a moment, then laughed along with them.

'So, the oil?' prompted Jack, gently.

'Well, as far as I understand it, Abramelin oil is a version of the holy temple oil, as described in Exodus 30. Its ingredients are practically the same.'

He picked up a bible from his father's library. He searched for the exact passage and then read out loud, 'It's in Exodus 30:22–29. *The Lord said to Moses, 'Take the finest spices: five*

hundred shekels of free-flowing myrrh; half that amount, that is,
two hundred and fifty shekels, of fragrant cinnamon; two hundred
and fifty shekels of fragrant cane; five hundred shekels of cassia-all
according to the standard of the sanctuary shekel; together with
a hin of olive oil; and blend them into sacred anointing oil, per-
fumed ointment expertly prepared. With this sacred anointing oil
you shall anoint the meeting tent and the ark of the command-
ments, the table and all its appurtenances, the lamp stand and
its appurtenances, the altar of incense and the altar of holocausts
with all its appurtenances, and the laver with its base. When you
have consecrated them, they shall be most sacred; whatever touches
them shall be sacred.'

'Those are all very strong fragrances and this oil could well
be it,' said Mina as she took another whiff of the vial.

Jack was mighty impressed by the young Cambridge scholar.
'I think you're right,' he said to Daniel.

'If these men managed to perform the so-called Abramelin operation, it means they know how to use it for magical
purposes.'

'Like what? Flying carpets?' asked Jack.

'...Like becoming invisible for a few hours,' replied Daniel.

They all went silent.

'Is that even possible?' said Jack.

'Who knows what is or isn't possible?' said Daniel. 'They
believe it is possible and that should tell you a lot about them.'

'Yeah. They're out of their fucking minds,' said Jack.

'We should all be extra careful from now on' said Daniel. 'If
Mina is right, and they took a fake tablet of some sort, they
might return.'

'They might,' agreed Jack, 'I think you should stay here with
your father tonight.'

'He's right,' said Mina.

'Alright,' said Daniel.

⌒

Around midnight, Jack and Mina returned to the fields with torches and shovels. The weather had taken a turn for the worse. With the force of the wind, the rain was falling almost horizontally.

'I wonder if this is such a great idea,' said Jack.

'We must try,' Mina answered, shivering under her umbrella.

When they reached the tree, Jack dropped the shovels and straightened his raincoat.

'Where should I start digging?' he asked Mina.

'Right here, a few paces from the tree.'

Half an hour later, Jack hit against some stones. He wanted to use the pickaxe to pull them out, but Mina showed him how, in standard archaeological fashion, to dig along the edges of the subterranean wall.

'We must follow the wall, to find the corners,' she said.

Jack was sweating profusely under his raincoat, as he laboured in the mud. From time to time, he looked down below at the riverbank, at the waters rising by the minute. After a while, he had uncovered the remains of a tiny stone walled room. On the room's ground level, below the vestiges of the roofing, which had caved in centuries ago, they found dozens of neatly arranged skeletons.

'I feel terrible doing this at night, in these conditions' said Mina.

'You're not the one digging,' Jack reminded her.

'That's not what I meant.'

'I know what you meant. Whatever we find, I'll cover the bodies when we've finished.'

'Thanks Jack,' she replied.

'Hey, what's that?' Jack said suddenly.

'What?'

'There, in the inner corner, one of the skeletons seems to be sitting upright, holding some rotting wood.'

Mina stepped down into the room, to examine the wooden remains more closely. She started digging between the skeleton's legs, and found a small metal box.

'The box must have been encased in wood,' she said to Jack.

'Well, pick it up!'

Jack held the umbrella above her, as she climbed out of the room, carrying the box. She pried it open with a screwdriver and to Jack and Mina's boundless joy, there it was: a baked clay tablet, covered with cuneiform writing.

⌒

Dark clothed men had been watching Mina and Jack all along. The time had now come for them to act. They crept slowly up towards the mound, but out of the corner of his eye Jack suddenly caught sight of their shapes moving below.

'Down, Mina,' he bellowed, 'get down! They're here.'

One of the men shouted from below, 'Miss Osman, Major, hand over the tablet and you will not be harmed.'

'You mean like Eli in Safed?' said Jack as he reached for the guy tucked into his waistband and tried to figure out through the pounding rain where they were.

'Hand over the tablet,' the man shouted again.

Jack assessed their situation. He was at the top of a tiny hill in the middle of fields. They had no escape route.

'Mina,' he hissed, 'take a photograph of the tablet, quickly.'

She was petrified.

'Mina!' he repeated.

'My camera's flash doesn't work. What should I do?' she asked.

'Don't you have your notebook?' he muttered.

'Yes.'

'Well get on with it,' Jack replied instantly 'while I think of something.'

Mina started copying the signs on the tablet as fast as she could, but it was hard work, writing while holding an umbrella at the same time.

'Hand it over,' yelled the man from below, 'and you have our word you won't be harmed. We're only interested in the tablet.'

'So you work for Shobai?' shouted Jack. 'He doesn't mind murdering old men?'

'That was a mistake, our brother shouldn't have killed the old man in Safed. All we want is the tablet.'

By this time, the river had broken its banks and overflowed into the fields, which were so flat the water quickly reached the lower part of the mound. Jack looked at Mina, scribbling away feverishly in her notebook. He had to gain more time. He heard the man shouting something from below.

'You're still there?' asked Jack to the voice down below.

'Yes,' said the man.

'You're still there?' repeated Jack, pretending not to hear.

'Major, I told you, I am not going without the tablet,' said the man.

'What do you want with it?' asked Jack.

'That is not your concern. We don't want to harm you. Just give us the tablet. You will never see us again.'

Jack turned to Mina and whispered, 'Have you finished?'

'Almost,' she replied. She looked up and saw the water rising almost to her feet. She yelped. 'How are we going to get out of here Jack?'

'We'll swim if need be,' he replied grimly.

Jack suddenly realised he shouldn't have wasted time talking to Mina. He had misjudged his opponents. There were two of them, but he had been speaking to only one. Where was the other man? He quickly turned around and there he was, climbing the other side of the mound. He had circled it while Jack was foolishly trying to gain precious time by bartering with the other man. It was too late. Before he could dive behind the tree, the man shot Jack twice. The force of the impact spun him around, and with a thud, he fell down on the sodden ground.

'Jack!' screamed Mina.

The man then took a shot at Mina, who instinctively flung her arms up to protect her face. The bullet hit the clay tablet still clutched in her hands, which shattered into tiny pieces and plopped into the rising waters. In shock, she watched the pieces sink into nothingness.

'Yakov, we must go. We're done here,' shouted the first man, from down below.

'I'm coming,' he called, throwing a last look at a pitiful Mina, who had crawled to Jack's body and was hugging him to her, her tears merging with the steady rain.

〜

'Are they gone?' muttered Jack.

'You're alive? Oh Jack, I thought you were dead!'

'Have they gone?' he asked again, weakly.

'Yes,' she answered.

'I think he shot me below the shoulder, I'm losing a lot of blood. The other bullet just grazed my wrist. We need to get back to the cottage.'

He was breathing heavily and his head was spinning. They waded through the muddy water, Mina supporting him most of the way, until they reached the main road which, fortunately, wasn't flooded. From there they managed to make faster progress back to the cottage. As they reached it, Jack slumped, unconscious, on the doorstep, finally overcome.

Chapter 27

December 20th. Hildersham. Mulberry Cottage

Mina stayed by Jack's bedside in the upstairs room for two days. When they had returned on that fateful night, Joshua had made up his mind quickly. Although Jack had lost a lot of blood he was confident he could take care of him at home rather than take him to hospital, where they would have had to explain the gunshot wound. Jack had drifted in and out of consciousness the first night and had slept through most of the next day. This morning Joshua had pronounced that he was out of danger and was recovering. Mina thanked the heavens in a silent prayer, and kissed Jack's brow.

Joshua and Daniel were sitting downstairs, discussing Mina's notes. The night she returned with Jack, she gave Daniel what was left of her soaked notebook. He had managed to salvage most of it, but some parts were missing. On the second day, Mina had translated *viva voce* what was left of the cuneiform inscription she had copied in the storm, and this was what Joshua and Daniel were now discussing.

'There you are, Mina. How's Jack?' asked Daniel.

'He's much better. We spoke a little, but he fell asleep again.'

'I'm still stupefied,' Joshua said to Mina, 'to realise that the tablet was hidden under Noah's Ark and not in the church.

'I still think it's horseshit,' said Jack, 'the only thing this
blet does is give a few exact moments in the sky. It's astro-
omical information.'

'He's right you know,' said Mina to Daniel.

'He might be right, but how did they find these dates or
laces, if not through astrology?' asked Daniel.

'That, I don't know,' she answered, 'it could be through a
umber of different observations. We don't have that part of
he text.'

'OK. Jack, what about dates?' asked Daniel.

But Jack had already fallen asleep.

I cared for this church all my life and my father before me!
Never mind, I'll probably never be able to resolve that mystery.
How do you feel about talking over your translation of the
tablet?' Joshua asked.

'Alright,' replied Mina.

'OK. Unfortunately, we've lost the introductory elements so
I don't know how the Babylonian scientists made their predictions,' said Daniel.

'They weren't really scientists, you know, Daniel,' replied
Mina.

'Are we going to quibble about terminology?' asked Daniel.

'No, no. So what do we have?'

'We have a series of omens and lots of equations. I don't
know if they are dates, astronomical precisions, places, or
something else. I just can't tell.'

At that moment, they heard footsteps coming down the
stairs.

'Jack,' said Mina, 'are you crazy? You should be resting right
now.'

'I've rested enough, and I can't leave the three of you to
figure it all out without me.' They laughed. Daniel fetched
cushions for Jack, as he fell into an armchair.

'Man, I'm exhausted,' Jack said. 'So where were you?'

'Well, we were just assessing what we've got so far,' said
Daniel.

'And?' asked Jack.

'Not much. Have a look,' he said, handing him Mina's
translation of the tablet.

After a few moments, Jack put the notes down, 'I have an
idea. It isn't really my field but I think some of these are mathematical equations, a little basic, but very effective in flood

management. I had no idea they were so advanced. I mean, really. Sure, there have always been floods, but we have always considered flood management to be something new.'

'But what about ancient dams, Jack?' said Mina.

'There's more to flood management than just a dam. How do you build a dam? Which material do you choose, inclinations, localisation, height, etc. and for each new variable, new equations. We're talking about complex systems.'

'And can you tell which equations have to do with flood management techniques?' asked Daniel.

'Maybe,' said Jack.

'Fantastic,' said Mina, 'could you do that while we work on the rest? But take it easy.'

'Alright. First I will take a nap,' he replied, smiling at Mina.

∽

Later that evening, Jack woke up in the armchair to find Mina and Daniel's heads almost touching, so focused were they on the translation. Mina turned around to see Jack's pointed gaze, drilling an imaginary hole into Daniel's skull. She gave him a look in return which said 'You're being silly.'

Knowing that he was still watching her, she pretended to yawn and stretched her back, lifting her arms above her head and arching her back towards Jack. He was mesmerised by the outline of her figure under her tight jeans. Had he not been recovering from a serious wound, he would have grabbed her by the waist there and then and pulled her to him. Instead all he could do was stare.

Daniel sat up suddenly, totally oblivious to what was passing between Jack and Mina.

'We've made some progress, but we'll need you the equations,' said Daniel.

'Alright, alright. I'll get down to it. I'll need a pen

'Here you go,' Daniel said, handing him what he

Jack read through Mina's translation and understoo had been so transfixed. It was a maze of calculations, within the biblical flood narrative. It was very weird, clearly it was done on purpose to hide their findings later, he had finished.

'Here you go,' he said. Mina and Daniel turne together.

'Can you explain what you've found, Jack?'

'Well, I've highlighted what I think are equations flood management, and what I think is astronomica

'That's great. Astrological information could be th Daniel.

'I said astronomy,' said Jack, 'don't go confusi with hocus pocus astrology.'

'What do you mean?' asked Daniel.

'I'll tell you what I mean,' replied Jack. 'The hundred and fifty billion stars in our own galaxy a hundred billion galaxies swirling about in space. T stars in space to be influencing or predetermining sonality, or his direction in life. How many plan did Babylonian astrologers know and use at the ti many are used today?'

'That's not the point,' said Daniel. 'Babylor focused on predicting events that affected the ent its cities. Whatever it is today, astrology then was predict future meteorological events, earthquakes,

Chapter 28

December 21st, 2004. Hildersham. Mulberry Cottage

Mina peeped through Jack's door. 'Morning Jack.'

Jack had had a rough night, but he felt better this morning.

'Morning beautiful.' She came and sat on the edge of his bed.

'We're making progress,' she said. 'Come down for breakfast and we'll tell you all about it.'

'You know, if you'd rather I stayed up here, just tell me. I'll leave the two of you alone,' said Jack.

'Jack, you aren't really jealous of Daniel, are you?' Mina asked, grinning.

'Me. Never. Why? Should I be?'

'No, you shouldn't,' she said, and she slowly bent down to kiss him.

Just as they were about to share their first kiss, they heard Joshua at the door and sprung up out like guilty teenagers. Joshua came in to check on his patient. After examining him, he announced that he was quite satisfied with his condition.

'Jack, I'm amazed by your recovery. You must be made of steel,' he said appreciatively.

'I know, doc,' it's my curse,' said Jack with a smile.

'You're almost as good as new,' said Joshua.

'It's all thanks to you. I owe you one.'

'Bring this whole matter to a close and you won't owe me anything.'

'I'll do my best,' said Jack.

⌇

When Jack eventually came downstairs, he found Mina and Daniel sitting at the breakfast table, arguing about the notes, which put Jack in an excellent mood.

'We're not getting anywhere,' said Mina.

'I don't agree,' said Daniel.

'What's going on?' Jack said, pulling up a chair.

But Mina went on regardless. 'Alright Daniel, maybe you're right, but how do you explain the term *ocean of water*?'

'It must be an image to describe the huge scale of the flood.'

'And the *mouth of the earth*?'

'That I don't know. I've thought about it the entire night and I still don't have a clue.'

'But what sort of river flood are they talking about?' asked Jack, 'what sort of flood could be that awful that they'd think of warning us thousands of years ago? Are we talking about a major city?'

'That's why we may be wrong in our interpretation of the text,' said Daniel.

'What if my first guess was wrong, and what I took for flood management measurements were actually successive dates, maybe crypted?' said Jack.

'Come on Jack, Daniel has been at this for days,' said Mina.

'I don't know,' said Jack, 'even if we had a perfect description of a star position, we'd still need another event to compare it with.'

'Mina, he may be right. Let me try out his theory.'

Daniel stayed at the kitchen table, covering sheets with calculations. Suddenly he looked up, dazed and rushed to his laptop. He opened the internet and typed in '1755 flood.' As he read through the results, his face drained of colour. Jack and Mina looked at him, as he frantically scribbled more calculations. After a while, he turned to Mina and Jack, horror-struck, and motioned for them to approach the screen.

'Jack was right. It is a date. I thought to myself, we have a date, 1755, the year the letter was sent to Safed from Hildersham. It's a weird letter. There's no other correspondence between the two places. What if Alejandro Cardozo and his family fled Portugal for some imperative reason and needed to write to say the tablet was safe? What if something dramatic happened in 1755? Well something did happen that year: the Lisbon earthquake. It's one of the worst earthquakes ever recorded in history and it was followed by a horrifying tidal wave on November 1st, 1755, at about 10.25 am. It killed over sixty thousand people.'

Mina did not respond. Her smile had vanished. She was thinking back to the letter Yeshua had written to his brother. It was dated December 1755. So Yeshua had left Lisbon with his family after the earthquake. Had he known how to use the tablet, surely he'd have left the city weeks beforehand. So why had he taken the tablet with him? She could only conclude that it was his duty to preserve the family's treasure out of respect for his ancestors. And, as it said in his letter, he'd keep on taking care of the tablet until the day it could be returned to the Jerusalem temple and used appropriately. 'Simply stupefying,' thought Mina.

'When and where will the next natural disaster hit?' asked Jack, whose brain, as ever, was trying to ignore the horrifying details and move to practical considerations.

'Oh I think I know,' said Daniel.

'So, tell us!' said Jack and Mina in unison.

'I calculated backwards from 1755 to find out what the date would have been in Babylonian terms... I used an online calculator. It seems that some astronomers spend a lot of time writing such software. To cut a long story short, the next gigantic natural disaster, whatever form it takes – earthquake, flood, eruption or other – will happen on 26th December, 2014. But we have no idea where it will hit. I wish we still possessed the stone tablet I found in Mosul. Maybe the clue was there? What are we supposed to do? I mean, we can't exactly make a list of all the great rivers, volcanoes, seismic faults in the world and warn everyone living nearby, can we?'

⌐

Daniel came running into the room where Jack was re-checking his calculations.

'Jack! Mina has found out where it will hit.'

They both went to the kitchen.

'Boys,' said Mina, 'I'm pretty sure it will hit in the middle of the Indian Ocean. I've calculated the planetary and star alignment described in the text, and it corresponds roughly to the sky map on the 26th above the middle of the Indian Ocean.'

Jack looked at her calculations dubiously, but Daniel seemed uplifted. 'Jack, let's assume Mina is right. How bad do you think this could be? I mean, really, an earthquake in an ocean isn't going to do much is it?'

I cared for this church all my life and my father before me! Never mind, I'll probably never be able to resolve that mystery. How do you feel about talking over your translation of the tablet?' Joshua asked.

'Alright,' replied Mina.

'OK. Unfortunately, we've lost the introductory elements so I don't know how the Babylonian scientists made their predictions,' said Daniel.

'They weren't really scientists, you know, Daniel,' replied Mina.

'Are we going to quibble about terminology?' asked Daniel.

'No, no. So what do we have?'

'We have a series of omens and lots of equations. I don't know if they are dates, astronomical precisions, places, or something else. I just can't tell.'

At that moment, they heard footsteps coming down the stairs.

'Jack,' said Mina, 'are you crazy? You should be resting right now.'

'I've rested enough, and I can't leave the three of you to figure it all out without me.' They laughed. Daniel fetched cushions for Jack, as he fell into an armchair.

'Man, I'm exhausted,' Jack said. 'So where were you?'

'Well, we were just assessing what we've got so far,' said Daniel.

'And?' asked Jack.

'Not much. Have a look,' he said, handing him Mina's translation of the tablet.

After a few moments, Jack put the notes down, 'I have an idea. It isn't really my field but I think some of these are mathematical equations, a little basic, but very effective in flood management. I had no idea they were so advanced. I mean, really. Sure, there have always been floods, but we have always considered flood management to be something new.'

'But what about ancient dams, Jack?' said Mina.

'There's more to flood management than just a dam. How do you build a dam? Which material do you choose, inclinations, localisation, height, etc. and for each new variable, new equations. We're talking about complex systems.'

'And can you tell which equations have to do with flood management techniques?' asked Daniel.

'Maybe,' said Jack.

'Fantastic,' said Mina, 'could you do that while we work on the rest? But take it easy.'

'Alright. First I will take a nap,' he replied, smiling at Mina.

⌒

Later that evening, Jack woke up in the armchair to find Mina and Daniel's heads almost touching, so focused were they on the translation. Mina turned around to see Jack's pointed gaze, drilling an imaginary hole into Daniel's skull. She gave him a look in return which said 'You're being silly.'

Knowing that he was still watching her, she pretended to yawn and stretched her back, lifting her arms above her head and arching her back towards Jack. He was mesmerised by the outline of her figure under her tight jeans. Had he not been recovering from a serious wound, he would have grabbed her by the waist there and then and pulled her to him. Instead all he could do was stare.

Daniel sat up suddenly, totally oblivious to what was passing between Jack and Mina.

'We've made some progress, but we'll need you to explain the equations,' said Daniel.

'Alright, alright. I'll get down to it. I'll need a pen and paper.'

'Here you go,' Daniel said, handing him what he needed.

Jack read through Mina's translation and understood why they had been so transfixed. It was a maze of calculations, imbedded within the biblical flood narrative. It was very weird, but quite clearly it was done on purpose to hide their findings. An hour later, he had finished.

'Here you go,' he said. Mina and Daniel turned around together.

'Can you explain what you've found, Jack?'

'Well, I've highlighted what I think are equations to do with flood management, and what I think is astronomical data.'

'That's great. Astrological information could be the key,' said Daniel.

'I said astronomy,' said Jack, 'don't go confusing science with hocus pocus astrology.'

'What do you mean?' asked Daniel.

'I'll tell you what I mean,' replied Jack. 'There are two hundred and fifty billion stars in our own galaxy and over one hundred billion galaxies swirling about in space. That's a lot of stars in space to be influencing or predetermining a man's personality, or his direction in life. How many planets and stars did Babylonian astrologers know and use at the time, and how many are used today?'

'That's not the point,' said Daniel. 'Babylonian astrology focused on predicting events that affected the entire nation and its cities. Whatever it is today, astrology then was about trying to predict future meteorological events, earthquakes, famines, wars.'

'I still think it's horseshit,' said Jack, 'the only thing this tablet does is give a few exact moments in the sky. It's astronomical information.'

'He's right you know,' said Mina to Daniel.

'He might be right, but how did they find these dates or places, if not through astrology?' asked Daniel.

'That, I don't know,' she answered, 'it could be through a number of different observations. We don't have that part of the text.'

'OK. Jack, what about dates?' asked Daniel.

But Jack had already fallen asleep.

Chapter 28

Mina peeped through Jack's door. 'Morning Jack.'

Jack had had a rough night, but he felt better this morning.

'Morning beautiful.' She came and sat on the edge of his bed.

'We're making progress,' she said. 'Come down for breakfast and we'll tell you all about it.'

'You know, if you'd rather I stayed up here, just tell me. I'll leave the two of you alone,' said Jack.

'Jack, you aren't really jealous of Daniel, are you?' Mina asked, grinning.

'Me. Never. Why? Should I be?'

'No, you shouldn't,' she said, and she slowly bent down to kiss him.

Just as they were about to share their first kiss, they heard Joshua at the door and sprung up out like guilty teenagers. Joshua came in to check on his patient. After examining him, he announced that he was quite satisfied with his condition.

'Jack, I'm amazed by your recovery. You must be made of steel,' he said appreciatively.

'I know, doc,' it's my curse,' said Jack with a smile.

'You're almost as good as new,' said Joshua.

'It's all thanks to you. I owe you one.'

'Bring this whole matter to a close and you won't owe me anything.'

'I'll do my best,' said Jack.

～

When Jack eventually came downstairs, he found Mina and Daniel sitting at the breakfast table, arguing about the notes, which put Jack in an excellent mood.

'We're not getting anywhere,' said Mina.

'I don't agree,' said Daniel.

'What's going on?' Jack said, pulling up a chair.

But Mina went on regardless. 'Alright Daniel, maybe you're right, but how do you explain the term *ocean of water*?'

'It must be an image to describe the huge scale of the flood.'

'And the *mouth of the earth*?'

'That I don't know. I've thought about it the entire night and I still don't have a clue.'

'But what sort of river flood are they talking about?' asked Jack, 'what sort of flood could be that awful that they'd think of warning us thousands of years ago? Are we talking about a major city?'

'That's why we may be wrong in our interpretation of the text,' said Daniel.

'What if my first guess was wrong, and what I took for flood management measurements were actually successive dates, maybe crypted?' said Jack.

'Come on Jack, Daniel has been at this for days,' said Mina.

'I don't know,' said Jack, 'even if we had a perfect description of a star position, we'd still need another event to compare it with.'

'Mina, he may be right. Let me try out his theory.'

Daniel stayed at the kitchen table, covering sheets with calculations. Suddenly he looked up, dazed and rushed to his laptop. He opened the internet and typed in '1755 flood.' As he read through the results, his face drained of colour. Jack and Mina looked at him, as he frantically scribbled more calculations. After a while, he turned to Mina and Jack, horror-struck, and motioned for them to approach the screen.

'Jack was right. It is a date. I thought to myself, we have a date, 1755, the year the letter was sent to Safed from Hildersham. It's a weird letter. There's no other correspondence between the two places. What if Alejandro Cardozo and his family fled Portugal for some imperative reason and needed to write to say the tablet was safe? What if something dramatic happened in 1755? Well something did happen that year: the Lisbon earthquake. It's one of the worst earthquakes ever recorded in history and it was followed by a horrifying tidal wave on November 1st, 1755, at about 10.25 am. It killed over sixty thousand people.'

Mina did not respond. Her smile had vanished. She was thinking back to the letter Yeshua had written to his brother. It was dated December 1755. So Yeshua had left Lisbon with his family after the earthquake. Had he known how to use the tablet, surely he'd have left the city weeks beforehand. So why had he taken the tablet with him? She could only conclude that it was his duty to preserve the family's treasure out of respect for his ancestors. And, as it said in his letter, he'd keep on taking care of the tablet until the day it could be returned to the Jerusalem temple and used appropriately. 'Simply stupefying,' thought Mina.

'When and where will the next natural disaster hit?' asked Jack, whose brain, as ever, was trying to ignore the horrifying details and move to practical considerations.

'Oh I think I know,' said Daniel.

'So, tell us!' said Jack and Mina in unison.

'I calculated backwards from 1755 to find out what the date would have been in Babylonian terms… I used an online calculator. It seems that some astronomers spend a lot of time writing such software. To cut a long story short, the next gigantic natural disaster, whatever form it takes – earthquake, flood, eruption or other – will happen on 26th December, 2014. But we have no idea where it will hit. I wish we still possessed the stone tablet I found in Mosul. Maybe the clue was there? What are we supposed to do? I mean, we can't exactly make a list of all the great rivers, volcanoes, seismic faults in the world and warn everyone living nearby, can we?'

∽

Daniel came running into the room where Jack was re-checking his calculations.

'Jack! Mina has found out where it will hit.'

They both went to the kitchen.

'Boys,' said Mina, 'I'm pretty sure it will hit in the middle of the Indian Ocean. I've calculated the planetary and star alignment described in the text, and it corresponds roughly to the sky map on the 26th above the middle of the Indian Ocean.'

Jack looked at her calculations dubiously, but Daniel seemed uplifted. 'Jack, let's assume Mina is right. How bad do you think this could be? I mean, really, an earthquake in an ocean isn't going to do much is it?'

'I don't know. Maybe you're wrong about the location.'

'Maybe. In any case, we have ten years to prepare, to do more research, and warn the appropriate authorities.' Mina smiled and felt more hopeful than she had in weeks.

⌒

Mulberry Cottage. Later that afternoon

Mina, Jack and the Bamarts were relaxing in the living room. They could at last enjoy a peaceful afternoon together, without fear. Jack kept stealing glances at Mina. He still could not believe they had survived their ordeal and were having tea and scones in this delightful cottage. They had a decade to prepare for the worst.

'Mina?' asked Jack, idly stroking her hand.

'Yes?'

'Would you like to spend the Christmas holiday with me?'

'I'd love that. With everything we've been through, I'd completely forgotten about Christmas. I'll need to call my parents first, they expected me to be back home over the holidays.'

'I don't know how you managed that in England!' said Daniel.

'Managed what?'

'Well, not noticing it was Christmas! People go nuts over Christmas in this country. You must have noticed the decorations, the Father Christmases and decorated crackers all over Cambridge?'

'Nope. I've been immersed in the ancient tablet world the entire time,' she replied. 'Where are we going?' She asked Jack, 'West Virginia?'

'No. I was thinking of somewhere more exotic,' he broke off, smiling.

'Won't your family be disappointed not to see you?'

'Not at all. They're expecting me.'

'But where?' asked a tantalised Mina.

'In Thailand. My mother and sister are already out there, on their first vacation outside the US.'

'I'll call my parents right away,' answered Mina, she jumped up and turned to Daniel, 'May I use the landline, Daniel?'

'Of course,' he replied, almost managing to conceal his jealousy.

She walked into the small study where Joshua kept his phone. It suddenly struck her that she hadn't spoken to her parents since she had arrived in Iraq earlier in the month. She felt awful. 'They must be terribly worried,' she thought. That said, they had no reason to suspect anything was wrong. She couldn't possibly tell them what she had gone through. Could she even let them know she was in Britain? She'd try not to lie, but she wouldn't volunteer any information they didn't ask her for directly.

'Hi Mum!' she said when the line finally connected.

'Mina! Are you alright?' asked her mother.

'I'm fine, Mum.'

She heard her mother excitedly call her father to the phone.

'Hi darling,' said her father.

'Hi Dad.'

'Professor Almeini called us two weeks ago,' he said, 'he was worried about you. He thought you'd left the country? Things look terrible in Mosul, at least from what we can gather from the news.'

'The media always exaggerate everything. You know that, Dad. I'm safe. I've met a very nice man. That's why I've been out of reach for a few weeks. His name is Major Jack Hillcliff.'

Mina's mother grabbed the phone.

'A Major?' she asked, excitedly.

'Yes Mum. He's a Major in the US army and he's invited me to join his family for Christmas. Do you mind?'

'Mina?' her dad was back on the phone.

'Yes?'

'Is this Major next to you? I want to talk to him.'

'I'll get him. He's in the next room.'

Mina took a deep breath and rushed into the living room. She quickly explained to Jack what had been said, and more importantly, what had been omitted from the conversation. They walked back to the study together.

'Dr Osman?' said Jack.

'That's me,' said Mina's father.

'Hi. I'm Jack Hillcliff.'

'I hear you've invited my daughter for the coming holidays.'

'Yes I have. I hope that is alright with you?'

'Well, young man, I need to know a little more about you, before agreeing to this out of the blue!'

'Well Sir, I'm thirty-five years old. I'm a retired Major from the US army, and I'm a trained water engineer. I'm currently working under contract with a few NGOs to bring proper water supplies to villages in the Mosuli countryside.'

'Good, good,' said Mina's father.

His wife picked up the phone again.

'Hi. I'm Mina's mother.'

'Hi Mrs Osman.'

'We are very happy to hear from you. Just make sure she returns safely to us, will you?'

'Of course, Ma'am,' said Jack.

'We would also be happy to welcome you after the

holidays in New York when Mina comes to see us' she said, and before he could say anything, she added 'could you pass me Mina.'

'Yes of course, goodbye Mrs Osman.'

'Goodbye,' she said.

'Mum?' asked Mina, picking up the phone.

'He sounds like a decent young man. Please bring him home after you've met his parents. Where do they live?'

'In West Virginia,' answered Mina.

'Oh. That's quite far away. When will you be back?'

'Probably mid-January,' Mina answered, cringing inwardly at the deception.

'We'll see you then. Do you need any money for the fare?' asked her mother.

'No mum, I'm fine. I've got a research grant.'

'Wonderful! Such good news. Your father and I are very proud of you. Take good care of yourself.'

'Yes mum. See you soon.'

She hung up, and looked guiltily at Jack.

'Well, that went well. I feel awful!'

'I'm not quite sure why you didn't tell them we were going to Thailand.'

'My parents are cool, but not that cool.'

'They seemed easygoing to me,' said Jack, grinning.

'Time to look for a flight then,' said Mina, refusing to pursue the conversation about her parents any further.

'That's all been taken care of my dear,' he said smiling at her.

'It's the 21st today, when are we leaving?' she asked.

'Tomorrow. I had to change my original flight. There's a flight tomorrow afternoon from Heathrow.'

'I'll get packing,' she said, climbing up the stairs.

Daniel had observed the entire conversation, 'You don't waste time, do you?' he said to Jack.

'She's worth it, a million times over, Dan.' said Jack.

'I agree. I've never met anyone like her…or you. I wish you both all the best.'

'Thanks,' said Jack.

'Do you think Shobai's men will return?' Daniel asked with a slight tremor in his voice.

'No. I don't think so. They accomplished what they had planned. We'll have a lot to do when we get back from Thailand. I'll be in touch then. We need to decide which authorities to contact and how to strike a deal at the highest level to keep us all out of harm's way, you and your father included, when Oberon Wheatley reappears.'

'What? I thought he was also out of the picture?' asked Daniel.

'No. That's what I told Mina to reassure her. She's gone through hell because of that bastard. We've been out of *his* picture. But it won't last.'

'You mean, from the moment we make our findings public?'

'Yes. He'll come back with a vengeance. He has no idea we found the Jerusalem clay tablet.'

'Of course. Well, don't worry, we have oodles of time to prepare,' said Daniel cheerfully.

'Yes. Listen Daniel, I can't thank you and your father enough for all your help.'

'What are friends for?' said Daniel, shaking Jack's hand.

'You've got yourself a friend too. Now, before we start weeping like girls, I'm going to pack up my stuff.'

Chapter 29

December 22nd. Hildersham, Mulberry Cottage

Jack got up at seven a.m. He felt irritable, having had a night of horrific nightmares about earthquakes and thousands of men and women screaming in agony. Still yawning, he threw some clothes on, made his bed – military habits die hard – and left his room. He knocked on Mina's bedroom door but she didn't answer. After a slight hesitation, he pushed the door open and went in. He sat on her bed, and waited until she opened her eyes. She was as beautiful asleep as she was awake. He brushed a strand of hair from her face, and caressed her cheek. She woke up, gently. 'Jack?' She murmured. He smiled. She looked at him, blinking her eyes, as if to make sure he wasn't a figment of her imagination. When she was quite satisfied it was Jack, she put her warm arms around him, and pulled him down by her side and curled up facing him. They kissed gingerly at first, and then more tenderly. For a moment Jack felt like tossing all his worries to the wind and losing himself in Mina's arms, but he stirred away from her embrace and sat up again.

'Sorry. Mina. It's not you. I'm worried.' He ran a hand over his weary face.

'Why? You look tired, Jack. Did you manage to get hold of your mother and sister last night to let them know you're bringing a guest?'

'No. They weren't in. I'll leave a message at their hotel, telling them we're on our way.'

'I'm sure they're fine. Don't worry,' she said.

'They've never travelled before. Of course I worry.'

'What flight did you find?' she asked, changing the subject.

'I managed to get two seats with Thai Airways, but the flight was overbooked. We might be on standby today and tomorrow.'

'That's good, isn't it?' Mina said, sitting up, her hair flowing down, covering her breasts.

'It's alright, but I'd rather be there already.'

'Me too!'

He kissed her, 'I'm going downstairs to have breakfast.'

⁓

After a short drive through the countryside, Jack and Mina had joined the M25, the infamously congested ring-road, which would take them all around London, westward to Heathrow. The departure from Hildersham had been an emotional one. As British as the Bamarts were, they had hugged both Mina and Jack for a long time and wished them the best of luck. They agreed to meet after the New Year to discuss future plans concerning the tablet.

'I wanted to ask you something,' said Mina, 'when you said your mother and sister had never travelled before, you meant abroad?'

'Yes. They've travelled a few times to Philadelphia, to see my dad's brother and his family, but that's about all.'

'So where are we going in Thailand?' asked Mina.

'Well, our final destination is Phuket, but we have a stopover in Bangkok.'

Jack thought about the last time he had travelled to Thailand. It was a covert operation in cooperation with the D.E.A. and Thai military forces. The operation had been successful in uncovering a drug smuggling ring with international connections. He had been sent as a military liaison officer, to make sure that their coordinated efforts would run smoothly. After the happy conclusion of the operation, he had spent a wonderful holiday travelling on a chartered boat in the Andaman Sea, stopping here and there in secluded coves to swim to his heart's content. He had been to Thailand a few times before for other, more personal reasons and always felt at home there. He smiled to himself, remembering his last conversation with his mother.

'Jack? A penny for your thoughts, as the Brits say?' asked Mina.

'I was just thinking of the efforts I had to make to convince my mum to go to Thailand.'

'And?' asked Mina, quizzically.

'It was so funny. How often do you have to convince people to go on holiday?'

'You didn't have to talk me into it!'

'Well, it was quite different with my mum. She could've stayed in any remote spot, without another tourist on the horizon. But instead, she preferred to be somewhere where other Americans stayed.'

'Ah?' said Mina, 'not very adventurous, is she?'

'Yeah. In the end, I bought them a package holiday to Phuket. She's terrified of anything new and exotic. Jen, my sister, is hardly different. Anyway, that's why I sent them to Patong beach: even if you'll find as many sex shows as restaurants there, she wanted to be somewhere full of tourists, rather than one of Phuket's more secluded beaches.' A few more miles and Jack had to slow down almost to a halt, as they were stuck in traffic. Mina had been thinking of her own situation for a time.

'I'm not sure I want to return to Iraq when we get back from our travels. I think I have enough material now to wrap up my PhD at Columbia and surprise the academic world.'

'You might want to be a little careful.'

'Why? Now that we're pretty sure that something will happen in a decade, and the secret will be out in the open before long, won't everything sort itself out?'

Jack looked at her. He didn't want to disclose his fears about Wheatley, so he chose his words carefully; 'I don't think the Intelligence services would appreciate us going public without preparation,' he said.

'I wish you hadn't contacted your… friend,' Mina said, speaking through gritted teeth.

'Who? Stella?' Jack asked.

'Yes Jack, Stella. Don't play dumb with me.'

Jack could not believe his ears. With everything they had gone through, Mina was fishing for information about another woman. He responded with just a hint of a smile. 'She's just a friend, a really old friend in the service.'

'Oh. That's it, just a friend?'

'Yeah.'

'Was she more than a friend, years ago?'

'Alright. We had an affair but it didn't work out. Come on Mina, don't tell me you're jealous?'

'You're right. Why should I be? First you put me on a train to Cambridge on my own and then you run off to meet some wonder-woman in a pub in London. Hey, why should

I be jealous of an operative who was previously your superior officer?'

He laughed and she punched him in shoulder.

'Why are you laughing?' she asked.

'I never thought I'd enjoy fighting with you so much.'

'You're impossible,' she blurted.

⤳

Heathrow airport. Thai Airways check-in desk.

Mina crossed her fingers, and prayed they would make the flight that evening rather than the next day. Unfortunately, around eight p.m. the final call for passengers sounded in the departure zone and their names weren't announced. Jack was quite dejected.

'Don't worry, Jack. I'm sure we'll catch tomorrow's flight and you'll find your mum and Jen are just fine. They probably went off on a fishing trip or something.'

'Yes, you're probably right,' he replied absent-mindedly.

The airline offered them a double room in a four star hotel near the airport at a reduced price. They accepted the offer, picked up the vouchers and walked out of the airport to hail a cab.

⤳

Heathrow airport, four star hotel.

After a quick but delicious dinner, Jack and Mina went up to their room. Mina had tried cheering Jack up throughout the meal, but he seemed out of sorts. 'Not a great start to the holiday,' she thought to herself. He seemed so remote. She wondered if he'd soon snap out of his mood. He sat on the corner of the bed, his arms hanging by his side. Mina sat down next to him.

'Jack? Please talk to me.'

He sighed and then looking away from Mina, began to speak.

'I know it might sound stupid, but I didn't really keep in touch with my mother and sister for almost a decade, until I quit the army. And even then, I only went to see them for the first time six months ago. That's when we decided to spend our first family reunion holiday together in Thailand.'

'So where's the problem?' asked Mina.

'I guess I feel guilty for not being there already.'

'Is something else bothering you, Jack?' she asked.

'Why do you say that?'

'You're not used to doing nothing with your time, are you? Wasn't it Daniel who called you an Action Hero?'

'Maybe. I felt at peace when I started my engineering work at the village.'

'You were still *doing* something.'

'So?'

'So, I think that instead of worrying for no good reason, you should embrace this time to think about where you'd *like* to be going.'

He searched her face for any signs of pity and found nothing but an inviting smile. Jack felt the wisdom in Mina's words, and understood what she meant, but he still couldn't shake off his worry. Where were his mother and sister? He still hadn't been able to get in touch with them. But maybe Mina was right and he was worried for other reasons. His family history didn't usually bother him that much. He just tended to avoid thinking about it. But right now, he felt that his tough guy act was crumbling under Mina's penetrating gaze.

She sensed he wanted to speak but couldn't find the right words.

'When did you stop speaking to your family?' she asked.

'It's complicated,' he muttered.

'Try me,' she continued, softly.

He sighed, 'When I left home. I was sixteen.'

'Where did you go?'

'I had a choice: jail time or the army. I don't regret my choice.'

'Why? What did you do?' Mina asked, a little taken aback.

'I hurt a guy pretty bad, outside a bar. He was drunk, he insulted me and it made me angry.'

'Why were you so angry?'

'Hey. Should I lie down? Do you need a note pad?'

'I'm not your therapist Jack, but I would like to know.'

'I'm sorry,' he said, sincerely. 'I suppose I had been angry a long time, ever since my dad died.'

'How old were you?' she asked, trying to keep her questions short.

'About eleven.'

'What happened?'

'He was gunned down in a drive-by shooting.'

She squeezed his hand softly.

'My dad could barely make ends meet at the best of times. When he died, we lost the house to the bank and ended up in a trailer park. I was angry at my dad for leaving us like that.'

'You must have missed him a lot?'

'I guess so.'

He felt something begin to thaw inside him. He had a

sudden vision of his father returning from the mill early one summer's day and playing baseball with him in the nearby school yard. He remembered his dad's large rough hands and the smell of freshly-sawn cedar wood on his clothes. They hadn't spoken much, but it was a good memory. He felt lighter at heart. He looked sideways at Mina, wondering what she was thinking now that she knew a little more about him. He hoped he hadn't driven her away. But she smiled up at him and he knew he was alright. Slowly, she put her arms around his neck and stroked his hair. He pulled her closer into him, feeling the swell of her breasts against his firm chest. He caressed her lower back. She pulled back to look at him, and then kissed him passionately. He lowered her down carefully onto the bed and started undressing her, removing her clothes, piece by piece, progressively kissing every newly bare area of her silky skin. Since the day – was it only a few weeks ago? – when Mina had seen him walking towards her in the desert with his shirt open wide, she had dreamed of Jack's firm body pressing hard against her own. Looking deep into his smouldering eyes, she undid the buttons of his shirt. They both breathed in unison, one last gasp before the leap, one last thought before losing themselves to the pleasure of the long-awaited moment.

⌒

Mina was curled tightly against Jack's warm chest, their naked bodies still intertwined.

'You know, after all we've been through, getting shot…I should be a total wreck, but there's something about being around you Mina, I feel I could do something amazing now.'

'You already have, Jack.' She said with a mischievous grin.

He laughed softly.

'So,' she said, 'are you ready to introduce me to your family?'

He held her in his strong arms and kissed the top of her head.

'Sort of.'

'What do you mean "sort of"?' she said, tensing up.

'My mum is quite sweet and so is my sister, but…'

'Yes?'

'They've never left their trailer.'

'So what?'

'Mina, they're not very sophisticated.'

'Please, don't been embarrassed by your family, not on my behalf!'

'Alright. What about your parents?' he asked.

'Oh. That's another story. They were polite on the phone of course.'

'But what?'

'You're a soldier you know, you're not a doctor or a lawyer… It might not work out.'

'You're joking, right?' said Jack, raising himself on his elbow.

She looked at the shocked look on his face, enjoying every second of it, and then kissed him hungrily as she climbed on top of him.

'Of course I'm kidding! They'll adore you, but not quite as much as I do.'

PART 4

THAILAND

Death carries off a person who is gathering flowers, like a flood carries away a sleeping village.

(Buddhist Saying)

Chapter 30

December 23rd, 2004. Thai Airways flight

The plane to Bangkok was packed with British tourists leaving behind their offices and heading for the beach. They were wearing shorts, t-shirts and flip-flops and were looking forward to a well-earned holiday in Thailand. Mina was amazed to see how lightly dressed they all were. In the shopping area of Abu Dhabi, where they had a short stopover, she was reminded of the variety of dress codes co-existing at airports all around the world. The contrast between her fellow travellers and the white-robed sheiks and their entourage was quite a vision to behold. Mina watched the queues of men of all ages and from all social classes waiting for a connecting flight to Mecca and felt quite moved. Was it their fervour? Or was it their anticipation of revealed mysteries, their communal faith? She clearly remembered her father's serene smile when he returned from the *Hajj*, many years before. She must have been ten years old and had kept asking her mother where daddy was, until one day he walked through the door and swept her off her feet in a long-awaited hug.

∽

December 24th, 2004. Don Mueang, Bangkok airport

Mina was trying to get her head around the time zone difference. The duration of their trip had been twelve hours, but because of the seven hour difference between Britain and Thailand, instead of arriving at ten p.m. it was actually five in the morning on Christmas Eve.

Having retrieved their luggage, Jack returned to the waiting room to find Mina, yawning on a bench.

'Mina, I finally managed to reach my mother at the hotel,' he said, his broad smile showing just how relieved he was. 'I told her we'd be with her for dinner. We've got a flight to Phuket around eight tonight, how about a little sightseeing in the meantime? I propose leaving our bags in a locker and going exploring.'

'That sounds lovely!' she answered, shaking off her drowsiness and picking up her bag.

〜

After a hair-raising taxi ride through Bangkok's busy streets, Mina marvelled at the strangeness of her surroundings and the beauty of the various temples along the Chao Phraya River. The driver came to a screeching halt just outside the National Museum. Jack paid the man and then turned to Mina, 'Believe it or not, even though I've been to Bangkok many times, and even to this park,' pointing at the leafy Sanamluang park opposite, 'I've never once visited the National Museum.'

'A good thing too, we'll discover it together. I always start a visit to a new city with a museum trip.'

'It's as good a place to start as any,' said Jack. 'I usually memorise the main streets and then go for a walk.'

'Museums make me feel more grounded. They reassure me, you know, the fact that all human beings have a sense of their own history, their own roots.'

'Well, you sure look like a fish in water the moment you enter a museum!'

She laughed and held his hand as they walked into the museum.

The collections were distributed in different buildings, some of which Mina found to be more refined than others. The Siwamokhaphiman Hall was an impressive ceremonial building made of traditional materials. In this case, she preferred the building itself to the prehistoric collection it contained. But what really impressed them was the Phra Buddhasihing, a famous sacred image of Buddha, held in the so-called Buddhaisawan Chapel, and a huge sculpture of Ganesh.

Jack knew this god well from his previous trips to South East Asia and had much affection for the elephant-headed god. He found this sculpture of the dancing deity particularly endearing.

All in all, Mina found the museum's collection fascinating but the descriptions, when there were any, amounted to no more than one-line legends. The city was utterly turned towards tourism. It was colourful and noisy, with gift shops, travel agencies and hotels. At every street corner, touts invited visitors and tourists to enter their establishments right off the street, whether to massage parlours or restaurants. In comparison, the national museum, at least in its presentation, felt almost like a cultural understatement. They sat at a table in the museum's inner courtyard and ordered a cool drink. Mina was finding it difficult to adapt to the weather, and felt more at ease indoors. It wasn't so much the temperature that bothered her but the tropical climate, humidity mingled with heat and the lack of any breeze. Her clothes stuck to her body and she wasn't used to sweating this much. One person's discomfort, however, is another's pleasure as it obviously appealed to Jack from the way he was checking out her glistening cleavage.

'It's a strange place, Jack. I know I haven't been here for more than a few hours, and call me callous, but I don't feel that people here are in touch with their past.'

'I'm not sure anyone really is, but it's funny you should say that. Most of Thailand has embraced capitalism and Western culture to such an extent that I've often had the same feeling. Someone once said to me that "the gods have left Thailand."'

'I know they're Buddhist, but what does it represent here?' asked Mina.

'What do you mean?' asked Jack in turn.

'As far as I understand it, Buddhism came from India, and was a monastic order. In India, lay people weren't Buddhists. How does it work in Thailand?

'You must have seen the beads and necklaces some men wear around their necks.'

'Yes, I noticed that the pendant was often the same, sort of triangular in shape.'

'It's a small image of a monk or a saintly man,' said Jack, 'while Buddhism is still monastic in its general form, it has little to do with what went on in India centuries before. A large section of the population is made up of monks. Many young men go to a monastery for a few years and eventually leave to get jobs.'

'I don't understand,' said Mina.

'Well, it's the best way for young people who can't afford to attend proper schools to get an education, free of charge. Some enter the orders for a year or two mainly to learn English.'

'So what's the main religion?'

'Well, apart from those who are Christian and Muslim, especially in the South of the country, you could say they worship their ancestors and I think that Buddhist monks sometimes officiate at weddings, but that's a recent change. You often find them at funerals.'

'You seem to know a lot about Thailand.'

'I had a good friend here. He taught me a lot about the country.'

'Had?' Mina asked, not believing her luck as Jack unveiled another layer of his mysterious past.

'Hon died five years ago.'

'I'm very sorry Jack.'

'It's OK. It's been a long time.'

'How did he die?' she asked.

'Quite tragic really. He was a doctor in Chiang-Mai. He went to a remote village to train local nurses and was bitten by a very poisonous snake.'

'I hope you don't mind me asking you about this?'

'Of course not Mina,' he said, kissing her tenderly. 'So, have you seen enough of the museum?'

'Yes, sir,' she replied, jokingly.

'Hungry?'

'Famished.'

'Good,' he replied, 'I know just the place to go.'

↜

Jack and Mina were sipping their double espressos after

a sophisticated meal at the Oriental Hotel. The exquisite outdoor terrace restaurant overlooked the Chao Phraya River. They both gazed for a while at the boats sailing past and tried not to laugh too much at the wealthy wives of western expats sitting at nearby tables, pouting disdainfully at everyone. They walked through the older parts of the Hotel, admiring the sepia photographs of the Hotel's rich and famous guests since Queen Victoria's time, and then into the foyer where they left the hotel and hailed a taxi.

'So where are we going next, Monsieur Jack?'

'My favourite,' he glanced at her mischievously, 'a massage.'

'I thought massages were kind of seedy in these parts?' she said, somewhat taken aback.

Jack laughed, 'They can be…but not where I'm taking you.'

'Where are we going?'

'Surprise,' he said, and stopped any further questions with a kiss.

Before long, they stood in front of the Grand Palace, in Bangkok's historic centre. Here was the beating heart of the city. Most monks lived nearby, within walking distance of this, the greatest of all the shrines and glittering temples in the City of Angels. Mina gazed with awe at the temples, or *wats* as the Thai called them, constructed with millions of small pieces of coloured glass and ceramic, and spectacular gilt roofs. There were many temples but the one that struck her the most was *Wat Pho*, or the Temple of the Reclining Buddha. It was the largest temple in the city and was famed for its gigantic gilt Buddha, which was over forty metres long. Even the statue's feet were more than three meters in size and its soles were covered with intricate decorations in mother-of-pearl. What surprised Mina most was the sound of money tinkling as pilgrims and tourists donated coins to the priests so as to gain merit from the Buddha.

'So where's the spa? I thought we were going to have a massage?' asked Mina, jokingly.

'Ah. Women, you lose all patience from the moment you hear of a good pampering.'

'I don't see you complaining,' said Mina.

'True. Follow me.'

After a short walk through the temple complex, Jack suddenly stopped in his tracks, 'Voilà.'

Obviously a great many visitors to the Wat Pho complex came for an invigorating massage rather than for religious zeal. Jack paid out two hundred *bahts* for each of them and they entered the real world of Thai massage, an odd mixture of yogic postures, deep muscle massage and body pressure points which the practitioners pressed on painfully hard with flat wooden sticks. Relaxing into the massage, Mina let her thoughts roam freely and through a curious association of ideas, started thinking about time-travel. They had lost a day, travelling to Thailand, although the actual journey had not lasted much more than half that time. She had the strange sensation of being a thought away from something important that she should remember. It was just out of her grasp. Trying to chase it down would never work, so she let go of her thoughts and focussed on enjoying the massage fully.

∽

Mina and Jack walked hand in hand on the river bank until they reached a pier, where a tiny booth offered boat tours exploring Bangkok's backwaters. Jack bought a two-hour tour. The boat moored and Mina and Jack boarded, waiting in line behind other tourists to show their ticket. Only one traveller got on without paying his fare, a chubby monk in saffron-coloured robes. No-one seemed to mind, Mina guessed that in Thailand monks probably didn't pay for public transport. He sat there, near the helm, his plump face looking out at the watery furrows on the boat's flanks, as it sliced through the river. Mina was mesmerised by this overweight monk, holding his begging bowl tightly against his chest. Most monks woke up early in the morning and left their monasteries to beg for food from passers-by on the streets of Bangkok. This one had obviously been collecting money, as his begging bowl tinkled every time the boat swayed in the wash.

The riverside landscape was fascinating, with many of the houses perched on stilts. Families were going about their daily lives, far away from the bustle of the city's tourist trade and big business skyscrapers. Stroking Mina's hair distractedly, Jack couldn't help thinking about the tablet and its meaning.

'Mina?' Jack said.

'Yes?' she answered, dreamily.

'How sure are we that *it* will happen?'

'Oh,' she said, a little disappointed that Jack had not opted for a more romantic sentiment. 'We can't know for sure, but Daniel's calculations have confirmed that past disasters were predicted by the authors of the tablet.'

'So what are we really talking about?' asked Jack, matter-of-factly.

'I hope nothing will happen, but if something does it will probably be an earthquake.'

'Can't you give me a more educated guess?'

'OK. The tablets describe events to come, as well as how to forecast them. Unfortunately the Mosul tablet was only partly preserved and the Jerusalem one... basically we don't know how they forecasted the events, but my personal feeling...' she broke off.

'Yes?'

'... The events described are incremental in magnitude and destructive power.'

'You mean they get worse over time?'

'Yes, they make me think of warnings.'

'Of what?'

'Of worse things to come.'

'And I thought you weren't religious.'

'I don't feel like joking, Jack. What time is it?'

'Almost time to get back to the airport to catch our flight. We're getting off at the next pier.'

Jack's mind drifted back to his time in Iraq. He wondered how the *qanat* work had progressed, if the villagers had followed his notes conscientiously and been successful in channelling the water. Since the fateful day he had met Mina, he had pursued an ancient tablet in four countries and come up against Wheatley and Shobai, possibly the deadliest foes he had ever faced. 'Some month,' he thought to himself.

~

Phuket airport.

Mina watched over their luggage as Jack bought two Thai SIM cards for their mobile phones. She looked around her, welcoming the warm and windy weather. 'A good thing Jack didn't send his mother on a skiing holiday,' she thought. Jack returned half an hour later.

'Let's get to Patong beach as soon as possible. We should make it for Christmas dinner as planned.'

As they walked out of the small airport to the taxi rank Jack noticed two men who seemed to be scrutinising the arrivals. The men's faces lit up when an old woman appeared at the gate. They were evidently greeting their mother. 'I'm becoming totally paranoid,' Jack sighed inwardly.

'Here's a tuktuk,' Jack said, hailing one of the strange looking motorised versions of traditional rickshaws. Their young driver greeted them, with the ubiquitous *wai* gesture, bringing both hands to his chest and bending his head slightly towards his hands. He then picked up their bags and stowed them behind their seats. He jump-started his engine and with a loud popping noise, the tuktuk was on the road.

'They're funny things aren't they?' Jack said, 'Tuktuks aren't as manoeuvrable as motorbikes, but they're really useful in areas where traffic congestion is a problem, like Bangkok. Here it's a bit for show, as it's a holiday destination and in fact there's hardly any traffic.'

Mina rolled her eyes. 'Boys and their toys,' she thought to herself.

'It may be tacky, but it's a lot of fun to feel the wind in your hair!' she retorted.

'I thought you'd enjoy it. Still, the journey will take roughly half an hour, just enough time to be covered from head to toe with dust. You'll definitely want to freshen up at the hotel after it.'

'I'm sure you will too, Jack. You seem to forget I don't spend all my time in libraries. You don't want to know what I look like after a three week excavation campaign.'

He smiled at her. The sun was radiant and the sea breeze cool and pleasant. He loved seeing Mina's evident excitement at being in Thailand. This was her first trip to South East Asia and Jack promised himself he would return with her another time, just the two of them. He knew some remote and majestic islands on the other side of the peninsula that would be perfect. He could not tear his eyes away from her striking profile, as she gazed at the landscape unfolding on either side of the open-air vehicle.

Twenty minutes into their trip and the driver turned around briefly. 'Here Hat Surin,' he yelled over the buzz of the tuktuk, pointing to a beach on his right, 'then we go Laem Sing, Hat Kamala and Hat Patong.'

Mina did not register any of the strange sounding names the driver had called out. She was just enjoying the ride.

〜

Patong beach. Hotel

Jack spoke with the hotel manager who confirmed that his relatives had received his message, but that they were off on a boat tour. They would be back in an hour. The contrast between the hotel's lobby and Patong beach's rowdy atmosphere was stark. Mina was overwhelmed by a tourist industry brought to its paroxysm. It was as bad as the infamous Pat-Pong quarter in Bangkok: noisy mopeds, techno and pop music blaring out from all sides, billboards sprouting in every language under the sky – advertising everything from go-go girls to smoothies and Singha beer. She was glad to have escaped to the relative peace of this hotel. After a while a porter came by to pick up their luggage. She followed him out of the hotel to a row of discrete bungalows. She savoured the warmth of the air on her skin, and was looking forward to swimming in the sea, only fifty metres away from the bungalows, which were built right on the beach. They reached their bungalow, hidden from prying eyes by wild tufts of bamboo and large, overhanging palm trees. It had a large porch and a beautiful view of the seafront. As soon as the porter left the room, she undressed and walked into the bathroom. It was a large room with stone flooring and tiled walls. With great relish, she lathered her entire body with soap and stood still under the powerful flow of the shower. Then, she sat on a flat rock, still under the shower and felt so relaxed she almost fell asleep. Jack entered the bathroom, got undressed and filled two wooden buckets with warm water. He turned off Mina's shower and told her to remain seated on the rock and close her eyes. He then poured the warm water from the buckets gently over her. He refilled the buckets and repeated this a few times.

'Mmm. That felt so good.'

'You're welcome,' he said, kissing her shoulder. 'I'll take a quick shower and then we can meet up with my mum and sister in the reception area.'

'Didn't I say you were worrying for nothing?'

～

Mina felt her hands shake ever so slightly when she saw Jack's mother and sister waiting for them at the reception. She adjusted her dress again. Was it too short, too long?

'Hi mum, Jen,' said Jack giving them both a hug. 'Jen, my Mum, Maureen, Mina Osman, my girlfriend.'

Jen was a plain girl in her late twenties, with mid-length

straw blond hair. She was very tall and her body moved slightly awkwardly as she approached Mina. Jack's mother, in her mid-sixties was a plump brunette with piercing blue eyes. She stood there, a little hesitantly and Mina saw straight away that they had thought Jack was coming alone. Mina could not decide whether she wanted to kiss Jack for confirming that they were a couple or punch him on the jaw for not telling his mother that she'd be coming. In the end she did neither and shook hands with Jen and Maureen.

'I'm delighted to meet you both,' she said.

'Same here,' answered Jack's smiling mother and pulled Mina into a big hug.

Jen gave Mina a hug as well and before Jack could under-stand what was going on, everyone was hugging each other.

'I'm so happy to meet you,' Jack's mother kept saying to Mina.

Jack couldn't take much more of the hugging, so he disen-gaged himself from his tearful but smiling sister, 'Right. Let's go for dinner.'

'We've already tried out lots of the restaurants, but there's a real nice place with authentic Thai cuisine, close by,' said Jack's mother.

'It's really awesome,' added Jen.

Knowing his mother, Jack could just imagine the restaurant: an ordinary joint with a congenial owner smooth-talking his mum into believing the most absurd things about 'traditional Thai cuisine.' But he was happily surprised by his mother's choice of venue for their Christmas Eve dinner. It was not at all the tacky restaurant he had imagined but a small well-estab-lished restaurant, owned by a Frenchman who had married a local Thai woman. They had opened the place a few years back, offering simple and well-prepared food, using only fresh produce from the island. It was a delightful meal. Jen kept smiling at Mina and Jack, she was so happy and proud to be spending time with her brother. When Mina went to the bathroom, both women starting peppering Jack with questions.

'One at a time, you're not making any sense!' said Jack.

'How did you meet?' asked Jen.

'In Iraq. She was working at the university in Mosul, on leave from Columbia University in New York.'

'They have a university out there?' asked Jack's mother.

'Yeah,' answered Jack.

'She's awesome,' said Jen.

'I like her. She seems real smart, but she's no snob,' said his mother.

The conversation went on and on in the same vein. Jack wondered if he could take much more of it. When Mina returned, she looked worried. Jack stood up immediately.

'What's wrong?' he asked.

'I'm not sure. My phone was on silent. I've just realised that I have twelve missed calls from Daniel.'

'What? You gave him your Thai number?'

'Yes. I emailed it to him, just in case.'

'In case of what?' Jack replied, frustrated by Mina's carelessness. 'What if the Bamarts' phone was tapped?'

'Well, I don't know. But Daniel's obviously trying to reach us, isn't he?' she said. 'I'm going to call him back' she added, and walked out to the beach front to make the phone call.

'What's wrong with her?' asked Jen.

'I'm not sure. She needs to make a phone call. She'll be back in a few minutes,' said Jack.

Mina dialled the Bamarts' number in Hildersham.

'Hello?' said Daniel.

'Daniel, it's Mina,' she said.

'Mina! Thank God! I've been trying to reach you guys all day,' he yelled down the phone.

'Can you call me back on this number?'

'Yes of course,' he said, and hung up.

She sat down in the sand, and tried breathing deeply through her nose, to calm herself. She jumped as the phone started ringing in her hand.

'Daniel?'

'Yes.'

'What's going on? Why have you been trying to reach us?' asked Mina.

'It's a catastrophe, a disaster!' he answered frantically.

'What? What's a disaster? You're not making any sense!'

'I made a terrible mistake in my calculations,' he replied, lowering his voice.

'What do you mean? Did you make a mistake when transposing the dates from the Akkadian calendar to the Gregorian or Julian calendars?'

'Nothing like that. I misread Jack's notes. I…' The line went dead.

Jack stepped out the restaurant and found Mina sitting in the sand holding her head in her hands. He knelt beside her.

'So?' he asked.

'The line went dead. He said he made a mistake in his calculations.'

Her phone rang suddenly.

'Mina?' said Daniel.

'Yes. Daniel, Jack is next to me. I'm putting it on loud-speaker, so the sound won't be that great.'

'Hi Jack. You both need to hear this.'

'What?' asked Jack.

'Well, I made a mistake. It's most embarrassing, I calculated everything but I misread two of Jack's figures.'

'You do have an appalling handwriting, Jack,' Mina said.

But Jack didn't take any notice of her. 'What mistake, Daniel?'

'Well, instead of the events happening in 2014…'

Mina and Jack looked at each other with growing unease.

'Yes?'

'… Guys, it's going to happen now, exactly ten years earlier, in 2004. In two days time in fact.'

Jack and Mina went dead silent.

'Mina? You still there? Jack? You need to contact the appro-priate authorities *right now*. You both need get out of there with your family. There's no way of knowing what's going to happen and how safe you are in Thailand,' Daniel said. He had obviously been thinking of nothing else since realising his mistake.

'I understand,' said Jack, 'but are you sure this time?'

'Yes, one hundred percent.'

'The problem, Daniel,' said Jack, 'is that we still don't know exactly *what* is about to happen, nor where exactly it will hit. That means I'm not sure who to contact.'

'But something is going to happen; think of everything you've gone through, Wheatley, Shobai's people scouting for this tablet through the ages…it must mean something! It must be for real!'

Jack felt his stomach churn. He had to spring into action.

'OK Daniel. We won't stick around to find out if it is or isn't,' he answered, 'we'll get back in touch once we land in the US. We'll try to contact the appropriate authorities.' Jack added, 'Not that anyone will believe us.'

'Alright. I'm really sorry about this,' said Daniel.

'It's not your fault,' answered Jack through clenched teeth, before hanging up the phone.

Jack reached for Mina, who was shaking violently. They held each other tightly, then stood up and returned to the restaurant, where Maureen and Jen were wondering what on earth was going on.

'Mum, Jen, don't freak out. We all need to return to the hotel right away and pack.'

'Why, what's happened?' asked Jen.

'I'll explain everything later. Hopefully we'll manage to get flights out tonight, or at the latest tomorrow morning. All you need to know right now, is that something catastrophic is about to happen in this region and we need to get the hell out of here.'

'Alright Jack,' said his mother, trusting her son instinctively.

They left the restaurant and separated near their hotel. Jack gave his mother and sister a few more instructions and left with Mina to find an internet café. They located one off the main street, next to a shop selling anything and everything from telephone cards to sandals. Mina realised she was still wearing winter shoes. She hadn't even had time to buy sandals. They sat at one of the terminals and Jack starting looking for flights.

'Who should we contact?' asked Mina.

'I'm not sure, Mina. We need to work that out.'

'Why don't you just call your "friend" in the secret service or whoever she is?'

'I told you. I can't do that,' Jack replied, 'it would start off a whole snowball effect of questions. Believe me, we're better off staying off their radar. No, we need to figure it out ourselves.'

'What would be the first point of call in a situation like this? Some sort of Earthquake centre, or Seismic tremors?' asked Mina.

'I guess, but then again, it's supposed to happen in the Indian Ocean, so maybe we should contact NOAA.'

'That sounds pretty biblical,' said Mina.

'N.O.A.A.' said Jack, spelling out each letter, 'not Noah! It stands for the US National Oceanic and Atmospheric Administration, or NOAA.'

'Ah, where are they based?'

'I'm not sure. Let's look it up online.'

Mina typed the word 'NOAA' and 'Indian Ocean' into Google. Lots of results came back, but searching some more, she found their switchboard number in Hawaii.

'Here's their number,' said Mina.

'Thanks.'

'I'll look for flights, while you contact them.'

Jack pulled out his phone and dialled the number in Hawaii.

'Hi, Major Jack Hillcliff here, US Army. I'd like to speak to your director.'

'I'm sorry, he's unavailable right now. Can I take a message?' said a man with an irritating nasal voice.

'It's an emergency, please patch me through.'

'An emergency? About what?'

'Listen carefully, man, I'm only going to say this once. A terrible earthquake is about to happen, in the Indian Ocean,' said Jack.

'Where exactly Sir?' he answered. 'Why do I always get all the nut jobs out there?' he thought to himself.

'I don't know,' answered Jack

'Well, It's a large area and we've had no readings so far about anything of the kind, Sir. Where are you getting your information from?' asked the man.

'Who am I speaking to?' asked Jack.

'I'm Bob Rear, the Centre's secretary.'

'Right, Bob. The earthquake will occur on the 26th. The source of this information is classified top secret.'

'Classified, hey. Two days from now? Do you think I'm stupid?' said Bob.

'No Bob, I don't think you're stupid.'

'Everybody knows it's impossible to get seismic readings two days ahead of an earthquake. Even if it were possible, we at NOAA would certainly know about it before anyone else, especially if it occurred in the Indian Ocean, and certainly before some dubious Major from the US army.'

'Now you're being unnecessarily rude,' said Jack.

'I'm sorry Sir, but I don't have time for crank calls.'

'This is not a crank call. Christ!' said Jack, losing his calm.

'Sir, you've seen too many movies! What was your major in College? Conspiracy theories and UFOs?'

Jack turned to Mina. He was fuming.

'I'm going to kill this guy,' he said.

'Calm down Jack,' said Mina, 'what's going on?'

'Listen,' Jack shouted down the phone, 'I'm deadly serious. I need to speak to your director, right now!'

The line went dead.

'He cut me off!' Jack said, 'that asshole of a pen-pusher cut me off.' He re-dialled the number but this time no-one picked up the phone.

'Will you try again?'

'I don't know. After all, we're trying to convince scientists, their eyes glued to the most sophisticated seismic detection instruments in the world, that a three thousand year old Mesopotamian tablet has foretold a devastating earthquake in two days time. I can see why they'd think we're crazy.'

'I guess so,' said Mina.

'I'll try again, but first we need to get flights out of here pronto!'

❧

Same day. Mumbai, India.

Oberon Wheatley was sitting at his desk, in his brand new offices in Mumbai, reviewing recent operations on his multi-screen, state-of-the-art computers. He smiled to himself, thinking that from the moment he had outsourced his computerised weather forecasting systems to India and to a number of other emerging countries, his company shares had skyrocketed. He had thousands of experts all over the world striving towards one goal, that of updating and calculating every possible change in the weather, even in the most remote regions of the world. His client list kept growing. In some areas, even the military needed his updates. Most weather channels used his systems, indirectly of course. They had no idea how he produced his results. Using his dedicated staff, together with his massively powerful supercomputers, it was certainly not qualitative research, but number crunching beyond what one could dream of. He had brought sweatshops into the modern digital era.

His thoughts drifted as he fantasised about what he could achieve if he recovered the Mesopotamian tablet. With a proper translation and some serious thinking, he'd surely manage to decrypt its untapped knowledge. And once that happened, the sky was the limit! He'd know when natural events would take place, and where. He'd buy up entire regions. The price of land and property would quadruple after a disaster struck nearby. Complex money-spinning schemes kept unfolding before his hungry eyes. He had to get his hands on the tablet at all costs.

Wheatley's phone rang. He checked the caller ID, and recognised his secretary's number in New York.

'Yes, Miss Dawson?' said Oberon.

'Sir, you have a call from a Mr Wilde. Should I put him through?'

'Yes please,' he said.

'Mr Wheatley? Wilde here.'

'Is this line secure?' asked Oberon.

'Yes, sir.'

'What's going on?'

'We're not sure, but you asked us to listen in on any unusual calls to all major weather centres. It seems that Major Hillcliff just called NOAA in Hawaii from a mobile phone in Phuket, Thailand.'

'Jack Hillcliff?'

'Yes, sir.'

'What was the call about?'

'We're not absolutely sure, as the line was very bad, but it seems he was trying to warn NOAA of a pending emergency, some earthquake, but they didn't take him seriously and finally hung up on him.'

'I want you to track his mobile phone immediately and find out exactly where he is staying in Phuket. Call Natasha as soon as you have results,' said Oberon, before smashing the phone down in its cradle.

'Damn!'. He dialled Natasha's number.

'Yes, sir?'

'Prepare the jet for Phuket, Thailand. We're leaving right away. Find us a yacht and get me the number of that Bangkok thug I did business with a few years ago.'

'Do you mean Ong-Tha, the lunatic guy with the cut-up face?'

'Yes. I'll explain everything when we're in the air. Meet me at the jet in half an hour.'

Two hours later. Phuket, Thailand.

Jack was still trying to reach NOAA, but nobody picked up anymore. He had even tried calling from a local phone box, but to no avail.

'Any luck with booking flights?' he asked Mina.

'There's nothing before tomorrow, late morning.'

'OK, let's take them.'

'Why don't we leave Phuket now and stay overnight in Bangkok?'

'No, we're better off staying here tonight. Let's go back to the hotel,' said Jack.

Mina needed a walk on the beach front. She wanted to hear the sound of the waves hitting the shore, it would help her calm down and gather her thoughts. Jack decided to accompany her and they walked for about an hour.

'I can't believe it's going to happen so soon,' she said.

'I know exactly what you mean. Until this evening and since leaving the Bamarts actually, I've felt almost no pressure. We had a decade to prepare and compare our notes with all sorts of specialists, agencies, either to confirm or deny our worst fears.'

'It just doesn't feel real. I mean, look at this beautiful beach! How can anything change this?'

'Don't forget that according to your and Daniel's assessment, the earthquake is going to occur somewhere in the middle of the Indian Ocean. Thailand may be completely safe.'

'Then why are we getting on the first flight out of here? Who are you trying to convince, Jack?'

'I'm not trying to convince anyone. I just don't like taking any chances if I can help it. That's all. Maybe nothing will happen tomorrow, maybe something will, and Thailand will be spared, but either way I'd rather hear about it from a safe distance.'

꒱

When they returned to the hotel, Jack left Mina packing her things and stepped out into the warm night air, heading for his mother's bungalow. Nothing could have prepared him for what he saw. The glass door was smashed open, chairs were upturned and the contents of their suitcases were strewn all over the floor. He looked in the bathroom and in Jen's room, both equally wrecked, but there was nobody to be seen. They had been kidnapped, he knew the signs only too well. Looking around he found a note near the phone. It read, *'No police or you no see women again. We call you.'*

Jack ran down the beach, back to their bungalow. Mina's

suitcase was ready, on their bed, but she wasn't there. He felt his mind was about to explode. 'It's impossible,' he thought. How could they have also taken Mina, in the few minutes he had been away? He sat on the bed, deflated and motionless for what seemed an eternity then he heard footsteps coming from the porch. He moved noiselessly to the bay window and hid behind the curtains. Someone was entering the room. Just as he was about to strike, Mina spun round to face him.

'Jack? What the hell?'

'You're here, you're alive! Oh my god!' he said, holding her tightly in his arms.

'Of course I am. I just needed say *au revoir* to the lovely beach. What's going on?' she asked, all her fear and anxiety returning in waves.

'Mum and Jen have been kidnapped. While we were in town booking the flights.'

'Kidnapped? By whom?'

'I don't know. Here's the note I found.'

Mina read it quickly.

'It's very rudimentary English. Probably written by locals.'

'I came to the same conclusion.'

'But why?'

'I don't know. They're American after all. Maybe their kidnappers thought they were wealthy and could fetch a nice ransom?'

'I'm so sorry Jack. I can't believe this is happening just as we are leaving the country!' said Mina.

'No. There's probably something else going on,' said Jack.

'I think we should call the police,' said Mina.

'No way. I know this place, there's corruption everywhere and thugs have contacts within the police departments. We'll have to play ball and pay,' said Jack.

'So what do we do now?'

'For now, we wait.'

⤺

An hour later, Jack was still standing next to the window, on the lookout for any strange visitors. Mina had been re-reading her notes on the Jerusalem tablet, and had now fallen asleep, fully clothed, on the bed. The silence in the bungalow was broken by the sound of Jack's mobile phone beeping in his jacket. He had received a text message, he looked at it, and immediately woke Mina up.

'Jack, what is it?'

'Read this,' he said, showing her his phone.

Dear Mina, I hope you have had time to rest. What a shame that we should meet again under somewhat strained circumstances. Major Hillcliff, if you want to see your family again, make sure you have a certain tablet with you and call me on +91191191191.
O. W.

'Is that a real number?' Mina asked Jack. She was shocked by the casual tone of the message.

'Yes. *91* is the international number for Thailand. What a sick joke, *nine eleven*.'

'I could kill the smarmy bastard!' hissed Mina.

'I know! I wonder how they knew we were here?'

'How did he get hold of your phone number?'

'The phone's the key. They must have intercepted my call to NOAA' said Jack, 'they figured out we were in Phuket and sent out the local mafia. We just happened to be out.'

'And they kidnapped your mother and sister instead,' she said.

'Maybe. The worst part is that he wants the clay tablet we unearthed in Hildersham…but we don't have it any longer. Shobai's men destroyed it.'

Mina didn't answer straight away. There was something odd about Oberon's message.

'I don't think so Jack,' she said softly.

'What the hell do you mean?' he snapped.

'Please don't lash out at me. I'm just trying to be constructive.'

'Sorry Mina, I'm just beside myself.'

'OK. No-one but Shobai, the Bamarts, you and I know about the Jerusalem tablet. So Oberon must be referring to the tablet he stole from me in Israel, the Mosul stone tablet.'

He looked at her quizzically.

'You think Shobai ran off with Wheatley's tablet?' Jack asked her.

'Why not? They've stolen everything else.'

'And…Wheatley thinks *I* am the one who stole the tablet back from him? I like this.'

'Yes. Seems logical to me.'

'But we need to be sure he really doesn't know about the Jerusalem tablet before I call him.'

'We can't be sure. We'll just have to assume our explanation is the right one.'

'It's quite a gamble.'

'We've got a bigger problem. We don't have any tablets,' Mina said.

'But he doesn't know that,' Jack replied.

'You know Jack, I might be barking up the wrong tree. Why would Oberon need the actual tablet? He must have had photographs taken of the stone one?'

'Damn. You're right. It doesn't make any sense.'

'So? What are you going to do?'

'I'll call him tomorrow morning, once I've taken care of a few things,' said Jack.

༤

In the middle of the night, three heavily armed men approached the bungalow's porch with extreme caution. On their leader's signal, they all rushed forward smashing down the front door. One of the men flipped the light switch. There was no sign of Jack or Mina. The leader lifted his hood, revealing a ravaged face, covered in scars. He dialled a number on his mobile phone.

'Wheatley?'

'Yes?'

'No-one here.'

'I see, they must have changed hotels.'

'What do you want me to do?'

'Nothing. Thanks for your help. My secretary will settle your expenses. It really doesn't matter. I'm sure they'll make contact tomorrow morning, they have no other option. Then we'll see who's the smartest.'

Chapter 31

December 25th, 2004. Patong Beach, Phuket

Mina woke up in Jack's arms. She kissed his lips and watched him wake slowly from his sleep. He opened his eyes to the sight of Mina's dark eyes looking down at him from under her long lashes.

'Mornin' you,' he said, 'what time is it?'

'About eight-thirty.'

He frowned, suddenly deep in thought. Mina looked at his furrowed brow and smiled.

'You should eat something before you run out the door to do whatever you're thinking about right now' she said.

'Am I that predictable?'

'Sometimes. I'm starting to know you Jack. So what's the magic plan you've concocted overnight?'

'I need to buy a laptop and I'd rather you came with me. I don't want you to be alone if they find out we're staying here.'

'They can't know we're staying in a bungalow belonging to the hotel manager's own brother, can they?'

'I'm not taking any chances. I promised your mum I'd bring you home in one piece. Come on, let's get some breakfast.'

They returned an hour later. Mina rested on the sand a few feet away from the porch, hidden from watchful eyes by a dense row of palm trees. Meanwhile, Jack was busy setting up his laptop, downloading and installing special software he needed for a secure communication. Luckily, the hotel manager's brother had a good broadband connection in this bungalow. He dialled a number on the laptop to start a secure call with someone he had not spoken to in a very long time.

'Hi Specs,' said Jack.

'Jack! My god! I haven't heard from you in ages!' said the crackly voice coming out of the speakers.

'D'you ever sleep?' asked Jack.

'You know me. I only sleep when my computer goes to sleep.'

'You haven't changed one bit.'

'Yeah. What's up?'

'I'm in trouble,' said Jack.

'What's new?'

'I need to track a mobile phone number, a number in Thailand.'

'Lucky bastard. Are you on the beach right now?'

'I can see it from here. I might go for a swim in a while, if I don't get killed before then.'

'OK. I'll instant message you a website address. You type 'C++' when a second pop-up page appears, type 'jacko' and password 'lolita,' all lower-case.'

'Lolita?' asked Jack with a chuckle.

'Shut up. It's a great book by Nabokov.'

'Yeah, it's also the name of that gorgeous boss of yours, isn't it?' Jack mused.

'D'you want my help or not?'

'Yes, sorry,' he said grinning. It felt good speaking to an old pal.

'Right. When you've done that, another window opens. Just type in the mobile phone number, and you should be able to track it, if it's turned on of course. If the person is in motion, it might be more difficult to localise.'

'Will it leave any traces on the owner's phone?' asked Jack.

'No Jack. Unless you called me to obtain the commercial version of the software?'

'Why? How does the commercial one work?' asked Jack.

'It simply asks the owner of the phone if he agrees to be tracked.'

'That's sort of stupid isn't it?' said Jack

'It's to avoid being tracked by your wife or girlfriend without your knowledge.'

'Come on Specs, that's even more stupid! She could just borrow your phone for five minutes, accept the tracking software then delete the text messages. You'd never know you were being tracked.'

'Jack. I hope your girlfriend isn't anything like you!'

'I wish. How do I localise the phone?'

'Once you've typed in the number, a map software will start running and if the person's in town, you should be able to pinpoint the phone within a few yards.'

'You're a life saver, Specs. I owe you one,' said Jack.

'No you don't, just keep in touch mate' said Specs and ended the call.

Within a few seconds, Jack received an instant message with a web address. 'Specs, you're my cyber god,' thought Jack.

He stepped off the porch, onto the beach. He loved the warm and gritty feeling of sand scrunching between his toes.

He approached Mina, lying half asleep on a colourful towel.

'Mina?'

'Hmm. I'm sorry,' she answered, 'I fell asleep. So tired. Found out anything?' she asked, groggily.

'No but I've sorted what we're going to do now. I'm calling Wheatley. You coming?'

'Of course,' she said, jumping up from her towel.

He explained carefully what she needed to do while he spoke to Oberon. She was to keep her eyes on the phone location and jot down the exact coordinates when he gave her the go-ahead. He plugged his phone into the laptop, started a GPS scrambling software, and dialled Wheatley's number.

'Welcome to Phuket,' said Oberon. 'I expected your phone call last night.'

'Where are my mother and sister, Wheatley?'

'You're a trifle direct, aren't you, Major?'

'You've made a big mistake attacking my family.'

'Don't fret. They're perfectly well, alive and kicking. Well, not kicking that much, as I had to have them restrained, you understand I'm sure.'

'Just you wait.'

'Threats? Now, now Major.'

'What do you want? Money?'

'Money? You know exactly what I want. Where is it?' asked Oberon, icily.

'It's safely tucked away, in London,' said Jack.

'Now that's too bad for Miss and Mrs Hillcliff. Don't you think?'

Jack looked at Mina, who confirmed she had pinpointed the location of Oberon's phone.

'Why do you need it so badly? Don't you have a copy of it already?'

'Don't provoke me unnecessarily, my boy. We both know exactly what happened to those photographs.'

Jack put his hand over the phone and turned to Mina with a quizzical look, 'You were right, he thinks we have it, and that we stole the photos of it.'

'Tell him we have a picture with us,' she whispered.

He was about to ask why, but she seemed so resolute, 'OK. We don't have the tablet here, but we have a photograph of the inscription with us.'

Wheatley didn't answer. Jack waited for a few moments, then blurted out, 'Listen man, that's the best I can do for the moment. When my family is safe, and we've all returned to the US, you'll get the real tablet.'

Oberon still didn't answer.

'I want,' said Jack, '*we* want out of this whole business. It was a terrible mistake to get involved any deeper than we already have with this tablet. I just want my mother and sister safe and sound. You won't hear from us ever again.'

Wheatley broke his silence, 'Tomorrow morning, nine o'clock. Bring the photograph in person.'

'Where will we meet?'

'I will text you the meeting place tomorrow morning,' he answered and hung up.

Jack immediately looked over Mina's jottings. The coordinates had changed quite a bit during the phone conversation. Oberon had been moving. But where? The first coordinates located the phone near Hat Kamala, a beach they had passed on the way from the airport. Then, the signal moved to another beach, Hat Surin, further north.

'It doesn't make any sense, Jack!'

'He's calling from a boat,' Jack answered. 'That settles it. There's no way of finding him before tomorrow's meeting.'

'At least we have our bargaining chip now,' said Mina.

'Yes. But how are we going to produce the photograph?'

'I'll make a fake one of the Mosul tablet. I know the damn thing by heart,' said Mina.

'But how?'

'I'll download a few images from the web and then use software to alter them, and produce a photograph that will look like just like the tablet Oberon stole in the first place.'

'Wouldn't he remember what it really looked like?' asked Jack.

'I can't see how. I don't imagine he took the pictures himself. With any luck he's never even looked at them properly,' she replied.

'OK. What do you need?' asked Jack.

'Download good image editing software. I'll take it from there.'

An hour later. Kamala beach. A luxury hotel. Oberon's suite

Oberon, wearing his favourite monogrammed bathrobe, was sitting comfortably in a wicker armchair. A beautiful Thai girl was massaging his shoulders. Natasha entered the room accompanied by a man built like a wardrobe.

'So, did you get a lock on their location?' asked Oberon.

'Yes sir, but he was using scrambling software.'

'He's still in Patong, but we don't know exactly where.'

'Clever Jack. I wish he worked for me,' said Oberon.

'I'm not sure he'd feel the same way, Sir,' replied Natasha.

'Everyone has a price,' he replied cuttingly. 'Never mind. We'll have to wait until tomorrow. Where are our guests?'

'Ong-Tha delivered them to the yacht. We'll bring them to the beach in the morning. We'll anchor the yacht at a safe distance and have a small motor boat ready. Sir?'

'Yes Natasha?'

'I think you should have stayed on the yacht. It's safer,' she said.

'God I miss my own yacht,' he replied.

'This one suits our purposes, sir. It's faster and although we won't go unnoticed, it is less conspicuous than your usual yacht.'

'It's tacky,' he replied stubbornly. 'I'll stay at the hotel until this matter is over.'

'Just don't use your mobile phone while you're here,' said Natasha.

'Fine. You know how to reach me if need be. We'll meet in the restaurant on Patong beach but I want you to be close by, with both women there. I must have line of sight from our table.'

'With binoculars you mean?' she asked.

'Yes. That Hillcliff is dangerous. We have underestimated him,' said Oberon.

Natasha thought to herself, 'I never did,' but said, 'At least we know who he is now, and he knows we can get to his family at any time.'

'As long as he doesn't ask for help from Intelligence.'

'He hasn't before, he probably won't in the future,' she answered.

'We have our man there anyway. Isn't it amazing what one can do with a little lubricating money?' said Oberon, cheerfully. 'What I still don't understand is how Hillcliff managed to steal the tablet from inside the vault.'

'Maybe the same way he got into the New York office unseen. Miss Dawson reckons he used a powerful electro-magnet to wipe out the CCTV data.'

'Yes, but how did he avoid the two teams at the mansion? They were real enough,' said Oberon.

'It seems that one of the men from team Beta...' Natasha started to say.

'Spare me the code names,' snapped Oberon.

'Sorry, the man guarding the main entrance was sick most of the night and may not have been at his post the entire time.'

'Sick was he?' Oberon asked white with anger.

'Hillcliff probably made him drink or eat something without him knowing.'

'Make sure you put the guard on an indefinite leave of absence.'

'Done. He'll never be sick again,' answered Natasha.

'Good. Still, I don't understand how he managed to approach the mansion unnoticed.'

'The CCTV footage had been wiped clean,' said Natasha.

'Never mind. Tomorrow, I might just ask him how he did it before you terminate his involvement, as well as that of his family and Miss Osman of course.'

'Yes Sir.'

'I'm glad that's all settled,' he said, 'now Natasha, would you mind leaving us?'

Natasha flashed a deadly look at the girl and left the room.

❧

Same evening. Patong beach restaurant.

Mina was trying to swallow her food, a Thai green curry with chunky king prawns. Jack was going on and on about Thai cooking and its diversity in an attempt to keep her mind off their worries. She tried playing the game, thinking it had to be even harder for Jack, as it was his family that was missing, not hers. They spoke of their shared experiences in Iraq and back home, their successes and failures. But, all the while, they both felt as if they were avoiding the real conversation, made up of muted fears of what awaited them the next day. Mina was beginning to understand Jack's ways, his military stoicism, how he lived in the present. He didn't waste his thoughts or strength on what-ifs. But she was different. Under the circumstances, she couldn't enjoy the food or even Jack's company. Every good thought was marred by anxiety over tomorrow's impending disaster. *What if* things went wrong? *What if* Oberon realised the photograph was not real? She had spoken about this at length with Jack and they had agreed that one frontal photograph of the main inscription would probably do the trick. As she herself had found the tablet and had an intimate knowledge of its measurements and appearance, she had been able to fabricate a good digital fake. She had downloaded numerous high-resolution images of cuneiform tablets from the internet. After copying, cutting and merging them one into the other, she had obtained a final picture, which was very similar to the original tablet in all aspects except one, the most important: it's content. She suspected that Oberon couldn't read cuneiform. All in all the result was pretty good and they had decided to print it out in black-and-white the next morning when the main shops opened.

Later that evening, they walked silently along the beach, side by side. Jack had rolled his linen trousers halfway up his calves, and Mina wore a long, orange and red dress, the hem of which trailed in the slow ebb and flow, as they treaded the wet sand. After a while, they returned to their bungalow and sat under the palm tree. They looked out at the shimmering sea and held each other under the star-filled sky. Deep down, they both felt the next day would be like nothing they had ever experienced before.

Chapter 32

December 26th, 2004. Phuket

Jack woke up at two a.m. He'd had a horrific nightmare. Although in life he was constantly in control, dreams were beyond any man's rule and they often revealed his innermost fears. The last image branded in Jack's mind was that of Wheatley, laughing madly from the edge of a crater, Mina in chains, looking on helplessly as Jack fell backwards into the volcano's roaring magma. He sat up, sweating heavily and trembling at the idea of losing Mina. He stroked her long, dark hair delicately. He got out of bed, turned on his laptop and started the scrambling software. He then turned on his mobile phone, but there were no new messages from Wheatley. He needed a drink. He puts some clothes on and sat down on the edge of the bed to tie his shoelaces. Mina stirred in her sleep.

'Jack?' Mina asked, 'what time is it?'

'Two a.m.,' he answered and kissed her softly, 'I'm just going out for a drink to wind down. I need to clear my head. I'll be back before you know it.'

'Any news?' she asked.

'No, not yet. I think Wheatley's going to wait until the last minute to let me know the meeting place.'

'That can only mean the meeting will be in Patong. We'd never have time to get anywhere else on the island,' she said.

'Yeah. I'm pretty sure it's going to be here somewhere. But it doesn't change a damn thing. After all I can't scout the whole town, hoping to find my mother and Jen.'

'Hmm,' she muttered.

'OK,' he said as he took the small rucksack containing the laptop with him, 'I'm off. Don't open the door to anyone. You know the drill.'

'Night Jack,' Mina said, before falling back sleep.

Jack left the bungalow quietly. His mind raging with thoughts, he walked slowly, twisting left and right through narrow alleyways. The only noises in the night were the muffled beat of dance music, the dying laughter of drinking parties and his rucksack brushing past coconut trees. He chose a bar in a slight recess, off the main street. It was less flashy than other places, but wasn't seedy. He was no moralist, but he couldn't stand the way prostitution was flaunted in tourists' faces as if it were something Thai people were supremely proud of, 'check out our temples, our great culture and our ping-pong banana shows!' He sat down at the bar, and ordered a drink. 'Poor mum and Jen,' Jack thought to himself 'their first trip outside the US and I've got them into this dangerous mess'. If only he could get his hands around Wheatley's neck, he'd crush his windpipe and every bone in his body. He asked the barman to hit him again with another shot of Jack Daniels. 'I'm feeling worse than before,' he thought to himself. Now he was assailed by even darker thoughts, morbid images of Wheatley's twisted face, covered in his own blood and guts. He opened his rucksack and pulled out the laptop. He looked at the JPEG file Mina had produced. She was quite the artist, Jack whistled in admiration. He'd never have thought it was a fake photograph.

It looked like the tablet he'd seen himself. He copied the JPEG file onto a small digital USB storage key and called the barman.

'Are you the owner?' he asked him.

'No, but I can get her,' the barman answered.

'Maybe you can help me, I need to print a good quality photograph right now.'

The barman looked at him thinking Jack was a lunatic.

'At this time? All closed Mister!'

'I'll pay good money,' said Jack.

'OK. OK. I call my friend and take care of everything.'

'Thanks, here's the key. There's only one document on there, it's the image I need to print in high resolution,' said Jack, handing him the USB stick.

The barman asked a girl working there to take care of the bar, and he left. Jack wondered if he really was going to call a friend or just go home and print it out on glossy paper on his own printer. In the end, he didn't care one way or the other. He'd have the photograph in hand before the morning. He suddenly remembered his conversation with Mina half an hour ago. He'd said he wasn't going to scout the whole island to find his mother and sister. Maybe he'd been wrong?

He switched on the WIFI connection on his laptop and picked a few signals from various modems in the neighbourhood. One of them was not password protected, so he connected his laptop to it. He clicked on the same special website he'd used the other day to track Wheatley's whereabouts but typed a different character combination. This website was a back-door into an hour-by-hour satellite photographic coverage of various regions of the world. He typed in the longitude and latitude coordinates of Patong Beach, 7° 53′ 24′ N, 98° 17′

24′ E, and was almost immediately offered a choice of fifty high resolution satellite photographs from the past five hours. As soon as he glanced at the first two, he knew his hunch was the right one. There was only one yacht of the kind Wheatley could be interested in and the detail of the photographs was such that he was able to identify men guarding the yacht, carrying submachine guns. He checked the last position of the yacht and it hadn't moved from its location in the past four hours. He had to go and check. Maybe that's where they were being held. He noticed the barman had returned but hadn't wanted to bother Jack while he worked. He gestured for the man to approach. He handed Jack the printed photograph and asked an exorbitant amount for it, which Jack paid without a murmur. The barman returned to his customers, a happy man. Jack called him again.

'Yes Sir?' asked the barman.

'I need a small boat, a rowing boat. Any ideas? I need to rent it for a few hours,' Jack said.

'With motor?'

'Yeah. Why not,' Jack replied.

'OK. No problem. You come with me and I show you,' said the barman.

Jack packed the laptop and the photograph into his rucksack and followed the barman, who was busy making a phone call. He hesitated about returning to the bungalow, to wake up Mina and let her know where he was going. But he guessed he would be back before morning, so there really was no point scaring her unnecessarily. The barman was waiting outside on his moped. Jack climbed on the back and off they went. He'd tried to find out how much this rental would cost him, but the barman had conveniently gone deaf. After a ten-minute ride, they drove down a path that lead back to the sea front. Jack could see a small boat, moored to a pier, made of a few odd planks of wood thrown together. They got off the moped. The barman walked over to the boat, followed closely by Jack. 'Here is boat,' said the man.

'But where's the motor?' asked Jack.

As he said these words he heard the approaching sound of another moped.

'My friend brings it now.'

Jack waited for the other man to fit the motor, start it and show him how it worked before paying his favourite barman. The price was as before, overwhelming, and Jack thought of the multiple ways he could knock out both men and disappear with the boat, but in the end he shoved a hand in his pocket and pulled out a wad of crumpled dollars.

Once both men had left, he stepped onto the boat and turned on his laptop. He needed to take another look at the satellite photographs he'd saved, comparing them to a coastal map he'd downloaded. He could roughly estimate how far he had to go to find the yacht. Hopefully it was Wheatley's. He couldn't bear the idea of navigating in the dark for an hour or more, covertly boarding the yacht to find a group of drunken Japanese businessmen playing cards. But did he have a choice? He started the motor and slipped away into the night. It was a good thing there was a relatively powerful torch at the front of the boat, but as he got closer to the yacht he would have to be discrete, which meant turning off the torch and also the motor.

Within an hour he found the yacht, roughly where he'd

guessed it would be. He spent twenty minutes or so observing the comings and goings but there seemed to be very few people on board. One guard stood on the main deck, another below and he also caught a glimpse of Natasha, Wheatley's head of security. Now came the difficult part. He needed to tie his boat to the yacht and get on board unobserved. After ten minutes spent approaching the yacht's port side as slowly and cautiously as possible, he looped a rope around a metal bar which ran along the lower deck. He had tied the other side of the rope to his boat's motor. He then checked his pulse, closed his eyes and started breathing slowly and deeply. When he was satisfied with his state of calm, he smoothly reached up on the port side, and grabbed hold of the brass opening of a cabin window, resting his right foot on a large bolt protruding from the hull. He suddenly heard some footsteps coming from the main deck, so he made as little noise as possible and waited. He tried relaxing as much as he could, but he couldn't remain in this position for much longer. He mustered his strength, and swung himself upwards, onto the deck. He looked left and right and didn't see anyone. He bent low and crawled to the door that lead to the stairwell. As he stood up, a guard appeared to his right. He quickly beamed his torch in the man's face to startle him, crouched down and felled him with a quick sweeping kick. Before the guard could get back on his feet, Jack kicked the man's gun out of his hand and knocked him out with a powerful blow to the temple. He grabbed the man's hand gun and stuck it in the back of his own jeans. He stood up and dragged the man to the side door, pulled him over the high step and dumped him in a corner of the stairwell. After knocking another guard unconscious in the stairwell, this time with the butt of his gun, Jack reached the lower deck.

There, through the bay window he saw his mum and sister, tied up and seemingly asleep on a large, white leather couch. He looked around, but saw no more guards. He ran into the room, woke them both up and untied them, urging them to keep quiet and remain as calm as possible. Jen shook as tears of relief coursed down her face. Jack put a reassuring hand on her shoulder and was about to usher them out onto the deck when Natasha appeared in the doorway. Jack immediately fired off two shots in her direction but Natasha was faster still as she ran into an adjoining room. Jack bolted after her and locked the door behind her. She was locked in. His panic-stricken mother and sister looked at him, waiting to hear what to do next. He reassured them, that he had everything under control now. He picked up a rope ladder lying nearby and returned to the spot where he had climbed onto the yacht. He secured the ladder to the railing, and made his mother and sister climb down onto the small motor boat. He followed and immediately started the motor. Before long, all that was left of their passage was a silvery trail on the sea's calm surface.

⸙

'Pick up the phone dammit!' Jack yelled frantically and slammed his fist down onto the dashboard in exasperation, frightening the taxi driver. His sister and mother were half asleep in the back, exhausted after their kidnapping and dramatic rescue.

'Hi, Jack? Is that you? What time is it?' asked Mina anxiously.

'Yeah. It's me. It's six a.m. I don't want to go into details over the phone. I've managed to rescue mum and Jen and we're off to the airport.'

'But…' Mina tried to interject.

'No buts. Get into the first taxi and meet us at the airport. Go!' he shouted.

He turned off his mobile immediately after the call and hoped with all his heart that Wheatley's thugs wouldn't have had time to track Mina's phone, which until now they didn't know about. He thought about what to do next. There were a number of flights out to Bangkok. From there he would try to get them home on whatever flights were available. All he knew was that they had to get out of there as quick as possible.

⌇

Mina jumped out of bed and felt queasy for a moment, her legs swaying underneath her. She looked around her. What should she take? Did she even have time to pack? Jack had rescued his mother and sister! She had only just digested what Jack had said. There was nothing stopping them now from leaving as planned. Who knew what disaster would strike today. She went for the simplest solution: leave everything behind. She slipped on a pair of jeans, a t-shirt and a good pair of sneakers. She checked that she had her phone, passport and money and slipped out into the dark maze of bungalows and palm trees. She took a wrong turn, and after a few more, hit the main road but too far down. She had to walk at least fifteen minutes to the taxi rank. She walked along the main road, avoiding a few drunken tourists returning from a bar to their hotel rooms. A taxi passed by her. She waved at the driver who slowed down and parked a little further on. She ran towards it, but two men were closer, opened the door and by the time she got there, the car had pulled away.

'You bastards!' she yelled, fuming.

She walked on and saw an empty tuktuk near the entrance of their hotel. The doorman noticed her questioning look, and told her the driver would be back soon. While she waited, she noticed a local squinting at her from the other side of the street. She thought for a moment the man had mistaken her for someone else, and she was suddenly afraid. But she was wrong about him; he seemed to have lost interest and before she knew it, he was talking on his mobile phone. She sat on a low wall waiting for the driver to return or another taxi to arrive. The man across the street was gone. The tuktuk driver came out of the hotel laden with boxes and wrapped-up gifts. Before Mina had time to speak to him, he had already fitted his load on the backseat and was ready to go. Mina was frantic. Would she ever find a cab to take her to the airport? Suddenly a taxi stopped at the rank. This time she practically tore the door open.

'Are you free?' she asked.

'Yes. Where you going?' he replied.

'The airport,' answered Mina.

But as she looked inside, she noticed someone was already in the front passenger seat.

'You come in?' the taxi driver urged her.

'Well, I was just waiting until your other customer left,' she answered.

'No. She my friend, going airport too,' he replied.

'Right,' said Mina.

She didn't feel as if she really had a choice in the matter.

As the car left the taxi rank, Mina took a better look at the veiled woman in front. She had a funny sensation of *déja vu*, or more precisely, she recognised the woman's perfume. It was quite distinctive, both edgy and classy; a fragrance that simply didn't seem right among the locals. Suddenly a cold sweat broke out over her entire body as she remembered when she had last smelled it. She tried opening the door, but it was centrally locked.

She screamed 'Let me out! Now!'

The woman turned around and pointed a gun at her. She lifted her veil and sunglasses and let her blond hair loose.

Natasha Mastrani smiled cruelly at Mina. 'Shut up and stay still,' she ordered.

Mina lost control and tried breaking the window with her mobile phone. The driver saw Mina wasn't wearing her seatbelt and slammed on the breaks. She was thrown violently against the front seat but she wasn't knocked out. Natasha suddenly plunged a needle into Mina's thigh and emptied the entire contents of the syringe. Within seconds Mina felt an immense weariness spread through her and a moment later she lost consciousness and was out cold.

'What was that?' asked the driver.

'At least we won't have to hear her moaning until tomorrow. Drive back to the yacht,' answered Natasha.

Chapter 33

Jack was a nervous wreck. What was Mina doing? He should have driven back to Patong beach to pick her up. His mother was asleep and Jen was stroking her head. Her eyes seemed vacant. They were still traumatised from their recent misadventures and Jack knew he'd have to find them some help when they got back to the States. Normal people don't get over kidnappings in a matter of moments. He was still amazed at Mina's resilience after all her ordeals at the hands of Wheatley. Maybe it was hatred for the man that kept her from collapsing. What was she doing? They couldn't wait that much longer, it was almost 7:30 and they had already missed one flight to Bangkok. He'd called her mobile phone many times and she'd never answered. He hoped she'd forgotten it in their room and that nothing more sinister had happened. After the tenth time of switching off his phone to avoid being traced, he turned it on again and this time noticed he had a text message. He opened it and immediately wished he hadn't.

I have Mina. Same deal. Meet me 9am. Patong Beach. Chiang Mai Restaurant. Don't forget the photograph.

Jack wanted to hurl his phone against the wall.

'I knew it,' Jack said out loud. 'I should've gone back to the bungalow.'

He looked at his mother and sister, and made up his mind in an instant.

'Mum, Jen, I'm putting you on the first plane to Bangkok. I've also organised your connecting flight back home.'

'But Jack, what are you going to do? Where's Mina?' asked Jen tearfully.

'You have a two hour gap between the arrival in Bangkok and your departure for the US. I have to stay here until Mina arrives.'

'We'll wait with you Jack,' she answered.

'No Jen. You must go. It's all arranged. You'll land in Phili. Uncle Frankie will pick you up. Mina and I will see you when we get back home. We'll be fine.'

One look at her stubborn brother left her defeated. Jen took her mother's arm and they walked briskly, passports in hand, to the departure zone. He stood there for a few more seconds, watching them go and then rushed out of the hall. On his way out he placed a few personal belongings, including his laptop, into a locker, but kept his small rucksack and the fake photograph of the tablet, which he placed in an envelope. He jumped into a cab and offered the driver triple the fare to get to Patong beach as fast as he could. He drove like a madman through the countryside and Jack arrived on Patong beach just before 8:00 a.m.

As he paid the driver the agreed fare, Jack heard his stomach growling. He realised he hadn't eaten since dinner the day before. He noticed a Starbucks café on the beach and decided to grab coffee and some food, as he still had one hour to go. As

Jack pushed the door open, he suddenly felt sick, as if all his insides had been turned upside down. A powerful tremor had shaken the café and the people sitting inside had felt the sharp rocking motion too.

They all looked at each other in surprise. Three American kids huddled around their parents, started screaming. The parents tried reassuring them, but they seemed as apprehensive as their children. They quickly ordered a few mango smoothies to distract their children, which seemed to work momentarily.

Two young Swedish men were having breakfast with an Israeli couple. The group's diving gear was scattered all over the floor. Markus, one of the Swedes, a tall blond hulk with a bronze tan, turned to the others excitedly:

'Did you feel that, guys?'

'Yeah, that was a close one! Maybe we shouldn't go diving after all?' the Israeli girl wondered.

'Don't tell me you're scared, Irit?' her boyfriend asked her.

'Irit? Scared of anything?' Markus laughed.

'What about you Stieg?' she asked the Swede, 'are you afraid?'

'No, dude. I don't feel anything anymore so it must've been pretty far away. Let's go!'

Jack's hands were trembling. He sat down, his hands on his thighs as he breathed in deeply. 'It's the earthquake!' he thought. 'It was true after all.'

But at least it meant that the earthquake was over now, and regardless of what it had caused in another country or island in the Indian Ocean, Thailand was now safe. 'It's over. Now I can focus on dealing with that Wheatley bastard.'

He thought about the restaurant, Chiang Mai. It was a swish

restaurant on the sea front and not very far from where he was. It was a slightly elevated building, isolated from bungalows and guest houses by a dense row of coconut trees. It had a good view of the beach and the seafront. As Wheatley was obviously a megalomaniac, Jack guessed he'd probably have booked the entire restaurant to avoid any witnesses. He caught sight of a local boy he'd seen hanging around the hotel the other day. He called him over.

'Hi! You remember me?' asked Jack.

'Yes Sir, I carried your luggage.'

'Ah. Of course you did. What's your name again?'

'Noi, sir.'

'Noi, I'm Jack. Could you do another small errand for me? I'll pay you well.'

The boy's eager eyes widened in anticipation, 'Yes Sir, no problem, Sir!'

'OK. I have a meeting at the Chiang Mai restaurant at nine, and I want you to wait for me here with this bag,' Jack said, handing him his rucksack. 'When I phone you, you come to the restaurant with the bag.'

'That's all sir?'

'Yes. I'll need your phone number and here's half the cash,' he said, giving him $40.

⤳

Patong Beach. Chiang Mai Restaurant

Oberon Wheatley and Natasha Mastrani were having tea on the outdoor terrace of the Chiang Mai restaurant. Oberon was reading a newspaper and Natasha was checking emails on her laptop when they felt the earthquake. Within minutes he had

received fifteen emails on his blackberry from various researchers and his centre in Mumbai. But none of them satisfied his
hunger for explanations.

'Information,' he thought, 'I need accurate information.'

Something was nagging Wheatley, a splinter in the back of
his brain; something he should be thinking of right now, but
couldn't recollect. The sky was blue and the sun was shining
on his face. He stopped checking his blackberry and tried to
remember this elusive fact. He placed his phone neatly on the
table, at equal distance between his cup of tea and the bread
basket. He had always liked space between objects to be exact;
it helped him think properly. Natasha noticed, but did not
comment; she liked his penchant for details and his exactitude
in preparing his plans and business strategies. 'Natasha, I'm
glad we have the place for ourselves.'

'I rented the entire restaurant for the day, Sir,' she replied
rather formally.

He smiled, seeming pleased with himself. 'I presume, my
dear, that our friend Jack didn't sleep much last night?'

'I guess. Waiting to contact him until the late morning was
a nice idea,' she replied.

He looked at her for a moment and could not decide if he
enjoyed her flattery or found it irritating.

'Is our lovely Miss Osman still asleep?'

'Yes sir. I'm sorry.'

'You had the Hillcliff women on board the yacht and you
lost them. You had that little Iraqi bitch in your grasp and you
drugged her up to her eyeballs!'

'The important thing is that she didn't have the photograph
with her. She was on her way to meet Hillcliff, so it was obvious
that he had it,' she said to Oberon.

'Yes,' he replied, 'but that's not the point. I wanted to question her about contacting NOAA. How much of the stuff did you inject her with?'

Natasha was about to answer when he suddenly felt he was on the brink of remembering the idea he was desperately searching for.

'Sir?' she said, breaking his chain of thought.

'What? Damn you! I was about to remember a detail,'

'My men have just told me that Jack Hillcliff is on his way.'

'Ah,' he replied, focusing his attention on the matter in hand and dismissing all other thoughts, 'good. Go now Natasha. I'll welcome the Major.'

⁓

Jack was in his element, now that the wheels of action had been set in motion. He looked at the boy, who returned his gaze with a reassuring air of confidence as he left the café. He took his time as he walked towards the meeting place, affecting an air of self-confident nonchalance. The beach crowd was a strange sight. 8:30 a.m. and the beach was already full of tourists from every country in the world; Belgians joking with Germans and Americans, the young Swedes checking their diving gear with the Israeli couple. He heard people speaking Spanish and French as he walked past the holiday-makers. Some were walking by the waterfront, others were laying down to get a back massage from a cute Thai girl. Now that he thought about it, he didn't see many Thai people enjoying the beach. They were too busy taking care of business. He passed a few British men lying on the beach snoring. He couldn't figure out if they were early risers who had just arrived and fallen asleep again, or if they had dropped dead drunk on the beach the night before after partying heavily.

He arrived at the Chiang Mai restaurant, a select establishment that catered for wealthy holiday-makers who enjoyed being cut off from the riffraff. Wheatley was sitting in the shade under a large parasol, flanked by two bodyguards. He saw Jack from a distance and waved to him to approach. Jack looked around the restaurant but didn't notice any other goons. He walked straight up to the table.

'Hello Major,' said Oberon condescendingly, as he stood up to shake Jack's hand 'I'm Oberon Wheatley, but call me Oberon. I feel like we've known each other for years.'

'Hi,' replied a stone-faced Jack, keeping his hands firmly at his sides.

'Not to worry,' Oberon said with a large sweeping gesture of the hand, 'there's no-one here but us. Would you like a drink?'

'Thanks, no. Where is Mina?' asked Jack.

Oberon nodded to one of his bodyguards, who handed Jack a pair of binoculars.

'If you look down the beach, right to the end, near the wall, you'll see a small shack. She's standing there.'

Jack took the binoculars and found the spot indicated by Oberon. He recognised Natasha standing next to Mina.

'That's not good enough. I want her here next to me when we do the deal,' said Jack.

'Hmm. Where's the photograph? No, let me guess. You don't have it on you but somewhere close by,' said Oberon.

'Correct. I'll call someone to bring the photograph when I'm satisfied that Mina is OK.'

'Fine,' said Oberon.

He picked up his mobile phone and rang Natasha.

'Bring Miss...bring Mina to the restaurant,' then raised an eyebrow at an irritated Jack, 'Satisfied?'

'I'll make the call when they're here.'

'Aren't you being overly suspicious?' asked Oberon.

Jack didn't react to Oberon's facetious tone. He chose to ignore him and remain businesslike. He watched Natasha and Mina walking down the beach, slowly approaching the restaurant. People on the beach weren't paying much attention to them as they were too busy staring out to sea, watching flocks of birds seemingly gone mad, flying frantically towards the coast and then inland. Jack shuddered with a sense of foreboding but kept his thoughts to himself, especially as Wheatley and his men hadn't noticed anything.

~

Hawaii. NOAA, Pacific Tsunami Warning Centre

Dr Jim Carson had received the first seismic data from stations in Australia earlier in the morning. This data had immediately been forwarded to his fellow seismologists in Indonesia, Thailand and Sri Lanka with a warning of a potential tsunami. Each of them in turn had called him to confirm they'd received his tsunami warning. But he didn't know more right now. There simply wasn't enough data. There he was trying to coordinate information from various local centres, but it would take much more cooperation between them to be able to issue an actual tsunami warning in all confidence. He rushed down to the main desk and asked the secretary for the telephone number of the South Indian bureau, which hadn't contacted him since he had first sent off the data. Bob Rear, the secretary, seemed very nervous and almost stuttered as he read him the number.

'What's wrong Bob? We've had other scares in the past,' said Carson.

'It…It… It's not that Dr Carson.'

'Well what is it?'

'Someone called two days ago. I thought it was a crank call. I'm still not sure what it was.'

'What are you talking about?' he asked impatiently.

'A major in the US army told me he had classified information according to which an earthquake was going to occur today.'

'Two days ago? That's impossible.'

'I know. I tried explaining this to him, but he hung up on me,' Bob lied.

'That's a real shame. Did you get his name or his number?' asked Carson.

'No. He didn't say.'

'That's not good enough. Bob, next time someone tells you a tsunami is about to occur, patch him through to me immediately. Maybe there is a classified military research project on earthquake detection that we are not aware of. We can't afford to dismiss information out of hand, especially when it turns out to be correct.

'With hindsight, I…' Bob began.

'Just do it next time,' said Carson cutting him off mid-sentence.

'I'm so sorry sir.'

Jim Carson was furious. Until five minutes ago he thought he was at the head of one the most advanced seismic detection centres in the world. But here was a secret military researcher who had somehow managed to detect an earthquake two days ahead of the event. As a seismologist he couldn't understand how that was possible, but as a scientist he had to accept the evidence when it stared him in the face. He would make every effort to find out who had called the centre two days before and what he knew exactly.

⤳

Thailand. Patong beach. Chiang Mai restaurant.

Natasha stepped onto the terrace, pushing in front of her a dishevelled Mina, who seemed to hesitate with every step. Natasha hardly concealed her gun. Jack walked up to them.

'Mina. Are you OK?' he asked her.

She seemed dazed, and tearful as if she'd been drugged.

'I'm not feeling very well,' she murmured weakly.

He turned around to meet Oberon's cold gaze and asked angrily, 'What's going on here? Did you drug her?'

Natasha took a step forward and answered for Oberon, 'Be happy nothing worse happened to her. She's been so out of it, I haven't even had the opportunity to have her raped.'

Jack turned around to face Natasha, brimming with barely restrained anger.

'I should've dealt with you on the yacht last night,' he spat.

'You should have, big boy,' she answered, keeping a safe distance between her and Jack.

Oberon was enjoying this banter but he had more pressing things on his mind.

'Don't you have a call to make?' asked Oberon.

Jack dialled Noi's number.

'Hi there.'

'Hello sir. Do you want me to come now?'

'Yes. Don't forget the bag.'

'I'm coming,' the boy answered and hung up.

'It's on its way' Jack said to Oberon.

'Good,' Oberon replied. He turned to Natasha. 'What's going on out there? What are all those people looking at?'

'I'm not quite sure,' she answered looking through the binoculars, 'the water's edge, which is normally right up close to the promenade has receded far out to sea. There was some frothing and bubbling, but most people don't seem to be particularly bothered. The locals seem to be focused on trying to catch fish trapped in the remaining pockets of water.'

'How strange,' said Oberon, feeling a shiver run down his spine.

Jack threw another cursory glance at the people on the shore, and turned pale as he realised what Natasha had just said. The frothing of the water and the sea suddenly receding had to be linked to an earthquake. Was it linked to the earlier tremor, or a sign of another one to come? They all looked at each other as the wind suddenly changed, and more birds, this time by the thousand flew inland. A rumbling sound like thunder seemed to roar from a distant place and the volume steadily grew. A number of people on the beach looked up for helicopters or airplanes, but the blue sky was as beautiful as it was empty.

The young boy Jack had called arrived at the restaurant. Oberon stood up to greet him. But Jack was quicker, and pulled him aside next to Mina. He stood in front of them.

Before Wheatley had time to pull out his gun, Jack had kicked Natasha's gun out of her hand, pulled a sharp knife from his pocket and grabbed Natasha by the throat from behind.

'Leave that gun where it is,' Jack ordered Wheatley.

Oberon looked at him with disdain. 'You have what you want. Give me the photograph.'

'Pass me the rucksack Noi,' said Jack to the terrified boy.

Noi handed him the small rucksack. Jack threw it over to Wheatley, still holding Natasha at knifepoint. She knew better than to move a muscle, Jack was not a man to be trifled with. One of Wheatley's men picked up the rucksack, opened it, and took out an envelope, which he handed to him.

'Oberon feverishly opened the envelope and pulled out the photograph. He examined it and seemed satisfied. He put it back into the rucksack, which he slung over his shoulder.

'I had planned a very different ending to this meeting. I don't think you fully understand who you are dealing with, Major Hillcliff.' Wheatley levelled his gun at Natasha's head. 'I'm sorry my dear,' he said.

'Mr W…Oberon, please!' pleaded Natasha, all her usual composure gone.

Oberon hesitated for just an instant. He lowered his gun a fraction but then he aimed and fired. Natasha was hit straight between the eyes and crumpled to the floor.

'She's out of the picture now, so what are you going to do with your little steak knife?' he taunted Jack, aiming his gun at Mina. He raised his gun, ready to shoot, but unexpectedly faltered. That nagging thought had finally struck him, it all made sense: Jack calling NOAA and warning about an earthquake, the tremors earlier on, the birds flying inland, the water receding far out at sea, the frothing and bubbling, the thundering

noise that had steadily been increasing and was now deafen-
ing. Oberon spun around and saw it. His facial expression
turned to one of absolute terror. A huge, grey wall of water
was advancing at an unimaginable speed towards the shore. It
changed appearance as it approached, seeming both to slow
down and grow in strength, shiny green then deep blue. By
then everyone had turned to face the shore and stood in frozen
horror, at the sight of this awesome wave racing towards them.
The tsunami was moving at almost 100 metres per second and
although it was slowing down as it approached the coastline,
its height was growing to something like ten metres.

By the time Jack screamed 'tsunami!' the wave had already hit
the beach and enveloped hundreds of people. Nothing could
slow down its progress. It swallowed everything in its path;
deck chairs, people, whatever stood in against it. Then the restaurant was hit. Windows exploded inwards under the terrible
pressure of the wave and the chairs, tables, even the platform
on which the restaurant was built, were swept up in a single
whirl.

Jack and Mina were swallowed by the wave and dragged a block
inland in a matter of seconds. Somehow they had managed to
hang on to each other as the water hit and Jack grabbed hold of
a metal railing set in a hotel's concrete outdoor terrace, which
they were now clinging on to desperately. He held fast, with
every muscle in his body screaming from the effort. As they
fought to keep their heads above the torrent, all sorts of float-
ing debris passed in front of them in the current. It lasted less
than fifteen minutes but it felt like an eternity. Jack had seen
Wheatley and his men vanish in a tangle of tables and chairs,

some of them smashing against a line of coconut trees. He looked for Noi in every direction but couldn't see him, they'd been separated when the wave had first hit. Finally the wave seemed to have run its course. Jack felt his strength leaving him, he couldn't hold on much longer. Suddenly he felt Mina's grasp slacken, her head slipped beneath the water and her eyes were closed.

'Mina! Please! Mina, wake up!'

In the distance, a young Asian man with a baby on his shoulders was frantically trying to tie himself to a palm tree. Closer to Jack, a German couple in their colourful shorts and monastic sandals, were helping one another scramble up to safety onto the balcony of a newly built hotel which, incredibly, had withstood the wave. The room was on the first floor, facing the beach. It was an absurd scene as the man stepped onto the nose of a speed boat which had somehow been thrown into the lounge area of the hotel, and was protruding from its side. His companion was pulling herself up to the balcony.

Mina stirred against Jack and looked at her lover's face, covered in cuts and bruises. She tried standing on her own, as Jack seemed at the end of his tether. She had just found her footing when something smashed into them and pushed her under water again. She could feel an object pushing into her back as she pushed up to the surface, trying to catch her breath. She turned around and a scream bubbled up in her throat – a woman's corpse, pressing into her. Her head was bent at a hideous angle and her long black hair floated on the water's surface like an old rag. A sudden current wrenched the body to one side and Mina caught sight of the woman's face. She had the most beautiful chiselled Eurasian features, high cheekbones and almost transparent skin. Faced with the wanton destruction of such beauty the scale of what had occurred hit her and Mina burst into tears. Jack was also horrified; the surrounding desolation was beyond comprehension but he would not, could not, break down. Would he have to carry Mina on his back? She was really struggling. He would have to keep life and limb together for them both. The beautiful corpse was finally swept away by the fast moving current.

Mina was sobbing uncontrollably.

'Jack, I can't go on. I'm sorry!'

'You must, Mina, one last effort.'

'It's too much,' she whispered.

'Mina, we can't stop now. I think the waters are receding but we still need to get to higher ground, fast.'

Sweeping the scene quickly, he noticed a few buildings not too far away. He suddenly recognised Noi, who was screaming to catch their attention. He waved to acknowledge he'd seen him and realised that the young boy had been lucky enough to land on a sturdily built hotel, with a high, flat concrete roof roughly forty metres away. If only they could reach it without losing their footing in the dark water they might just be out of danger, and would have time to assess their injuries.

They pushed hard, feeling submerged objects scratching and cutting their bodies under the water, as they moved through the path of the dissipating wave. The level of the water seemed to be dropping. They were almost there. Noi was on his knees and stretched out his hand for Mina to grasp. Just as their hands touched, Jack felt a sudden shift in the current of the water. By the time he realised what was happening it was too late. He gave Mina a shove in Noi's direction and the boy caught her and pulled her clumsily onto the landing.

Mina had also felt the change in the water and turned back

to grab Jack, but it was too late – with an immensely power-ful sucking force the waters, receded all at once to the sea. Jack was wrenched from them with an irresistible force and dragged back. He screamed at Mina to stay put. She screamed his name. Noi tried to restrain her, but she had already jumped down into the puddles and mud left by the fast-receding wave. She thought she could see Jack's head bobbing about, far away. She set off as fast as she could, trying to avoid the debris, upturned cars, smashed furniture with jagged edges that lit-tered the way back to the shore. She barely noticed the snakes slithering rapidly down into the surrounding chaos.

'It's over,' Mina thought to herself. 'The wave has come and gone.' She shivered and pressed forward, desperately looking for any sign of Jack. Her progress was slow but she managed to keep close to a row of trees that were still standing. It seemed hard to believe that the trees could withstand God's wrath but so many man-made constructions had not.

When she came across mangled bodies, she looked away. Many people had perished but many had also survived, albeit in terrible conditions. She noticed a middle-aged couple hugging a young girl who was in a state of shock, bleeding from a large gash in her forehead. She walked on. 'Where are you Jack?' she thought, as tears streamed down her battered face.

She finally arrived at the point where she thought she'd last seen Jack when he'd been washed out to sea. But he was nowhere to be seen. Suddenly, a deep rumbling sound engulfed her. It was much louder than the previous wave. She froze. Was it an earthquake? But as she turned to the shore she saw to her horror a second, huge wave returning with a vengeance. It was mightier than the first and was crushing anything that had been left standing. She frantically tried climbing up one of the trees, but her shoes kept slipping off the wet bark and then it hit, blue oblivion. It ripped Mina like a rag doll from the tree she was holding on to with her last strength, and swept her into the road.

∽

The second wave had carried Jack like a cork back towards the shore, much farther this time, two blocks inland. He was unable to move left or right, pressed and paralysed by the ferocious current that was pinning him against the wall. Stricken with horror, he watched as a huge Coca-Cola lorry was washed away sideways like a matchbox toy and literally crushed on the hotel's outside wall, just a few paces from where he was trapped.

Mustering his strength, he clawed his way back around the side of the building, inch by inch, to avoid being taken further inland by the current. He heard high-pitched screams nearby. As he turned the corner, he saw them: two boys, one about fifteen and the other around ten. They were stuck by the hotel entrance, screaming for help. Two mangled motorboats, which had been sucked in by the force of the tsunami were hurtling towards them. Jack calculated that if he could let go of the railing and let himself be taken by the current he might just get close enough to help the boys. A torn volleyball net was entangled in what was left of the entrance to the hotel. The free end of the net was thrashing about in the water. He jumped forward, and was immediately taken by the current with tremendous force. He had just a few seconds to reach out for the net. He caught it and pulled himself forwards to the hotel entrance. He felt one of his fingernails rip as he made one last lunge towards the boys and yelled at them to join him. The older one did but the younger was frozen in panic. Jack pulled the elder one around the corner and safely into the restaurant. 'Climb the stairs and go as high as you can' he barked at the terrified youth. He saw the smashed boats arriving at full throttle. He reached out, searching for the younger boy's hand and yanked him towards him. They struggled around the corner together and the young boy managed to get in and run to the stairwell. Jack wasn't so lucky. He had managed to avoid the thunderous crash of boats into the hotel lobby, but a huge splinter of carbon fibre from the smashed hull had pierced his right thigh.

The two boys huddled on the roof, watched their saviour's body drop back into the waters as he passed out from the pain. That was the last they saw of him, as he was carried away by the wave. They could see other people vainly trying to swim in the debris but being cut to pieces by all manner of sharp objects and shards of glass from smashed car windscreens and hotel windows. The two boys looked at each other as surviving soldiers do after a raging battle, without feelings, but with the palpable relief that life was still pumping through their veins.

Chapter 34

December 26th, 2004. Noon. Patong Beach

Mina was being pulled up onto the top of a truck by two men. When she reached the top and looked around her, she counted four other people in their small group of survivors. One of the men said to her with a strong French accent, 'This is my brother, and this is his wife and this is her two cousins.' The wife was screaming relentlessly.

'What happened to her?' asked Mina.

'The baby, she lost the baby,' said her brother-in-law, tears running down his cheeks.

'Oh my God,' said Mina.

The truck was very heavy and was lying on its side, having been knocked over by the first wave. But now it was grinding slowly inland with the force of the new wave. They could all hear the screeching of the metal container against the ground and the sound filled them with dread.

Mina moved to the edge of the container to get a better look at their surroundings. She had never felt so helpless in her life. Although never a religious person, today, for the first time, she felt like a tiny speck in the fury of God's path. If the authors of the tablet were right and this was just a foretaste of worse events to come, she could not begin to fathom what they might be.

∽

Jack was barely alive, but had somehow managed to lift himself up onto some wooden planks. He examined the shard sticking out of his thigh. Thankfully, it hadn't hit the artery but he was bleeding heavily. He clenched his teeth and took hold of the shard, trying to ignore the excruciating pain. He pulled it out and then, having torn his shirt, he bandaged his thigh as best he could. It was a very nasty wound. It would soon be infected and he needed urgent medical attention, but he had no idea where he was. He felt his life and strength ebbing away.

∽

Late afternoon. Patong Beach

Jack slipped in and out of consciousness. He was lying on his back, staring at the vastness of the sky. His body was bruised and broken beyond anything he'd ever experienced. He couldn't even remember how he'd landed on this pile of dirt. He hoped with all his heart that Mina was safe and wondered if he'd ever see her again. Images of the first time he met her came back to him, when Professor Almeini had left them together in her office. How much had happened since that day in Iraq. He thought of all his accumulated hatred towards Wheatley and Natasha. He had fantasised so often about how he would make them suffer. But in the end, Wheatley's devious plans, his own bloodlust, Mina's quest, the few truthful moments they had lived together, all of it had been washed away in one fell swoop. He couldn't think anymore and felt the drowsiness creeping over him again.

⌒

Mina and the French survivors were air-lifted to safety. As the helicopter slowly rose into the air, the full horror of the scene unfurled before her eyes; ruined remains everywhere. Mina made a silent prayer for Jack, hoping against all odds he was still alive, somewhere on the beach. She saw the bloated, drowned bodies of men, women, children and babies, scattered all over the place. Apart from a few hotels, all that was left of this popular beach resort was a huge pile of wreckage.

It would only be later that evening and over the coming days that she would learn the full extent of the devastation caused by the tsunami in South India, Indonesia and Sri Lanka, and the hundreds of thousands of lives lost to this cataclysmic event. As the helicopter flew over a row of swaying trees and left Patong beach, she couldn't help but keep her eyes fixed on the ground far below in search of Jack, even though she knew it was hopeless. With a heavy heart, she raised her eyes to the sky.

It was bright blue and peaceful, as if nothing had happened. A majestic rainbow arched over the scene below. She followed the rainbow's curve through the sky, and wondered how such beauty could emerge from so much devastation. In a flash she heard the words, the covenant between God and Noah, and a shiver ran down her spine.

My rainbow I do give in the cloud, and it shall be for a token of a covenant between me and the earth…And I will remember my covenant, which is between me and you and every living-soul among all mortals; and the waters shall no more become a flood to destroy all living creatures. (Genesis 9:13–5)

Epilogue

6 months later. New York. East Village. Café Mogador

Mina played nervously with her cigarette. She felt restless, sitting on the terrace of Café Mogador, her favourite hang-out. She fidgeted with her soft pack of Camel filters, not like an addict, but more like an actor in need of a prop. She'd been suffering from anxiety for months, and her state of mind had hardly improved. Whenever someone alluded to or spoke about the tsunami her head would start spinning. Sometimes, all it took were a few simple words, 'sea', 'wave' or 'blue sky' and she'd start to feel queasy. The only person with whom she'd even tried to talk about the tsunami was her counsellor. But every time she was about to speak, she froze up. She'd bottled it all up inside her, and thought about the tsunami like something that had happened, but not really to her. Even worse, as far as her parents were concerned, she'd been to visit Jack's family in West Virginia for Christmas. She didn't know how to begin to explain that she was in Thailand on December 26th and was, in fact a tsunami survivor. Not being able to talk about her experience made it impossible for her to deal with the existential questions that had haunted her ever since that day.

When she finally made it back to the US, she had stayed a

few weeks with her parents in the East Village, before finding a cosy apartment in the Upper West Side, closer to campus. During those first weeks at home, they'd gently tried asking Mina why she had cut short her holidays with her new boyfriend. She had not said a word, even when they had asked her directly about Mosul. She preferred to let them think that she'd kept silent about her last month in Iraq because things hadn't worked out with Jack. She had also written a letter along those lines to Professor Almeini, thanking him for the opportunity he'd offered her at the Department of Cuneiform Studies, and for his constant support. She knew that he would guess there was more to her sudden flight than this boyfriend story, but she also knew he wouldn't pry. On the positive side, she had made up with Nigel, her doctoral supervisor, and she was back on track, working harder than ever on her dissertation. She had also managed, with Nigel's help, to secure a three-year grant for Hassan to pursue his studies in New York. She had delivered on what she had promised. After that, Hassan could make anything he chose to of his life. She wasn't too worried about him; he would always land on his feet. Hassan's personality would always lead him to success. He was clever, wouldn't let anyone tread on his toes, and yet his heart was in the right place. She took a sip of mint tea and lit another cigarette. She inhaled the smoke and then watched its blue-grey plume rise swiftly, and vanish into the air. Her arms dropped limply by her side. The sky was deep blue and peaceful, just as on that fateful day. She sighed deeply, and her thoughts drifted away to forgotten places. Eventually her gaze hardened as it returned to the table, the street and the people around her. None of the people who walked by her table could possibly imagine what she'd been through. How could they picture the indomitable power of nature destroying all humans, regardless of race, age or culture; indiscriminately tearing their constructions and beliefs to shreds?

She had survived, and like many survivors felt guilty about the very fact of having survived. She couldn't stop thinking of all those who hadn't made it. But something else tormented her. The more she tried to avoid thinking about it, the more it made her mind reel. The naked truth was that she had had prior knowledge of the event. So had Jack, Daniel and Joshua. It was predicted in the 13th tablet. Of course, none of them knew that a tsunami would actually happen for a fact, nor what shape the disaster would take, but they had held the strong belief that something terrible would happen and knew precisely when it would strike. Could they have done more? Had they still possessed both tablets intact, or even Benjamin of Tudela's letter, maybe they'd have stood a better fighting chance. But Shobai and his men had made sure that their vision of what they believed was God's plan would run its course smoothly, unhindered by humans. But was it God's plan? This was no Deluge. It was a flood, a horrendous one, certainly, but nothing as awesome as Noah's Flood which had destroyed all of humanity. As the rabbis had correctly concluded in Safed, so long ago, whatever God's plan was, it was beyond human reach. Nature proceeds for better or for worse, but it is up to mankind to do everything in its power to save and perpetuate life on earth. She would never know if Oberon had lied about there being other tablets around the world, as he had disappeared that day in Phuket with all his men. Was Shobai aware of these other tablets? Was he still tracking her whereabouts? These were the questions that had been tormenting Mina almost daily since she'd returned to New York.

She was suddenly brought out of her reverie by a light tap on her shoulder and a familiar voice from the past. She couldn't quite put her finger on who it belonged to and yet she did recognise it.

'Hi Mina,' the voice said quietly again, 'your parents told me I'd find you here.'

Mina was afraid to turn around. She was frozen to her chair. A few seconds passed before she could summon up her courage. She slowly turned round, raised her eyes and saw her dear friend Liat. Mina had tried contacting her many times since she'd returned from Thailand, but Liat had made it clear she needed time and space, while she recovered from her wounds. Mina thought Liat would never want to speak to her again. She'd suffered greatly at the hands of Oberon's henchmen in their attempt to make her reveal anything she knew about Mina's tablet. Another wave of guilt swept over Mina.

As Mina looked at her friend, the fine-tuned speeches she'd prepared in the unlikely case she'd meet her again, all the words of explanation and justification vanished. Tears began to stream down her face. Liat's face still carried the thin scars of her ordeal. They didn't make her less attractive. On the contrary, they made her look wiser.

'Liat, I'm so, so sorry,' whispered Mina, her gaze dropping to the floor.

Liat stroked her hand, trying to soothe her sobbing friend. Slowly lifted Mina's chin with her hand and looked into her eyes.

'It's over, Mina,' said Liat softly, by this time also weeping profusely, 'I forgive you, but this time I want the whole story,' adding 'and a cigarette!'

Mina burst out laughing amid her tears. She stood up clumsily and gave Liat a long hug.

'I can't believe you've taken up smoking!' said Liat, 'Miss my-body's-my-temple!' she grinned and snitched a cigarette from Mina's packet.

They sat down and Mina ordered two drinks. Liat watched her friend smile. It was odd, as if all the smiles that had been locked away had been bundled together. She wasn't far wrong. Mina beamed, unbelievably happy to be reunited with her friend. She also smiled because she knew that this time she could take Liat on a shopping spree in New York – Oberon's grant money was still being credited to her account every quarter. And last, but certainly not least, Mina smiled because she'd finally be able to properly introduce Liat to Jack that evening.

Acknowledgements

I would like to thank first my agent Sharon Galant from Zeitgeist Media Group for her constant support and creative input.

My learned, energetic and efficient team at Haus Publishing for all their wonderful work.

My brother Ben who encouraged me to write a work of fiction on that fateful day in 2009 standing in front of Hannah Courtoy's mysterious funerary monument in Brompton cemetery; my friend Bernard Gowers for reading and discussing early versions of The 13th Tablet sometimes at three in the morning in his awe-inspiring flat in Oxford; my parents and particularly my father Irving Mitchell for his unflinching courage in (re-) reading my work and making suggestions.

I am indebted to Rabbi Avi Tawil from the European Jewish Community Centre in Brussels for his precious time and expertise in Hebrew and kabbalist lore; James A. Matthews, the talented and good-willed sculptor who produced a faithful copy of The 13th Tablet; Anne-Sophie Reinhardt my great friend and Parisian film director for making the book trailer and Geraldine Beskin from The Atlantis bookshop on Museum Street for letting us film on location. Special thanks to the staff at the University Library in Cambridge and the Sackler Library in Oxford (a library I miss from the very moment I set foot in another: may its collections prosper!) for their kind help while I was researching this novel.

And last but not least, my beloved Lila who is always on my mind and inspires me daily.

Haus Annex is a carefully selected combination of visual and textual extra material which complement a Haus hybrid book. It is downloadable for **free** in pdf, epub and mobi formats.

In the case of *The 13th Tablet*, the additional information provided in the Annex focus on the archaeological research which underpins the plot, and explore the universality of the Flood Story. The Annex also recounts stories which are related to main theme and includes a wealth of photographs featuring the places which appear prominently in the story.

Scan this code to access the Annex for *The 13th Tablet* or visit www.the13thtablet.com